S0-BEG-817

FAREWELL PERFORMANCE

Books by Ernest Lehman

SCREENING SICKNESS
THE FRENCH ATLANTIC AFFAIR
NORTH BY NORTHWEST
THE COMEDIAN
SWEET SMELL OF SUCCESS

FAREWELL

Ernest Lehman

PERFORMANCE

McGRAW-HILL BOOK COMPANY

New York · St. Louis · San Francisco
Toronto · Mexico · Sydney

Copyright © 1982 by Chenault Productions, Inc. All
rights reserved. Printed in the United States of America.
Except as permitted under the Copyright Act of 1976,
no part of this publication may be reproduced or dis-
tributed in any form or by any means or stored in a
data base or retrieval system, without the prior written
permission of the publisher.

1 2 3 4 5 6 7 8 9 DOC DOC 8 7 6 5 4 3

ISBN 0-07-037074-5

LIBRARY OF CONGRESS CATALOGING IN PUBLICATION DATA

Lehman, Ernest, 1915–
Farewell performance.
I. Title.
PS3562.E4283F3 1983   813'.54   82-7871
ISBN 0-07-037074-5   AACR2

Book design by Roberta Rezk

To Arnie Rosen, who gladdened the
world with laughter . . .

"They say best men are molded out of faults,
And, for the most, become much more the better
For being a little bad."

WILLIAM SHAKESPEARE
Measure for Measure

FAREWELL PERFORMANCE

chapter 1

LYING ON HIS BACK in the sand with only a thin film of Coppertone and a white bikini between his well-bronzed body and the warm September sun, he came awake slowly, first becoming aware that the dull booming sound was no part of the dream but rather the breaking of waves on the rocks offshore, and then once he realized that he had indeed been asleep and drifting through a vaguely sexual dream, he came up to complete wakefulness and determined immediately that the other sound, the ringing telephone, was coming from inside the house behind him, and for an instant he felt anger that Diane wasn't picking it up until he remembered that she had walked out on him the night before, the little bitch, or had he *thrown* her out, who the hell could recall unimportant details and what was the difference anyway, the main point being that the phone was going to go on ringing unless he got up from the sand and went inside and answered it, which was the last thing he felt like doing now, or any other time for that matter, hating telephones as much as he hated acting and knowing that it was only when the phone rang and it was Kramer telling him that he had a couple of days' work for him in some fading sitcom or a half-assed bit in a Movie of the Week or even a commercial for some goddam supermarket or used car lot, never anything classy like Xerox or Prudential, only then did he have to leave the beach house and get in the car and make the long ride from Malibu to one of the studios and stick his face in front of a camera and make believe he didn't hear every script girl and second assistant and sound man on the set whispering my God, he looks so much *like* him, isn't it *uncanny*, which always bugged him, really bugged him, because why *shouldn't* he look so much like him, they were identical, for Christsake, it was enough to make *anyone* hate acting and certainly hate ringing telephones, which was probably why he had just decided not to answer this one now, unless it was more because he was feeling so deliciously lazy and languid and sun-warmed and comfortable, and wanted to fall back to sleep again and maybe pick up on that same

1

dream he had been in, so that he wouldn't have to sort out whether Diane had left *him* or he had left *her*, they had both been so stoned last night neither of them would ever be able to figure out *what* had happened other than the fact that it had happened in the middle of a particularly nasty, violent, loveless fuck, which was the story of his life, wasn't it, and wasn't he going to have to start thinking about which of the zillion broads he knew was going to be chosen to move into his empty bed unless he fell back to sleep immediately, as soon as the phone stopped ringing, which it should have done by now but hadn't and obviously wasn't going to, not ever, it was just going to go on ringing and ringing until he went inside and picked it up and heard Kramer telling him to drive over to Universal and play a coke-snorting antique dealer who knew the murdered woman, or over to Twentieth to be a robbed filling-station attendant who tells the cops one of them had a limp and the other had a scar on his left cheek about this big, shaped like a crescent moon, Christ, what dialogue, what roles, what garbage, and to think that there wouldn't even be *that*, he'd be sweating at the poker tables in Gardena or hustling some rich Beverly Hills widow with his pecker if his brother hadn't leaned on a few people now and then, not very hard, it was true, never hard enough to make him a Pacino or a Nicholson or a Redford, just hard enough maybe to keep him in tequila and grass and the Malibu pad and the steaks in the freezer on the back porch, let's have no uncanny resemblance to a bum, God forbid, a *handout*, an *embarrassment*, a skeleton in the closet of the upwardly mobile brand-new president of the only studio in town *he* could never work at because it would smack of nepotism, which is the only word you could have used for giving him *any* kind of acting job inasmuch as, aside from total lack of talent, he had this other ability of being able to act his way *into* a paper bag, especially if it was a brown one and there was a bottle in it but let's not go into *that* now, not with that goddam phone ringing, and if it wasn't going to stop he wasn't going to be able to fall back to sleep again and avoid the facts of his waking life, so he rose slowly to his feet and adjusted his bikini so that the remnant of the hard-on of his broken dream wasn't so obvious and climbed the wooden stairs to the patio and went into the house through the open sliding door past the unclean odor of dead roaches in the ashtray and the diluted dregs of interrupted drunkenness on the coffee table before the sofa and over to the shrilly ringing telephone and he picked it up and said hello, and who should it be but, well whaddaya know, his brother . . .

BLUESTERN NEVER LIKED to phone Teddy *personally* if he could avoid it. Whenever he *hadn't* been able to avoid it, like now, he always seemed to come away from the conversation feeling vaguely guilty, as though his own success were an act of hostility toward his brother, as though twins were supposed to stay *even* or something. He usually had one of his secretaries place the call *for* him, and not all that often at that, mostly when he wasn't using the Dodger tickets and no one around the studio wanted them, or when there was a night screening that he knew he wouldn't be attending and there were some seats left over, or when word filtered through to him that only his quick intervention could head off another embarrassing firing and Teddy's replacement by another actor who would have enough interest in eating regularly to memorize his lines rather than the printing on a wine label. But he didn't think that this was the time to have a secretary call, even to get Teddy on the line. This one called for the private phone behind his desk. Even in the old days, when Bluestern had been first an independent producer and later, one of four veepees, he had had an uneasy feeling that many of his calls were being monitored here, if only by the girls at the switchboard—on orders, of course. And now that he was president and chief operating officer, he felt even more vulnerable, for the more powerful you became, the more dangerous were your secrets. And when he heard his brother's voice greeting him on the other end of the line, Bluestern knew that he was about to add still another secret to a list that was already far too long.

"Did I wake you?" he said.

Teddy came back a little too sharply. "Hell no, I was studying a script out on the beach and didn't hear the phone until it rang a long time."

"How could you know it was ringing a long time if you didn't hear it?" It was the kind of remark Bluestern could never resist making, even when he was about to ask for a favor. Maybe that was why he always felt a residue of guilt after talking with Teddy, guilt over his *own* covert hostility, not Teddy's.

"I'll have to give that one some thought," Teddy said, and Bluestern imagined he heard a silent "you prick" in Teddy's voice before he went on to say, "So how you doing, Howard?"

"Your guess is better than mine," Bluestern replied, toying with some of the papers on his desk. "My new office here would dwarf the Coliseum, I've got three, count 'em, three secretaries, one of them *très intéressante* but not your type—"

"No such thing, they're *all*—"

"—And a hand-picked (but not by me) group of euphemisms in charcoal-gray suits called executive assistants, each of whom obviously harbors an intense dislike for my intestines—"

"Ain't we got fun."

"—And so I won't know how I'm faring here until I've sampled Miss Kallen (that's her name), flushed the little turds in the Brooks Brothers suits down their executive assistant toilets, and found out how many of the six projects I just okayed get shot down by New York. Never mind about *me*, Teddy, what've *you* been up to?" He heard his brother's throat-clearing stall. "I mean, in matters Malibu, not Hollywood. Diane behaving?"

"We split last night, Howard."

"Jesus, I'm sorry."

"Don't be."

"All right, I'm not." He didn't want to hear about it anyway. He had no time for trivia right now. "When I see you you'll tell me."

"Or not."

"Or not. Look, I don't want to keep you from that script you were reading . . ."

"Yeah."

"So I'll tell you why I called."

"Shoot."

"Are you alone?"

"Yes."

"You're not going to believe this, Teddy. It's urinal-smoothie time."

"You're kidding."

"Warm up that golden stream, pal. You're going to be on."

"When?"

"Like tomorrow?" Bluestern felt himself relaxing. He could tell that Teddy wasn't going to be a problem . . . not that he had ever been one. Just the same. . . . "The legal department sprang it on me a few minutes ago. Corporate policy, they said, to insure the life of the president for the term of his contract, with the company as beneficiary. They're willing to have Mutual of Oklahoma's doctor do it in my office, blood sample, urine specimen, blood pressure, and a portable EKG. The rest they take on good faith. After all, it's only a five-million-dollar policy . . ." He couldn't resist.

"Five *mill?*"

"What's the matter, didn't you know how valuable I am?"

"Why don't you just avoid the whole thing?" Teddy said.

"Because it turns out, old boy, and I didn't know this, that my new deal is not valid unless I'm insurable."

Bluestern was aware now of the long silence at the other end and the subtle change in his brother's voice when he finally responded, bolder, but only marginally so, inhibited by whatever it was that had always been the limiting factor in Teddy's life and had kept him on the beach instead of in the main arena.

"I guess that makes me valuable too, huh Howard?"

Bluestern forced a laugh. "Indispensable." Be jocular. Don't for Christsake let him know that you know how valuable he really is. "Why else do you think I'm going to buy you a lobster at the Palm after it's over?"

"I'll settle for a quarter-pounder at All-American Burger with everything on it," Teddy said.

"You've gotta raise your sights, kiddo."

"You've got them high enough for the both of us, Howard."

"Listen, I hate like hell to give you such short notice, Teddy, but that's what *they* gave *me*. I think you'd better get in the car and get your ass over here in a hurry."

"Oh, shit, when?"

"Five minutes ago."

"Must I?"

"Yes, must. I told you, the medical is tomorrow, tomorrow morning in the office, and you've never even *seen* the setup here. I barely know it myself after three memorable weeks. I know how much you hate rehearsals, but if you expect to win an Academy Award for best-pissing—"

"Okay, okay, I'm coming."

"You'll spend the night at my place . . ."

"Your booze is as good as anyone's," Teddy said.

". . . And I'll use yours. The place, that is. Though I don't know if I like your bed when it's *empty* . . ." Hating himself immediately for having said it.

"You want it *not* empty, say so, Howard."

Bluestern waited for his pride to rescue him, but it didn't have a chance. "You mean that?"

"Just say the word."

"What was her name again?"

"Who?"

"Last year? The afternoon before Christmas? Dark blonde with streaks in her hair? Lanie? . . ."

"Linda. No problem . . . I don't *think*. Consider it done."

And make believe it hadn't even been mentioned. "How's your health, Teddy?"

"Don't worry. You'll pass."

"Drive slowly," Bluestern said.

"Fuck you, Howard."

Bluestern laughed and hung up, but his face wasn't even smiling. He swung around slowly in the swivel chair and gazed out the window, allowing himself to wonder for a moment what his feelings toward his brother would have come to finally without this ridiculous, hilarious, deadly serious need for the occasional use of his sugar-free urine.

There had always been an invisible wall between them, since the year one, but he'd be goddamned if *he* was always going to take the blame for it. The very glass that mirrored their physiological samenesses had always seemed to refract their psychological differences into wedges that had slowly pushed them apart and placed them in competition with each other, with neither of them ever *really* winning or losing, only appearing to do so according to which set of value judgments was being used as the yardstick.

Okay, so Teddy had been born with the secret of instant popularity. He, Howard, had acquired the skills to earn it and buy it. With Teddy, sex had always been as natural as eating, and women had flocked to him. Hung-up and shy, he, Howard, had *sublimated* his way to power, which was sex appeal of an equally effective kind, you better believe it. It hadn't been *his* fault that the world wouldn't let it go at that, had insisted on declaring *him* the winner and Teddy the loser. From that had come nothing but tension, uneasiness, stickiness, with no way out for either of them.

Howard helps Teddy because Teddy needs help, but Teddy no *like* help, no like *Howard* for giving it to him, no like *himself* for accepting it. Howard feels guilty if he *doesn't* help Teddy, and Howard no like to feel guilty, and resents being *disliked* by Teddy for helping him, and resents Teddy for needing help, and Teddy no like his brother's resentment and blames his brother for weakening him with his support, and instead of going out and *doing* something about it, like getting stronger and not needing this support, he makes excuses and gets weaker while Howard gets stronger and feels guiltier and the resentments get more resentful, and how do you get out of that mess? You don't. It only gets worse.

Had they *no* good feeling toward each other?

Bluestern hated that question. He could hardly face it now, sitting at his desk. And when it began to come through to him that in all probability he wouldn't even be *speaking* to Teddy much less seeing him, if it hadn't been for the kidney dysfunction, the awareness of his own cold-assed lack of familial loyalty became more than he could accept. He quickly leaned forward and pressed a button on his telephone.

"Yes, Mr. Bluestern?"

"Come in, please, Miss Kallen." He could have given her the instructions on the intercom, but that would have been a waste of an opportunity.

He kept his head slightly averted toward the window, using only his peripheral vision to watch her as she came in from the outer office and made the long walk to his desk, her long slim legs wobbling a little at the knees. Was it possible, he wondered, that she had no idea how she affected men, *must* have affected them, not just him, despite the horn-rimmed glasses that were large but not stylish, the sparing use of make-up, the plain white blouse and the skirt that was a little too short? He glanced up to look at her face, lovely but expressionless, thinking he'd be able to understand instantly what it was about her, that excited him, but her gaze was so open and challenging that he immediately looked away and said, "My brother will be coming in in about an hour. Will you leave a pass at the gate for him, please?"

"Certainly, Mr. Bluestern." It couldn't have been her voice, which was soft but ordinary.

"He uses the name Teddy Stern."

"Yes, I know."

"I should say his name *is* Teddy Stern now."

She smiled faintly, but said nothing.

"Thank you, Miss Kallen."

She turned and walked away from him and he watched her go and knew suddenly, as certainly as he knew anything, that one day soon he was going to take her, in every way possible, had to, *had* to, it was only a matter of time, why couldn't *she* be the one tonight instead of that Laura or Linda or whatever her name was that Teddy was setting up for him?

SURELY it must have been showing. Her cheeks felt flushed, her legs were weak. She sank down quickly in her desk chair and fumbled with the telephone, and her voice was hardly recognizable as she gave the guard at the gate his instructions.

You've got to stop this, Jo Anne.

But she did not *want* to stop feeling the way she was feeling now, no matter how risky. Because while it was upsetting, and dangerous, and distressing, it was also unendurably exciting. Unendurable . . .

The way he had pretended again not to look at her when she came into his presence. The shock of his eyes meeting hers, possessing her wordlessly as he threw a coverlet of formality over the both of them. Had he read the truth beneath the lie of her cool but trembling show of disinterest? Did he *know*, the way *she* knew, what was surely going to happen between them? In the three weeks since their eyes had first met, she had told herself over and over that she could not stand another day, another night of not having him. And such uncontrollable madness was not typical of her at all.

For too many years of her young life, Jo Anne Kallen had been the kind of girl her mother and father would have been proud of even if they had been indecent enough to pry into her most intimate personal existence. They had never had to, nor would they have wanted to. They had always sensed their daughter's love and admiration for them, and her unconscious dedication to their simple, solid, unremarkable concepts of right and wrong behavior.

Jo Anne had never stinted in showing them how much she valued her father's stubborn courage in the face of forced early retirement from his busy life as a plant manager, and his heartrending refusal to show *anyone* the terrible hurt of his arthritis-ridden body and the wounds it had inflicted on his pride as a man and provider. As for her mother, a retired high-school teacher, Jo Anne had always adored her, from earliest childhood, had even gone to the University of Michigan because her mother had gone there, even though secretly she had preferred to stay in her native Southern California.

Marianne Kallen had rewarded her daughter's affection by not growing old, just older, gracefully, handsomely, uncomplainingly, and by being there for Jo Anne whenever she had needed her. She had seen Jo Anne through a quickly failed, much-too-early marriage to a boy, not a man really, whom she had met in her senior year at Michigan. No harm, no large regrets. And she had been Jo Anne's nonintrusive confidante during her surprisingly few and far-between infatuations and brief affairs that ultimately had gone nowhere for the probable reason that few young men, if indeed any, then floating around Los Angeles, Hollywood, Beverly Hills, or Pasadena could quite live up to Jo Anne Kallen's private image of the man she thought her father had always been. It is doubtful whether Bill Kallen could have lived up to that image either.

It was three years ago that Jo Anne had undergone her sea change, when her parents had been forced by inflation to give up their modest house in the Valley for a modest apartment in the Valley. Jo Anne had taken her own place in West Hollywood, and not a moment too soon either, for she had heard her twenty-fifth birthday coming ominously around the corner and knew intuitively that the shape of her life had to be altered.

She had never quite found her place in the workaday world after graduating from Michigan. A stint in a Beverly Hills bookstore, a year in a Sherman Oaks nutrition-counseling center, and a spell as a reader for an independent film producer in Century City had not really tested her mettle and had seemed socially limiting. And so, more in order to pay the rent on her new apartment and pay her own way for everything else than for career purposes, she had landed a job in the secretarial pool at the busy studio, never dreaming that she had accidentally found an arena, and the games to play in it, that would turn out to be just perfect for her. Spurred by enthusiasm, and using nothing more than her own easygoing, unthreatening charm, a few modest skills with an IBM Selectric, and a way with a telephone, she had leapfrogged in no time at all to the prideful position of executive secretary to the head honcho himself, Steven Cramm, and now to his successor, Howard Bluestern.

She had vibrated to the constant stimulation of life in an entertainment factory, to the interpersonal sparks and challenges of daily office dramas with ever-changing casts of characters, the vicarious thrills of victory and the despairs of defeat that were part and parcel of a close working relationship with a high-altitude executive whose career was forever on the line. She had discovered new strengths and abilities in herself. And that was not all that Jo Anne had found out about herself in the three years since moving out of the home of the father and mother she still adored, and for whom she still secretly harbored the dream idyll of a little house in the country with a workshop for her father to putter around in and a lovely little garden for her mother to wear her big floppy hats in.

Jo Anne had discovered her own sexuality.

It had never occurred to her how subtly she had pushed it onto the back burner of her existence, partly through choice but mostly, unconsciously, because of her intense closeness to the two most important people in her life. Once she had separated from them, the damped-down fires had begun to glow. Too many vibrant men and women streamed through her daily life who simply refused to allow her to be oblivious to her own powerful attractiveness. At first she had had difficulty adjusting to this new self-image. Gradually, her outdated resistance to invitations and overtures softened into acceptance and experimentation, and before long she found herself possessed of an active, healthy determination to make up for wasted time and lost delights, with no trace of guilt whatsoever. More quickly than she would have dreamed possible, she had evolved into a selective, discriminating young woman who sought, welcomed, and enjoyed intimate, adventurous physical relationships with her own carefully chosen opposite numbers, with responsibility but without restraint.

Jo Anne had not only *discovered* her true inner nature. She had reveled in it, and treasured it, knowing that it would lead her eventually, no hurry, to a partner for life. But all along she had confidently assumed that she was in complete control of her passion and her choices, and she had been right, up to a point—until Howard Bluestern had come along.

She had tried to fight it. She had even tried to understand it and reason it away, telling herself that it was nothing more than the excitement of his power and his palpable lust for her. But where had *that* gotten her?

Here she was, still fighting it.

Stop it, Jo Anne.

She took her handbag from the desk, rose to her feet, and went quickly past Mrs. Griffin's desk to the outer door saying, "Cover for me, will you, Dorothy?"

She'd go to the commissary and get a cup of coffee or something. Maybe that would break the spell. A glass of cold water would do even better. She knew just where to pour it, too.

Good, Jo Anne. That's better. Laugh *at yourself. Laugh at* him. *Laugh at the whole idea of the two of you together, you and the head of the studio. What a ridiculous joke. Laugh at it, Jo Anne. Where's your sense of humor?*

She got into the elevator and started down, and she couldn't even manage a smile. Because there was nothing funny about it, nothing funny at all. The truth was, she wanted to make love to Howard Bluestern in the worst possible way, and nothing on earth was going to change that.

Nor prevent it, either.

And realizing that, suddenly she started to smile.

chapter 2

HE BROUGHT the yellow Porsche to a stop at the main gate, lowered the window, and waited for the gray-haired studio cop in the glass booth to notice him. Staring straight ahead through the windshield, Teddy could see that the lot was crawling with activity, and he quickly banished from his mind the first faint tinge of sadness at feeling left out, not that he really wanted any part of this scene any more. It just felt more comfortable not to know that it was going on without him, which was why he hated to leave the beach for *any* reason. The old geezer finally decided to look at him, did the inevitable double take, and started to say, "For a minute there I thought—"

"Yeah, I know, I know. Teddy Stern. Appointment with Howard Bluestern."

The cop glanced down at the list on his desk, then looked up. "Sure, *I* know you, Teddy. You're the actor fellow, aren't you?"

"None other than." He shoved the car into second with an impatient thrust.

"You know where to go, Teddy?"

"Approximately."

"Okay, Teddy. Turn left up there, then make another left and take the first parking place you can find."

"What's your name, mister?"

The old cop blinked rapidly. "Louis H. Carmichael."

"Okay, Louie. Tell me, Louie. Do you call my brother Howie?"

"What?"

"Fuck off, Louie." Teddy gunned the motor and shot forward, startling a covey of blue-jeaned chicks in high-heeled boots who were showboating their tight behinds past the messenger boys, fourth assistant nobodies, and two-bit actors loafing around ogling the action and picking their teeth. Subjects, all of them, whether they knew it or not. Formerly of the kingdom of Steven Cramm, who had committed the unpardonable blunder of getting caught wrist-deep in the Famous Amos

11

jar. And so they were now, every last twelve thousand of them in this phantasmagoria factory, the subjects of one Howard Bluestern, whose chief qualification had been that no one had ever managed to catch him at anything, though God knows, and all that. The king was dead. Long live the lucky schmuck.

Teddy emerged from the elevator at the penthouse level and made his way with difficulty across the deep pile of the carpeting, like walking in a snowdrift, toward the wide-eyed stare of the dark-haired young woman at the reception desk. The fact that he was wearing shades, Western-style boots, and a cowboy hat didn't seem to make a damned bit of difference. There was something about him, *always*, it seemed, no matter to what lengths he went to deodorize it, that smelled of brother Howard, and rare was the nose that failed to pick up the scent.

"Mr. Bluestern is expecting me," he said to the upturned face.

"You must be his brother," she said.

"Fantastic," he said, and waited while she dialed a number and said some magic words.

Presently the door behind her opened and a honey-haired girl wearing spectacles that were much too large for her flawed but beautiful face and a skirt that was too short for her perfect legs came toward him saying, "Mr. Stern?"

His eyes took her in in one big bite as he nodded, and quicker than a dying meteor, the ridiculous thought that his life had somehow just changed, for better or for worse, flashed through his mind and was gone.

"Come with me, please."

"Any time, Miss Kallen."

She threw him a puzzled look. "How did you know my name?"

"I read it in your eyes," he said. "Right beneath where it says Pittsburgh Plate Glass."

She regarded him for a moment without expression, then walked back into the office and held the door open for him.

"I know," he said, going in past her. "Real stupid, I'm sorry."

She nodded toward a closed door. "In there. He's waiting."

"Forgiven?"

She said nothing and went back to her desk. Through the open door of a smaller adjacent office he could see two older women staring at him over their typewriters. You are looking, he said to them silently, at the once and future nothing who is about to become king for a day. And with that, he opened the door and went inside.

Howard Bluestern looked up and tossed the memo he was reading back on the desk. "Jesus, you must've done eighty," he said.

Teddy grinned. "Only when I spotted a police car following me and slowed down."

Bluestern grimaced. "Sit down. Can I get you anything?"

"Nope." Teddy sank down on the sofa and looked around appraisingly. "All *right*. A touch much, but I think I'm going to like it."

Bluestern was eyeing his brother with faint distaste. "What's with the Wild West costume?"

"Just to make it easier for *you*," Teddy said. "Even at a costume ball, no one would suspect you were president Howard Bluestern, not in *this* outfit. By the way, my car is parked behind the building and across the street." He took out his car keys, tossed them in the air, caught them and ostentatiously returned them to the left breast pocket of his fringed light-suede jacket.

Bluestern nodded and said, "Still driving the Porsche?"

Teddy shrugged. "I couldn't go for the colors on this year's Rolls."

They looked at each other for a few moments in silence. "You've got a helluva tan," Bluestern said. "Lucky I've been playing a lot of tennis or one of us would have to use make-up. By the way, am I liable to run into any trouble out at the house?"

"Not unless you call Linda Carol trouble, and she's none whatsoever, believe me," Teddy said. "It's all set for tonight."

Bluestern blinked rapidly. "That's nice . . . I think. What's your relationship again?"

"Fun and games, impure and simple. She just started a new job at Holman-Meyer in Beverly Hills, assistant to the buyer in leather goods or something. She'll arrive around seven, expects to cook me . . . *you* . . . a spaghetti dinner. A hundred-dollar bill afterwards, for perfume and stuff, would not make her furious."

"You got any grass around, foolish question? I may need it."

"Below the bar, behind a couple of jugs of Gallo," Teddy said. "But you won't need it. The chick has magic in her tongue. Worry not."

Bluestern glanced at his brother. "Speaking of worry, shouldn't I be concerned about Diane?"

Teddy scowled. "Only a psychiatrist should be concerned about *her*. She cleared out all her clothes, so I guarantee you she went home to equally crazy momma in Palm Springs. I mean, we weren't living together for more than a month before she was beginning to get a ringing in her ears . . . wedding bells, can you beat it? *That* one, of all creatures.''

"You probably told her you were in love with her or something. I know you, kiddo.''

Teddy stirred uncomfortably. "So what?''

Bluestern shook his head slowly. "You'll never change, will you?''

"Look, don't give me any of that shit.''

"What are you getting so angry about?''

Teddy got to his feet. "I say just enough to them, no more, no less, than it takes to get them to lie down . . .''

"You'd be better off saying less and doing it to them standing up,'' Bluestern said.

"And what have *you* got to show for all your wisdom, huh, Howard? Two dirty divorces and a double dose of alimony . . .''

"Single dose, single. The Hufnagle guy *married* my Frances, remember?''

"Terrific,'' Teddy said with sarcasm.

Bluestern frowned. "Look, what the hell are we talking about?''

"I don't know. You started it.''

"And finished it. Right now. You want some coffee? I do.''

"No.''

Bluestern pressed the intercom and asked for an all black, nothing in it. To his brother he said, "Sit down, will you please? You're making me nervous.''

Teddy flopped on the sofa again and took off his sunglasses. The door opened and Jo Anne Kallen came in with a mug of coffee and set it down on the desk.

"Thank you,'' Bluestern said. "You know my brother, don't you?''

"Yes,'' she said tersely, and left.

Teddy shrugged.

"Well, what do you think?'' Bluestern said eagerly.

"Miss Kallen?''

"Yes.''

"I think maybe you better tell me what you know about her,'' Teddy said.

Bluestern frowned. "Absolutely nothing. Why?''

"Just so I don't go putting my foot into anything around here, including my own mouth.''

Bluestern's expression darkened. "Just keep the door to this office closed, and bear in mind that I'm very uncommunicative with the help. The less you have to do with them, the easier the strain will be on your questionable acting skills . . ."

"Thank you, Howard."

"Naturally, I'm going to brief you on the few problems that may come at you around here in the way of company business during your brief sojourn . . ."

"This'll be a first for me," Teddy said. "I've never played anybody more important than the chief dispatcher for a taxicab company."

Bluestern's voice turned sour again. "What makes you think a dispatcher is any less important than a company president with shit in his urine?"

"My guy had leukemia and didn't know it," Teddy said. He glanced around. "Say, don't the phones ever ring around here? I'm gonna get lonesome."

Bluestern's nose twitched slightly. "I instructed the girls to hold my calls. After all, you told me you were an important person."

Teddy noted the hostility and filed it away under So What Else Is New. "Oh yes, very large."

"Then suppose you rise and shine," Bluestern said, getting up from behind the desk. "First lock that door over there, if you will."

"Yes, your majesty." Teddy got to his feet slowly, ambled over to the door and turned the button in the knob. "And then . . . ?"

"I'd like to leave early and beat the traffic if possible," Bluestern said. "Shall we change partners and dance?"

"Now?"

For an answer, Bluestern removed his suit jacket, and Teddy picked up the cue. They began to peel off their clothes, tossing them on the sofa, until Bluestern was down to his undershirt and boxers and Teddy stood in his jockey shorts, grinning foolishly.

"Underwear too?" he said.

"Everything," Bluestern said. "It's just as easy to do this thing right as it is to screw it up."

In a moment they were both nude.

For men of dissimilar life styles, their bodies were remarkably similar, lean, hard, flat-bellied and attractively muscular. Teddy's addiction to daily five-mile sprints along the water's edge was matched by Bluestern's competitive mania on his tennis court. The marijuana that put something of a ceiling on Teddy's booze consumption had its equivalent in the obsession with work that kept Bluestern from eating and drinking when everyone around him was committing slow and secret suicide. At thirty-nine, they were both considered handsome by men and turn-ons by women. But those who knew them intimately were embarrassed by the self-contempt that lay too close to the surface of Teddy's flippancy and were made uncomfortable by Bluestern's smugness, and by his apparent belief that a sense of humor was nothing more than a worthless butter knife in a jungle that called for machetes.

Naked, without their clothes on to distract and confuse the senses, they were indeed identical, give or take Bluestern's slightly paler body and Teddy's inch or two of longer hair. But as they began to put on each other's costumes now, their personalities appeared subtly to change, became easily misreadable in the eyes of the average careless beholder, consumed as he or she would be with self.

It had ever been that way, since the age of eight, when they had first fooled even their now long-dead father and mother, and then their schoolteachers, and of course every willing, unwitting female they could lay their perverse, tricky hands on. But the pleasure of deception had faded years ago, as their mutual dislike stole up on them and quietly grew, fed by disparate interests and unequal fortune. Since making the move west to California, they had exchanged names and physical identities only out of medical necessity, when Bluestern had felt himself sufficiently prosperous to purchase an extravagant disability-insurance policy, or the major medical hospital policy that would protect him against any dangerous inroads into the money market funds and sophisticated tax shelters his business manager had put him into.

If Teddy was jealous, it certainly never showed up in his wee-wee, which was always pure and abundant. Nor did he ever crow, even secretly to himself, over the twist of fate that had spared him his brother's tainted stream even as it had spared him his brother's wealth. The only true amusement they had actually shared, down through the years, had not been over a glass of beer or champagne but over a beaker of urine in the dumbbell presence of some unsuspecting examiner for Equitable Assurance or New York Life.

Bluestern had found out about his condition early on, when the family was still living in Chicago. A close friend, who had lost too many jobs too quickly and had become an insurance salesman, had managed to get his company to return Bluestern's application for a small whole-life policy and destroy all evidence of the application's ever having been made after the insurance company doctor had found sufficient albumin in Bluestern's specimen, and in a second one after that, to warn the agent that his client would probably be, forevermore, uninsurable, particularly if his medical history found its way into the ever-vigilant insurance industry computers.

Using another name, Bluestern had gone to a GU specialist in nearby Galesburg, had heard uttered for the very first time the words *benign albuminuria*, had been told that it would be chronic but never kill him, and every year or so after that, always when he was traveling, always using another name, always paying the doctor's bill in cash, Bluestern had had checkups with other physicians, just to make sure that the condition was under control.

Meanwhile, Teddy had pinch-hit for him—whenever there had been insurance company runners on base.

And now, as he finished buttoning Howard's shirt on himself, Teddy said, "The question is, do I remember how to tie a tie?"

"Don't ask, just go over to the mirror and do it," Bluestern said. "I'm not coming over to the house tomorrow to dress you." He had struggled into Teddy's jeans and boots and the Western shirt and slid now into the suede jacket, put on the shades, and donned the hat. "Hot damn," he said softly. "Like right on, man . . ."

"Like shut up, Teddy," said Teddy, turning away from the mirror. He slipped on the suit jacket and buttoned it. "Wait a minute, we forgot wristwatches."

"I always did admire your thoroughness, Howard," said Bluestern. He removed his tank watch and exchanged it for Teddy's Seiko digital, then walked over to the door and unlocked it. When he turned, Teddy was seated behind the desk. "Jesus, if the stockholders could see you, they'd crap in their pants."

"Must you be so insufferably vulgar?" Teddy said. "This corporation has never been in more capable hands."

"By the way," Bluestern said, "I told David to do a steak and salad and half a grapefruit for tonight. I hope that meets with your approval, Mr. Bluestern."

"Would he feel hurt if I had dinner out?"

"You mean in a restaurant?"

Teddy smiled. "I kind of thought I'd practice forging your signature at Ma Maison."

Bluestern frowned, and his voice grew hard. "You're supposed to hate acting, right? So tonight you're going to live up to your reputation. You're going to stay home and watch TV, and you're going to let my answering service take any calls and you're going to go to bed early . . ."

Teddy forced his smile to widen. "No faith in me, huh?"

"Goddam it, Teddy, if you can't lie low for one lousy night, if it's asking too much of you—"

"Come on, Howard . . ."

"—Maybe we better make the switch early in the morning, even if it means getting up at six o'clock—"

"Howard . . ."

"I was trying to make it as easy as I could for you. I know you like to sleep late. But if you're going to—"

"Will you stop it?" Teddy said. "I was pulling your leg, can't you tell? How the hell are you going to pass yourself off as *me*, especially with Linda, if you're going to be so *ridiculously* straight?"

"You forget," Bluestern said, his voice still shaking a little, "I *am* ridiculously straight. And *you* better be too while you're around this office."

Teddy came up out of his slouch and sat stiff and upright behind the desk. "You have my assurance, sir, that I will take the matter under consideration. My secretary will call you as soon as the executive board arrives at a decision. And now, if you will excuse me, Mr. Stern, I have to go into a meeting."

Bluestern nodded, cooling down. "Not bad, not bad."

"It's fucking perfect."

Bluestern glanced at the Seiko digital on his wrist. "If you don't mind, I'm going to blow now. But first let me take about ten minutes to brief you and show you the lay of the land . . ."

"I already met her," Teddy said.

Bluestern reddened. "Look, I'm *warning* you—"

"Howard, Howard," Teddy wagged a finger, smiling sadly. "Unstraighten a little, will you? Bend a little, get crooked a little."

Bluestern's lips tightened. "Maybe I'll be able to afford that luxury some day, when I don't have to worry about carrying the both of us."

Teddy looked away reflexively, as though a sinking feeling in the pit of the stomach were something visible that could be seen in the eyes and betray you. "Yeah," he said quietly.

The briefing took almost thirty minutes. Then Bluestern left.

OH LOVELY SKY, lovely clouds, peaceful, peaceful, the shimmering sea far below her on her left, and through the window on the other side, the rolling hills and the ribbonlike highways covered with little crawling things, little bugs scooting every which way, how she needed this, to be alone up here, snug and comfortable in the beige vinyl bucket seat of her beloved bird, with her hands resting lightly on the control yoke and her feet on the rudder pedals and the sound in her ears of the deep-throated, reassuring thrum of the engine and the whistling bite of of the clean pure air rushing past the wings and Plexiglas windows of her sanctuary, her haven, her only escape.

Diane peered down at the world of majestic beauty gliding by beneath her and thought how much more beautiful it was from this distant vantage point than when you were close in and a part of it, when you were right in the middle of it, trying to live with it and endure it, how much better to be able to take off from it, to ease the throttle in and gather speed and soar away from it and look down on it and know that it could no longer touch you.

Teddy could not hurt her up here, nor she hurt him. Nor could she hurt her mother either.

Why was it that she could not stop hurting people and thereby hurting herself? Diane would never know the answers, because they were unknowable to her, but she had to go on asking herself the questions just the same. They went around in her head all the time and troubled her and confused her and made her say terrible things to everyone, which shocked them and hurt them and made them strike back at her, and their striking back was painful to *her* but she did not know how to stop, she could never seem to stop no matter how hard she tried, and she did try, she tried very hard to be kind and decent and loving, but she just couldn't sustain it for long, something would happen inside her, and the best she could do then, for herself and for the others, was to run to her Cessna, to her faithful big bird, and let it take her aloft to safety, where the worst that could happen was that she could not stop thinking, and the only person she could hurt was herself, and she was glad that she was up here now because she hadn't wanted to hurt Teddy. It was the unknowable something inside her that had driven her to do and say the things that she had the night before. It only *seemed* that her drinking had been the cause of it all, the cause of everything that was painful in her life.

She knew it wasn't the drinking. She knew it was something else. But if she could make everyone else think that it was the drinking, maybe she could make herself believe that too. Then she could stop looking inside herself, and stop asking herself all those dangerous questions and go back to Teddy, where she really wanted to be, of course she wanted to be with Teddy, her darling Teddy, how could she have stormed out on him that way? He needed her so, needed her love and her caring and her protection and her understanding of all his weaknesses and vulnerabilities. No one understood him the way she did, no one could read the deep hurt in his eyes at the way everyone in the movie community treated him with pity and scorn just because he wasn't *some*body, just because he wasn't his brother, just because he hadn't *made* it and never would. Well, *she* knew him for what he was, and he was adorable and tender and funny and touching and crazy and cruel and dangerous and . . . and *what* . . . incapable of loving anyone? Who said *that*?

You said that, *you*, Diane, last night. How could you have *done* that to him? It was the drinking, Diane, you really should stop. You've *got* to stop. I mean, why do you *do* it?

I do it to fool everyone.

To fool myself.

She let the questions come, she did not mind them at all, as she floated through the sky on the wings of her friend. She was going to be banking and turning in a very short while, and take her bird back to its nest at the sprawling airport in Santa Monica. She was going to try to get back with Teddy again, so let the questions keep coming if they wanted to, for in one of them, perhaps, she might find a clue that would help her to make the relationship go *right* this time.

What was this knack she had, this splendid skill, this marvelous ability to make everything in her life go wrong, no matter how hopeful things seemed? What was she trying to prove about herself, and who was it who was always to blame for these failures?

Not she. Oh never, not she.

Was there any *better* way—admit it, Diane—any better way of holding someone in thrall, a captive in chains of guilt, if that someone were bound up in your welfare and cared what happened to you, any better way to make someone *miserable* than always to fail that someone's hopes for you, always to be self-destructive and nonproductive, forever disappointing?

That would teach the vain, self-indulgent, pleasure-loving, adulterous *bitch* to love her as much as she always had and still did.

Suddenly Diane felt anger rising in her. The hell with it. She kicked the rudder pedal hard, rolled over into a steep banking turn and headed for home. She was going back to Teddy, if he would have her.

And even if he *wouldn't*.

chapter 3

IT WAS Method acting all right. Not Lee Strasberg's Method, Teddy Stern's Method. The way to be unmistakably Howard was to think pretentious bullshit in your head at all times, even when saying something as simple as, "Would you hold my calls please and bring your pad in?"

He had wasted *enough* time, almost a whole hour, reading the trades, staring out the window, using the executive toilet, and fielding phone calls, the one from Lazar mostly a listening job, the others from people who apparently hadn't known Howard any better than *he* had known *them*. No problems had arisen, but each time Jo Anne Kallen's voice had come through to him announcing the call, he had felt more frustrated by the closed door between them.

He had, he thought, exercised admirable restraint. He deserved a reward for good behavior. And so he had given it to himself by asking her to come in. The fact that he was being deliberately disobedient to Howard by so doing, even risking the possibility of a quick unmasking, only served to add to his anticipatory enjoyment. Good boys finished last. Naughty boys had all the fun.

Teddy watched her approaching the desk now, and saw nothing on her fair-skinned, sensual face that hinted at puzzlement or suspicion, only a strange kind of breathless nervousness, as though she were planning to ask for a raise, and a glitter in her eyes that he had not noticed before. He gestured toward the chair beside his desk and swiveled to watch her sit down and cross her legs. Her short skirt hiked well above her knees and immediately rekindled the free-floating lust that had pervaded his earlier dream on the beach. A moment later her perfume washed over him, bringing back memories of other creatures, other rooms. Eyeing her with studied indifference, as he imagined Howard would have done, he said, "Well, what did you think of my pseudo-cowboy brother, Miss Kallen?"

The question seemed to startle her. Her face flushed slightly. "We hardly even met," she said softly.

21

"*Impression*, then . . ."

She thought about it for a moment. "Sort of offbeat. *Different* than you in many ways, Mr. Bluestern . . ."

He knew, of course, that he should drop the subject, but instead he moved on to where the ice was even thinner. "In what ways?"

"Well . . . he seems a little fragile, or is the word *brittle*? You're more solid . . . *together* . . ."

"Uh huh . . ."

"I don't think he *likes* himself very much, or anybody else, I suspect. . . ." She hesitated. "He has none of your *strength* . . . *attractiveness?* . . . Is that the right word?"

He shrugged. "*I* like it." He held her gaze, then glanced away and ran a hand through the unanswered mail on Howard's desk. "I don't see how I'm ever going to catch up with all this. I wonder, would anyone object if I asked you to stay on and work with me tonight?" He dared to look at her again, and her eyes were still on him.

"Who would object, Mr. Bluestern?"

"Well, you for one," he said, smiling. "Or the head of your department? Or a gentleman friend perhaps?"

She pushed her hair out of her eyes. "Where would you like to work?"

Teddy could feel the beating of his heart. "Here would be all right," he said evenly. "But frankly it would be more convenient, and *comfortable*, if we met over at *my* house and managed a little dinner in between dictation. How does that strike you?"

"That sounds fine to me," she said.

"Are you sure?"

"Very sure," she said.

"You know the house?"

"I know where it is. I'll be able to find it. Shall I go home and change first or—?"

"No, Jo Anne, you're perfect just as you are."

Something in his voice made her look away. "What time do you want me, Mr. Bluestern?"

He tried not to say it, but it came out anyway. "Now," he said quietly.

She glanced at him with uncertain expression.

"Right now, Jo Anne," he said.

Her whole body started to tremble.

He held out a hand to her. "Come over here."

She hesitated.

"Please?"

Slowly she rose and placed her pad on the chair and went around the desk to him and he could smell her other, more personal fragrance now. He put his hands behind her on the soft curve of her and brought her very close to him and pressed his lips to her skirt just below the buckle of her belt, and then suddenly he felt her hands seizing his hair and pulling his head back and she was leaning over him and finding his mouth with her own and moaning, "Oh God, what are you doing to me? . . ."

He rose carefully to a standing position, still in her grasp, and buried his hands in her hair and kissed her hungrily, and then they broke apart, pale and shaken, and he said thickly, "I better call the house."

Her voice was a whisper. "I'll get it for you."

She started away but he reached out quickly and seized her wrist and pulled her back to him and took her into his arms and devoured her savagely until he heard her faltering voice, "The door isn't locked . . ."

"I know," he murmured. She tore out of his arms and moved quickly to the door and opened it and went out, leaving him standing there, his heart pounding.

He sank down in the desk chair and for a few moments he tried to make believe that he hadn't been planning this all along. Howard had told him to lie low at the house tonight and stay out of harm's way. So what the *hell* was he doing? He was being seduced, that's what he was doing. By a girl who obviously wanted him as desperately as he wanted her. Wanted *Howard* desperately. It came with the territory, no?

Yes, goddam it. Don't blame *me* . . .

The buzzer sounded and he picked up the phone.

Her voice had regained its composure. "Your houseman on two," she said.

"Thank you." He closed his eyes, shook his head to clear it, willed himself back together again, vividly imagined himself smelling fresh dog-do, punched the phone button and immediately became Howard, saying, "David?"

"Yes, Mr. Bluestern?"

"Don't change the menu for tonight, just double it. My secretary, Miss Kallen, is coming over for dinner to clean up some work with me."

"Very well. Shall I change the wine then? We were going to finish up the Margaux."

"Whatever you say, David." How the hell would *he* know? Once you got past José Cuervo he was over his head.

"Morgon perhaps? Moulin à Vent?"

"Moulin à Vent. Perfect." Only don't ask me to spell it.

"Very well, sir. Anything else?"

Yes, he thought, you might open your veins and serve us some ice water, too. "No, that's it. See you later."

He was going to have to be on his toes around the limey bastard tonight. The few times that he had met him, he had not been surprised by the man's hostility toward *him*. What *had* surprised him was the little turd's obvious contempt for his employer. The evening promised too much sheer, wanton delight to be interfered with in any way by a former British safecracker, blackmailer, bookmaker, and pimp who considered working for one of Hollywood's most powerful executives somehow beneath him and made no secret of the fact that he was on the lookout for something better.

Why the devil had Howard kept him around so long?

Obviously, what the man needed was a little slapping around.

chapter 4

JUST BEFORE he stepped into the shower, David Stanner removed the wad of Kleenex that was stuck to his detumescing penis and noticed thin streaks of blood in the already drying semen around his crotch and belly. He would have given the matter immediate thought, adding it to all the other puzzlements of the evening, but getting squeaky clean had priority right now, and he gasped as the hot water hit him. Quickly his body adjusted to the extreme temperature, and then he began to feel good again, felt himself coming back from the exhaustion that always overtook him when he mixed too much cocaine with intercourse.

He started to lather himself with the thick green bar of Roger and Gallet soap that he used only because Bluestern had brought back several boxes of it from London just for him. The round bar was too large for his relatively small hands, and quite often had slipped from his grasp and fallen on his bare feet, usually the right one, hurting him painfully if not seriously. He had decided to keep using the fragrant soap anyway, telling himself that he did not believe in waste, or in looking gift-soap bars in the mouth, when he knew bloody well that he continued to suffer the occasional blows to his instep only because he still harbored hopes that he would one day soon be successful in persuading Bluestern to take a shower with him. No need to insult and confuse the luv unnecessarily when you were working so hard to break his fingernail grasp on his heterosexuality.

Working his smooth, fair-skinned body over with the perfumed lather, enjoying the feelings his sensuous hands created, Stanner idly reviewed whatever highlights of the evening presented themselves now to his receptive musings.

Bluestern and the girl had gazed at each other across the table with embarrassing nakedness all during dinner, barely speaking, scarcely picking at their filets, obviously obsessed with each other, or with thoughts of what they would shortly be doing to each other. Every time Stanner had returned to the kitchen after stealing glances at them

25

in the dining room, he had been aware of the swelling of his sex, and had finally recognized it as the invitation to the party, self-extended and eagerly accepted. No matter that the girl was nothing spectacular in the face or bosom. There was promising hunger in her deep blue eyes and in her full wide mouth, and her long legs and arching ass seemed to be made for all kinds of sinuous wonders.

Then, too, Bluestern had not been his usual rigid self tonight, seeming more relaxed and loose, a little disheveled even, less formal, actually wild-swinging with biting, sadistic putdowns that had left Stanner positively quivering with wounded delight. Had it been this verbal whipping that had excited him so? Had it been his master's preoccupation with the girl and she with him? Or had Stanner been unwittingly taken by Bluestern's never-before-seen slouch, a kind of lazy grace when he entered the house and walked across the entrance hall that had caught Stanner's eye and caused a sudden unbidden quickening?

Stanner soaped his underarms, placed the Roger and Gallet foot-destroyer in the soap receptacle, and started to turn slowly, face upraised, under the hot cleansing spray. He had wondered, at first sight, what qualities there were about this secretary that had gained her an entrance into the hall of fame hitherto reserved by Bluestern exclusively for ravishingly beautiful aspiring young actresses, and for older, less physically desirable superstars. But when Stanner had heard her love-cries all the way from the closed-off master bedroom to the kitchen, and when he had then stood quietly outside the bedroom door and listened to her ecstatic weeping, her endless moaning, "Oh God, Howard, I love you love you darling darling . . . ," he knew how powerful her attraction must have been for Bluestern if he himself had suddenly felt the pounding of his own pulse and an overwhelming, irresistible need to share immediately, without a second's delay, what the girl was feeling for Bluestern and he for her.

His hands had trembled so badly that he had fought with his clothes to get them off, and his fumbling fingers had spilled some of the precious dust that he inhaled on such occasions for animal strength and the power to soar to heaven. But once inside the almost-dark bedroom, with the door quietly shut behind him, with the smell of their flushed and sweating bodies in his nostrils and their groaning sighs in his ears, inflamed by the sight of Bluestern's body, buttocks upreared, head burrowing between squirming milky thighs, Stanner was all poise and purpose, stiff and directed, advancing noiselessly to their side in the darkness, his swollen member throbbing before him as he eased himself onto the bed.

In his mind's eye and in the quickening between his legs as he stood beneath the shower now, he saw it all again and felt its wonders as well as its mysteries, mysteries that would be solved at some future time when there were less pleasurable reveries to luxuriate in.

Bluestern's head rears up in the darkness and turns. "Who is that?"

"Oh God, don't stop!" she cries.

" 'Tis only I, luv."

"Come into me, Howard, come into me!"

"David! What the hell are you . . . ?"

Ah, silly boy, it's only my hand with the Vaseline, ah nice, ah how lovely you be . . .

"Howard, please!"

And she pulls Bluestern toward her and their mouths are glued together and her long legs around him are locking him inside her and her body heaves beneath the double burden of master and slave and in her beautiful agony she is unaware or uncaring of the presence of the stranger who is nothing more than the lock at the back door that keeps her Howard oh God Howard from withdrawing and now the hands that are too small for Roger and Gallet are on the undulating male hips and the throbbing phallus finds its mark and fights its way in past the sphincter that is tight, so unfamiliar, so tight, where is the soft corridor we know so well, and why the screaming with pain, luv, who are you trying to fool, you know you adore it, you know that nothing on earth can keep you from exploding when you feel me moving inside of you when you're inside the loved one underneath you, that's more like it, luv, ah yes, that's more like it, luv, ah yes, scream and shout with pleasure and pain, that's it, ah beautiful, luv, there we go, there we go, listen to her, marvelous woman and now you, yes *you, you, go, go, go,* yes, scream, yes, shout, ah *good,* oh *Jesus Howard* . . .

They had died together, the three of them, in the strange, mysterious darkness of the steamy, sweet-smelling, sex-smelling bedroom, with only the sound of their labored breathing and the dying-down sobs of the grateful girl, and then his own noiseless feet padding on the thick gray carpeting and the closing door, as quiet as when he had opened it to come in. And now he was clean and coming down hard from the diamond-sharp high with only the smarting of his nostrils to remember it by.

He toweled himself gently, not wanting to disturb the train of his gathering thoughts, trying to decide whether he had only imagined the look of total surprise on Bluestern's face when Bluestern had reared up and turned to see who was joining the love play. It had been dark enough for him to have read more surprise on that face than had really been there, just as Bluestern himself could have mistaken him in the dark momentarily for someone else. There was an explanation for everything on God's earth, Stanner knew, once you had all the facts. Bluestern's acting surprised, his pretense that back-porch loving was new to him, could have been for the girl's benefit. More difficult to account for, though not impossible, was Bluestern's strangely virginal tightness inside. Apparently the mind had strange ways over matter at times, trying to shut out the very intruder who, a few moments later, would bring you ecstasy.

He moved the towel softly over his genitals, drying his parts and at the same time soothing them. The streaks of blood bothered him. They were gone now, but he had seen them there, no doubt about that. True, his phallus had felt huge and he had been wild with lust. But he could not recall having thrust with undue violence, certainly not more than Bluestern had ever received from him during the almost two years that they had been working their miracles in tandem on the lucky women of filmland who knew how to open their legs and keep their mouths shut.

Back in his insultingly small bedroom, annoyed with himself for being so incapable of tolerating mystery but resigned to living with it until the morning, when no doubt Bluestern would explain everything, Stanner turned on the telly, lay back on his bed, all warm and dry and naked, and waited for sleep to put a temporary end to the puzzlements that still nagged at him. He had no way of knowing that a part of his brain which had always been beyond the reach of his consciousness was already at work, analyzing and synthesizing the events of the evening in order to create new and highly profitable tools of survival for him at some future, undetermined date.

I'LL *kill* HIM! She shrieked inside her head, I'll kill them *both*! Diane cried out to herself with her tear-stained face pressed against the cold window pane to block out the reflection of the streetlights behind her that was threatening to prevent her from seeing everything that was going on inside the bedroom in all its beautiful ugly magnificence, everything she could not bear to look at yet could not tear her eyes from as she watched them on the bed through the imperfectly drawn curtains that were meant to hide their naked bodies from the outside world as she shivered in the windy darkness with the waves booming on the rocks and sand beyond the warm and cozy beach house she had thought would be her own one day and now knew would never be hers, nor him, not ever, him on the bed with that gorgeous creature whoever she was with her golden-streaked hair, he had lied to her, she had been *right* to leave him, but he could have mourned her loss, suffered her walking out on him for at *least* a few days, not like *this*, my God, with the bed barely cold and the perfume of her own body still in the sheets and him with another one now, easing her back and down now, rising above her spreading thighs and thrusting into her and joining his mouth to hers, oh God, she couldn't bear to look, she couldn't bear *not* to watch them, how beautiful, how beautiful, oh Teddy, you bastard, how *could* you, oh darling, she cried, turning away from the window, and she stumbled across the sand toward her car, waiting up the road where she had parked it beside the dunes earlier that evening, where she had sat, watching and waiting, first seeing him arrive in the yellow Porsche, then sitting there in her car drinking Wild Turkey out of the bottle until she had thought her throat would burn away, drinking and weeping and trying to make her numbed brain compose the words, the dialogue that would make him understand that she had not meant what she had said to him and what she had done to him the night before as they had tried to come together in love and hate and misunderstanding, and just as she had decided that she would leave the car and go inside and confront him with her love even if she knew not what the words would be, she hadn't cared what she would say or what he would say, just as long as she could be in there with him again, hear the sound of his voice, feel his hands on her again, just as she was getting out of the car feeling sick and dizzy but filled with fiery love and courage and determination to forgive him and rejoin him and take care of him and marry him and spend the rest of her harrowing, fear-ridden, Mommy-ridden, screwed-up life with him, the other car had come up the road and turned into the driveway and entered his garage, *his* garage, and she had seen the girl get out of the car with the large grocery bag in her arms, she had seen the long streaked mane and the flash of her legs and the lewdly inviting curve of her bottom and had known without evidence, had known with certainty what would go on between her and Teddy, what would happen that night with the spiked heels removed and the tight-fitting green jersey dress peeled off and the breasts exposed and the legs around him, oh the son of a bitch, what a fool you were, Diane, you disgusting, simpering, loathsome excuse for a woman, you doormat, you pitiful, hateful, sniveling fool you, you knew what they would be doing with each other when they were sated and stoned and dizzy with wine, you knew your Teddy, you *knew* girls who looked like that one did, you knew but you had to see, didn't you, and now you've seen, haven't you, and all you can do is choke and gurgle and let your nose run all over your wretched face, is that all you can do, is that all you're going to do, you mean you're going to let him do this to you, you're going to let him get away with this, you're going to live with the memory of this for the rest of your life, is *that* all you're going to do, knowing that she'll be leaving him and going home soon, of course she will, sluts like that don't stay long, not like you, Diane, they put their clothes on and go home, they don't even bathe or shower, they just put their clothes on and take the money off the dresser and slip out of the house and disappear into the night, taking their whore-smell with them while he lies on the bed sound asleep, unmindful of the wet spotted sheets or the sound of the door closing quietly or the car starting away, unmindful of anything, not really *giving* a shit about anyone or anything, sound asleep, alone like he always wanted to be, even when you had lain beside him, alone, that's all he had ever wanted of you, to be left alone, he had never wanted you, he had lied to you all along, used you and lied to you, the son of a bitch, she sobbed, leaning against the car, you can't do this to me, she wept, not to *me* you can't, not to *me* you won't . . .

chapter 5

ONCE THE LAST FEW NOTES of the musical alarm clock had finally brought him awake, it took Teddy several moments to add the absence of the familiar thunder of the Pacific to the absence of the damp and musty odor of his own bed and come up with the luxurious silence of Howard's subtly scented bedroom in Bel Air. He turned his head to the pillow beside him, where last he had seen the lovely face, and now there was only a note there, written in pencil in her elaborately graceful penmanship. He glanced first at the tank watch on the bed table, noted that it was only ten minutes to eight—he had plenty of time—then propped himself up in bed and plucked the note from the pillow.

> *Howard dear,*
>
> *Whatever it may or may not have been for you,*
> *I want you to know that for me, last night was*
> *sheer heaven (despite the inconsequential but*
> *SURPRISING complications). You are a lovely*
> *being, Howard, and I hope I am not overestimating*
> *my command over myself to assure you that*
> *nothing that ever happens between us on a personal*
> *level will ever affect our professional relationship.*
> *Please don't allow my cool office demeanor*
> *to persuade you that I am indifferent to you. I*
> *am a firm believer in hidden feelings, wherever*
> *and whenever the hiding seems appropriate. (Weren't*
> *"hidden feelings" INDESCRIBABLY BEAUTIFUL last*
> *night, once we revealed them?)*
>
> > *Yours,*
> >
> > *Jo Anne*

He got out of bed, pulled the drapes open onto another sunlit day, took the note into the bathroom with him, tore it into many small pieces, dropped the pieces into the toilet and flushed them away with

31

his urine. His first inclination, to regard her words with the cynicism born of too many encounters with treacherous females, somehow did not work. He felt strangely touched by her fairness and decency (the shrewd and clever little broad), just as he had been moved almost to tears last night by the nakedness of her wild emotions (what an actress). It saddened him now, gave him a gnawing sense of personal loss, to realize that she would be in no way his if he should want her (you deluded asshole). It was Howard she was taken with, not him. Howard would have her in his life every day, and any night that he chose. He had set her up for Howard without even intending to (you're welcome, you prick).

As he slipped into his brother's navy blue terrycloth robe and the matching slippers, he became aware of the ache in his rectum that had been there the moment he woke up, and he allowed himself to think again of David's sneak attack. But as much as he wanted to ponder the significance of the event—the possibility that his brother belted them into the *left-field* stands as well as the right-field bleachers—his brain stubbornly refused to dwell on the subject. Either he secretly feared that what could be true for Howard could always be true, if not now then later, for him. Or else it was too early in the morning and too nice a day outside for him to accept the fact, and it *was* a fact, that he had *allowed* the insidious limey to bugger him, no matter that it had been uninvited, no matter that he had been afraid to overreact to what apparently was not an extraordinary happening in the bedroom of Howard Bluestern.

You son of a gun you, he thought. *I* called *you* straight? You're a closet pretzel.

He smiled wryly as he shaved; then showered, blew his hair dry, went into Howard's vast dressing room and selected one of the three dozen suits that Norman at Dorso's had created for Howard to make him appear a little less stiff than he really was (or was he, really?). At eight forty-five by the wall clock in the breakfast room, he sat down at the table and immediately immersed himself in the *Times* sports section and in his bacon and eggs, so deeply that the paler-than-usual David Stanner would have had to be rude and intrusive to get a conversation going if he had wanted to, and there was no indication that he really wanted to, thank God. With the orange juice he had offered Teddy a tentative "How are *we* this morning?" To which Teddy had replied, "As thoroughly spent as an Arab's thousand-dollar bill on Rodeo Drive."

And if you mean am I hurting, the answer is yes, you cockney bastard.

"Could I have a large glass of water, David, with no ice in it?"

"Certainly, sir."

The least he owed Howard's insurance examiner this morning was a decently filled bladder.

He gulped the water down, finished off his coffee and got up from the table. Glancing at the telephone on the sideboard, he thought for a moment of calling Howard out at Malibu to see how he had fared with Linda Carol, but decided against it. He might wake him up. Also, he ran the risk of stirring up a flurry of admonitions and last-minute, fretful instructions that would only bug him and spoil the whole morning. And anyway, the longer he could put off confessing to Howard that he had brought Jo Anne Kallen into the sacred temple the better it would be for all concerned. Unzip your fly and do him the favor first. *Then* plead for mercy.

"I'm leaving," he called out to the kitchen.

David appeared in the doorway. "Is it home for dinner tonight, Mr. Bluestern?"

"I . . . can't really say yet. I'll let you know." The houseman was looking him over from head to toe. "What, David, what?"

The pale face smiled insinuatingly. "I must say, you do look unusually smashing today."

Teddy threw him a little answering grin straight out of every TV role he had ever played. "After last night, why shouldn't I?"

Driving toward Sunset in Howard's iridescent gray Bentley, Teddy wondered how long the unpleasant afterimage of the limey's suggestive smile would linger in his thoughts. He turned on the stereo radio, found the Bee Gees shrieking away, and that did the trick for the time being. But he had no confidence that the cure would be permanent . . .

Stern, it looks like they're bringing in Tug McGraw. I'm gonna have to lift you for a right-handed hitter.

You don't have to, Lasorda. I can switch.

You a switch hitter? Are you outta your friggin' mind?

I hope so, Tommy. I sure hope so.

THEY WERE in the outer office waiting for him when he walked in, Seligman of Legal, the insurance company doctor, the nurse from the studio hospital, and the little bald-headed guy who had to be the agent from Mutual of Oklahoma.

"Good morning, boys and girls, am I late?" Teddy sang out in his best Bluestern manner.

"As a matter of fact, right on the button, Howard," said Seligman.

"Can you give me just a couple of minutes, Scotty?" Howard had briefed him not to call the lawyer Edgar.

"All the time you want."

Jo Anne Kallen looked at Teddy and flushed as he approached her desk. "Would you come inside, please?" he said quietly.

He went past her into Howard's office, wondering how a girl could be that wild in bed all night long and look so refreshed and totally *great* the morning after, and immediately he realized that the thought reflected a negative attitude toward sex, as though it could be something destructive to one's health or appearance.

He heard her entering behind him and closing the door, and when he turned and saw her coming toward him with a quizzical, expectant look on her face, he said quickly, in a low voice, "I just want you to know that your note was beautiful, and *you* were too, and still are, goddammit . . ."

"Why 'goddammit'?" she said softly, moving closer.

"Look, don't come near me, don't touch me, you drive me out of my fucking mind and I'm going to take a physical in a couple of minutes and—"

But she had already walked into his arms and suddenly they were ravishing each other hungrily with their hands and lips and tongues just as though they hadn't done it in a thousand years . . .

"Ah Christ you wonderful . . ."

"Darling love . . ."

"All I want to—"

"Yes . . ."

"Just as soon as they—"

"Yes darling . . ."

She broke out of his arms, ashen-faced and breathless. "They're waiting outside, Howard . . ."

"I know. . . . Jesus, my heart is pounding so. . . . Go on, go ahead, but give me a minute or two. . . ." He sank down in the desk chair, still breathing hard, and watched her unbearably desirable body in motion on the way to the door, and he called out to her softly, "We'll have the whole morning to ourselves," and then she went out, leaving him sitting there in swollen silence, wondering how he was going to hang onto her forever, because he knew that that was what he was going to try to do, and the rest of it, the pedestrian, logical *facts*, all the reasons why *not*, were the crap that you told yourself until you had it all worked out in your head.

He took a deep breath and pressed the intercom and said, "I'm ready for them now," and hoped that his systolic wasn't 180 or something even worse.

Seligman led the others in and did the introductions, blinking like an owl behind his horn-rimmed glasses. "Howard, this is Dr. Franklin Kimmel, and I believe you already know Miss Seeley of the hospital here, and this is Marvin Gerber of Mutual of Oklahoma. Mr. Howard Bluestern."

Teddy shook hands all around and then started to strip to the waist, old pro that he was.

Seligman rubbed his hands together. "Marvin, you don't need me, do you, or you, Dr. Kimmel?"

"No, we're fine, Mr. Seligman," the bald-headed insurance agent said with a heavy New York accent.

The physician nodded assent.

"In that case, I'll leave. Howard, you're in good hands. If you want me for anything, give a holler."

"Thank you, Scotty."

The lawyer left hurriedly, before they could change their minds.

Bare-chested, Teddy braced himself as the doctor, a pink-cheeked, white-haired man of about sixty with rimless spectacles and a high-pitched voice, came at him with the cold end of his stethoscope and started listening to his heartbeat and the sound of his cough-on-request in a perfunctory manner that quickly labeled the scene, in Teddy's mind anyway, a Cursory Examination. If this doctor ever turned a Howard Bluestern down for a five-million-dollar policy, Teddy decided, Mutual of Oklahoma would probably sue the guy for malpractice.

Teddy breathed in, coughed, breathed out, and watched the little man named Gerber sitting on the sofa idly leafing through the morning's trade papers as though he couldn't care less about this physical, while Florence Nightingale, all starchy and gray-haired and white, stood with her hollow needle waiting to get into the act. "If you listen a little lower down, Doctor," Teddy said, "you can probably hear KFWB."

Kimmel recoiled as though shot and whipped the stethoscope from his eardrums. "Mustn't talk while I'm listening, Mr. Bluestern," he said in a quivering voice.

"Sorry," Teddy said.

A hell of a way to talk to a corporate president. Who did he think he was, an insurance doctor?

Act two was called Blood Pressure, starring the sphygmomanometer. Teddy played the scene sitting on the edge of the desk.

"One thirty-five over seventy," Franklin Kimmel announced, loosening the cuff around Teddy's arm. "For a man in your position in this business, I'd say that that was mighty remarkable."

"Don't tell the board of directors, Doctor. They'll think I'm not working hard enough."

"I mean it . . . really remarkable."

You should have had that thing on me ten minutes ago, Teddy thought. The mercury would have exploded. Which was what *he* was planning to do, ah yes, just as soon as these people left.

"Why don't we sit down on the sofa for this, Mr. Bluestern?" said Miss Seeley, trying to hide the needle as she approached him.

Marvin Gerber sprang to his feet saying, "Am I in the way?"

Teddy sat down, held out his right arm, made a fist and waited while the nurse poked at his flesh with her index finger.

"Here we are," she said finally. "All right, open your hand, please."

He looked away, felt the sting of the needle, saw in his mind's eye his lifeblood draining off, and immediately thought of better things to come. The needle hurt on the way out, and then he felt the wad of cotton, and the woman said, "Just press down on this please, Mr. Bluestern. That wasn't too bad, was it?"

"You have the touch of an angel, Miss Seeley."

"Well, thank you." She beamed as she tucked the vial of blood away in her shoulder-strap cold pack.

Franklin Kimmel opened the portable electrocardiograph machine he had brought in with him and set it down on the floor beside the sofa. "If you'll lie flat now, Mr. Bluestern . . ."

Teddy lay back and allowed the nurse to daub his chest with gooey gel and then press the rubber suction cups into place to act as electrodes for the wires.

"We're ready, Doctor," she said.

"The condemned man ate a hearty breakfast, and would like to live to eat a hearty lunch," Teddy said.

"Oh, it's not as bad as all that," Kimmel said, switching on the machine.

Actually, there'd be very little time for any meaningful lunch, what with the long drive out to Malibu and Howard's probable insistence on hearing every last detail spelled out for him. Howard had proclaimed that the reverse switcheroonie take place in the safety and privacy of the beach house during the lunch break, and that was that. Still, there would be what was left of this morning for Jo Anne. After that . . . question mark.

He listened to the clicking of the electrocardiograph machine and decided to think about nothing at all, but Jo Anne kept waltzing into his head, sometimes with, sometimes without her clothes on, and he wondered how she looked on the squiggly lines of his heart patterns as the white tape slowly uncoiled. He closed his eyes, and finally heard Kimmel saying, "That should do it," then opened his eyes and watched the nurse disconnecting him from the machine. She removed the electrodes, wiped his chest clean with some tissues, and Kimmel thrust a small glass flask at him.

"Shall we take a trip to the water closet, Mr. Bluestern?"

"I'm game if you are, Doctor."

All right, this is it, Stern. I want you to give it everything you've got, don't hold back. Remember, you're the star, and this scene is the whole *raison d'être* of the picture. Give it strength, give it power, give it *feeling*. Are we rolling? All right. *Action.*

"I hope you're not insulted by my coming in here with you," Franklin Kimmel said in the bathroom. "We've had some cute tricks played on us."

"Listen." Teddy unzipped Howard's trousers. "I hope *you're* not insulted by my taking a leak in front of you."

Kimmel cackled appreciatively.

It could have been worse, Teddy thought. David Stanner could have been in there with the two of them.

He had a little trouble delivering at first. Though Jo Anne was not in his thoughts at the moment, obviously she must have been lurking somewhere deep in his scrotum, because he could feel a slight swelling, and a subtle desire to come forth with something more pleasurable than the occasion called for. But then the situation cleared, and it was twinkle-twinkle time.

"A little present for you, Doctor." He handed Kimmel the full flask.

Five million dollars' worth, fresh from the goose that laid the golden stream. Someone should have incorporated him, or harnessed him, or invented an automobile that could run on him. They should have done a comic strip about him, and then two movies.

Superpiss One and Two.

He put his shirt back on in the office while Kimmel and the nurse gathered their paraphernalia together, and then he eased them toward the door, wondering why the little insurance agent, Gerber, was hanging back near the desk.

"Well, thank you for your time, Mr. Bluestern." The white-haired doctor shook hands with him at the door. "A busy man like you . . ."

"No, thank *you* for the convenience of doing it here, Dr. Kimmel. And you too, Miss Seeley."

"It was lovely, sir," the nurse said.

Teddy closed the door on them and turned to face the agent. "So."

"Do you have a few minutes?" Marvin Gerber said. "I have a few matters I'd like to go over with you."

Teddy hesitated.

"They could be important," Gerber said.

"Why don't you sit down?" Teddy said.

Heaven can wait . . .

The insurance agent started toward the sofa, then changed his mind, came back, and took the chair a few feet from the desk, moving his body around to make himself comfortable.

Teddy peered across the desk at him. "Did everything go off all right? I mean, are there any problems?" He noticed a thin film of perspiration on the man's face.

Marvin Gerber shrugged. "Why should there be problems? You don't want them, I don't want them, the studio doesn't want them, and Mutual of Oklahoma doesn't want them . . ."

"I thought maybe if I were at death's door or something . . ."

The insurance agent gave a little laugh. "*I* should be so close to that door." He leaned forward, knocked wood on the desk top, then settled back in his seat. "I grant you, appearances can be deceiving with these physicals, but if there is a sucker around who wants to put up money, I will lay odds of fifty to one, a *hundred* to one and I'm still stealing the money. So there you are, Mr. Bluestern."

"Here I am. Right. Wondering what it is you wanted to discuss." He stole a peek at Howard's tank watch. The day wasn't getting any younger. "Excuse me a moment." He picked up the phone and buzzed Jo Anne.

"Yes?"

"Hold the calls please. This won't take much longer."

"Miss you," she whispered.

"That is correct." He hung up and turned to the insurance agent, who was dabbing at his face with a handkerchief. "Sorry."

"That's all right." Gerber cleared his throat. "Mr. Bluestern, what I'm about to tell you I tell to all my clients in situations such as this one . . ."

"Such as which one?" Teddy shifted in his chair.

"Short-term policy taken out by the corporation on the life of a new executive, two million, three million, five million, seven million, depending on the company . . ."

Teddy stared at him, waiting.

"Number one, as the agent, I feel responsible that nothing should go wrong. Who needs a no when we all want a yes? Right? Number two, why shouldn't the executive being insured have all the privileges of the situation, even though the underwriter is too big and too busy and too impersonal to bother *telling* the man about it? And as for the corporation, whether they know about it or don't know about it, they couldn't care less because it's no skin off *their* behind one way or the other. You follow?"

Like a blind man in the dark with his legs cut off. "Keep going," Teddy said.

"If I'm wrong, I'm wrong, but I don't think so," Gerber went on. "I don't *think* Mr. Edgar Seligman or anybody else around here bothered to tell you, *if* they know about it, that you *can*, if you so desire, Mr. Bluestern, take out an equal amount of life insurance for your own personal use *matching* the policy the studio has applied for . . ."

Teddy shook his head. "But what would I—?"

"In plain language," Gerber interrupted, "that means you can decide right now to apply for an *additional* five million dollars—"

"But—"

"—And all you have to do is pay the premium out of your own pocket, and when you pass that cockamamie little physical you just took you automatically *got* it, Mr. Bluestern. Now is that a privilege or is that a privilege, I ask you?"

"But suppose it just so happens that I don't need any more insurance than I already have?" Teddy said.

Gerber blinked. "You got a family, don't you, Mr. Bluestern?"

"As a matter of fact, no, I don't, Mr. Gerber."

"No family?"

"A *brother*, if you can call that a family," Teddy said.

"What's wrong with a brother?" Gerber asked, with great reasonableness.

Well, you see, he drinks too much and he smokes too much and he whores around too much and he's lost the ambition he never had and, Jesus, I could go on like this forever but what's the use, he's never going to change, he's just a fucking bum and it's in his blood and the fact that *I've* made it big, that Howard Bluestern is an *important person* in this community just makes it *worse* for him because that's half the battle, that's what started him off on the wrong sneaker from the very beginning when we were just kids and he was such a charming, popular little bastard and I was so shy and serious and unpopular that I had to make up for it by *becoming* somebody, by studying harder, trying harder, by getting good marks and getting good jobs, and I'll be goddamned if I'm going to blame myself for my success and his failure, *let* him hate me for it, *I* can't stop that, I don't owe him *anything*, I've heen taking care of him *as best I can*, so get off my back, do you *hear* me?

"No," Teddy blurted out, and rose quickly from the chair.

"No?" Marvin Gerber was peering at him. "No *what*, Mr. Bluestern?"

Teddy blinked. *He* wasn't Mr. Bluestern. What the fuck was all *that* about? He was Teddy Stern. Let's not overdo it. Let's keep things *straight* around here. Honey, did you happen to see my script lying around? A suit of clothes, a suite of offices, a secretary and a kingdom for a day do not a king make. Let's not get carried away when the cameras aren't even rolling, okay buster?

"Nothing. There's nothing wrong with a brother," Teddy said to the perspiring face that was looking up at him. "It's just that he's . . . . he's well taken care of, even if I should get hit by a truck tomorrow . . ."

"God forbid," Gerber said.

"So you see, inasmuch as he's the only beneficiary I can possibly think of, I don't need any more insurance at this particular time, though I do appreciate your giving me the opportunity."

"Listen, I kid you not," Gerber said. "The seventeen thousand dollars' commission on the premiums wouldn't hurt me one bit."

"Well, I'm sorry about that," Teddy said, and thought, five million dollars, cash on the barrel, if Howard got hit by a truck God forbid, wouldn't hurt *me* one bit either when you consider the price these days of a lid of the green stuff or a gram of the white stuff or a whiff of the pink stuff that was always up there where the bent and outstretched golden gams of Southern California's sweetest and dearest came together in moist and perfumed confluence. The thought vanished almost as quickly as it had come, and good riddance.

"There was this other thing I brought up," Marvin Gerber was saying.

Teddy glanced at the tank watch again. "What other thing?" He started to pace back and forth impatiently.

"That nothing should go wrong," Gerber said. "How we don't want a no on the medical you just took when we're looking for a yes. Remember?"

Teddy came to a stop. "You mean a turndown from Mutual of Oklahoma?"

Marvin Gerber nodded slowly while shrugging his shoulders.

"What is *that* supposed to mean?"

Gerber shrugged again.

Teddy looked down at the man. "You said the odds were better than a hundred to one, Mr. Gerber."

The insurance agent met his eyes. "So I did. But the odds that Marvin Gerber is always right are only three to one, and even *that's* stretching it . . . ."

Teddy slowly sat down.

"One thing I *do* know," Gerber said. "And on this you can bet everything. My company would find it much much more difficult to say no to a *ten*-million-dollar policy than they would to a fiver."

Teddy felt the blood rushing to his face and it wasn't even *his* face, for Christsake, it was Howard's. "Look, there's nothing wrong with me. There's nothing they're going to turn me down on. I'm perfectly fit. I'm totally insurable. I'm a healthy man . . ."

"There's no need to get excited, Mr. Bluestern." Gerber spoke quietly and calmly. "I agree with you one hundred percent. But just as *you* know *your* business well enough to become what you've become— which is why I am sitting here—*I* know *my* business, the insurance business, and I know it well enough to know that I don't trust the judgment of computers that have electronic instead of *human* reasons for deciding that a person is a bad risk, and I don't trust a business that listens to these computers like they are God. I have already given you my advice, Mr. Bluestern, namely to double the face value of the policy. Your personal application, and the studio's application too, of course, will receive my *closest possible private attention*, the kind of detail work that will see us through to a happy conclusion, instead of a possibly unhappy one. That I can guarantee."

Teddy felt goosebumps crawling up his spine. His mouth had gone dry, and the words came with difficulty. "And if I elect *not* to apply for this extra policy?"

Marvin Gerber's face took on a sad expression. "Why let your whole existence be at the mercy of a computer, Mr. Bluestern?"

Teddy stared at the man. Gerber stared right back, unblinking.

"You realize, of course, what you're implying," Teddy said.

"Exactly," Gerber said evenly. "Except that I am not merely implying it, I am giving it to you as a sincere recommendation. For a hundred and six thousand dollars, payable in five annual premiums, your life will be insured for an additional five million dollars, with your brother, I presume, as the beneficiary. It's a bargain, Mr. Bluestern, all things considered. I would go so far as to call it a *necessity*. Don't you agree?"

Teddy had to look away for a moment, so badly did he want to seize the man by the throat. But that wouldn't have gotten Howard anywhere. "When do I have to make this decision, Gerber?"

The insurance man's expression did not change. "The sooner the better. Right now is better than sooner."

Teddy stared at him. "Could you give me just a couple of minutes in private to think this through?"

"Certainly." Gerber rose.

It wouldn't take Teddy longer than that to call Howard and tell him about this little weasel who was trying to hold him up for over a hundred grand. Howard would have to make the decision himself. Howard would have to decide whether he wanted to give in or take a chance and call the guy's bluff and accept the danger of a turndown, of having his whole deal with the company aborted. Sure, Howard would bawl the shit out of him for making the call from the studio, for taking what Howard would call "unnecessary risks." But he had no choice, none that *he* could see, anyway.

As soon as the door to the outer office had closed on Gerber, Teddy swiveled around to the private phone and dialed his house in Malibu. His own palms were sweating now. He had caught the mysterious malady known as Marvin Gerber's disease. Immediately after the third ring he heard the connection being made, and then he heard Howard answering with a familiar greeting, and it took him several moments to realize that it wasn't *Howard* impersonating *him*, it was his own voice on the Answerphone, on the recording he had made yesterday before leaving the house . . .

". . . And if you leave your name and number, I'll call you right back. Promise."

He heard the beep, and then the silence, and said, "Hello? Hello?" and muttered to himself, "Come on, Howard, I know you're there. Pick up the phone, it's safe, it's only me, come on, gutless, pick up the goddam phone, this is *important* . . ."

But it was useless.

He slammed the receiver down, got up, and went to the door to the outer office, wiping his palms dry on Howard's trousers. Gerber was thumbing through some magazines on Jo Anne's desk.

"Mr. Gerber?"

The insurance agent thanked Jo Anne quietly, turned and walked past Teddy back into the office, going directly to his seat. Teddy followed him and remained standing beside the desk, watching him.

Gerber looked off with vacant expression. "Well, what did he say?"

Teddy blinked, without replying.

"What advice did Edgar Seligman give you?" Gerber said, looking at Teddy and smiling at his own brilliance.

Teddy felt his face reddening. "I didn't call Seligman. I didn't call anyone."

The little man shrugged. "Didn't I tell you Marvin Gerber isn't always right?"

Teddy walked over to the window, clenching and unclenching his hands. He looked out over the lot, teeming with activity now. "I want you to do me a favor, Gerber," he said quietly.

"If it's something I can do, consider it done, Mr. Bluestern."

"I'm going to have to get back to you on this decision," Teddy said to the window. "What is the latest I can do that?"

"Five o'clock," Gerber said in a firm voice. "I'll be in my office all day until five o'clock."

Teddy turned to him and nodded.

Gerber took some papers from his breast pocket, unfolded them and placed them on the desk. "If you'll just sign this application and fill in the beneficiary, I'll do the rest and hold the papers until you call me."

Teddy went over to the desk, sat down, and glanced over the application. The son of a bitch had been so confident of success he had come with the application all prepared and ready, a five-year wager of a hundred grand or so against a five-million-dollar payoff. Teddy picked up a pen, wrote his own name in as beneficiary, signed Howard's name in the lower right-hand corner, and filled in the date.

"Once you have given me the go-ahead and the company has your application processed and we have your check for the first premium, all we'll need is word from the medical department that everything is hunky-dory," Gerber said. "At that moment you will be covered, even before we get the policy physically in your hands."

"I'll get back to you," Teddy said coldly, handing him the signed papers.

"Before five o'clock, please," the agent said, rising.

Teddy remained seated.

"About the first payment," Gerber said. "It will be all right if I have a certified check on my desk by tomorrow morning. Twenty-one thousand two hundred and fifty dollars. Would you like to write that down?"

"Good-bye, Mr. Gerber," Teddy said.

Tucking the papers back into his breast pocket, the little insurance man walked at a leisurely pace to the door and went out.

chapter 6

SHE HAD TAKEN IT beautifully. Her whole attitude—calm, mature, reasonable, had impressed the hell out of him. He had told her—and let's face it, it was the truth—that something extremely urgent had come up that demanded his immediate presence off the lot. The disappointment in her eyes had been heartfelt, but without hurt or reproach.

And then she had been all business, reminding him of the appointments she would have to cancel for him, suggesting the proper ameliorating words she would use, giving him the afternoon lineup that (little did she know) *he* would never be facing, even offering to have a sandwich sent up for herself so that she could remain at her desk while he was gone.

"Now you don't have to do *that*," he had said.

"I know I don't have to." She had felt his cheek tenderly. "I want to."

Gripping the wheel of the Bentley now, his eyes fixed on the road ahead, he found it hard to believe there was a possibility he might never see her again. Certainly as *Howard*, it was more than a possibility, it was a certainty. But as Teddy—"fragile," "brittle," "offbeat" Teddy—he couldn't see any hope at all. He'd think about it later. First things first. Right now he had to concentrate his attention on Howard, how to keep Howard from quickly jumping to the conclusion that his ineffectual brother had somehow fucked up again and caused this sticky situation with the insurance man.

Speeding up the coast highway toward Malibu, squinting in the sun and glancing occasionally in the rear-view mirror to catch that all-important first glimpse of a California Highway Patrol motorcycle cop, he reviewed what had taken place in the office and decided that he had been not only blameless but also completely intelligent in his handling of Marvin Gerber. He had bought time for Howard, and he had done it without antagonizing the man.

Yes, but what I don't understand is how you got into this discussion about a personal life insurance policy in the first place.

45

I didn't get into any discussion, Howard. The guy brought it up himself, that's all there was to it.

Yes, but how did this business of you as the beneficiary come into it?

I *told* you, he was trying to sell me on the idea of taking out the goddam policy for my *family*, and I told him I *had* no family—that is, *you* had no family—except your brother, that's *me*, so *he* said what's wrong with a brother as beneficiary? It wasn't *my* idea. I mean, look, even if you didn't have one fucking relative in the whole world, the guy was *still* going to try to muscle you into popping for the extra hundred and six Gs, even if the beneficiary had to be the Motion Picture Country Home or United Jewish Appeal.

But it wasn't, Teddy. The beneficiary *isn't* going to be the Motion Picture Country Home or UJA. It's going to be *you*.

Hey, wait a minute! Are you trying to say that I *maneuvered* all this into happening just so I could wind up with a five-million-dollar insurance policy on your life? Is that what you're saying?

I am saying no such thing. Why do you always read the worst possible construction into everything I say?

Maybe it's because of the way you say it, Howard.

Well, it's goddam insulting, and I want you to cut it out.

Okay, but one thing I know for sure: if you decide to go along with this cocksucker Gerber, you're going to have to change the beneficiary to Permanent Charities or whoever else you want—David Stanner, there's a good one for you—because *I want absolutely nothing to do with that policy* . . .

Oh for Christsake, stop being ridiculous, Teddy.

I am not being ridiculous. I am telling you right here and now that I refuse to be the beneficiary of *anything*. Are we understood on that?

All right, all right, you've made your point.

And I'll make another point. This is the last time I step into your shoes. From now on, take your *own* leaks, okay?

HE SWUNG OFF the highway onto Old Malibu Road, drove north for half a mile, and parked the Bentley across the street from the house. The garage door was closed, but he could see the yellow Porsche inside as he walked past the side window on his way to the house.

He rang the kitchen doorbell—Howard had his keys—and, getting no answer after a couple of minutes, went around to the waterfront side. He stood on the patio shielding his eyes from the sun and scanned the beach from right to left. Not a sign of Howard, either in the water or out. Just a few children challenging the waves as their eagle-eyed mothers stood at the water's edge watching for the first signs of impending disaster.

He turned and peered into the living room through the tinted glass, but saw no movement inside. He tried the sliding door. It was unlocked. He opened it and went inside.

"Hello? . . . Howard? . . . It's me. Teddy . . . Hello? . . ."

The living room looked uncommonly clean, everything in place. There was an orderliness about it that bespoke Howard's presence and *his* absence. Howard had always been the neat one. You could do a paper on the two of them and get yourself a Ph.D. The Teddy Stern Study: On the Incidence of Sloppy Genes in One Half of an Identical Pair and Its Relationship to Intelligence, Effectiveness, and Bank Balance.

He sniffed his way through the empty powder room and detected the fragrance of expensive perfume still lingering in the air, the good stuff that Linda Carol probably got at cost from Holman-Meyer with some of those C-notes that sprang from her mouth and her darting tongue like colored handkerchiefs from a magician's empty hand. He thought for a moment of Linda's empty hand and decided it would be nice to fill it.

That's how much you really care about Jo Anne, you shallow prick.

The door to the bedroom was closed. He started to open it, then drew back. Suppose they were in the kip? Much as he'd like to watch, he was no David Stanner. Anyway, Linda's car hadn't been parked outside or in the garage. She was probably long gone.

He knocked on the bedroom door. "Howard? . . ."

Nothing.

He knocked again. "Howard, it's Teddy . . ."

Five after twelve, for Christ's sake.

He turned the knob and pushed the door open part way. "Howard, I've got to talk to you . . ." Getting no answer, he pushed the door all the way back and went into the room.

Sure enough, Howard was in bed, alone, fast asleep, with the covers pulled all the way up over himself against the daylight.

Teddy went over to him. "Come on, man, we've got problems." He reached down and shook him. "Wake up. It's after twelve." Howard didn't respond. He shook him again, a little roughly this time, and felt his hands sending a message to his brain and to the pit of his

stomach that he could not understand. "Goddam it, Howard," he
heard the whine of fear in his voice. "Will you get up? I've got to
talk to you. Get up, get *up*." He shook him again, and again, and the
cold dread spread from the pit of his stomach to every part of his body,
and he became rougher and rougher with Howard but the dread wouldn't
go away, he couldn't shake it away, it became worse and worse, he
was sick from it, frightened from it, he couldn't stand it any longer it
was so frightening, it was *unbearable*, he had to *do* something about
it, he had to pull the covers off, he had to look down at Howard,
anything, he *had* to, he had to do *something*, he just *had* to, so he
pulled the covers off, whimpering with fear. He looked down and let
out a strangled cry, he looked down and saw what he knew he was
going to see, only it was worse than he had expected, oh my God oh
my God oh my God, he saw his poor naked brother lying there with
his head so strange-looking and misshapen on the bloodstained pillow,
so peaceful, so silent, so unmoving, oh God Teddy groaned oh no oh
Jesus God help me God help me oh no Howard no oh no Howard
please, as he sank down on the floor beside the bed and tried to die
please let me oh please, holding onto his face and waiting for the tears
to engulf him but all that came was the icy coldness in his hands and
the chill of fear in his stomach and a numbness in his head thank God
for the numbness mustn't think mustn't think go away didn't happen
never never didn't happen help me help me Jesus Christ Howard what
happened wake up get up you son of a bitch wake up I have to talk
to you please I want to talk to you Howard please Howard please
Howard please, and then he realized that the awful sound he was
hearing was the sound of his own choking and gasping and retching
and he hated himself for the sounds he was making, you sniveling
bastard, get up off the floor, get on your feet, blow your nose, shut
up and do something, *do* something . . .

He held onto the side of the bed and pushed himself to an upright
position and stood there shivering in the cold clammy sweat that had
soaked his body. He forced himself to look again at Howard and he
pleaded with him to wake up but Howard wouldn't wake up and then
he pulled the blanket over Howard's body and stumbled out of the
bedroom into the living room and went right to the bar and found a
half empty bottle of Sauza Gold and tilted it back without even using
a glass.

Ah Christ, ah good, ah Jesus . . . good . . .

He fell back on the sofa and dropped the empty bottle on the carpet and waited for Howard to come out of the bedroom and ask him what all the commotion was about, and he'd tell Howard what a scare he had just had, you know, not much light in the room with the blinds drawn, and then Howard would ask him if everything had gone well at the studio with the insurance people and he'd have to tell him about Marvin Gerber and the gun at Howard's head . . . the . . .

No . . . not the *gun . . .* the *poker . . .* yes, the *poker . . .*

He struggled to his feet and made his way around the coffee table to the fireplace, feeling the tequila whirling dizzily through his brain, and he looked down and said out loud, "Son of a bitch, of *course. . . ."* *The wrought-iron poker.* His eye had gone to it first thing when he had entered the house. The poker was where it belonged, resting across the andirons right above the shovel, but someone had *removed* the poker and then replaced it *backward.* The handle was supposed to be on the right, not the left.

And so you see, ladies and gentlemen of the jury . . .

He went back to the bedroom doorway and stood there staring in at the lifeless lump beneath the blanket and felt his hands growing cold again, felt the icy clutch of fear. It wasn't Howard who had been murdered. That was *him* on the bed, that was Teddy Stern. Whoever had killed Howard by bashing his head in with the fireplace poker had thought they were killing *him.* Who hated him that deeply? Who regarded *him,* Teddy Stern, important enough to *kill,* for Christsake? Linda Carol? Come on. Diane? Yes . . . no . . . maybe. . . . Had it been a prowler? No sign of robbery. What would happen when the killer found out that he, Teddy Stern, was still alive? Would the killer strike again? Jesus . . .

He turned away from the doorway, went unsteadily back to the bar, found a fresh bottle of tequila in the cabinet, cracked it open, poured some into a tumbler, and downed it in one gasp. He poured some more into the glass, walked it carefully to the club chair and sat down.

Suppose they'd think *he* had killed Howard? Why not? Why *not* him? Did he have an alibi? Could he prove that he hadn't done it? No, but why *him*? Why would *he* have wanted to? *His own brother . . .* What motive would *he* have had?

"Jealousy, ladies and gentlemen of the jury. He always *envied* his brother . . ."

Bullshit!

"A huge life insurance policy."

"I haven't *taken* the policy. It doesn't even *exist.*"

"But if you *had*—"

"*If nothing. I haven't.*"

"But if you had—"

"If I *had,*" he said to the glass. "If I had and it went through okay and nobody found out about Howard until afterwards, I'd be worth five million dollars."

"You *see?*"

"See *nothing.*"

"Ladies and gentlemen of the jury, I ask you this: Why didn't he call the police immediately?"

"Give me time, give me time," Teddy cried out to the empty room.

"Why didn't he call the police immediately?"

"Because," Teddy cried, struggling to his feet again and spilling some of the liquor on Howard's suit.

"Because *why?*"

"Because," Teddy cried as he stumbled to the telephone and grabbed the receiver, feeling the room begin to spin.

Information told him to please look it up in the directory and he started to argue with the man, but then he realized that it was only a recording, and then a live voice came on, a woman, a live woman, not dead like Howard but alive, a live woman asked him what city he wanted and he said What city do you think the Malibu police station is going to be in, Chicago? and finally they gave him the number and he managed to dial it and he got this Sergeant Prattker or whatever his name was, and Sergeant Prattker said, "What can I do for you, sir?"

"I wanna report a murder," Teddy started to say, but instead, to his surprise, he heard his voice saying thickly, "I want to report a stolen car," and the Sergeant said, "One moment please, I'll transfer you," and as soon as he was put on hold, Teddy hung up and turned away from the phone.

"And the motive, ladies and gentlemen, the only possible reason for his action, his *lack* of action, was the five million dollars . . ."

"How else am I gonna get through life without Howard?" he cried to the glass in his hand. "Who'll pick up the tab?"

"For the money, ladies and gentlemen. He did it for the *money.*"

"And if you want to be *fair* about it, you heartless bastard, he was *drunk* at the time. Tell them *that.* He didn't know what he was doing."

"The hell he didn't."

"You can say *that* again."

"The hell he didn't."

Teddy frowned woozily as he set the glass down on the coffee table, peeled off his suit jacket, threw it aside, rolled up his shirtsleeves, and made his way back into the bedroom and right over to the wardrobe closet, careful not to look at the bed, careful to keep from crying, couldn't stand the sounds he made when he cried, so weak, so ineffectual, so Teddylike. He slid the door back and pushed the shirts and slacks and jackets aside and found the huge oversized plastic three-suiter in the far left-hand corner, hanging where he'd placed it after the location trip to Durango.

He hauled it out and laid it on the floor next to the bed and unzipped it straight down the middle, all six feet of it, and then he closed his eyes tightly as he leaned down over the bed, but that was ridiculous, because he wasn't going to be able to do it with his eyes *closed*, he was just going to have to open his eyes and *do* it, go on, *do* it, goddam it, *do* it . . .

Oh God, what am I doing, what am I doing?

What do you mean, what are you doing? You know *goddam well* what you're doing and *why*. Don't give me any of that shit. Just put him in here, that's right, just slide him in here like this; now you're talking, man, now you're cooking. Just do it like this and zip it up, that's it, zip it all the way up, what's so tough about that? Why do you make such a big deal out of nothing at all? Who are you playing to? Who's your audience? Who's watching, who's listening, who *gives* a damn?

He felt better now. He felt dizzy but better. He was pissed to the eyeballs but he felt better, because he couldn't see Howard any longer. Howard was in the plastic suit carrier. Howard was just a shape, a weight, something to haul across the floor. He dragged the garment bag slowly, carefully, holding onto the brass hook that served as a handle. He didn't want to bump Howard unnecessarily. The least he could do was be gentle about it. He'd get rid of the bed linens later, the mattress too if necessary. He'd get rid of anything that might prove embarrassing. That was a good word. Embarrassing . . .

"This is embarrassing, Howard . . ."

The plastic bag slid smoothly across the kitchen floor, thumped a little as it landed on the back porch, then came to a stop as Teddy let go of the brass handle and turned to the freezer.

It was a big son of a bitch with a nasty vibrating hum, about eight feet wide, four feet deep and three feet high. It was chipped and peeling on the outside, but on the inside it did its work so well that hell would have frozen over with something to spare. Teddy threw back the lid and forced it into the clamps that held it in the open position, and then he leaned in and began to empty the freezer rapidly, mindful of the painful ice burns that threatened his fingers as he tossed sirloin strippers and TV dinners and frozen vegetables and pizzas and lamb chops and all the crap that he never ate anyway but Mrs. Mahoney the housekeeper insisted that he keep *just in case* . . . Mrs. Mahoney . . . Jesus . . . she'd be coming in at two o'clock tomorrow . . .

The brick floor was strewn with half the contents of the Colony Market by the time he had the freezer emptied out.

He leaned down over the plastic bag, tucked his hands underneath, carefully held his knees together, grunted and groaned but didn't pull anything, didn't go the old hernia route, took it slowly and carefully, raised Howard as gently, as lovingly as he could, and laid him down inside the freezer at the very bottom. And then, taking great care not to drop anything on Howard, being very careful not to hurt Howard in any way, he covered him completely with the still-frozen foodstuff, putting back in the freezer, on top of his brother, everything he had taken out, with the exception of six boxes of frozen broccoli, six boxes of Stouffer's spinach soufflé, four quarts of Rocky Road ice cream, four loaves of Pioneer sourdough bread, and six one-pound packages of chopped chuck steak.

What the hell was he going to do with all *that*? There was no way he could safely *give* it away, or eat it. He'd simply have to let it thaw out without using it, and then get rid of it somehow in *someone's* garbage, not his. As for Howard, he wouldn't be thawing *him* out and using him until it was time, later on.

He closed the lid tightly and frowned as he noticed the two hasps that had never, as far back as he could remember, had a padlock inserted in them. Much as he hated the idea of a brand-new lock springing into being where there had never been one before, he knew he'd never rest easily as long as Mrs. Mahoney or anyone else could wander at will through Howard's icy grave. He'd buy something by nightfall.

There was so much to do, so much to remember. What to do with all this frozen food? What to do with the bedding? And he mustn't forget to call Marvin Gerber before five o'clock and tell him the answer was yes. And what about Linda Carol? Maybe he should surprise her at Holman-Meyer and see if she fell over in a faint when she saw him alive. *That* would be a dead giveaway. But for that he'd have to change into his own clothes. No time for that now. She was a long shot anyway. Why would *she* want to do anyone in, especially him? It had to be Diane. She had been really pissed off at him. She still had a key to the house. Of *course* it was Diane. He looked down morosely at the freezer.

I'm sorry, Howard. I told you she was nothing to worry about and *now* look at you, pushing up TV dinners.

He turned away, feeling a terrible need to lie down somewhere and cry. If tears wouldn't come, he still needed to close his eyes and go to sleep. Even a half hour would do it, get him over the hump, enable him to go on. God, how he needed to lie down.

He went to the living room, slid the glass door closed, locked it, pulled the drapes shut against the brightness of the sunlit sand and the sparkling water outside, went over to the sofa and lay down on his back. His heart was still pounding. Would it ever slow down? He closed his eyes, tried to wipe everything from his mind, but Howard kept coming back, mute, unmoving, reproachful. At the count of ten, he told himself, you're going to go to sleep. This is Pat Collins talking to you, your lids are getting heavier, you can't open your eyes even if you want to and you don't want to, you're going to sleep, deeper and deeper, deeper and deeper.

The telephone rang.

He bounded to a sitting position, eyes wide open.

He stared at the instrument. The ringing stopped. The Answerphone had taken over, giving out his recorded spiel. Should he override it? Should he pick up the phone and answer the call?

No.

Yes. Why not?

Who *was* he, Howard or Teddy?

Teddy was dead.

No, Teddy was *supposed* to be dead. *Howard* was dead. *Howard* was in the freezer.

No, *he* was Howard, *had* been all night, all this morning, was going to be when he returned to the studio . . .

Returned to the studio?

Of course, you fool. What did you think?

Hurry. That recorded spiel doesn't go on *forever*.

But who *was* he?

He wasn't Teddy *or* Howard.

He was Teddy *and* Howard.

Of course. He was *both* of them. *Had* to be. For at least as long as it took for the policy to go through, plus a decent interval afterward.

Right now he was Teddy. In Malibu he was Teddy.

In Bel Air, or at the studio, he'd be Howard.

Answer the fucking phone.

But be careful. Listen first.

Quietly, he raised the receiver to his ear and listened.

It was Diane. She was leaving a message on the tape. Her voice sounded funny but it was Diane.

". . . I just got back from Palm Springs a few minutes ago and would love to see you, darling. . . ." (So it *hadn't* been Diane. Linda? Never. Then who had killed Howard? He could have sworn—) "Please call me, Teddy, as soon as you get home. I miss you so much. 'Bye now."

Quickly he broke in. "Hi, honey, it's me. Don't hang up."

He heard a little gasp, and then nothing but silence, the heaviest, most palpable silence he had ever heard in his whole life.

Was he imagining it? Had she hung up?

"Hello? . . . Diane?"

He heard a whisper. "Who is this?" And then a shriek, a scream: "*Who is this?*"

What in the name of—? "It's Teddy."

"Teddy?" she cried.

"Yes."

"Oh my God oh my God *OH MY GOD . . .*"

"Diane . . ."

But she wasn't listening, she was sobbing and choking, "Teddy . . . Teddy . . . Teddy . . . Teddy . . ."

"Diane!"

"Thank God oh thank God . . . I . . . can't talk . . . I have to—"

"Are you home, are you home?"

"Yes, I—"

"Hang up. Hang up, Diane. I'll call you right back. Did you hear me? Hang up."

He heard her phone clatter. Then he hung up, got to his feet, drew a very deep breath and let it out slowly. Okay, come on, wake up, get your head clear, gotta know what you're doing. He went to the windows, opened the drapes again, flinched in the glare, turned and went back to the sofa.

It *had* been Diane. It *had* been her after all.

Okay, now *think*. What does this *mean*?

It means nobody knows about Howard except you and her.

No, wait a minute. She *doesn't* know about Howard. She thought it was *you* she'd clobbered and *you're okay now*, she just *talked* to you. She doesn't know *anything*, and that's the way it's gotta be. Nobody must know except *you*.

Had to be.

You. Only you.

He picked up the phone, dialed her number, heard it start ringing, paced back and forth with the phone in his hand, and felt himself coming to nervous life again. The phone kept ringing. Where the hell was she? He glanced at Howard's wristwatch, the tank watch, *his* watch now. Almost one o'clock. He hadn't had a bite. All that tequila and no food. He'd have to get back to the studio, to Howard's office, to Howard's desk, to Jo Anne. Christ, he'd almost forgotten about Jo Anne. And all those meetings that would be waiting for Howard. He really had to get to the studio and keep the illusion of a living Howard Bluestern alive. And there was so much to do here beforehand.

Finally she answered. "Teddy?"

"Yes, are you all right now?"

"I think so. Yes. Much better. Oh God. Teddy. How about you? I still can't believe it. How *are* you? Oh darling, are you all right? Please tell me you're all right . . ."

"Let's just say I have a bad headache, okay?"

"Oh Teddy, I feel so *awful*. I can't just say I'm sorry, because that's just plain *meaningless* compared to the way I really feel. I know I want to ask you to forgive me but I can't, because *you* can't, because what I did was *unforgivable* . . ."

"It's okay, Diane."

"But I was insane, absolutely insane, seeing you with that girl . . ."

"It's okay, honey . . ."

"Are you sure you're all right? Have you seen a doctor? Are you going to see a doctor? Oh Teddy, is there something I can do . . . ?"

"No."

"Anything at all? I want to do something to make up for—"

"Diane?"

"Just let me do *something* . . ."

"Diane?"

"Yes, Teddy?"

"One thing I don't understand."

"What, darling?"

"Why did you call? Why did you just call here? What was that message you were leaving on the tape about just getting back from Palm Springs and all the rest?"

"You won't believe it, Teddy. I thought I had—God, I can't say it . . ."

"What?"

"*Killed* you last night when I hit you with that fireplace iron."

"Jesus."

"And I wanted to go on record, on *tape* actually, as having been in Palm Springs at the time . . ."

"Smart cookie."

"I wanted your playback to have me sound as though I expected you to call me back, as though I had no reason whatsoever *not* to call you . . ."

"Diane?"

"Yes, darling?"

"If you're that smart, and that *is* smart, *really*, why couldn't you have been smart enough not to get so fucking angry that you had to do something *dumb*, like hit me over the head?"

"You're furious with me now, aren't you? I can tell, I can hear it in your voice, and you're right, you're absolutely right—"

"I'm not furious."

"It's the drinking, Teddy. You know that. I'm like two different people. I was blind last night, blind and stupid and horrible and I'll *never* be like that again, I swear I won't, Teddy. I'll prove it to you. I'll bring sober little me over there right now and kiss your poor dear aching little head and make it feel all wonderful and perfect again."

"No, Diane."

"Pretty please?"

"Absolutely not. I'm not feeling all that terrific and I don't want to see anyone right now. I don't want to see anyone until I'm all better. I don't want to have to make *explanations* for bruises and black-and-blue marks and things like that."

"Well you don't have to make explanations to *me*, for God's sake."

"Obviously not."

"So why can't I come over then?"

"Because I don't want you to."

"Ever?"

"I didn't say that."

"I know you didn't, but is that what you meant?"

"I meant what I said, that's all, nothing more."

"You're avoiding the question, Teddy."

"For Christsake, do we have to go into this *now—?*"

"Yes."

"—When I'm not feeling well?"

"When am I going to see you?"

"I don't know."

"You don't know?"

"That's right."

"Are you going to see *her* again?"

"Who?"

"The girl you were fucking last night, in *our bed* . . ."

"*Our* bed?"

"Yes, our bed, you miserable bastard you . . ."

"Honey, listen to me—"

"How *dare* you, you prick—?"

"Diane . . ."

"—You loathsome prick, how *dare* you—?"

"Diane!"

"Yes!"

"Will you *listen* to me?"

"Go ahead, make excuses, go ahead, I'm *listening* . . ."

"I want you to stop this now . . ."

"*Me* stop, when you—?"

"I want you to go away, go to your mother's place in the desert, you're all worked up—"

"You think you're going to get *rid* of me, is that what you think, you son of a bitch you—?"

"Diane . . ."

"Well, you've got another think coming. I don't get lost that easily, you don't drop me like a piece of dirt, I mean, who the fuck do you think you are—?"

"If you ever come near this house again—"

"*What?*"

"You heard me."

"I'll come there any goddam time—"

"No you won't, Diane."

"I *won't*, huh?"

"No, because you tried to kill me, honey. You broke into this house . . . my house . . . and you attacked me with a weapon and tried to murder me—"

"And you *deserved* it, you bastard!"

"And if I ever see you around here again, if you ever so much as call me on the telephone—"

"*Are you threatening me?*"

"Threatening you? I'm *telling* you: stay away from me, stay the hell out of my life, don't ever come near me again, because if you do—"

"You'll *what*? Go ahead, you'll *what*, you son of a bitch?"

"I'll turn you over to the police for attempted murder."

"And you think they'll listen to *you*, believe *you*, you two-bit drunken no-talent *nothing*?"

"They won't have to, Diane. I've recorded this whole conversation."

There was a moment of sudden silence.

"Like hell you have."

"Yes, Diane."

"Bullshit."

"No, Diane. Every single word."

"Don't make me laugh . . ."

"Why do you think I told you to hang up so I could call you right back?"

"You're such a liar. You're lying to me. Isn't that right, Teddy? You're lying, you're putting me on . . ."

"Now are you going to hang up like a good little girl and never call here again and never have to go to jail for the rest of your life, or am I going to have to hang up this phone right in your face . . . ?"

"Now wait a minute . . . Teddy . . . honey . . . listen to me . . ."

He slammed the phone down and cut off her head and screamed hoarsely, "You killed my brother, you dirty cunt! You killed him, you killed him, you killed him . . ." And then he was sinking down on the sofa shaking his head slowly from side to side crying you killed him you killed him you killed him and weeping piteously, not caring how it sounded, not caring about the tears streaming down his face, not caring about anything now, just letting it all come out finally . . .

Howard . . . why did you leave me? How could you leave me all alone like this? Look at what you're making me do . . .

chapter

7

HE DROVE in the slow lane with excessive care. Not that he was still smashed from the tequila. A pot of black coffee had taken care of that. And a quarter of a pound of cheddar cheese and a few large hunks of French bread had done it for the lunchtime hunger pangs. He was drained, that was all, emotionally exhausted, empty, wiped out. Getting a radio-dispatched locksmith to come over and change all the locks on the outside doors and sell him a combination-type padlock for the freezer had been an effortless matter of thirty minutes or so. What had *really* done him in, what with charcoal-starter fluid that wouldn't pour and matches that wouldn't stay lit, was the burning of the sheets and pillowcases and the pillows themselves in the living-room fireplace without burning the goddam house down or attracting attention on the beach. Where there's smoke, there's fire, and where there's fire in the middle of a warm September day, there's something rotten in the state of Malibu, no? Yes. Thank God for the kiddies who went out too far and for the nervousness of their mothers, none of whom had been born with eyes in the back of her head.

The mattress had appeared to be free of bloodstains, but he had turned it over on the box spring anyway, just to be on the safe side. No worry about Mrs. Mahoney. Her bones were too lazy to even *consider* turning a mattress. As for the blankets, only someone with a large magnifying glass, a Meerschaum pipe, and Dr. Watson standing nearby with a needle could have found anything suspicious in a few little dark smudges. Nevertheless, he had stowed the blankets away in the attic for future cleaning or burning (God forbid) and had put fresh ones on the bed in their place, along with some spare pillows.

Finally he had done the most difficult thing of all. He had stood on the back porch beside the freezer, head bowed, and said a tense, tearless, carefully controlled farewell to his brother, remembering long-forgotten prayers and uttering them from a heart that he would not let undo him. There was too much to do now, all of it impossible enough, without the added burden of further grief.

He hunched over the wheel of the gray Bentley, watching the road
ahead, looking for the parking lot where he would dispose of the last
of the foodstuff that had been displaced by Howard's body. After that
he would head back to the studio, with equal parts of fear and chutzpah
in his heart. He was going to have to establish with Mutual of Oklahoma,
by way of the film community, that both he and Howard were very
much alive, active, and omnipresent, and it was not going to be a
mere one-day performance either. It would be an extended engagement,
with holdovers, with the closing date coming whenever circumstances
indicated that it was now safe and beyond suspicion for poor Howard
to die his accidental and public death.

Why are you doing this to me, Teddy?

Howard . . . please . . .

Playing a studio head was not totally outside his ken. Anyone who
had been in and around "the industry" as long as he had been, who
had read as many trade papers as he had read over the years, and gone
to as many Hollywood parties, could spout the jargon just as convincingly
as any of the former agents, former stockbrokers, former fashion models,
and former idiots who were currently in vogue as presidents or vice-
presidents in charge of production. And he had the added advantage
of having heard Howard's secretly cynical, pseudo-optimistic, football-
coach approach to dealing with people every time they had been together.
Howard had rarely talked about anything but the picture business,
unless it was about his waistline or his backhand.

But Teddy wasn't kidding himself. He was trying to, but not
succeeding. He knew damn well that he was minimizing the dangers
grossly in order to smoothe the quaking of his entrails. If he was all
that qualified to act the role of a lifetime, how come he occupied the
place that he did in his chosen profession, which was *no* place at all?
Was he not truly as incompetent as everyone thought he was, or had
he merely lost his at best tenuous confidence early on, searched for it
at the bottom of a bottle, and thereby accidently made wise men of
his critics, not the least of them Howard? Which had come first, the
chickenshit or the egg?

Right now he needed time to think and to plan.

Above all, he needed quiet in his head . . .

*Why are you doing it? She murdered me, Teddy; she murdered
me, your own brother. How can you let her get away with it and go
free? My God, Teddy, how can you do this to me?*

Don't talk like that, Howard. I'm not doing *anything* to you. It was already done. What good would it do you now if that screwed-up broad went to jail? She never meant to harm *you*, it was an *accident* . . .

Teddy, she killed me. How can you—?

Please, Howard, please, you're past hurting, past caring. I'd never do anything to hurt you, you know that. Have I ever done anything to you, have I ever hurt you?

Yes. You never liked me. You needed me, and hated me for it. Didn't you think I knew? Didn't you think I could tell? Didn't you know how much it hurt me to feel that in you ALWAYS?

I hated *you*? How can you say a thing like that, *you* who never had anything but contempt for *me*, ever?

I want a decent death, Teddy, I want a decent funeral. Don't rob me of that.

You'll have it, you'll have it . . .

I'm so helpless now, Teddy. No power. No voice. No life. Nothing. You're all I've got, Teddy. Don't forget all I've done for you. Take care of me. Please take care of me.

I'm keeping you *alive*, for Christsake, isn't that *something*? Don't I get *any points at all*?

He leaned forward and turned on the windshield wipers.

What are you doing that for? It's not raining out, it's a sunny day.

I'll turn on any goddam thing I want. I'll turn on the *radio* if I want to. I'll turn on the *air conditioning*. I'll turn on any goddam thing I want. Just leave me alone and don't tell me what to do or what *not* to do, okay?

Don't do this to me, Teddy . . .

There it was, up ahead on the right, just before the Sunset Boulevard turnoff. He slowed down and turned into the half-empty parking lot, turning off the windshield wipers at the same time. The only food still remaining in the luggage compartment of the Bentley were three one-pound packages of chopped chuck steak and two loaves of sourdough bread. The rest of the thawed-out stuff lay at the bottom of seven different trash receptacles in three separate parking lots along the coast highway.

He handed a dollar bill to the attendant, drove to a far corner of the lot, got out of the car, unlocked the luggage compartment, and carefully consigned the last of the movable feast to two of Santa Monica's public garbage cans. Then he got back into the Bentley and continued on toward the studio.

IT WAS TWENTY TO THREE when he finally got there.

He had worked everything out. He had rehearsed his attack on the role in his mind's eye and it was going to play. He was going to *make* it play. That's what he had told himself all the way to the studio and into Howard's parking space. But the moment he entered the administration building, it didn't mean a goddam thing. It was strictly whistling-in-the-graveyard time. He was no more Howard Bluestern than he was the man in the moon. Who the hell was going to be fooled by *his* performance? They'd see right into the hollowness inside, smell the fear of discovery on him the way animals picked up the scent of cowards.

He went up in the elevator and strode past the receptionist into the office of the president feeling like the impostor that he was, and because his stage fright was about to overwhelm him he flew right into the teeth of it. He walked right up to Jo Anne's desk and met her searching gaze head on. "Before I do anything, I want to talk to Marvin Gerber at Mutual of Oklahoma."

"Certainly." She stared at him intently, and kept her voice low. "Are you all right, Howard?"

I just lost my only brother. I never felt better. "Of course I'm all right. Why do you ask?"

"You look tired," she said.

"I always look like this after three too many at lunch . . . women, that is."

She didn't smile.

"Get me Gerber," he said, and started for Howard's private office. This morning he had lost her, and now here she was back in his life again, and he hadn't even been nice to her, just shitty and cold. He'd make it up to her later, once he got over his daze and figured out which feelings were more important than others, what the priorities were. First he had to handle Gerber and all the studio crap that was sure to follow. Then he'd get to Jo Anne. He needed her in so many ways.

God, if only he weren't so *weary* . . .

Marvin Gerber must have been sitting with a hand on the phone, waiting. He was on the line almost before Teddy could get a chance to glance around Howard's handsomely decorated office and become accustomed to the fact that he was actually back here, that all the internal good-byes had been canceled, all bets were off—except the *big* one, of course, the new one, the challenging one, the frightening one.

That bet was on, no matter what the odds.

"Good afternoon, Mr. Bluestern. . . ." The voice sounded too pleased with itself.

The answer is *no*, you prick . . .

"I've thought it over, Mr. Gerber," Teddy said. "And I've decided that you gave me some very sound advice this morning."

"Thank you. That's a very thoughtful way to put it. That's very kind of you," Gerber replied. "Just as soon as we hang up I'll put the applications through for immediate processing, and from here on in you can count on everything flowing automatically without a hitch."

"That's fine," Teddy said. "One little favor."

"Of course, Mr. Bluestern."

"Not that you insurance companies spread these things around, but I'm saying it to you anyway: namely, I'd just as soon keep the fact of my personal policy a private matter. I don't think it's any concern of anybody around here . . ."

"Oh, I agree with you completely," the insurance man said. "We never divulge such information unless we're specifically instructed to. Nevertheless, I appreciate your reminding me of your feelings in the matter."

"Now, about the first premium, the certified check," Teddy said.

"Yes, as I told you earlier," Gerber said, "that would come to twenty-one thousand two hundred and fifty dollars . . ."

"Right."

"But while we're on the subject, and now that you've come to your decision, I just want to point out an additional option that is available to you which may or may not interest you . . ."

"What's that?" Teddy said warily.

"I don't mean to insult your intelligence," Gerber said. "No doubt a man of your experience has heard of something called an accidental-death rider. In more common parlance, we refer to it as double indemnity."

Teddy didn't dare to speak, didn't trust his voice. The blood was rushing through every part of his body.

Gerber moved into the silence. "For an extra five thousand a year you can double the payoff value of the policy to ten million in the event, God forbid, there is an accidental death involved. You follow?"

"Yes," Teddy said, fighting the dryness in his mouth and the trembling of his hands. *Ten . . . million . . . dollars . . .*

"I'm only offering this as a suggestion, Mr. Bluestern, nothing

more than that, please understand me; I'm not *selling* you on the idea.
I'm not pressuring you in any way. Do I make myself clear?''

"Yes, of course, Mr. Gerber, I understand." He ran his tongue
over his parched lips. "Frankly, I'm thinking, I'm weighing it. My
gut feeling is that I don't really need or want anything like that. And
yet, who knows? Driving the freeways? Hopping to New York and
back every five minutes? Slipping in the bathtub? *I* know the statistics.
But still, five thousand dollars a year. Let me ask you something: if
you were me, would *you* go for it? I mean, is it a sensible expenditure
of assets for me to have that kind of additional coverage at that price?
What's *your* recommendation?''

Without a moment's hesitation Gerber said, "I think if you can
afford it, it would be foolish—penny wise and pound foolish—*not* to
take it, because in these crazy times there is no predicting what can
happen to anyone, anywhere, anytime. But as I said, it's only a suggestion. The decision is entirely yours.''

"I know that, I know.'' Teddy gave it a reasonably long pause.
Then he said, "The trouble with me is, I can't think of a single good
reason why I should ignore your thinking in the matter. I guess what
I'm trying to say is I agree with you, Mr. Gerber, the answer is yes,
and therefore I'm going to go ahead on it. There. That's that.''

"Whatever makes you feel comfortable,'' Gerber said calmly.

"Now that changes the first premium, doesn't it?''

"Yes,'' Gerber said. "Make the check out for twenty-six thousand
two hundred and fifty dollars.''

"Twenty-six two-fifty,'' Teddy repeated.

"May I congratulate you on your sound judgment, Mr. Bluestern?''

"You may if you include yourself in,'' Teddy said.

"Thank you,'' Gerber said. "Now, as you know, the coverage
won't go into effect until we get the official okay from the medical
department, which as far as you and I are concerned is a foregone
conclusion. I should have the good word for you by Monday, Tuesday
the latest, so don't go driving any motorcycles this weekend. And
better lay off the sky-diving too.'' Gerber chuckled at his own humor.

"I won't even use the bathtub,'' Teddy said.

Gerber continued to chuckle. He was such a chucklesome fellow
Teddy hated to say good-bye to him, but finally he forced himself to.

Ten . . . million . . . fucking . . . fantastic . . . dollars!

He buzzed Jo Anne.

"Yes?''

"Nothing,'' he said, somewhat giddily. "How are you?''

"I'm fine." She sounded happy to hear him back among the living. "You've got people out here waiting."

"I know," he said.

"I mean, in *addition* to me."

"I know," he said.

"I was thinking," she said. "If you're pooped, maybe you won't really feel like tennis at the end of a day like this."

He tried not to sound too mystified. "Tennis, tennis . . ."

"Shall I call them in alphabetical order?"

"How would that go?"

"Evans . . . Turman . . . Zanuck."

"No," he said. "Dick doesn't like to be last in anything."

"I'll call him first then," she said. "If they get another fourth, shall I tell them it's all right at your house, or would you rather have peace and quiet?"

"P and Q, definitely," he said.

"Howard?" He could barely hear her.

"Yes?"

"I like minding your Ps and Qs."

They were back together again.

He felt a warm rush of pleasure at the thought of it.

"Get me Victor Lampkin, please," he said, and hung up.

Howard's business manager spent most of his workdays on the back nine at the Brentwood Country Club. His clients rarely complained, for their fortunes unaccountably improved even as Victor Lampkin's golf handicap stayed stubbornly in place. Though Teddy had never been able to figure out what anybody saw in the man, other than his incongruously elegant suite of offices in one of Hollywood's oldest and most rundown buildings and his ability to hit the long ball from the fairway with a number-one iron, Teddy did admire Lampkin for the promptness with which his office always managed to get the monthly check to Teddy on the first—never on the thirty-first, or the second, always the first.

"Yes! What can I do for you, Howard?" Heartiness and a steadiness on the greens were two of Lampkin's chief assets.

"I'm going to tell you, Victor, and you're probably going to get upset, and then I'm going to have to do a lot of explaining and defending, and it's going to take more time than I've *got* right now . . ."

"Do you realize how much time you've wasted already? Tee off, Howard. What is it?"

Teddy swallowed hard and plunged in. "I want you to have a

certified check for twenty-six thousand two hundred and fifty dollars, made payable to Mutual of Oklahoma, delivered to the office of one Marvin Gerber, that's G-E-R-B-E-R, at Mutual's main office on the Miracle Mile first thing tomorrow morning. Do you follow me so far?''

"Of course I do," Lampkin said, his feathers ruffling through the phone. "But may I ask you, why are you so confident that you have twenty-six thousand dollars lying around when only yesterday—?''

Teddy blanched. "Do I or don't I?''

"It so happens you do, but—"

"Then pay it, Victor."

"As you say," Lampkin said in a small voice.

"It's the first premium on a five-year term life insurance policy for five million dollars with double indemnity. The beneficiary is Teddy, but that is strictly between you and me . . .''

"But why did you—? Never mind, I don't want to know."

"Now, what else do you don't want to know?''

"Whether I can go now," Victor Lampkin said. "I've got exactly forty-five minutes before the bank closes.''

" 'Bye, Victor." He hung up and sat there for a moment gaining heart, thinking: Not bad, not bad. Howard was taking on color, coming alive, at least over a telephone. But hadn't he been neglecting Teddy Stern a little?

He swiveled around to the private phone behind him, dialed Howard's house in Bel Air, and mentally slipped on a pair of sunglasses and a bikini and maybe three or four shots of tequila on the inside.

The snotty voice answered. "Mr. Bluestern's residence.''

"David, m'lad, this is Teddy Stern. Would my brother, by any chance, be out on the tennis court making a fool of himself?''

"No, Mr. Stern.''

"No what, David?''

"He is not on the tennis court, sir.''

"Smart move. Is he haunting the premises elsewhere?''

"No, he is not.''

"Do you expect him?''

"I couldn't say, Mr. Stern.''

"Aw, come on, I'll bet you could if you tried.''

"Was there anything else you wanted, sir?''

"Much, David, very much. But I'll settle for talking to your master.''

"I suggest you try the studio.''

"I already did. They said he's left for the day.''

"Then I'm afraid I can't help you."

"Do *not* be afraid, my boy. Just tell him, please, to call me as soon as he gets in. Is that a Roger?"

"Very well, Mr. Stern."

"Eternally grateful, David."

He hung up, feeling a temporary surge of renewed energy coursing through his veins. Maybe the incredible surprise from Marvin Gerber had been good for his circulation, or his ailing soul. Whatever it was, he wasn't going to question it, he was going to swing with it and let it carry him along. He liked working without a script or rehearsals. Maybe it had been badly written roles that had held him back, not the drinking, not the paucity of acting skills. The writers had screwed him up. Everyone else in the industry blamed the writers for everything that turned out lousy; why shouldn't *he*? It was the *writers*. He felt far more effective doing it off the wall.

He turned back to the desk, pushed the intercom button, and said, "Who's on first?"

"Barnett and Hough," Jo Anne said in a low voice. "They've been frowning a *lot*."

His heart sank. He ordered it right back up. Without the necessary moxie, he could parlay a slim credibility gap into a yawning chasm and fall right into it. "Ready," he said.

The moment they walked in Teddy knew what *anyone* would have known: they were two of Howard's four executive assistants. The foulard ties, the short-tab collars, and the discreet threads—not quite charcoal gray but not exactly wild strawberry either—were dead giveaways. They wore matching serious expressions, and there was bitching in the air. Teddy could smell it.

"Gentlemen," he said expansively, rising.

"Mr. Bluestern," they said in unison.

" 'Howard,' for God's sake, please." Teddy shook hands with them. "And what have I been calling *you*?"

The tall one with the tinted glasses said, "Frankly, nothing, sir, and that's why we wanted to see you today. I'm Jeff Barnett. This is Larry Hough, as in huff."

"Are you *in* one, Larry?"

"I wouldn't exactly call it *that*." The pudgy face ran scared and smiled nervously.

"Then sit down, guys."

They all sat, and Teddy scrutinized them quickly and carefully.

He and they were going to be cellmates for a while, at least until he decided that a reasonable interval had elapsed and it would look kosher for Howard to come to some untimely and, perforce, fiery end. Why not use the hell out of them and make his brief term in office a breeze for himself? Come to think of it, thank God for executive assistants. How would he ever be able to do it without them? Two of them anyway. Four would be an unmanageable crowd.

"Let me anticipate you here with a short speech," Teddy said, wondering what the hell it was going to *be*. "And then you're on."

They nodded agreement.

"I don't know *what* your relationship was with the previous occupant of this throne, and I don't *want* to know," Teddy began. "But I can tell you this: in the short time *I've* been here, my relationship with you, Larry, and you, Jeff, has been just about as bad, as nonexistent, as *neglected*, as every other relationship I've had at this studio, with the possible exception of the night cleaning women and the guards at the gate. I've been so busy trying to figure out where the wall sockets are in my john, and which way the doors open, in or out, and how the hell you pre-empt the tieline to New York without offending *anybody*, that I frankly haven't had time to run the company properly, meaning I haven't had time to call *you* men in to run it *for* me, while *I* sit back and take all the bows, because that's what I plan to do, fellows—be warned."

Jeff Barnett fussed with his glasses to cover up his sudden elation. Larry Hough just grinned and said nothing, probably afraid a whoop of joy would escape if he opened his mouth.

"Question is," Teddy said, watching them. "Are you guys interested, and ready, to take on the burdens and miseries of important decision-making, because that's what I'm talking about, nothing less? The worst part is, if you guess *right* now and then, you're liable to wind up as executive vice-presidents, or even, God help you, behind *this* desk. Enough. I've said my piece. Let's hear yours."

Howard, you should've heard me. You were great . . .

The two men exchanged quick glances, and then Jeff Barnett said, "As far as I'm concerned, and probably Larry too, I think you've said it *for* us, Mr. Bluestern. *Howard*. Excuse me. Right, Larry?"

"Absolutely," Hough said. "If we've had any complaint at all around here, and that's long before *you* moved in, sir, it's that we've been *wasted*, paid too well, treated too politely, and totally ignored. That's hard to live with when you think you've got something to offer."

"Don't I know," Teddy said, shaking his head slowly. "Look, what have I got on you guys, maybe ten years? I remember exactly what it felt like in the early days. I'm not going to put either of you through that. What I'd like you to do from now on is consider yourselves extensions of *me*. There, I've just cloned myself. I want you to start right now finding properties, putting together packages, melding the right people with the right people, coming up with winners, *big* winners, and let it be known around town immediately that you're in a position to make deals, not just talk about them but *make* them. You don't have to come to me—I don't *want* you to come to me—not until everything is ready to be closed, just the way *I've* got to turn to New York before *I* give the big yes. You've got the pigskin, fellows. The team may be mine, but it's your ballgame, and you better get us into the Superbowl because if you don't, it's my ass, not yours. Now will you please get the hell out of here and go make umpteen hundred million dollars for this studio and make me look so good no one will ever find out I don't know shit from Shinola?"

Jeff Barnett sprang to his feet. "We sure as hell are going to try, Howard. Christ, this is terrific. This is really terrific. I'm afraid I'm going to wake up and find out I've been dreaming."

"Would you believe it, sir?" Larry Hough was grabbing at the desk in his excitement. "I told my wife this morning that I was going to *resign* today. You couldn't get me out of this job now with a *court order*."

"Way to go, team, way to go," Teddy said, starting around the desk to escort them to the door. "And while we're still in an office that isn't, I don't *think*, *bugged*, how do we feel about certain *other* players in your category?"

Barnett looked at Hough, Hough looked at Barnett, and Barnett looked at Teddy. "Marty Wallach and Liam O'Toole, who are right guard and right tackle on your team, have everything going for them . . . youth, experience, hustle, chutzpah, good looks, the right friends, the right enemies, and red-hot ambition. The only trouble with *them* is, the only teeny-weeny little drawback is, they don't know a fucking thing about the motion picture business and don't even know that they don't know."

"That's a damned shame," Teddy said gravely. "I'm very, very disappointed to hear this . . ."

"You can imagine how disappointed *we* are," Larry Hough chimed in.

That, Teddy thought silently, would take the combined imaginations of Lewis Carroll, Ray Bradbury, Isaac Asimov, Arthur C. Clarke, and H. G. Wells, with an assist by Harlan Ellison and a putout by Robert Jastrow.

"I'd hate to have to say something crummy like it's them or us," Jeff Barnett said.

"What would you *like* to say?" Teddy asked him.

"It's them or us."

Larry Hough shrugged sadly.

Teddy looked from one to the other. "I guess there's nothing we can do then but trade them to the Miami Dolphins for a twenty-sixth-round draft choice."

"*If* you can get that much," Jeff Barnett said.

"You're a hard man, McGee," Teddy said.

"Vicious," said Larry Hough.

Barnett shrugged. "Nice guys go to the toilet bowl."

"The sound you just heard was Wallach and O'Toole being flushed." Teddy opened the door for them. "Not a peep to anyone, please. Now go make some miracles."

He slapped them both on the back and sent them forth to prowl the jungle and maraud and kill for him.

On the way back to his desk, he thought You're gonna go out *good*, Howard. Not with a whimper, but a bang. . . . He pressed Jo Anne's button. "Would Edgar Seligman be back from lunch yet?"

"Possibly from dinner too, Mr. Bluestern."

"Will you get him for me, please?"

"Phone or in person?"

"Phone will do. He's already *had* me once today."

"Some people have all the luck," she murmured.

He didn't say anything.

She said, "While you were in conference there were calls from Mr. Wallach and Mr. O'Toole. They want to see you, either separately or together, before you leave the studio."

"Call their secretaries right away," he said. "Unfortunately you just missed me. I've left for the day."

"All right."

"Now Seligman."

"Do you know that Joe Van Allen is out here waiting for you?"

"Joe Van Allen. . . ." Who was *he* again? "Fill me in."

"Directing *The Madison Bunch*."

"*That* I know. What does he *want?*"

"I *think*, I mean I've *heard*, that he and Bemmelman are having a major disagreement on some casting."

Bemmelman . . . Bemmelman . . . he couldn't come right out and *ask* her. "How come this kind of junk food winds up on *my* table?"

"Your not just the president, Mr. Bluestern."

"No, I'm also the garbage disposal."

"And chief operating officer in charge of worldwide production . . ."

"I should have read the fine print. Pour a glass of iced tea over Van Allen to cool him off and get me Seligman."

The lawyer came on apologizing all over the place for running out on the medical examination, but Teddy cut him short. "Scotty, please, no problem. It was a breeze, except you *did* miss holding the flask while I peed."

"You see? I knew I never should have left. What's cooking, Howard?"

"What kind of arrangement do we have with Martin Wallach and Liam O'Toole?"

"You and I just *reviewed* those commitments last week."

Damn. "Does it say anywhere that I have a memory?"

"Hold on just *one second*." Seligman left the phone for about a minute, then returned. "Howard?"

"Yeah."

"Seventy-five thousand a year, first year firm, with an option to pick them up for another two years at a hundred and a quarter. As of today they've got, let me see, twenty-nine weeks and two days to go on year one."

"Okay, here's what I want, Scotty. As amicably as possible, with you handling everything *personally*, no phones or memos or anything like that, they're to be told this afternoon they're terminated as of Friday close of business . . ."

"Jesus, Howard . . ."

"Total payoff, no hondling whatsoever, and the only reason, the sole reason, the *true* reason to be given: tightening of studio operations, the fight against inflation begins at home, et cetera. *I'm* out of it *completely*. Advised but not consulted. New York again. That's it, Scotty."

"But what about the other two, Barnett and Hough?"

"What *about* them?"

"Nothing, nothing, I was just asking." Seligman sighed.

"Have you got it all?"

"Yeah," the lawyer said morosely. "Right in my lap."

"Thank you, Scotty."

Teddy hung up quickly. Don't stop to think. About *anything*. Particularly about the back porch at Malibu. Just keep going. And don't look over your shoulder. They may be gaining on *you* now that Satchel Paige is gone . . ."

"Is Mr. Van Allen still waiting?" he asked Jo Anne.

"Yes, he is."

"All right, while he's in here, please call my brother out at the beach and see if he'd like to have dinner at my place tonight around nineish."

There was a pause at the other end.

"Anything wrong?" he said.

"No," she said.

They both clicked off.

So far, he felt that he knew what he was doing, and why. But at the same time he was not unaware of the dangers of going too far, getting too cute, too confident, and pulling the rug right out from under himself. It was one thing to advertise to those around you that they were getting two brothers for the price of one. It was another to get caught at it, to get nabbed for violating the Truth in Advertising laws. You could wind up facing Ralph Nader and get the electric chair— powered by solar energy, no doubt.

Joe Van Allen walked in hopping mad. Or hopped in walking mad. Either way, he looked like a fifty-five-year-old bear dressed in a powder-blue jumpsuit. No threat to Teddy. A director was a director was a director.

"Sit down, Joe," Teddy said.

"I don't wanna sit," Van Allen growled.

"Stand up, Joe," Teddy said.

"Look, Bluestern, I don't have time for any bullshit. I start shooting on Monday and I want Louise Fletcher to play the dance-hall hostess and Bemmelman wants Jennifer O'Neil, who is not only too young and too beautiful and too—"

"Wait a minute, is Bemmelman directing the picture?"

"He's the fucking *producer*, are you putting me on?"

"Then what is this conversation all about? What are you doing in this office when you start shooting on Monday?"

"I just told you—"

"You told me you're the director on this picture and you told me you want Louise Fletcher and haven't gotten her yet. If I had more time, and I *don't*, and *you* don't, I'd ask you how come you haven't had Bemmelman thrown off the set or barred from the lot yet, for Christsake." He leaned over the desk and buzzed Jo Anne. "Miss Kallen, tell Edgar Seligman to sign Louise Fletcher immediately for the role of the hostess in . . . uh . . . ."

"*The Madison Bunch?*" she said.

"Naturally, and I don't want to hear another word about it, so don't put Bemmelman through to me if he calls. All right?"

"You forget, Mr. Bluestern. You've already left for the day."

"And listen," he said in a loud voice, "can you make believe I'm wanted in a meeting somewhere so I can get Joe Van Allen out of my office?"

"What?"

"Nothing." He turned to the bear in the blue jumpsuit. "Go make a picture, will you, for Christsake, and stop bothering me?"

Van Allen shook his head, grinning. "Bluestern, I don't know what's happened to you or what you're taking, but whatever it is, get *me* some, will ya? Provided it's not more than a grand an ounce." He went out still shaking his head.

Teddy sank back in his chair, drained.

Jo Anne's voice came through. "I called your brother. His answering machine said he's not home. So I invited his answering machine to your house for dinner."

"Funny," he said, and tried to smile but couldn't.

"Are you ready for another customer?"

He closed his eyes and shook his head slowly. "Jo Anne?"

"Yes, Mr. Bluestern?"

"Not another soul in here. Finished. That's it."

"Certainly," she said. "No problem."

"I'm sorry," he said.

"Please," she said.

"I'm going to lie down now and try to nap . . . ."

"Wonderful idea."

"Don't let me oversleep."

"Promise."

"You won't leave early, will you?"

"I wouldn't dream of it," she said, and something in her voice made him want her badly.

With what? he thought ruefully. I'm all used up.

He closed the shutters, snapped off the lights, tossed his jacket on a chair and flopped down on the sofa, utterly astonished at the depths of the fatigue that had suddenly overcome him. He had been playing over his head, that's what it was. He had been running too hard all day long, running not *toward* anything but away from, running away from the memory of a dreadfully misshapen, pitiful, bloody figure that had looked so much like him, but wasn't him, no, wasn't him . . .

Stop thinking about him. You're too tired to think about him. Did you hear what I said? Stop thinking about him.

He closed his eyes again and, helpless to prevent it, started to relive each moment of this day, *everything*, beginning with his waking up in the morning in the quiet bedroom in Bel Air.

By the time he got to breakfast, he was fast asleep.

HE WOKE UP in the semidarkness and found her standing quietly beside the sofa looking down at him. She had removed her glasses, and her hair hung down all soft and loose about her shoulders, and there was a lovely loving expression on her face.

"Hi," she whispered.

He started to rise.

"No, don't get up," she said softly.

"What time is it?" The few rays of fading daylight that leaked through the closed shutters were tinged with reddish gold.

"Twenty after six," she said.

"God . . ."

"You had a delicious snooze. You needed it." She sat down on the edge of the sofa and smiled at him. "You put in a rather remarkable day, Howard, do you realize that?"

"Yes, I guess I did," he said. If she knew, if she ever found out what he had done and was doing now and was going to do, would she hate him forever, or longer than that?

"I haven't been around you that long," she was saying. "I didn't *really* get to know you until yesterday, last night, but I have this feeling that you've changed, Howard, you really have, suddenly and marvelously. I never dreamed, and I had many wild dreams about you, darling . . . I never dreamed that you could be so tender and vulnerable and . . . so touching . . ."

"Me?"

"Yes, you."

"Beware of the touch of touching men," he said, trying not to feel the deep shame that was within him.

"I'm serious, darling."

"I know you are."

"You're changing," she said.

"I wonder what's come over me?" he said.

"I hope it's me," she said.

"I think it is," he said, knowing that that was only partly true.

"I want to come over you again, right now," she said softly. "No, don't move. Please, darling. Lie still. Just rest, and relax and don't move. Promise me you won't move?"

"I promise," he said, wanting to lie there for the rest of his life, not moving, never leaving her or the peaceful stillness of this reddish-golden-tinged semidark office. What a terrible thing he was doing to her. . . . Was there a chance he could resist?

"We're all alone," she was murmuring as her hands undid his belt. "The door is locked and everyone has gone home. Isn't that thoughtful of them?"

"I like your perfume," he sighed helplessly, beginning to surrender.

"I put it on just for you," she said. "All my thoughts today have been just for you. I've been thinking about *now*, and it's been a wonderful day, because no matter what I was doing or saying, I was always thinking about you, and what I wanted us to do together. Are you comfortable, darling?"

"Beautifully," he said. Let me stay here forever, please. . . . Don't make me ever face the truth . . .

"Close your eyes," she said.

"Must I?"

"Yes, close them, and relax completely."

And he did as he was told, because he found it impossible to do otherwise, and felt her hands taking off Howard's shoes and socks and heard the shoes thumping on the carpet, and then she was slowly working his trousers off and casting them aside, and gently peeling off the boxer shorts, and tucking his shirttails up underneath the thin undershirt he wore next to his skin, and the slight coolness of the air in the quiet office caressed his nakedness and made him feel good there. He imagined her eyes looking down on him where he was so open and exposed, and he luxuriated in the feeling of exposure under the warmth of her gaze, and yearned to be touched there, and to be held, and fondled, and kissed, and he opened his eyes so that she could look into them and see all of him, and he saw the tender smile on her face as her gaze wandered over his legs and thighs, sprawled out, relaxed, resting, and his vulnerable sex, wanting to be touched by her, yearning to be held by her soft gentle hands . . .

"How beautiful," she murmured, feasting on him with her eyes. "You beautiful man, you. Oh God, Howard, how beautiful you are . . ."

And his sex yearned toward her, rising now, reaching toward her, aching to be held by her, to be taken into her.

"Don't move, darling," she whispered. "Lie still and let me, please let me . . ." She moved up on the sofa and knelt over him, her knees on either side of his hips, her hair tumbling down over his face, her mouth moving slowly over his, their mouths opening for each other, tongues loving each other, moving deeper and deeper into each other. He reached up to hold her head in his hands and she murmured, "Lie perfectly still, my darling," and slowly, carefully, she raised her skirt and he saw that she had removed everything underneath and his sex yearned toward her and she smiled down at him with her lips parted and her eyes looking deeply into his and he gasped as he felt the first velvet touch of her sex on his own and she lowered herself ever so carefully, ever so gently, down onto him, taking him slowly, inside her warm moist grasp.

"Ah, beautiful . . . ," he sighed.

"Ah, darling, oh Howard darling . . ."

"Jo Anne . . ."

Their warm bodies slowly melted together and met and held in motionless embrace, and he looked up at her and she was too beautiful, too beautiful . . .

"I can't stand it . . . " he moaned.

"Isn't this lovely?" She smiled down at him.

"I can't stand it . . ."

"Yes you can."

"Oh God . . ."

"Just lie there. That's it, just like that, darling Howard, look at you, beautiful man, beautiful Howard, if you could see the look on your face, ah lovely, isn't this heaven . . . ?"

And more than he could bear, he had to close his eyes, he couldn't look at her, couldn't bear to look at her and hear her voice caressing him so softly, so tenderly, how she felt inside, oh Christ how she felt inside. . . . "I want your lips, Jo Anne . . ."

"Don't move, darling."

"Your mouth . . . come here . . . give me your lips . . . come to me . . . Jo Anne, come to me . . ."

And he felt her leaning down and her hair brushing his cheeks again and then her lips were gently kissing his eyelids and his forehead and his cheeks and the tip of his nose and then her head was resting on his shoulder even as they lay deeply united in loving clasp and her voice in his ear whispering, whispering, "Lie still, lie still, lie still, my darling . . ."

"Oh, God, Jo Anne, I want you so badly . . ."

Their mouths found each other and came together and opened wide and they stayed that way, joined together, their tongues exploring each other, exchanging wordless, sinuous, ardent currents of passion that flowed through their bodies and met where her moistness enfolded him, and then he moved with her gently toward the back of the sofa and lay on his side facing her, with her on her side facing him, and their arms went around each other and their mouths met again and his hands went down and drew her skirt up and clasped the soft curve of her and drew her tightly to him and he went harder and deeper inside her and they lay that way in loving embrace, feeling an aching and wanting and longing that they knew could not be denied much longer no matter how hard they tried.

She knew it even as he did. She could see it in his shining eyes and the flush of his cheeks and feel it in the soft demanding looseness of his lips and tongue and the power of his grasp on her buttocks and the quickening pulse of the hardness inside her and the murmuring of his wandering needy mouth, groaning oh God how I want to come inside you, oh God Jo Anne, how I want you, Jo Anne, Jo Anne, I have to have you, darling, I can't help it, darling, I have to, I have to, I'm going to take you, darling. . . . And knowing that he had to, that he was going to, that he couldn't help himself any longer, was so unbearably exciting to her, so deeply, beautifully, savagely in rhythm with her own wild hunger to ravish him and be ravished by him that she was suddenly ready now to answer his growing abandon with her own, and she announced this to herself and to him by kissing him slowly and deeply, and then gently drawing back and allowing his throbbing sex to escape her grasp.

And then she reached out for his hands and drew him to a sitting position and then onto his feet along with her and they stood facing each other beside the sofa, looking into each other's eyes, and they began to disrobe each other, kissing each other and fondling each other's yearning sex, silently, without words, too filled with joy and desire to be able to utter a sound. And, naked now, she stood before him with her legs slightly apart and gazed with longing at his swollen love for her and watched his eyes devouring her hardening breasts and her parted lips and her tawny thighs and long slim legs and, moving close to him, she opened her mouth on his bare chest and began to taste him with her tongue while her hands roamed over his lean hard body and his own hands moved all over her, sending shivers of delight through her, and the mounting delirium in her soul gave slow and subtle movement to her body which he answered with his own and her hips swayed slowly from side to side with him upright and hard against her, firmly held between them as they moved in rhythm together, hands on each other, mouths glued together, coiling tongues moving slowly, slowly, flushed with the thrilling certainty that nothing could stop them now, they were on their way and nothing could stop them and there was all the time in the world for their slow deliberate wet warm insistent mounting rising inescapable undeniable growing hardening firming hungry movement and touching and tasting and looking and wanting and wanting and wanting more and drawing back and gazing at each other and murmuring hello darling and her moaning, "I want you so badly, come into me, darling . . ."

And his hoarse whisper: "I want to devour you, darling. I have to, Jo Anne, I have to . . ."

"Oh, yes, take me, darling, please take me . . ."

And she sank into the club chair and leaned back with her eyes closed and her hands behind her holding onto the back of the chair and her breasts all full and firm for him and her tawny legs and thighs spread wide for him, and then he was down on his knees before her and she felt his hungry mouth finding her and she shuddered with delight and cried out oh my God as he began to feast on her as he had wanted to, devoured her as he had wanted to, his tongue hot and hard and demanding, wanting all of her, all of her, her legs slowly closing around him oh my God oh my God oh my God, and then finally he rose slowly and came up over her and his mouth was on hers and she tasted herself on his tongue and she reached down and seized him and held on to him, feeling him moving slowly in her hands, and then he was helping her to her feet and taking up the soft pillow from the chair and leading her over to the desk and she knew now that he wanted her and was going to take her and she could not bear not having him a moment longer so she sat up on the pillow on the edge of the desk and held out her arms to him and opened herself up to him and begged him, implored him, to take her and come into her and love her . . .

"Oh God, I can't bear it, I want you so much . . ."

And he walked into her open widespreading welcome and looked into her eyes and put his hands on the back of her head and, crouching slightly, moved into her warm wet hunger and felt her hands on him and her mouth opening wider and her tongue on his and he moved slowly and gently deeper inside her and told her he was going to take her now and her hands tightened on him and her legs went around him and her mouth went slack and vulnerable and he strained inside her passionate embrace, wanting to go farther into her, farther, farther, straining to reach way beyond his aching love oh Jo Anne he groaned oh Jo Anne and her womb became hollow and overflowing and insatiable and needed filling, needed more of him, she wanted more of him, she wanted all of him, she tightened her legs around him and her arms and her mouth and the clasp of her sex trying to take all of him inside her, all of him, all of him, and move with him, yes, she wanted to move with him, yes, and move onto him, yes, and over him and love him, oh God, darling, she moaned into his mouth, I want to love you and make you come inside me, please let me, darling, I want to love you into coming, please, darling, please, she cried, and moved him down, slowly they moved down together, never leaving each other, joined together, moving together, easing him gently to the soft warm carpet, loving the heavy-lidded look in his eyes as she helped him lay back on the soft warm carpet and came to rest on top of him, kissing him softly on his open lips as she lowered her wet and hungry love down onto him and took him into her as deeply as she could, feeling the warmth of him and the hardness of him and the soft velvet of him, oh my darling, she moaned gazing down at his face, loving him so much for letting her do this to him, oh my darling, oh God what it felt like loving him like this, moving on him like this with voluptuous abandon, hearing his groans of agonized delight, having all of him hers to love and devour and torture, ah listen to him cry out, oh what heaven loving him this way, oh I love you darling, I love you darling, deeper and deeper, oh you beautiful man, oh heaven, oh God, oh heaven, and his voice in her ear groaning with ecstasy Jo Anne darling Jo Anne darling I'm going to oh yes oh Jesus oh Christ I'm going to come Jo Anne darling I'm going to come and she felt him yes darling stiffening stiffening stiffening oh yes she cried I'm going to come with you darling oh Jesus he shouted oh Christ he shouted and started to rise up and turn her over and she let him do it wanted him to do it and he rolled her over with him on top of her moving inside her shouting oh my God and taking her so beautifully faster and faster, faster and faster, and suddenly he stiffened and shuddered and cried out and burst inside her and her legs tightened around him and she cried out oh my God and felt the wonder of him exploding deep inside her and oh my God she was going to oh my God she cried out oh my God oh my God and his love pouring out inside her throbbing throbbing and her mouth open and crying out oh . . . oh . . . oh . . . oh. . . . And they clung to each other in wild and passionate embrace, making wordless sounds of ecstasy, all flushed and sweating and kissing each other savagely and moving together, moving together, bathing each other with their flowing love for each other and crying out to each other, I love you darling, lovely woman I love you, moving together with slow and deliberate rhythm, sending each other into new transports of joy and delirium, flowing and spending and throbbing as one, ah darling she cried and took his fevered kisses and crushed her lips to his and pulled him to her, not wanting it to end, not ever, darling, my darling, they continued that way, intertwined and intermingled, until there was nothing left to give to each other and they came to rest finally, with her hands on the back of his head stroking him tenderly and his lips on her throat kissing her gently and his sex held lovingly in the clasp of her own, and they lay there resting, hearts beating together, on the soft warm carpet of the hushed, semidark room, with the world someplace else, far away . . .

He had never felt this way in all his life, and he clung to her now, letting her hold him and enfold him in her warmth and love and tenderness, knowing that as long as he lay there with her he was safe and protected. He rested his head on the pillow of her breasts, and for a while there was no nightmare of his own making out there, waiting to close in on him, no treachery and deceit and perilous masquerade of his own invention in which he had unwittingly become loved for being someone he was not, someone who no longer existed, and who would publicly die again in a horrible accident and tear her heart in two, leaving her with memories in a world where there would be a brother she did not like, who would be rich in dollars beyond all belief, but without her and alone, and contemptible in his own eyes for what he had secretly done to her.

For a brief moment, he had a glimmer of awareness in which he sensed that he was on the verge of weighing all the risks and telling her everything now, before it was too late, even though now would be too late too. But the glimmer vanished almost before it came, for he had never made a right move, a wise decision, in his whole life, and there was no reason to believe that he was going to start doing it now.

Burrowing into the softness of her womanliness, he moved his head slightly and parted his lips and took her breast into his mouth as though for sustenance. And when he felt her hardening and felt the ache of his own desire renewing and growing inside her, he knew then that they were going to make love to each other all over again, and he forgot his sadness and was filled with happiness again as they slowly embraced and began to move together, murmuring sounds of rapture and endearment, taking each other with unhurried sureness and confidence toward the consummation they both yearned for and which, each moment, became more and more agonizingly irresistible, and then finally, oh God, oh darling, oh darling, so exquisitely inevitable . . .

chapter 8

SITTING at the kitchen table nursing a weak gin fizz and a sizable grudge, David Stanner heard Bluestern's Bentley pulling into the circular driveway and announcing its arrival with a characteristic squeal of its expensive brakes. He glanced up at the kitchen clock. Ten minutes past eight, the fucker. He rose from the table reluctantly and made his way in slow motion toward the foyer, as though his body would show Bluestern how *he* felt even if his body's proprietor, the mind in the brain, would be too shrewd to show any feelings at all. Stanner was annoyed with Bluestern. The inconsiderate bastard could have called, as he usually did. He could have said I may be home for dinner or I may not, but don't worry about it, I'll let you know. Or he could have said I'm dining out tonight, don't expect me, make your *own* plans. Instead, he had said nothing.

I'll show him, Stanner's body said, arriving at the front door much too late to save Bluestern the trouble of fumbling with his key to get the burglarproof lock open. "Good evening, sir," Stanner's mouth said and formed Smile Number Two, the weak one, which was more than the man deserved.

Big Shot brushed past him, looking all fagged out, in the poorest sense of the word. "Any calls?" he demanded.

"Your brother . . ."

"Teddy? What did *he* want?" With more than the usual annoyance.

"He'd like you to call him as soon as you get in . . ."

"So I'm in."

"I'll get him for you, sir."

"Never mind. Stop rushing me."

"*Nobody* seems to be rushing you today."

"What's *that* supposed to mean?"

"Absolutely . . . nothing, sir." Stanner smiled inwardly. "You do look a little tired, if you'll pardon my saying so."

"This morning I looked smashing. Make up your mind, will you?"

"This morning was a *long* twelve hours ago, sir."

The Powerful One glowered at him. "When you get cute, you're not very cute, David. If you're trying to tell me I've come home late, say it. The bush you're beating around may be your own." He started for the bar.

"Vulgar vulgar, sir," Stanner said, following him. "All right, you *have* come home late, but what's the diff, say I. Where there's a microwave, there's a way. Shall it be some Red Snapper, perchance? Or a bit of tender chicken with oregano?"

"Red Snapper will be fine." Teddy poured Sauza Gold heavily over ice cubes and gulped some of it fast, staring at himself in the mirror behind the bar, wondering whether the sweat on his face read as humidity or as the inner tension he was feeling. Here in Howard's home in Bel Air, he'd never be able to pull it off for long. The British pimp was too intrusive, too hostile, too unsettling. He could see himself doing something foolhardy and disastrous just to get himself out of the man's presence. The timing of the accident and the producing of Howard's body were of vital importance. He must never, *never* get suckered into making his move prematurely merely because David Stanner was unendurable. The obvious solution would be to fire the man immediately, yet the thought made him strangely uneasy. He did not fully trust the possible consequences of such an overtly unfriendly act. There had to be an easier way, a safer way.

Over the top of his glass, he stared at the man, who was staring at *him*, too curiously for comfort.

There *was* a way.

He'd have the creep kicked upstairs.

The *studio* stairs.

What a wonderful idea.

Meanwhile there was the weekend to get through.

He looked at Stanner. "Get my brother on the phone, will you? No, never mind, I'll do it myself."

My, aren't *we* the impatient one tonight? Stanner watched him step to the phone and pick it up, apparently overriding his customary passion for privacy, as though he were glad now to have someone within earshot while he talked to his brother. He watched him punch the touchtones and wait for the connection to be made, scowling as Stanner, ever the one to oblige, moved closer.

"Teddy? I hear you called. . . . Hopelessly. The job is too goddam much for one man. . . . You are? When? . . . Pretty short notice, isn't

it? . . . Uh huh . . . uh huh . . . could have been worse. Could have
been Ensinada. . . . Oh? . . . Really? . . . Well, thank you, I may
just take you up on that. I've got about four hundred scripts to read
over the weekend, and maybe the beach could do the trick for me.
Before you can change your mind, I accept. . . . Right. . . . When're
you getting back, Monday or Tuesday? . . . I see. . . . Well, have
fun, steal the money, and I'll do my best not to burn your house
down . . . I will. . . . You too." He hung up and turned to Stanner.
"You can do what you do best this weekend, David . . . loaf . . .
after you throw some hot dogs and hamburgers at the tennis-court
leeches. I'll be relaxing out at my brother's place."

"I do wish I could have known sooner, sir. I could have made
plans."

"Well I'm *very* . . . *sorry*, David." The nerve of the son of a
bitch. "You can always work the streetcorners on Santa Monica Boulevard." He started away.

"Oh, I almost forgot," Stanner called after him. "Bea Magnin
called a few minutes before you got in." *That* stopped the sadistic
bloke in his tracks. "She wants to know if you're coming alone or
bringing a lady to the thing tomorrow night."

"The thing? Tomorrow?"

"The dinner party, Mr. Bluestern?"

"Oh . . . *that*."

"She said that Meryl Streep and Princess Diana are in town at the
Beverly Hills Hotel, and alone. She also said, 'Tell your boss that if
he can manage to bring either one of them, he can have me in the
powder room right after dinner.' "

"Tell her I've already got someone."

"She'll want to know who."

"You mean *you* want to know who."

"It's for eight o'clock, dressy informal, in case you've forgotten
that too, sir."

Irritable One gave him a vicious look that thrilled him to the core,
and said, "I'll be going there straight from Malibu, so pick out some
clothes for me, head to toe, and put them in the car. But try to remember
that it's *me* who's going, not you. There won't be any bleachboys
there."

Stanner repressed a powerful urge to tell his employer to go down
on himself. "You realize, sir, that this is a first for you."

"What is?"

"You've never deigned to let me select your wardrobe before."

The annoyance on The Face seemed out of all proportion. "You got something against firsts?"

"Not at all." Stanner put on one of his nastier smiles. "I could suggest a few of my own if you'd care to hear them."

"Some other time, huh?"

"Patience," Stanner said, "is my last remaining virtue." And on his way back to the kitchen he found himself wondering, among other things, when his employer had switched from a simple Perrier or a very watered-down vodka martini to a tidal wave of tequila on the rocks. And when had the man's memory gone from frighteningly sharp to early senile?

Will wonders never cease? Stanner asked himself.

Or wondering?

In the bedroom, Teddy slowly divested himself of Howard's clothing and gave his annoyance with the needling snotnose time to evaporate. He was beginning to feel better about the immediate future, and only ninety-five percent of it was due to the Sauza Gold reaching his brain. By the time he stepped into the shower, he was ready to dwell on what had gone *well* instead of obsessing on what *might* go badly. The fake phone call to himself in Stanner's presence had been sheer artistry, worthy of a Sir Laurence Olivier or, at the very least, Bob Newhart. As for the idea of having Teddy offer Howard the use of the Malibu beach house for the weekend, that had been a fucking inspiration. It would rescue him from Stanner and the relatively stressful, unfamiliar scene of Howard's drop-in tennis crowd, and he'd have Jo Anne all to himself in his own natural habitat. His only problem would be to forget the freezer and remember that he wasn't Teddy.

Oh God, so soon?

I said forget the *freezer*, I didn't say I'd forget *you* . . .

I know what you meant . . .

I didn't say you, Howard, I didn't mean you . . .

I know what you meant . . .

Quickly Teddy turned his face up to the shower spray to wash away the soap, or whatever it was, that had gotten into his eyes.

SHE CALLED HIM at eleven, as she had said she would. She was in her apartment now, fresh from dinner with her parents at a restaurant in Studio City. He took the call on the extension in Howard's bedroom and told her about the weekend they'd be spending together at the

Malibu beach house. The cold and instant silence at the other end of the phone was curiously painful to him, which must have been what he had wanted, for he had neglected to mention up front that the chief occupant of the house would be away in Mazatlan doing a television commercial.

"Oh, that's different," she said. "How wonderful."

And that had hurt too.

But why hadn't he told her *first* that the house would be empty? Was it his own deep-seated perversity in the face of things going well? Or had he needed this reminder of her antipathy toward Teddy Stern in order to justify his determination to continue deceiving her?

How could I not have, honey? How could I have told you when I knew how much you disliked me?

How could I not have, honey? How could I have told you when I knew how much you disliked me?

Enough. Over and out. "Honey?"

"Yes, darling?"

"I know I should know things like this, but which department at the studio actually runs the executive dining room?"

"Studio manager. Stan Howe calls all the shots," she said.

"Think you can press some buttons and make him appear in my office tomorrow morning?"

"Watch me."

"You're terrific."

"Some of the time."

"Guess what *I'm* going to do now," he said.

"You're going to go to sleep," she said.

"You're too smart, Miss Kallen."

"Some of the time, Mr. Bluestern."

They made kissing sounds, lots of them, and finally hung up.

But he didn't go to sleep. Not then, he didn't. He left the house quietly, drove out to Malibu in the Bentley at a steady fifty-five on the relatively deserted coast highway, let himself into the beach house, wrote out a note for Mrs. Mahoney and left it on the kitchen table: "I've gone away for the weekend. My brother, Howard Bluestern, will be using the house with a friend. Please take good care of them, and yourself too. See you next week. (signed) Mr. Teddy . . . P.S.— Please don't drink all my booze." Then he went into the living room and punched the playback button on the Answerphone for possible messages. There had been one recent call . . . from Linda Carol.

"You can call me anytime up to midnight, Teddy bear. Please do," said the tape.

He did. And obviously woke her up.

"I'm sorry, baby," he said.

"Don't *be*, silly. Where are you, home?"

"Uh huh. Just got in. Busy busy busy."

She yawned, long and loud. "Oh God. Excusez-moi."

"Hey, me and my lousy memory," he said. "I *did* take care of you last night, didn't I?"

She gave him the old Triple-L, Linda's Lascivious Laugh. "In more ways than one, love. You shouldn't *save* it so long, Teddy bear. You were absolutely overflowing."

"It was you, baby."

"Bullshit, but I love it. If it wasn't so late and I wasn't in bed, I'd come right over there and fuck you into kingdom come."

"Is that the way you talk to the customers at Holman-Meyer?"

"You know where my hand is right now?"

" 'Deed I do."

"Why don't you get in your car and come over? I mean it, sugar. I'll leave the door unlocked, and you can steal in and wake me up with that big cock of yours. Please, Teddy?"

"Don't you think I'd love to? But I'm ready to collapse."

"Tomorrow, then?"

"I'm leaving for Mexico in the morning."

"What do you want to go to Mexico for when you've got *me* here?"

"Bread, baby, the much-needed sourdough. A scuba-diving commercial."

"Ah love, ah beauty, this feels so . . . good . . ."

"I'll call you when I get back, okay?"

"Oh Jesus . . . oh Jesus . . . don't hang up yet . . . oh Teddy . . ."

He held the phone away from his ear and waited until her noisy orgasm came and went, and then he said good night to her and dropped the phone back into its cradle as though it were something hot and unclean, which it was. The irony of it, he thought as he went to the garage. The last two persons on earth to see Howard Bluestern alive—President, Chief Operating Officer, Mr. Success himself—were a couple of X-rated females who hadn't even known it was him.

He got in the Porsche this time and drove out to Los Angeles International Airport and checked the yellow sports car with Valet

Parking. Then he had the attendant drop him off at the United Airlines terminal, where he caught a taxi back to Malibu and the waiting Bentley. By twenty after one he was coasting the big gray car up the driveway in Bel Air, and very soon after that he fell into a deep sleep in Howard's bed. It was the first time in months that he hadn't needed a Seconal or a Nembutal or a fifth of *something*.

"WILL YOU HAVE two saccharins or one, sir?"

"One will suffice," Teddy said, trying to concentrate on Sylvia Dragon's fence-straddling review of *Bloodthirsty and Beautiful* in the Los Angeles *Times*.

"Seems we've got a bit of low clouds with our oatmeal this morning, don't we?" Stanner placed the mug of coffee before him on the breakfast-room table.

"Uh huh."

"Some pretty late comings and goings last night . . . "

"I'm reading, David."

"Thought I heard a car in the driveway shortly after one. Actually woke me up."

"Maybe it was burglars," Teddy said to the *Times*.

"Burglars?"

"Come to steal your virginity, David. Obviously they left empty-handed."

"If it was me, sir, their hands would have been full."

"Modest, aren't we?" Teddy reached out automatically, found the mug, and brought the coffee to his lips.

"What's the verdict?" Stanner said.

"Just a so-so review."

"No, the coffee, sir."

"Oh. Not bad."

Never took a sweetener in his coffee *or* his tea, not ever, not once.

Teddy folded the newspaper and glanced at his tank watch. "I'm late." He rose from the table.

"What have you done with him, sir?"

Teddy looked at him blankly. "Who?"

"Howard Bluestern," Stanner said.

Teddy wiped his mouth with the napkin and tossed it on the table. "I've dressed him, fed him, and now I'm going to take the little devil to the studio, *if* it's all right with you." He turned to leave.

"What *have* you done with him, sir?"

Teddy wheeled. "What the fuck are you talking about, you insolent little cocksucker?"

Stanner blinked. "The cock calling the kettle black?"

"Look, I know you're looking for a better job—"

"But, sir, I haven't even—"

"—And I don't blame you, it's a bloody bore around here. So I'll *do* something for you, all right? You can *count* on it, okay? Just be patient."

"I haven't said a thing, sir," Stanner said quietly. "I only wanted to know where is the Howard Bluestern I used to know so well, we both knew so well? You've changed, sir, that's all . . ."

Teddy stared at him, tight-lipped. "Into a *pumpkin* if I'm not out of here in two minutes."

He went out the front door fast, without looking back, knowing that he hadn't handled Stanner well at all, but he didn't *give* a shit, because it had felt *good*, and the only way he could imagine that it would have felt even better would have been if he had *killed* the son of a bitch. He knew now how Diane must have felt when she seized that poker from the fireplace. And driving to the studio, he told himself over and over again that he goddam well *better* get David Stanner another job, not to save his own neck but to save Stanner's.

But with no guarantees that it would.

chapter 9

JO ANNE WAS SOFT and warm and as fragrant as a flower garden.

"All right, what is this going to be, good Friday or bad?" he said to her, when she finally took her hands off him and backed away from his desk chair a little.

"So far so good," she said, smiling.

He couldn't stop looking at her. "I don't know about you, but I find it difficult enough to run this studio under ordinary circumstances. With a hard on, it's impossible."

She laughed. "You can't fire me, I quit."

"Seriously," he said, "don't you find it a little bit awkward stepping out of my loving arms into the role of secretary? I mean, one minute we're in heaven together, and the next, I'm giving you orders and you're calling me Mr. Bluestern."

"Women are more adaptable than men in these matters, Howard darling Mr. Bluestern. If it ever gets to the point where I can't handle it, I'll send you a memo."

"I'm not worrying about *you*," he said. "I'm worrying about myself."

"Why don't we try this?" she said. "Let Mrs. Fahnsworth take over as your secretary, and I'll sit in *her* office."

He grimaced. "I'm not *that* worried." And, pointing to her pad, "You were about to say . . . ?"

"Stan Howe, the studio manager, will be here in twenty minutes . . ."

"And not a minute too soon," he muttered to himself, thinking of Stanner, and the need to get him *placed*, goddam it.

"A Miss McWorter called . . ."

His heart sank. . . . *Diane?* . . . What could *she* want of *Howard?* . . .

"She said she's a friend of your brother's."

"I know who she is. What does she want? Did she say?"

90

"Urgent that she see you. She didn't say why. Fifteen minutes at the most. Or if you're free for lunch today."

Christ, of all people to risk his act on. "I was planning to take off for Malibu early," he said.

"Then by all means do it," she said.

"You'll meet me there after prison lets out?"

"Darling, what do *you* think?"

He looked up at her. "By the way, I didn't tell you, we're going to Bea Magnin's for dinner tonight. Eight o'clock. Dressy informal."

She frowned. "That's some by-the-way, Howard. How come you didn't mention it?"

"I was afraid you'd say no and leave me with a lonesome weekend."

"Why would I say no?"

He shrugged. "I wasn't sure you'd want to go public . . . with me, that is."

She looked at him and probably saw right through his lie. Actually, he had truly thought she might turn him down, because from all he had heard about Bea Magnin's dinner parties, Jo Anne would be a nobody among supersomebodies, and to some girls that could be an ego-crusher. Queen Bea herself would probably soil her panties when she discovered that a mere studio secretary had been Trojan-horsed into her vaunted home. And probably never forgive Howard Bluestern for doing it to her (even after he was dead and gone).

Teddy saw the thoughtful expression on Jo Anne's face. "Any problems?"

She smiled. "No. Fine. Fortunately, I brought the correct dress along with me in the car."

"Even if you wore nothing at all, you'd be the center of attention," he said.

She reached over and tweaked his nose. "Now what about Miss McWorter?"

No escape. Why put it off? "Tell her I can make it for one drink and that's all. The bar of the Polo Lounge at noon."

"No booth? No table?"

"Nope. And right now, I'd like to talk to Victor Lampkin."

"Oh. He already called, first thing. The message is. . . ." She read from her pad. " 'I delivered the check myself, in person, to the gentleman in question, early this morning. He seemed grateful, and why shouldn't he be? Signed, your critical but obedient servant.' "

"Good. Is that it?"

"No, there's Marty Wallach and Liam O'Toole, who, I gather, are about to become your *former* executive assistants. They want to come up just to say good-bye. I told them you were busy, and Wallach said so was he, looking for a new job . . ."

"What did O'Toole have to say?"

"Something about a new broom sweeping dirty."

"God, do I have to see them?"

"I think you better," she said. "Really."

"You're a big help," he said, knowing that she was. Howard would have seen them. That's all he had to know. He was going to have to go through with it. "Okay. Go get 'em."

She left quickly and he sat there, counting his blessings while there was still time.

He came up with exactly one.

Marvin Gerber had the check in his hands.

He was halfway home.

Well, not quite halfway.

About one-thousandth of the way.

"Mr. Wallach and Mr. O'Toole are here."

"Send them in," he said. "And buzz me when Stan Howe arrives."

He got to his feet—no sense being seated if either of them took a swing at him—and reminded himself that the cameras were rolling and this had better be a good take, because these two guys were potential enemies who would blow the whistle in less than five seconds if they so much as *smelled* impostor.

They came in reeking of Scotch and bitterness with deceptive broad smiles on their faces, Wallach rumpled and unshaven, O'Toole showing yellowing uneven teeth.

"Fellows . . . hi . . ."

"We know you're up to your ass, Howard," Marty Wallach said, "but we didn't want to desert the sinking ship without waving good-bye." He reached out a hand. "Thanks a hell of a lot, man, we mean it."

Teddy shook his hand warily, then shook O'Toole's outstretched paw. "I don't know what you're thanking *me* for, I didn't have anything to do with this. It was New York all the way."

"You're too fucking modest, Howard," Wallach said thickly. "No sparrow falls on this lot without you knowing about it."

"With a knife in its back," O'Toole murmured, still smiling.

"I hope Seligman told you how shocked I was," Teddy said. "I was really counting on your hearts and your minds, your drive and your spirit . . .''

"You would've got *bupkis* from us,'' Wallach sneered. "We were ready to spend twenty-four hours a day trying to figure a way out of here without being in breach—''

"Twenty-five,'' said O'Toole.

"—And you handed it to us on a silver platter, with a hundred-percent settlement yet. We *owe* you one, Howard, I mean it, a big one, anytime you want it or need it, and you're gonna need it, man, believe me. This studio is headed for the crapper, with you the chief crapper—''

"Now just a second—.'' Howard *certainly* would have been in a rage.

"Just a second, *shit*, you're gonna hear us out, you miserable son of a bitch—''

"Miss Kallen, get me Edgar Seligman on the phone wherever he is . . .''

"You think you're gonna get away with trying to embarrass us and humiliate us in front of the whole fucking town just so's you can crawl up the ass of Hough and Barnett . . . ?''

"It's two asses, Marty,'' said Liam O'Toole. "You left out an ass.''

"Why don't you take your *sick friend* out of here, Mr. O'Toole?'' Teddy gave it the old Bluestern disdain.

"I don't think it's safe to move him, sir.''

"Mr. Bluestern, Edgar Seligman is coming on . . .''

Marty Wallach's face turned dangerously red. "You can tell him for me he's a worse liar than he is a lawyer.''

"Scotty, Marty Wallach and Liam O'Toole are here with me now, and I want them to hear me giving you these instructions, which replace my *previous* instructions to you. As of now, they are fired for breach of contract. They are not to receive a single dollar, not a penny. Let them sue us if they can afford it, and I don't think they can, because this was the only studio in town that had an administration dumb enough to hire them in the first place. . . . That's all right, as soon as you hang up, call accounting and tell them to tear up the checks immediately. Thank you, Scotty.'' He hung up and turned to the two men. "*Adios, muchachos.*''

Wallach started around the desk, cursing.

O'Toole grabbed him. "Hey hey . . .''

They grappled as Teddy watched them.

"Get your goddam hands—"

"Easy, Marty . . ."

"That tenth-rate prick—"

The buzzer sounded.

"End of the round," Teddy said.

"Stan Howe is here," said Jo Anne.

"Send him in."

"You haven't heard the end of this, Bluestern," Wallach cried hoarsely.

"I didn't even hear the beginning," Teddy said quietly, and to Stan Howe, entering, "Stan, say good-bye to Marty Wallach and Liam O'Toole."

The studio manager, a tall, iron-gray man of fifty, stepped back with a startled expression to let the grappling pair go past him through the doorway. "Jesus, what was *that*?"

"They do not go gently into the ranks of the unemployed," Teddy said. "Have a seat, Stan."

The big man sat down and crossed his legs and stared straight ahead with steely eyes. "I got people in my office waiting for me."

Teddy stayed on his feet, trying to size the man up, feeling the sweat running down his back. The guy looked like a bitch.

Come on, Howard. This one I *need*. Don't let me down.

"Stan, I've been giving some thought to our executive dining room, or should I say *your* executive dining room?"

"What kind of thoughts, Mr. Bluestern?"

"The name is Howard, for Christsake . . ."

"What were your thoughts?"

"I was wondering, how do you feel about the, uh, the *personality* of the room, the mood, the atmosphere?"

Howe's face twisted in a cold little smile. "I've been in a lot of executive dining rooms in this town . . . studios, book publishers, big corporations. I've had lunches, dinners, buffet suppers, you name it. Never had better food than ours, anywhere . . ."

"Stan, I didn't ask you about the cuisine."

"No, you didn't, but I'm telling you, because I know what's important, a hell of a lot more important than—"

"Do you think we could improve the character of our dining room?"

"The what?"

"The character."

"You can improve anything. Nothing is perfect in this world. Those pictures you made when you were an independent producer, did you think they were perfect?"

"No, I didn't. How do you feel about the man who runs it?"

"Runs it?"

"The executive dining room."

"My *department* runs it, Mr. Bluestern. If you're talking about the maître d', Mario is as fine as they come."

"How much does he get?"

"Twenty thousand a year."

"That's a lot of money."

"For a pack of cigarettes maybe. Not for Mario."

"That's a matter of opinion."

"That's true . . . mine," Howe said. "What's wrong with him?"

"I didn't say anything was wrong with him. It *is* possible, though, that the Italian style—"

"Mario Jovanek is as Italian as you and me. He's a Yugoslav . . ."

"Maybe that's what bothers me . . ."

"Only thing that bothers *me* about our operation is that we only break even. I'd like to see us show an annual profit without giving up anything, without sacrificing consistent high quality."

"I think I have just the man for you," Teddy said. "He's British, his name is David Stanner, and he's been running my kitchen, my whole damned household, for several years now. I'd like to put him in as soon as possible . . ."

"In where?" Howe uncrossed his legs.

"Replace the Yugoslav."

"Mario has nothing to do with profit and loss. He's practically a figurehead."

"That's just the trouble. I think we need more than a figurehead. We need a take-charge kind of guy, with charm, someone who can turn a sterile, characterless, good-but-dull dining room into a class restaurant with ambiance, something this studio can be proud of."

"Ambiance? For a bunch of actors and directors and agents talking movies and TV shows and deals? You gotta be kidding, Mr. Bluestern."

"I am not kidding, Mr. Howe."

"Who is this man?"

"His name is David Stanner."

"And he's your . . . what?"

"My houseman . . . but worthy of better things."

"I didn't know we were in business to help worthy people achieve their goals, or whatever you want to call it. I thought we were in business to do business, profitably."

"Is your executive dining room returning us a profit, Mr. Howe?"

"Not yet it isn't."

"Which is why I'd like you to see Stanner on Monday morning to work out the details of his new position."

"What's he got on you, Mr. Bluestern?"

"Beg your pardon?"

"I said, what's he got on you? That's from the movie, no man is a hero to his own valet."

"What time would be convenient for you to see him?"

"No time. There's no sense in my seeing him. I have no intention of firing Mario Jovanek. He's too good a man, and they're too hard to find. Why don't you make your houseboy an independent producer or something?"

"I got a better idea," Teddy said. "Why don't you start cleaning out your desk?"

"No need to do that," the studio manager said, getting to his feet. "We'll let your *sister* do it when you put her in as a cleaning woman."

"I'd tear your head off if I had a sister," Teddy said.

"You don't know how lucky you are," Stan Howe said on his way to the door.

Teddy's hands were trembling when he called Seligman, and they were *his* hands, not Howard's.

"You should have called me *first*, Howard. We just renewed him for four more years at a firm hundred and fifty thousand a year. You can get *angry* at a man, Howard, but not six hundred thousand dollars' worth. It won't wash on the Eastern seaboard, not for a minute."

"So what am I supposed to do?" Teddy said. "I want that shitheel responsible to *me*, where I tell *him* and he executes."

"Kiss his ass and make up," the lawyer said. "That's the *first* thing I'd do. Then pray."

"All right, get over to his office right away and do it."

"Wait a minute, Howard, it's your fight, not mine."

"It's your kiss and his ass, Scotty. Stop wasting time."

He hung up and put his head in his hands.

David Stanner was still in the kitchen. He hadn't moved him one inch.

Suddenly the studio, this office, the tan worsted gabardine suit of

Howard's that he was wearing, every little thing he was wearing, every little thing he was doing to keep the fraudulent fantasy alive, were insufferable. For the first time, he knew with some small measure of conviction that he was in a hurry to have Howard die, come what may, so that he could put an end to *being* Howard. The hell with decent intervals to allay suspicion. Decent intervals were for people who could shrug off the kind of life his brother had been made for. Howard had risen to the top by knowing how to deal in comfort with the Stan Howes and the Marty Wallachs and the Liam O'Tooles and *Christ* knew what with the David Stanners. He, Teddy Stern, had wound up on the beach because he had never been able to hack it. And he *still* couldn't hack it, didn't *want* to hack it.

Right now, he longed for the beach more than ever before.

A few more days. If he could only hang on for a few more days . . . a *week* maybe . . . until word came through from Marvin Gerber that the insurance company was legally on the hook for ten million dollars, and *he* had time to pull himself and the whole damned thing together, and stage the accident.

You can do it.

You've *got* to do it.

He reached for the phone and buzzed Jo Anne.

"Will you call Miss McWorter please and ask her to make it earlier if she possibly can? I'm going over to the Polo Lounge right now."

"Now?"

"Yes."

She lowered her voice. "What for, Howard?"

"What do people usually go to a bar for?" he said.

He got up from the desk, went into the john, relieved himself of unimportant matters, stared at himself in the mirror over the sink to see if he could find out who he really was, then returned to the desk, took some scripts from the pile there and stuffed them into Howard's gray attaché case. He didn't know what the scripts were and he didn't care, because he had no intention of reading them. They were props that might come in handy, that was all. Sometimes an actor needed a few to play a role convincingly.

On the way out he paused at Jo Anne's desk and said, "Well?"

"I reached Miss McWorter. She'll be in the Polo Lounge by the time you get there."

"Good." He held up the attaché case. "I'll be at Malibu reading scripts for the rest of the day, in case you need me."

"I'll be there at six-thirty," she said in a very low voice, "in case *you* need *me*."

"I already do," he said, and hurried out.

DIANE HAD MET Howard Bluestern only once, about a year ago, at some large affair at the Beverly Hilton with a few thousand people milling around spilling drinks on each other. It hadn't occurred to her, that night, how amazing the resemblance was to Teddy. But seeing him walking into the Polo Lounge now, she could have sworn it was Teddy himself. Not that there weren't subtle differences. Anyone as sharp as she was about people (when she was sober) and who knew Teddy as well as she did could spot those differences right away.

Howard dressed so much more conservatively (naturally he *would*), and there was something stiff, almost rigid, in the way he carried himself. Even before he spoke, she was aware of the arrogance and hauteur in his manner, none of Teddy's blatant informality about *him*, nor any of Teddy's inherent warmth either (she had to give the bastard credit for *that*). When he smiled, as he spotted her now at the bar, she saw coldness in his eyes.

Uneasy suddenly, she clutched her glass and took more than a sip of bourbon as he approached, far more than she had intended, filled as she was with a resolve to stay sober and not fuck this meeting up.

"Diane?"

"*Yes.* Howard, darling, how *are* you?" She offered her cheek and he gave it a peck.

"How nice to see you again, dear," he said. "It's been much too long."

"It certainly has."

Why do I have such trouble believing his effusiveness? she wondered as she watched him glance around the half-empty room and ease himself onto the barstool beside her. He turned his blue eyes on her, and she felt a little shiver go up her spine at the downright eeriness of the resemblance.

"You're looking marvelous," he said.

"Thank you. You too."

"Still contributing to the energy shortage in that plane of yours?"

"Every opportunity I get. How did you know about that?"

"I . . . uh. . . ." He seemed nonplussed. "Teddy must have told me. What are you drinking?"

"Oh, just a little Wild Turkey on the rocks."

"Is that a Scotch?"

She laughed. Poor dear. "No, it's bourbon."

"Oh." He turned to the bartender. "I'll have whatever Miss McWorter is having."

"Certainly, Mr. Bluestern. Same way, sir? A double?"

"Whatever she's having." He turned to her. "Forgive me. I'm not much of a drinker."

"Lucky you," she said. "Don't let me corrupt you."

"I'll be careful," he said. "Listen, dear, I want to apologize for being somewhat on the run. I feel like a heel for not even having time to take you to lunch."

"Please, Howard, I'm so grateful that you could manage to see me at all."

She saw him steal a peek at the time, and she couldn't help noticing his classic tank watch. No digital for *him*, like Teddy.

"I may be getting a call here from New York in the next few minutes," he explained. "But I hope not. Now . . . let's get to *you*. Don't tell me, let me guess. You and Teddy are getting married."

Oh God, Diane, be careful. Don't start to cry now and fall in a heap. "Not quite, Howard. Not really quite that at *all*."

"Oh?"

She took a drag on the bourbon and avoided his gaze. "Teddy hasn't told you anything about us?"

"Not really," he said. "First of all, we don't communicate all that much . . ."

"When did you speak to him last?"

"Yesterday. He called to say good-bye."

"Good-bye?" She felt a sudden chill.

"He's gone off to Mexico on a job for a week or so . . ."

Of *course*. Suddenly she realized. Not a *job*, but to recover from his head wounds.

"Matter of fact, I'm using his house at the beach this weekend."

"Lovely," she said, thinking, *his* house? *Our* house. No . . . no . . . that was all over. . . . She reached for her glass, stalling for time.

Howard was taking the double Wild Turkey from the bartender, turning and clicking his glass to hers. "A toast to you and Teddy. Happy happy," he said, then gasped and made a face. "My *God* this is strong."

"I could've told you," she said, and took another big bite out of her own drink. The hell with her resolve. She *needed* it. She mustn't blow this opportunity by being too nervous and cowardly. It was probably her last chance. "Howard, I know we don't have much time, so I'll get straight to the point. Your brother and I have had a terrible falling out, a really *bad* one . . ."

"Oh, I'm sorry to hear that . . ."

"Frankly, when I called your office and left word that I had to see you, what I was planning to do was ask you to *talk* to Teddy, to *plead* for me a little bit, to do whatever you could to patch things up and maybe get Teddy and me together again, because I think I'm good for him, and I was feeling kind of desperate . . ."

"You know I'll do whatever I can, Diane." He must have been awfully upset by the news, because he was *really* pouring the Wild Turkey down.

"But now that you tell me Teddy is going to be away for a while," she said, "and you're going to be using the house—"

"Just for the weekend," he said quickly.

"—There *is* something you can do . . . that is, if you can find it in your heart to help *me*. After all, he *is* your brother . . ."

"Tell me how to help you, Diane."

"Can I have another one of these?"

"Certainly." He summoned the bartender. "Another for Miss McWorter please."

"And you, sir?"

"Sure, I'll keep her company." He turned to Diane. "Go on, dear, tell me."

"Well, yesterday, I said some awful things to your brother over the phone. And Howard, when I say awful I mean *awful*. I was *not* what you would call cold sober at the time, if that's any excuse, which it isn't." She put her hand on his thigh and—God, how that Wild Turkey was flapping its wings in her head. For a moment there she had forgotten it wasn't Teddy. "So I said these terrible things to him, and as bad luck would have it (my luck has been *so lousy* lately) *Teddy* had the *recorder* on, *you* know, that goddam machine he uses to answer the goddam telephone? And he made a *tape* of our conversation with all those *horrible things* I said to him and he told me he was going to *save* that tape and *use* it against me as *evidence* that I tried to *kill* him or something if I ever try to see him again . . ."

"Oh, come on, he'd never do a thing like that, Diane, even if he said he would."

"You don't know your brother, Howard. He's not like you at all. You don't know him the way I do, and when he drinks, well, I don't want to say it but he *scares* me, he really does . . ."

"Speaking of drinking . . ." He pointed to her refilled glass.

She took it, and he clicked his own to it and drank with her, probably just to make her feel more comfortable, she thought. He wasn't such a bad guy, just a little stuffy, a little pompous . . .

"You know something, Howard, you're not such a bad guy . . ."

"Thank you."

"I really mean it."

"I'm sure you do."

"So do you think maybe you'd be willing to do this big favor for me?"

"Which is what, honey?"

"Get me that terrible tape," she said eagerly. "Look through all his cassettes, the ones he keeps in the drawer beneath the answering machine, in fact, anywhere in the house you think he might keep his tapes, and find this one lousy cassette that has this phone conversation with me where he makes believe I hit him over the head with a poker from the fireplace and *I* make believe I really *did* do that, Jesus, were we blotto, the two of us, and then I bawl the shit out of him because of this other woman, I won't go into *that* now, anyway that's the tape, and Howard, if he should ever play it again and listen to it, he's gonna hate me all over again, and we don't want that, do we, do we?"

"Of course not. Of course we don't." He drank right along with her.

"You won't tell Teddy we had this little talk, will you?"

"Not if you don't want me to."

"Swear that you won't, Howard?"

"Absolutely, Diane."

"And you'll find that tape for me and give it to me, so I can know for sure that Teddy will never hear those awful things I said ever again?"

"I'll try, Diane. I'll do my very best, I can promise you that."

"Oh God, you're terrific, Howard." She was feeling so relieved now, so dizzy and so relieved. "Shall I come over and help you?"

"Help me?"

"Find the tape. I could come over. I know the house so well—"

"No, Diane."

"Why not?"

"No, I'll find it, don't worry."

"But I can help you."

"I don't need help."

"How do you know you don't?"

"I really don't want any visitors this weekend, Diane."

"I'm not a *visitor*. I'm your brother's fiancée."

"I'm sorry, I won't be there alone. A friend is going to be there with me all weekend."

"You mean a lady friend."

"Exactly."

"So what's the diff? I'm not going to *stay*. I'll just come over and we'll go through all the drawers together and we'll find that tape and that'll be it. I mean, the minute we find it I'll leave, I promise. It's just that you have no idea how worried I am about that tape. It scares me to death. . . . Wait a minute, where are you going?"

He was on his feet, tossing money onto the bar, acting all fussy and bothered.

"Howard, what's the matter?"

"I'm late. I gotta go."

"Listen . . . Howard. . . . All right . . . I *won't* come over. You're right, you don't need me, you can find it yourself. All right?"

"Good-bye, Diane."

"Wait a minute." She struggled to get off the barstool. "Howard, you're gonna get the tape for me, aren't you?"

"Yes, yes . . ."

"You haven't changed your mind, have you?"

"No."

"You'll call me as soon as you find it?"

"Yes."

"You're not mad, are you?"

"No, but I'm late."

"Right. Gimme a kiss."

He brushed her cheek with his lips.

"G'bye, Howard. You're wonderful. I really appreciate it."

"Good-bye, Diane."

He walked away so fast she wouldn't even *try* to follow him. Besides, she needed another one right away. She tried to climb back onto the stool but she couldn't make it, too much trouble. She held onto the bar and looked at the bartender, who was watching her. She knew that expression. She had seen it so many times.

"Please?" she said weakly.

He shook his head slowly. "Sorry."

"Please?"

"No."

"Goddam you . . ."

"Lady, I'm saving your life . . ."

The room was beginning to fill up. She pushed people aside who got in her way as she walked uncertainly to the entrance.

She had fucked it up.

No . . . no . . .

Yes, Diane.

No.

She started across the lobby, weeping softly. He'd do it, of *course* he would. She *couldn't* have spoiled it, it was too important. Never mind whether Teddy ever talked to her again, as long as she had that tape in her hands. Howard would get it for her, wouldn't he? Hadn't he said he would? She was *not* going to have to go on living with *that* threat hanging over her for the rest of her life, was she? No. Never. She *couldn't*. He'd get it for her, he *had* to . . .

Stop crying, you idiot, he'll *do* it.

chapter 10

AH YEAH, this was more like it. If only Mrs. Mahoney weren't due any minute. If only he didn't have to shed the bikini that meant Mr. Teddy to her and get back into the trousers and shoes and shirt and tie that would add up to Howard Bluestern. Perhaps for the first time in his life he had truly *luxuriated* in being Teddy Stern, sprinting along the water's edge under the hot sun with the sea breeze biting at his face, doing the five miles in what felt like record time for him, plunging into the bracing Pacific afterward, battling the waves with powerful strokes, then drying out under the solar furnace until the Wild Turkey was long gone from his bloodstream. Puttering around in the kitchen, he had made himself a Reuben sandwich and washed it down with a tequila sunrise, all the while hearing the reassuring hum of the freezer on the back porch, seeing in his mind's eye, but not wanting to see, the freeze-frame of poor Howard's suspension between death and death-to-come.

He had allowed himself only one very brief glimpse of the vibrating white mausoleum, enough to convince himself that the padlock was still in place. After that, he had tried to put the mental picture out of his head, to be evoked on command only when needed, if at all. What had been slightly more difficult to put out of his head was the specter of Diane.

You're *Howard*, he had to keep reminding himself. She gave the assignment to *Howard* to find the goddam tape. *Howard* had no way of knowing that the tape didn't exist. Only *Teddy* could know that. Only Teddy knew that it was all a bluff, that there *was* no tape. All *he*, as Howard, would be able to tell her at the end of the weekend was that he had searched and searched and hadn't been able to find it. So stop thinking about it, for Christsake, and stop worrying about *her*.

As he tossed his trunks on the floor of the wardrobe in the bedroom, his glance fell on the navy blue blazer suit that David Stanner had placed in the Bentley for him to wear to the Bea Magnin thing. It

104

would be his costume for the most difficult role he had ever played and he wondered, not for the first time, how wise he was being in going through with the evening, instead of ducking out of it with a last-minute excuse. It was one thing to tell yourself that a flamboyant, high-profile appearance at Bea Magnin's was a heaven-sent opportunity to establish to the whole film community, by word of nasty mouth, and therefore to Mutual of Oklahoma, that Howard Bluestern was alive and well and living in Bel Air, thank you, on this night. It was another thing though to risk taking all the chances the evening would provide for him to put his foot in his mouth and blow the whole masquerade.

Pulling his necktie tight, the only necktie, he was sure, in all of Malibu Beach that afternoon, he heard Mrs. Mahoney's twelve-year-old Chevrolet pulling to a noisy stop before the garage, and then she was rattling at the back door and entering the kitchen.

"Hello," she called out. "It's just me . . . Mrs. Mahoney. Are you home, Mr. Teddy?"

He didn't answer, waited quietly in the bedroom, giving her a chance to find his note and read it. Then he broke the silence finally and called out, "I'm here, Mrs. Mahoney. Howard Bluestern."

She appeared in the bedroom doorway with the note in her hand and stared at him for a moment, her gray hair straggly as usual, her deeply lined face damp with perspiration.

"Teddy's brother," he said, in case she needed a diagram.

"How are you, Mr. Bluestern?" She came closer, eyeing him. "Why yes, of course, Mr. Teddy mentioned all about you. Well, not all that much, but everything he says was highly complimentary; he's very proud of you, Mr. Teddy is. Many times I overhear him talk about you to Mr. Kramer, that's his agent, as you no doubt know. It's true you're the spittin', but I don't have no trouble at all. I mean to *me* you don't look like Mr. Teddy all that much, I can tell the difference easy. So, Mr. Howard, where's your *friend?* You don't mind, do you, if I call you Mr. Howard, same as I call your brother Mr. Teddy?"

"No, Mrs. Mahoney. By all means call me Mr. Howard." And please remember well, if anyone should ever question you, that it was Mr. Howard who was in your presence this day.

"Thank you," she said. "And about your friend . . ."

"She hasn't arrived yet," he said.

"Oh, it's a she, is it?"

"Yes, it is."

"Well, that's perfectly all right with me," she said. "I don't go messing into Mr. Teddy's life, though it could use a little dusting and cleaning up, believe me, and I certainly don't intend to interfere with yours, Mr. Howard . . .''

He could feel himself bristling. Thanks a hell of a lot, Mrs. Mahoney.

"Now can I fix you something for lunch perhaps?"

"No, it's way past my lunch."

"Well, I don't never get here earlier than this because Mr. Teddy sleeps such crazy hours, y'know, and he never eats no lunch to speak of anyway, but if he'd only of said something to me about going away and you coming here and all, I could've arranged—"

"Mrs. Mahoney . . . ''

"Yes, Mr. Howard?"

"It's all right. I don't want lunch. I ate before I got here."

"Well, is there anything I can get you now?"

"No, there isn't."

"Some grapefruit juice? We got some good grapefruit juice."

"No, nothing."

"How about a nice piece of fruit?"

"I don't want anything, Mrs. Mahoney. It's too close to dinner."

"Will you and your friend be having dinner here tonight?"

"No, Mrs. Mahoney, we're going out for dinner."

"I see. Then I'll get started on what I have to do. There's always a lot to do around here. Mr. Teddy has his own peculiar way of making filthy little messes every place he goes in this house."

"It looks pretty goddam clean to *me*," he said loudly.

"You're just like your brother, Mr. Howard. Mr. Teddy can never express nothing without he swears right to my face, he does."

"Well what the hell can you expect from an actor?"

"Yes, but you're a refined gentleman, Mr. Howard, and an important one too."

"Not so goddam important, believe me."

"Well if you don't mind, I'll go about my work now, and if there's anything you want you'll let me know."

"You bet your ass I will, Mrs. Mahoney."

"Mr. Teddy left written instructions I was to take good care of you, and that's what I aim to do, no matter what."

"What do you mean by no matter what?" he said.

"Never you mind," she said, and went back to the kitchen.

One thing she had over David Stanner. She only used her mouth for talking.

The telephone rang, and he felt an almost adolescent surge of hope that it would be Jo Anne calling for Howard, and he'd be hearing the sound of her voice again. He went to the Answerphone, quietly picked up the receiver and, instead of Jo Anne, heard Sam Kramer's secretary delivering a message to the recorder. He walked the telephone on its twenty-foot cord around the corner of the room out of Mrs. Mahoney's range and overrode the machine, speaking in a low voice, his own voice, not Howard's.

"I'm here, tootsie," he said.

"I wish you wouldn't call me tootsie, Mr. Stern. Hold on, here's Mr. Kramer."

"Sorry, Ruth."

Kramer came on, already talking. ". . . You know it's getting to be ridiculous trying to find you. Aren't you *ever* home?"

"What are you talking about, Sam? I haven't gotten any messages that you called."

"I don't *leave* messages unless I'm desperate. I don't talk to machines. They make me ill. Why don't you get an answering service like other people?"

"Why don't you get me the kind of roles Redford's agent gets *him*? Then we'll talk about machines and answering services, all right, Sam? Now what's the terrible urgency?"

"Look, I know you're not going to be crazy about this but the money is good and it should be an easy few days' work . . . "

"Stop apologizing. What is it?"

"Now don't get angry, Teddy . . ."

"Who the fuck said I was angry? What is it?"

"A small part in *Trixie and the Sergeant*, but they're willing to go seventeen-fifty for three days just to get you . . . "

"Shit."

"*I* know."

"Is it firm?"

"Almost."

"What do you mean almost? Either it is or it isn't."

"The director, Jud Fleming, wants to say hello to you first, just as a matter of routine. This afternoon, in fact. Four o'clock over at Universal."

"In other words, I have to *audition* in the bargain."

"Why do you insist on putting it that way? He just wants to say hello."

"Sam, I don't mind *your* swallowing bullshit. Just don't feed it to *me*."

"You going to be there or not?" Kramer said.

"Hello to Jud Fleming at four o'clock. Okay, goddam it." There went a perfectly fine afternoon at the beach, which he needed badly. But, what the hell, maybe just as badly he needed every opportunity that came along to establish the unmistakable existence of Teddy Stern as counterpoint to the existence of Howard Bluestern. He'd know how to handle a snot like Fleming and free himself in no time at all to be Howard Bluestern again. "And listen, Sam," he said, "not that anyone will be interested, but just in case someone should ask you *or* Ruth, I am not here, not in California, for the next few days. I'm in Mazatlan doing a commercial for some Canadian outfit, got it?"

Kramer sighed. "*Now* what?"

"Nothing. I'm trying to duck a broad who can't get enough of my cock, that's all."

"Have you ever considered working in porno flicks? We should be getting *paid* for all the screwing you do."

"I'm with *you*. Just get me some firm offers, Sammele, but remember, I come high."

"You think I'm kidding, don't you?" the agent said.

"No," Teddy said. "You think *I* am."

"Do the thing at Universal, and we'll talk dirty pictures next week."

"Don't forget, Sam . . . Mazatlan."

"I already wrote it down."

Teddy hung up and glanced at his wristwatch. Back on the goddam merry-go-round again. Pushing his own image onto a disinterested world had always come hard to him. Projecting *two* identities at the same time now was truly a pain in the oosh. Maybe it would help if he started thinking of ten million dollars as something real and tangible instead of only as a set of numbers.

He went into the bedroom again, grabbed some blue jeans, a Western shirt, and a pair of boots from the wardrobe, stuffed them into a canvas carryall, and went out to the living room, calling out to Mrs. Mahoney, "I'll be back in a few hours if anyone wants me."

"You needn't rush for *me*, Mr. Howard," her voice answered from the kitchen.

"Please take any messages," he said.

"Don't worry," she said.

"Who the hell said I was worried?"

He heard her turn on the garbage disposal in reply.

He went out by way of the patio with the canvas carryall in his hand and drove the Bentley as fast as the Friday afternoon traffic would permit to the Sheraton Universal Hotel parking lot on the outskirts of the big studio in Universal City. In a toilet stall in the men's room of the hotel, he changed from Howard Bluestern to Teddy Stern and returned the canvas bag to the car with Howard's clothes rolled up inside. Then he walked the few blocks to the studio and made it to Jud Fleming's office by ten after four.

"He's been waiting for you," the secretary said with a reprimand in her voice. "Go in, please."

Fleming didn't even bother to look up from the trade paper he was reading at his desk. He was a pale-faced man of forty with rimless glasses and a full, graying beard that was rumored to conceal a nonexistent chin. "You're late, Stern," he said to the trade paper.

"Sorry about that." Teddy put on a sheepish grin. "I was trapped into an audition for a new series over at Columbia."

The director looked up at him with a cynical smile. "Is that right?" he said. "Kramer told me you were very available."

"I didn't say I wasn't," Teddy said.

"Why don't you sit down?" Fleming said.

"I don't mind standing," Teddy said. "Fighting gravity is good exercise."

"Suit yourself."

"Have you ever been an actor, Fleming?"

"Hell no," the director said.

"Then you don't know what an embarrassment it is to be looked over like a hunk of meat or something."

"Is that the way they do it at Columbia?"

"I'm talking about here, with you, right now."

"I'm not looking you over," Fleming said. "I just wanted to get a chance to talk to you."

"About what?" Teddy said.

Fleming picked up a paper clip, bent it open, and started to clean his fingernails. "There's a feature over at your brother's studio that appeals to me, called *Legerdemain*."

"Yeah, I've heard of it."

"I've never directed a feature before," Fleming said. "I'd sure like to start with that one."

Teddy looked at him for a moment. "And I'm getting this role, this three-day career, because you think I might put in a word with my brother, is that it?"

"How do you suppose you *ever* get a job, Stern? You think it's your acting ability anybody wants?"

"I happen to think I'm goddam good," Teddy said.

"What has being good got to do with shit like *Trixie and the Sergeant*?" Fleming said.

"If it's such shit, why are *you* doing it?"

"Because you haven't had that talk with your brother yet," Fleming said.

"I don't know," Teddy said.

"What do you mean, you don't know? Your agent sounded hungrier than a starving Armenian. I upped the price to fifteen hundred—"

"Seventeen-fifty."

"—Seventeen-fifty to keep him from dying right over the telephone."

"I don't know," Teddy said.

"You want the part, don't you?"

"If I'm gonna have to sell you to Howard Bluestern as a movie director, maybe you should tell me some of the things you've done in TV . . . "

"You're putting me on."

"I know you by name but not by reputation, Fleming."

"Let's not overdo it, Stern."

"Why don't you tell me a little bit about yourself?"

"Look, I think you've made your point . . . "

"How about taking a little scene from one of those scripts on your desk and showing me right here in the office how you'd direct it? I'll be the camera."

"Don't call *me*, I won't call you," Fleming said, picking up the trade paper.

"You mean I don't get the part?"

"In the middle of your ass you get the part," Fleming said to the trade paper.

By the time Teddy had changed back into Howard's clothing in the men's room of the Sheraton Universal and coaxed the Bentley through the late-Friday-afternoon crawl on the Hollywood Freeway, the Ventura Freeway, the San Diego Freeway, Sunset Boulevard, and the busy coast highway north to Malibu, Jo Anne was already at the beach house waiting for him, lying on a chaise on the patio watching the sun getting ready to plunge below the horizon.

"I'm sorry," he said, leaning down and kissing her on the lips.

"No, I'm fine," she said. "Mrs. Mahoney fixed me a drink, and I've had a chance to sit here and unwind. I like your brother's place. It's quite charming."

"Good." He sank down on the chaise next to hers.

She looked at him and studied him. "And you?"

"Called to a damned meeting at the producers' association."

"How did they know where to get you?"

"I made the mistake of calling *them*," he said, a little too quickly. "Did you try to reach me?"

"No," she said. "The only incoming call of note was from Mr. Van Slyke in New York . . ."

The chairman of the board? Number One himself? "How come you didn't call me?"

"His secretary said there was no need for him to speak to you personally. He merely wanted you to be officially notified that you're to be in New York next Thursday at noon to appear before the board of directors to discuss your proposed film projects."

New York . . . before the board . . . Jesus. . . . "Officially notified, huh? Was that the expression used?"

"Yes," she said. "And to tell you the truth, he didn't say 'discuss,' he said '*defend*' your projects."

"That's nice." He stared off, thinking.

Don't worry, Howard, with a little luck you'll be dead by next Thursday, beyond the reach of Winthrop Van Slyke and his well-publicized humiliating board of directors. But *without* that little luck . . . ?

Unaccountably, he felt anger rising within him, and he wasn't sure why, but somehow it seemed to be anger on Howard's behalf, not his. He wondered whether the Winthrop Van Slykes of the world aroused an atavistic reflex of defense and attack in anyone they came up against, maybe even a powerful desire to kill.

Who the *fuck* did Van Slyke think he was, summoning him to New York like some lackey?

Well, not *him* exactly. Howard.

He waited until he had simmered down. Then he looked at Jo Anne and studied her face. "Is that why you're being so glum?" he said. "Empathy for *me*?"

"Do I seem glum?"

"A little."

She gazed out to sea. "Maybe it's because I had visions of you lying on the beach all afternoon waiting for me. Instead . . . Mrs. Mahoney."

"Who talks a lot."

"More than you do, Howard."

He looked at her sharply. "What are you trying to say?"

She turned her head and met his gaze. "Mrs. Mahoney said you got a phone call around three o'clock, that you were very obvious about trying to keep her from hearing you, which was an insult to *her* because she *never* listens to other people's phone conversations, and you left here in a big hurry right after you hung up. Yes, she *does* talk a lot."

"I seem to be missing the point," he said.

"I'm not so sure I know what it is myself," she said. "I *think* it's that I'm depressed by the realization that I'm already capable of feeling terribly jealous where you're concerned, and very ready to think the worst about every little so-called mystery . . ."

"Mystery? What mystery?"

"Oh . . . like who is this McWorter girl, and why did you have to hurry so to meet her this morning, and who phoned you here today, and what were you *really* doing all afternoon, and why did I *know* you weren't at any AMPTP meeting the moment you said you were? I'll be all right, Howard. It's probably something called falling in love. I need another drink."

"You and me both," he said, hoping that the chill of fear inside of him wasn't showing on his face. He got up, went to the open sliding door, and called Mrs. Mahoney until she finally answered and came running.

"You're back, Mr. Howard. I didn't hear you."

He handed her Jo Anne's glass. "Miss Kallen would like another, and I'll have three jiggers of tequila in a tall glass of orange juice over ice, if there *is* any tequila around here."

"There better be," she said. "Mr. Teddy swims in it, he does."

"Is it absolutely necessary to air all my brother's private habits in public, Mrs. Mahoney?"

She snorted, "*I* don't air them, *he* does," and stalked off to the bar.

Teddy flopped down on the chaise again and held out his hand until Jo Anne took it in hers. He waited for her to say something, but she remained persistently silent.

"You know," he said, "there's a lot I don't know about you too."

She glanced at him. "All you have to do is ask me, Howard."

"I intend to," he said, and turned his gaze to the sun, a crimson fireball partially obscured by deep purple clouds, beginning its final slide into the sea.

"Do I hear the same offer from you?" she said.

He felt his lips tightening. "There could be risks in full disclosure. I suppose you know that."

"For you or for me?"

"For the both of us," he said.

"I can live with a lot of things," she said, "but not with mystery."

He looked away.

Why is it that you can't get away with *anything* in this life? he asked himself. For all its inequities and injustices, the world was like one big fucking grand jury, nailing you for everything you tried. Usually when you were convinced that you'd actually managed to pull one off, they closed in on you from the least likely direction, and suddenly you were in jail, or the poorhouse, or the cemetery. What good was it to guard yourself against your worst enemy when you could just as easily be destroyed by someone you loved? It was as though some goddam *presence* were watching over earthly affairs and playing this sadistic little game with people, luring them into foolproof schemes for putting one over on society, for getting something for nothing, and waiting until they were in the very act of celebrating their successful chicanery, and then, without warning, pulling the trapdoor out from under them and laughing, laughing, laughing . . .

I can hear you out there, you son of a bitch, he said in his head. I can hear you smiling in the dark and rubbing your hands together, but it's not time for your laughter, not yet it isn't, and maybe it never will be if I get lucky for once in my life. It's time you lost one, you merciless prick, just to keep the game honest.

Mrs. Mahoney arrived with their drinks. "Here we are . . ."

He reached out, took his own glass and handed the other to Jo Anne, and when the housekeeper remained on the patio, apparently in no hurry to leave, he looked up from his drink and forced her hand with a questioning stare.

"Will you be wanting anything else, Mr. Howard?" she said finally.

"Not that I can think of," he said. "Are you finished with everything you're supposed to do around here?"

"I get my work *done*, not like some people," she said.

"Then why don't you just take off and . . . have a nice weekend?"

"That's about what I had in mind, Mr. Howard. But I wonder if I could speak to you in private for a minute."

"Miss Kallen is family," Teddy said. "You can say anything you want right here."

"Shall I go inside?" Jo Anne said wryly.

"Don't be ridiculous. Stay where you are. Now what is it, Mrs. Mahoney? Has my brother been mistreating you, or underpaying you?"

"Nothing like that, sir. Excuse me, miss, for imposing on you this way . . ."

"Not at all," Jo Anne said.

"Mr. Howard, I got my two daughters and my two son-in-laws and all my grandchildren, five of them, coming to my little house for a barbecue on Sunday, also some of the neighbors' children, and I been planning and preparing for over a week now, and the one thing I can't do *without* is these very special cuts of beef I ordered a *month* ago from Superior in downtown LA, two of the most beautiful strippers you ever seen . . ."

"My mouth is watering," Teddy said, feeling the air suddenly getting cooler.

"Well, I picked them up at the butcher's last Tuesday morning when I make my regular visit to clean up for Mrs. Black over in Hancock Park, and then when I come *here* in the afternoon like I always do, I stored the strippers in the big freezer Mr. Teddy keeps on the back porch, figuring they'll stay nice and fresh and frozen while I clean up Mr. Teddy's mess, and I don't say nothing to *him* about the strippers because he couldn't care less about food unless you can pour it from a blender, and then, wouldn't you know, like the fool I am, I plumb forget all about my meat and drive off without it, and when I get home I *remember* and I say to myself, Mary, you'd forget your *behind* someplace if you didn't keep it in a girdle. Excuse me, miss . . ."

"That's quite all right," Jo Anne began to laugh.

Teddy's face was unsmiling. "Honey, if you'd rather go inside and start dressing now . . ."

"No, really," Jo Anne said. "Sorry, Mrs. Mahoney. Continue."

"Anyway," the woman went on. "I figure to myself it's all right, they're safe in Mr. Teddy's freezer, those strippers are. I'll pick them up on Friday when I come here. Plenty of time, nothing to worry about. So I come here today and I don't even give it a thought until a few minutes ago, and I go out to the porch to take my strippers out of the freezer to put them in the car, and what do I find but a *lock* on the freezer . . .''

"Oh dear . . . ," Jo Anne said.

"Can you imagine that? After all these years, why in tarnation does Mr. Teddy put a *lock* on the freezer before he goes away, when always he says to me, Mrs. Mahoney, why do you keep piling food in there when I tell you I go *out* to eat? And *I* say, because the rocks may come sliding down from the cliffs and you'll be trapped in this house someday and you'll *thank* me for the common sense that keeps you from *starving* to death. So *he* puts a *lock* on the freezer and goes off someplace and here I am with a *houseful* on Sunday and my beautiful meat locked in the freezer instead of sizzling on my broiler. What in the world am I going to do, Mr. Howard?''

Teddy could feel Jo Anne's eyes on him as he frowned at the ice cubes in his glass. "Did you look in the kitchen drawers?" he said. "I'm sure he left the keys around someplace.''

"Keys? There *ain't* no keys,'' Mrs. Mahoney said. "Not to *this* one. It's one of them fancy combination locks where you turn all the little dials to the right numbers and open it.''

"Howard?''

Teddy turned to Jo Anne. "Yes?''

"Everyone *I* know always uses their birth date for those combination locks, like on luggage, you know?''

Mrs. Mahoney's sagging face brightened. "You think maybe you could call Mr. Teddy and ask him how to open it?''

"I don't know where to reach him,'' Teddy said. "Look, what are we making such a problem out of this for? I'll give you the money and you *buy* yourself all the strippers you want.''

"Oh no, Mr. Howard, that's impossible. Superior isn't open tomorrow and besides, you gotta order them way in advance.''

"So you'll go to a supermarket. How much were they, Mrs. Mahoney?''

"Mr. Howard, you don't understand. This is no ordinary meat. This is the finest top-quality triple-A sirloin strippers in all of California. This is not just—''

"How much were they?'' Teddy rose from the chaise, fishing in his pocket.

"I don't remember such things, really I don't.'' Mrs. Mahoney's voice had become strained. "Forty-two dollars for one of them, I think. Thirty-six something for the other. I ain't gonna let you do this, Mr. Howard. It's wasteful, that's what it is, wasteful . . .''

"Why don't we try to *open* the thing, like a pair of safecrackers?'' Jo Anne said cheerfully.

"Never mind,'' Teddy said.

"Darling, it may be easy.'' She got to her feet as Teddy started peeling money from the wad of bills in his hand.

"I really don't want it, Mr. Howard.''

"Take it,'' he said. "Take it, will you please?''

The elderly woman tried to turn her body away but Teddy seized her by the shoulders.

"Darling, listen to me,'' Jo Anne was saying. "I have an idea. What's your birthday?''

Mrs. Mahoney broke out of Teddy's grasp. He looked at Jo Anne. "Forget it, will you?'' he said sharply.

"No, really, I mean it,'' she said with brightness. "Your brother's date of birth would be the same as yours, wouldn't it? I'll *bet* we can open that lock. Let's take a look at it.'' She started into the living room.

Teddy went after her quickly, leaving Mrs. Mahoney behind. "Just a minute . . .''

Jo Anne stopped and turned to him. "I'm only trying to *end* this nonsense and *help* the poor woman,'' she said in a hushed voice. "Let's at least give it a *try*.''

"I said no,'' Teddy said quietly.

She laughed at his utter seriousness. "But, darling, why not?''

"If Teddy wanted that thing locked, he must have had a reason,'' he said. "It's not our business to pry into things.''

"Pry? Into a freezer?'' She stared at him, the smile on her face turning to puzzlement.

Mrs. Mahoney had entered from the patio, and was trying to get past them now, saying, "I'll be getting my things together . . .''

Teddy stepped into her path. "My dear woman,'' he said. "Are you going to spoil my whole weekend by making me think of nothing but your disappointed grandchildren? And can you imagine how my brother is going to feel when he returns home and finds out what he unintentionally did to you? Here.'' He thrust the money into the pocket of her apron. "Now don't argue with me. I'm younger than you are and stronger than you are . . .''

"And you're richer than I am too, that's for sure, Mr. Howard, throwing your money away like that.'' She smiled wearily. ''All right, all right.'' She turned. ''Good-bye, miss. Have a lovely dinner tonight, the two of you.''

''And you have a marvelous barbecue Sunday, Mrs. Mahoney. I'm so glad to have met you.'' Jo Anne watched her go, then turned. ''Howard?''

He was moving away from her toward the patio. She followed slowly and stopped in the open doorway a few feet away from him, and watched him move up to the rail to look off at the darkening sea with his back to her.

''You're not angry with me, are you?'' she said quietly.

He shook his head.

''Then what is it?'' she said.

''Nothing,'' he said without turning.

''Don't you think we better start getting ready?''

He nodded. ''I'll be right in.''

She backed away and left him there, and he stood at the railing staring off, not hearing the breaking waves, not hearing anything but the sound of the smiler in the dark, chuckling softly, warming up for a good loud laugh.

chapter

11

IT WASN'T LIKE HER at all.

She had always had an abiding respect for the privacy of others, because that was what she expected and demanded for herself. Of all her shortcomings, and she had many, certainly sneakiness was not one of them, not even ordinary, garden-variety nosiness. And yet she had known with utter certainty, even as she had walked away from Howard on the patio, that she was going to find some way of looking into what she thought of privately as "the mystery of the freezer" before this weekend was over.

Perhaps it was because the appliance belonged to Teddy Stern, not to Howard, that she was able to contemplate doing something so alien to her nature. She'd be invading the purely impersonal domain of someone she scarcely knew. *Howard's* only connection, indirect at that, was his unaccountable nervousness and defensiveness over something that couldn't have seemed more trivial to her. It was his *overreaction* that had stayed with her, wouldn't let go of her. No doubt the mystery would turn out to be something perfectly silly, but still, she felt she *had* to clear it up, not for its own sake, or hers, but for the two of them. Until she got to the bottom of it and had a chance to look at it squarely, it would inevitably come between them, as it had begun to do already, and introduce distance where she wanted nothing but closeness, and *more* closeness . . .

While Howard had been on the phone with his houseman, David, to see if anyone had called his home in his absence, she had roamed about the beach house inspecting things admiringly, so that it would not look too obvious if she happened to wander out to the back porch. From the guest powder room she had heard Howard saying to David, "Are you sure the studio operator said this is his *home* number I'm to call?" And from the den she had heard him telephoning this someone else and apologizing for disturbing him at dinner, then thanking him for his thoughtfulness in calling so late just to give him some kind of news before the weekend started.

"No, you're *wrong* there," she had heard him saying. "I was *not* worried about it at *all*. I don't know where you got the idea that I was. But I still appreciate your letting me know."

His spirits had seemed to lift so perceptibly after that second phone conversation that she had been unable to resist wanting to share it with him, whatever it was. "Don't tell me. You've won the Irish Sweepstakes," she called out brightly.

"No, nothing like that," he said as she approached him.

"Well, what *was* it?"

He tried to shrug it off. "Just that insurance agent, Gerber, about the studio's policy on my life. He wanted me to know that the medical report came through at the end of the day. It seems I'll live."

"Well, *that's* good news for the company." She went up to him and gave him a little hug. "You may even allow yourself to have a good time tonight."

His expression sobered. "Look, if I've seemed a bit *preoccupied* this afternoon, for want of a better word—"

"How's 'moody'?"

"—It's that damned board of directors meeting coming up in New York. I could have done *without* that call from Winthrop Van Slyke. The trouble is, the studio can't do without the two hundred million a year he makes selling cornflakes—"

"Not cornflakes, Howard. Wheat-Toasties."

"Well, it ain't movies, and I wish to hell you hadn't been so *verbatim* with his words, like 'defend,' for example . . ."

"I thought it was vital that you should know, darling. To be forewarned, et cetera, et cetera . . ."

"I know, I know. I'm just bitching," he said.

She kissed him on the cheek. "Go take a shower, you male chauvinist."

She watched him go to the bedroom, and when she heard the shower being turned on, she knew that it would be all right to saunter to the kitchen area . . . for a glass of water or something.

She heard the big Frigidaire on the back porch even before she saw it, and it was a tossup whether it looked uglier or sounded uglier. Either way, it was a monstrosity that must have come with the house years ago, hardly the sort of thing whose sanctity you'd expect Howard to defend as though it were Fort Knox and he the Secretary of the Treasury. At least the padlock, with its six little thumb dials, looked shiny and new, if a bit incongruous.

She stared at the freezer. Teddy Stern was a drinking man, wasn't he? Some people saved postage stamps, or Baccarat crystal paperweights. Maybe *he* saved ice cubes, and had a valuable collection.

She started back toward the bedroom in no way the wiser, but no less thoughtful.

She saw Howard's wallet lying on top of the dresser and had a strong impulse to peek at his driver's license and find out the exact day on which he had come into this mysterious world. It *could* be the numerical key to his brother's lock. She glanced toward the closed bathroom door . . . and decided to resist the impulse. She might hate herself in the morning. It had to come to her more naturally, spontaneously, at the very least in a way she could live with . . .

All this she was remembering and turning over in her mind as she sat beside him in the Bentley, driving through the night to the dinner party at the Magnin woman's house, feeling his gaze occasionally stray from the road ahead to her profile.

"Are we okay?" he said.

"Of course," she said.

"Stop talking so much."

"Thinking," she said.

"Never heard of the stuff."

"I was just thinking of something that would make a marvelous present for you."

"Good. I like presents."

She gave him a little smile. "When's your birthday?"

"I hate birthdays," he said. "Give it to me for Christmas, if I'm still talking to you by then."

"Too chancy. When is it, darling?"

He hesitated for a split second. "January third, dammit."

"Nineteen . . . let me see . . . forty-three?"

"Come on, someone told you."

"You mean I hit it?"

"Right on the schnozzola. Now what's the present?"

"Unh uh. Surprise," she said.

"That's no fair," he said.

She shrugged. "No fair in love or war."

He looked at her without smiling. "Or in playing devious little games with someone while he's driving?"

She stared straight ahead at the road. "Just for that, I'm going to return your present and get a credit for it."

"Nice try anyway," he said easily. "The name of *my* game, in case you're interested, the one I just played with *you*, is called lying about your age. In Hollywood, second only to backgammon."

She smiled inwardly, holding firmly in her mind the image of a wallet lying on top of a dresser, to be invaded sometime in the immediate future, like at the end of the evening, perhaps? The hell with liking yourself in the morning.

EVEN THOUGH the Dodgers were leading 5 to 1 in the bottom of the fourth and the two kids were sleeping over with friends and his wife was off at the movies with her sister, Marvin Gerber was aware of a strange uneasiness in his soul as he sat before the television set in his West Hollywood home nursing a glass of Loewenbrau beer and watching the subscription channel. Ordinarily when Gerber had the house all to himself he felt a great calm settle over him. And when the Dodgers were comfortably ahead, this calm usually approached euphoria. But tonight, one and one were not adding up to two. He was bothered, and he didn't know exactly why.

It couldn't have had anything to do with the game. Not the way Gangelin was pitching. This one wasn't going to blow up in Gerber's face. He groped around in the dark, listened for his ulcer, and couldn't hear a thing. His lousy sex life? So what else is new? Maybe it has something to do with Bluestern being in the bag, he mused. Too much good news may be too rich for my blood.

In his twenty-five years as an insurance salesman, and a goddam good one at that, Gerber had never scored so big, so fast, with so little effort. He wouldn't have even had to *telephone* it in. He could have sent it by parcel post, Bluestern had been such a trembling pussycat. Easy come or tough nut, the studio's five-million-dollar policy on the movie man was larger than anything Gerber had ever sold. Add to that the second five million for Bluestern's *personal* policy, and the triumph became staggering.

Like all American males addicted to spectator sports, Gerber was a superstitious man and, like most superstitious men, he believed that there was danger in victory and safety in defeat. When you suffered defeat, that was all that could happen to you, you didn't have to worry about the consequences. You lose, which is what you expect, because it's what you deserve, because you're a no-goodnik and you know it. But when you win, and win big, *anything* can happen to you, *terrible* things, because you're a no-goodnik and you know it and you don't deserve to win, and you will be punished for putting one over on the gods.

The more Gerber thought about this, the more uneasy he became. He couldn't stop thinking about the small fortune in commissions that would automatically be added to his annual income now that the doctors had declared Bluestern insurable. He went to the kitchen, took another bottle of Loewenbrau from the refrigerator, returned to the living room and polished most of the bottle off, but that did nothing for him, just made his uneasiness more flatulent. He tried rooting for the Giants for a while, thinking that perhaps he could make their impending defeat his own, but he was unable to deceive himself. Even as he rooted for the Giants, another part of him was feeling pleasure every time the Dodgers stomped on them.

Gerber sat there on the sofa, his shoeless feet up on the coffee table, gazing distractedly at the television screen, and allowed his thoughts to drift wherever they wanted to drift, and eventually they came to rest on the telephone call he had received from Howard Bluestern earlier in the evening in response to his own call. It had been a unique experience for Gerber to get up from the kitchen table where he had been having supper with the kids and pick up the ringing telephone and hear the voice not of his brother-in-law or of Lou Mindlin trying to sucker him into a gin game, but of the president of a major motion picture company asking for *him*, Marvin Gerber.

So what about it? Gerber asked himself.

Nothing about it. Just a surprise, a pleasant surprise.

What was so surprising? You left your home number with the studio operator, didn't you?

Yes, but I never expected him to call me, and so soon. It was a pleasant surprise.

Then why do you feel so uncomfortable as you think about it, if it was all that pleasant? What bothered you about the phone call?

Bothered?

Sure, you're bothered, right now, thinking about it.

Oh, that. It's nothing.

What's nothing?

Oh, just the way Bluestern made such a big thing about not being worried about passing the medical, when obviously he cared so goddam much that he called *Marvin Gerber*, for Christsake, at *home*.

Gerber was something of an amateur psychologist. You had to be if you wanted to stay alive selling life insurance. Life insurance was something people didn't even want to think about, much less talk about, because it involved thinking and talking about croaking. So Gerber had become a self-taught student of human behavior and how to outsmart it. And if there was one pattern Gerber the psychologist had never seen fail it was this: When a guy makes a big megillah about how he couldn't care less about something, *that's* when he cares.

So why had Howard Bluestern been so worried about passing the medical? Did he *have* something? Jesus, could that fart of a doctor who had examined him at the studio have overlooked some hidden disease? Was Bluestern secretly living in Tumor City? Was Marvin Gerber's biggest victory Mutual of Oklahoma's greatest impending disaster in disguise?

Gerber got up from the sofa and turned off the television set. It would make no difference who won the ballgame. He was going to fret all weekend no matter what. And probably on Monday he'd drop into Grover Tillock's office and infect Tillock with his own anxiety and make the guy wish he were back in Tulsa instead of running the California division. The pressure on Gerber grew. Most of it was in his bladder. He went to the bathroom and urinated for a long time, and along with the two bottles of Loewenbrau, he suddenly got rid of most of his worries. For suddenly he remembered.

He remembered all the commissions he would collect.

If he made Tillock's feet grow cold and Tillock hauled out some technicality and canceled the policies before delivery, then what?

The Big Nothing for Marvin Gerber, that was what.

Gerber zipped up his fly and left the bathroom, cursing himself for the fool that he had almost become. Stop worrying, he told himself. Stop inventing things out of thin air just to make yourself feel lousy for having scored a big one.

Fuck the gods.

Howard Bluestern was not only healthy, he was going to live forever. Or at least for the five-year term of the policies. After that, who gave a shit?

Gerber smiled to himself as he turned the television set on again and sank down on the sofa and waited for a happy image to fade in on the screen, like the bases loaded with Dodgers or something.

Stop worrying, he said to himself.

And, ten minutes later, said it to himself again.

*   *   *

FROM THE OTHER SIDE of the silent house, David Stanner suddenly heard the front doorbell chiming and raised his head. "Who the hell . . . ?"

"Oh God, David, don't stop, I'm almost in heaven . . ."

"I know, baby, I know, but I have to see who it is . . ."

"Oh, but look at him, *look* at him, he wants to shoot *so badly* . . ."

"I'll be right back, you silly little cock . . ."

"Don't leave me, I'll *die* . . ."

Stanner hurried out of the bedroom, struggling into his robe, and went through the darkened living room to the foyer, calling out to the insistent chimes, I'm coming, I'm coming, pushing at his rock-hard penis to make it more inconspicuous, but it wouldn't go down, not with that darling boy waiting for him back on the bed. He snapped on the outdoor lights, peered through the peephole in the front door and saw the face of a dark-haired attractive girl he had never seen before, and behind her, her car, parked in the driveway.

"Who is it?" he called out.

"A friend of Mr. Bluestern's," the girl called to him.

"Mr. Bluestern is not here," he said.

"Open the door, will you," she said.

"There's nobody home," he said.

"Will you please open the door?"

Christ. He quickly tightened the belt of his robe to bind his impossible hard-on upright against his belly, undid all the locks and chains and pulled the door open.

The girl stood there looking at him with an uncertain smile on her face. "Hi, I'm sorry," she said. "I hope I didn't wake you or something."

"Not at this hour, for heaven's sake." He caught her eyes flashing on the bulge of his crotch. "What can I do for you?"

"I'm Diane McWorter, a friend of Howard's," she said. "And you're . . ."

"Mr. Bluestern's houseman, David Stanner."

"May I come in?"

"He's not home now."

"I was hoping, but I didn't think he *would* be," she said. "I didn't have his unlisted phone number, so I thought this would be the next best thing. If you don't mind . . ."

"Here, wait a minute . . ."

But she had pushed right past him into the foyer saying, "Look, I know that Howard, Mr. Bluestern, is spending the weekend at his brother's house in Malibu . . ."

"That's right."

". . . And I just called him there and of course he wasn't in, my dumb luck, so I thought maybe, just maybe, he might have returned *here* . . ."

"No, he hasn't," Stanner said, keeping his hand on the open front door.

". . . Or that maybe someone here would possibly know where I might *reach* him . . ."

"Reach him when?"

"Now. Right now. It's important."

Stanner hesitated, hating himself for the confusion he found himself in. Too goddam much to sort out too fast, and the girl was unsettling, pushy, not at all Bluestern's type.

"You say you're a friend of Mr. Bluestern's?"

She laughed nervously. "Actually I'm more of a friend of his brother Teddy."

He stared at her. "I see."

She moved closer to him. "You're British, aren't you?"

"Rather sounds that way, doesn't it?" he said.

"I love the way you sound, David."

"Thank you very much," he said.

"Now do you happen to know where Mr. Bluestern is, David?"

"Well, yes, he's at a dinner party, ma'am."

"By the way, my name is Diane, in case I didn't tell you."

"You did tell me," he said.

"A dinner party . . . " she said.

"Yes, or just about arriving there right now."

"I see. And would you have the telephone number there? Perhaps I could use the phone right here . . ."

"Well, frankly, Miss McCutcheon . . ."

"It's McWorter, Diane McWorter, like in squirter. And do we have to stand here in this hallway, with the door open?"

"No, not if you don't want to." He waited. But she didn't leave. So he shut the door and said, "Why don't you come right in here?" He led her into the living room and snapped on the wall lights.

"More like it," she said, and saw the telephone. "Now if you'll give me that number . . ."

"I'm not sure he'd like to be disturbed, Miss McWorter."

"What did you say?"

"I said I'm not sure he'd like to be disturbed."

"What is *that* supposed to mean? Why do you assume I'd be

disturbing him? I mean, do I sound *disturbing* to you? Do I disturb *you*, David?''

''Not at all, not at all.''

''Then be a nice guy and give me that number, will you?''

''You're really making it very awkward for me. You really are.''

''No I'm not.''

''Well you are. Now can't you call Mr. Bluestern in the morning, out at the beach?''

She flashed him an angry look that gave him the shivers. ''You're not going to give me the number, is that it, David?''

He shrugged. ''I'm afraid I just can't do it, ma'am.''

She turned away from him. ''Shit.'' She grabbed a cigarette from the lamp table, lit it, exhaled furiously and began to pace back and forth. ''Look, will you do *this* much for me? Will you call him *yourself* and *ask* him something for me and give me his answer?''

''Gee, I don't know about that,'' he said.

''What do you mean, you don't know about that? Surely you can do *that* much, for God's sake. Look, David, this is *important* to me, and important to Mr. Bluestern too.''

''I believe you,'' he said.

''Then why don't you do something about it?''

''Well, I can't call right now . . .''

''Why not?''

''Because I *can't*.'' He pulled the belt of his robe tighter. ''Maybe in a half hour or so.''

''All right, in a half hour then,'' she said eagerly. ''Will you do it in a half hour?''

''Yes,'' he said.

''You promise?''

''I *said yes*.''

''All right, I'll be at a restaurant in Santa Monica. At the bar. It's called Pal Joey's.''

''I know it very well,'' he said.

''You do?''

''*Very* well.''

''I'll give you the number.''

''You don't have to. I know the place very well.''

''You sure?''

''Now what is it you want me to ask Mr. Bluestern?''

''Very simple. Just ask him this: *Did you find it?*''

"Find what?"

"David, just *ask* him. He'll know. *Did he find it?* That's all I want to know. Is that clear, David?"

"Yes, it is."

"I'll be waiting to hear from you."

"Right." He started to ease her toward the front door.

"Good-bye, David."

"Good-bye," he said.

"Diane McWorter."

"I know," he said.

" 'Bye."

He closed the door after her and bolted the locks and turned out the lights, and as soon as he heard her car pulling away, he started running through the darkened house toward the bedroom, pulling off his robe as he went and tossing it aside and calling out I'm coming, baby, I'm coming . . .

And in a way he was, but in another way, alas, he wouldn't be at all, not tonight he wouldn't. For David Stanner was distracted now. He had, as it were, lost his concentration. His head, which should have been otherwise occupied, was busy thinking. He was thinking about the strange, frenetic girl who had barged in so unceremoniously and who would be waiting for his telephone call at Pal Joey's.

chapter 12

AT FIRST he thought it was just normal anxiety that was creeping over him as the car neared Bea Magnin's house on Copa de Oro Road.

He would have had to be a goddam fool not to have been feeling *some* apprehension. After all, who was he supposed to know or not know at this party, who was he meeting for the first time or the twentieth, and which pair of eyes (maybe every last damn one of them) would be looking right through him and saying, Come on, Teddy, cut the shit, *you're* not Howard?

But then he began to realize that it was something deeper than anxiety he was feeling, something more like sadness, almost like grief, a loss that had already happened to *him* but hadn't happened to the others yet, to Howard's friends. He would be moving among them now, carrying a death they knew nothing about. He would be Howard still alive, moving among them with the foreknowledge of his impending end, giving them moments to remember and talk about after Howard died next week.

Yes, *definitely* next week.

Why hadn't he given the evening more thought? He hadn't given it *any*, for Christsake, only a lot of worry. He was unprepared, as usual, totally unrehearsed. It hadn't occurred to him until now that whatever he did and said tonight, however he looked, sounded, appeared, behaved, would provide the final images of Howard Bluestern for his peers, the last and most vivid memories that Howard would leave behind with the only people who had ever counted to him (say what you will about them), in the only community where he had ever made a splash during his brief appearance in the universe.

How would Howard have wanted to be remembered if he had had any choice in the matter? (*It makes no difference . . .*) What would he have hoped they would say about him after they sat at his services and stood around his grave, preoccupied with their own endings? (*Who cares . . . ?*) Would he have hoped they'd say you had to be smart to be as lucky as he had been, did it the hard way, never played the

128

Hollywood game, never kissed a single ass? (*Forget it . . .*) Would he have crossed his fingers and said to himself, Maybe they'll think I was a nice guy?

Teddy didn't know. He didn't know because he had never really understood Howard, and now, of course, he never would. He had never been able to look at his brother without seeing something of himself in the mirror. Anything he had ever felt or thought about Howard had always been less or more than the truth, altered by whatever the margin of jealousy, resentment, neediness, misunderstanding, or confusion of identities.

I'm sorry, Howard, I'm just not up to it. I'm going to have to be myself tonight . . .

Who's stopping you?

It won't be the first time you made a mistake in casting. It won't be the first time I let you down . . .

I don't know what the hell you're talking about, Teddy, why you go on this way. Can't you get it into your head that nothing matters to me any more, that nothing ever will ever again . . . nothing . . . ever . . . ?

But I thought you wanted me to take care of you. I thought you said—

I SAID NOTHING. I'M DEAD, YOU FOOL.

As the big house loomed up ahead, lights blazing, Teddy glanced at Jo Anne beside him and said, "If I had a brain in my head I would drive right past this place." But his foot pressed down on the brake pedal and the Bentley came to a stop before the lineup of red-coated parking attendants waiting at the side of the road.

"We can always leave early," Jo Anne said just before the car doors flew open.

"Have a nice one, folks," said the attendant, handing Teddy a parking ticket.

"Can I get this validated inside?"

He followed Jo Anne up the flagstone path to the front door, which opened under the magical touch of a waiting butler.

They weren't the first to have arrived, nor even the forty-first. The stark, ultracontemporary living room was jam-packed with bodies, and the din was incredible.

"Don't leave me," Jo Anne said.

"You may never see me again." Teddy peered about, searching for the bar. He hated houses that were strange to him. They put you at such a disadvantage when you had to have a drink in a hurry, or take a leak.

He heard a voice calling out, "Oh, there he is," and saw the tall, dark-eyed, olive-skinned beauty who called herself Bea Magnin pushing her way toward him through her chattering guests, saying, "Howard, love, before you even get *started*, there's a telephone call for you, my God, what timing, for the rich they ring. Why don't you take it in there?" She pointed to the den. "Just close the door and stick a finger in your ear, and I'll watch over this gorgeous young thing for you." She turned to Jo Anne as Teddy started away, a puzzled look on his face. "I'm Bea Magnin and you're, don't tell me, Miss Kallen . . ."

"Jo Anne. Hi, and thank you so much for having me here tonight. I'm really excited."

"Oh my God, you're too much." The big woman put her arms around Jo Anne and hugged her. "I don't even know you and I love you already. What did Howard ever do to deserve *you*?"

"Left me in the lurch for another woman on the telephone, no doubt."

Bea Magnin wrinkled her expensively sculpted nose. "His houseboy, the outrageous David. You have nothing to fear but fear itself, darling. Damn, I have to leave you, Jo Anne, what a lovely name, but only for a moment. Don't go away."

She hurried toward the entrance to greet new arrivals, and Jo Anne moved over to the closed door of the den and opened it.

Standing with the telephone at his ear, Teddy saw her in the doorway and called out, "In a minute," and then into the phone he said, "Never mind that. Do as she says and call her right away, and David, here's what I want you to tell her. Tell her I searched high and low for it, spent half of my day doing it, and *could not find it anywhere*. . . . Right. *No* place. Tell her I'm very sorry, but I've done all that I can for her. . . . Correct. And David, I'd be pleased if she doesn't call me, or ring my doorbell, ever again, but be *very* careful with that one, all right? . . . Okay, thank you. . . . Stop apologizing. I told you it was all right."

He hung up and started toward Jo Anne, frowning. "My brother and his sick friends. I wish he'd come home already."

"Miss McWorter?"

"You're too smart."

"I listened."

"How'd you do with the hostess with the mostes'?"

"I think everyone in this town is jealous of her because *she* has a personality and they don't," Jo Anne said.

"Mind if I quote you?"

"To whom?"

"Bea Magnin."

"Please do."

He took her hand, and together they left the den and plunged into the party.

A bubbly, vivacious woman with piles of shimmering blonde hair turned and smiled as they passed her. "You must be Howard Bluestern," she said.

Teddy brought Jo Anne to a stop. "That's right," he said.

"Then I must be Rona Barrett. How *are* you, Howard?"

"Thirsty," he said. "This is Jo Anne Kallen."

"Charmed," the commentator said. "What should I know about you, Jo Anne?"

"My life is an open secret."

"Ah hah."

"Miss Kallen is my intended," Teddy said.

The blonde woman's face brightened. "Can I write that down, or do I have to memorize it?"

"What I mean," Teddy said, "is that I intend to sit next to her at dinner."

"You sure know how to hurt a working girl, Mr. Bluestern," said Rona Barrett. "If it's all right with you, I'm going to save a couple of places for you two at Bea's table . . ."

"Why not?"

"I want to ask this girl what she sees in a man who has the chutzpah to think he can run a movie studio these days, and then I want to find out from you, Howard, how you've managed to hold on to the job for three whole weeks."

"Very simple," Teddy said. "Miss Kallen handles everything."

Rona Barrett looked at Jo Anne. "What do you do, dear?"

"I'm Mr. Bluestern's secretary."

The woman stared at her. "You're serious."

"Deadly," Jo Anne said.

"You wouldn't know where the bar is?" Teddy said.

"Don't interrupt me, Howard. I'm thinking," Rona Barrett said, and slowly wandered away.

"I like her," Jo Anne said.

"You like everyone," he said.

Someone told them there were four bars and the nearest one was out on the terrace, and they were halfway there when, unaccountably, they found themselves trapped and frozen to a few square inches of breathing room by a young auburn-haired actress named Samantha Frye, who insisted on explaining at inordinate length why meeting Howard Bluestern meant far less to her than it ought to have, because she was not really interested in working in films, only in the *theater*, and more specifically only if Gordon Davidson were the director.

Teddy simulated the act of listening to her, but his eyes wandered, and suddenly, through an opening in two conversation groups a dozen yards away, he saw the ugly gray beard even before he saw the head that went with it, which was momentarily turned away from him, but he knew immediately that it was Jud Fleming, and more out of instinct than for any well-worked-out reason he started to shift his position to present his back to the man, but saw out of the corner of his eye that the director had already turned and spotted him and was staring at him now. Teddy glanced at Jo Anne, saw that she was giving all her attention to the talking actress, and decided to pretend to do the same during the few minutes that it would probably take before Fleming made his initial move.

Presently the TV director appeared in Teddy's sightline as background to the nonstop Miss Frye and then moved unsteadily forward, drink in hand, until he was standing behind and to the right of the girl, his eyes fixed on Teddy, scrutinizing him through his rimless glasses, face smiling to indicate that he would welcome being invited into the conversation. He had probably ridden in here on the pantyhose of some woman more celebrated than he was, and to Teddy it was obvious that he had been drinking heavily.

When the girl named Samantha Frye paused for a moment to catch her breath, Fleming spoke up in a loud voice. "You get around, Stern, don'tcha?"

Teddy glanced over his shoulder, then back to the man with the nonexistent chin, and said nothing.

"You don't *know* me?" the director said thickly, moving closer.

"I'm afraid not," Teddy said. The man stank of Scotch.

"You were in my office just a coupla hours ago."

"I don't think so," Teddy said, feeling Jo Anne's eyes on him.

"I'm Jud Fleming. Are you kidding?"

"Hardly."

"Oh, the hell with it," Samantha Frye said, annoyed at the interruption, and moved on.

"You're Teddy Stern," Fleming said.

Teddy smiled and shook his head. "Most people have no trouble telling us apart. Teddy is better looking and a lot smarter. I'm Howard Bluestern, and this is Miss Kallen."

The man ignored Jo Anne. "Come on, Stern, what's the gag?"

"I don't hear anyone laughing, Mr. Fleming." And to Jo Anne: "Shall we?"

"I may be smashed but I'm not that smashed," Fleming persisted. "I'd know that voice anywhere, and I remember the hairs of your right eyebrow all squiggly just like they are now, from sleeping on them or something. That was some performance you put on in my office this afternoon."

"I'll tell Teddy you were pleased." He took Jo Anne's arm.

"Pleased, hell! You were *ridiculous*. Can't even take a joke . . ."

"I don't mean to be rude, Mr. Fleming, but *we're* headed for the bar." He eased Jo Anne away.

"Catch ya later," Fleming called after them.

Teddy's face was flushed. He could feel it.

"What was *that* all about?" Jo Anne said evenly.

"Apparently the sins of the brother are visited upon the brother," Teddy said, thinking furiously but coming up with nothing. When they finally arrived at the bar on the terrace, he pushed his way through a little too desperately and realized for the first time that he was sweating heavily.

Jo Anne eased her way up alongside him and said to the bartender, "I'll have white wine please."

"Make mine a double tequila in a little orange juice," Teddy said in a strained voice.

"You've got it," the bartender said.

Teddy mopped his damp forehead with a handkerchief, feeling Jo Anne studying him.

"I thought you said your brother had gone out of town," she said. "That man said Teddy was in his office late today."

"That man is pissed to the eyeballs. That man said a lot of things," Teddy said. "With a little luck, he'll fall on his face and roll back under the rock he came out from under."

She looked at him for a long moment, but she didn't say anything.

He took her glass of white wine from the bartender and handed it to her and took his double tequila and drank some of it immediately, and then together they set out again through the minefields on the perilous journey to nowhere. He kept wishing she would say something . . . anything . . . but she remained strangely silent amid the rising din of the party.

He spotted another of the four bars and made a mental note of its location. He was going to need it.

THE SON OF A BITCH was a bigger liar than his brother. She had known it the moment she had laid eyes on him at the Polo Lounge today. Deep in her bones she had sensed that he had just been going through the motions with her, making her think that he was her *friend*, that he really *cared* whether she got back together with Teddy again. But he cared about nobody but himself. That's the way big shots got to be big shots.

Big *shits*.

She hadn't spoiled it, *she* hadn't done anything to queer it. It was all *his* doing, his *not* doing. He had never intended to find that tape for her. He never was even going to *look* for it. He was just going to string her along, and that's what he had done, only he hadn't fooled her, not for a minute. Sitting at the bar at Pal Joey's, waiting for that snide servant to call her, she had nursed her Wild Turkey and steeled herself for the inevitable, so that when the call finally came she wasn't even disappointed. In fact she was *pleased*. It proved that she had been *right* about Howard Bluestern.

"I'm afraid the news is rather gloomy," his flunky had intoned. "Mr. Bluestern looked everywhere, and it, whatever *it* is, is nowhere to be found, and he can do nothing further for you."

"You don't say," she said, smiling nastily to herself.

"Oh but I do, and I just have."

"Well, I just may call your poor, overworked, looking-everywhere, high-and-mighty boss *myself*, tomorrow, and make him say it to my face."

"I wouldn't do that if I were you, Miss McWorter."

"You wouldn't? Why not?"

"Trying to see him again, or calling him, are simply not advisable."

"Who asked you for your advice?"

"I'm giving it to you out of the generosity of my heart, and I suggest that you take it, Miss McWorter."

"You should get yourself a new bathrobe," she said. "That one you were wearing tonight makes you look like a fag . . . even with your little prick sticking out.''

"Spoken like a true lady," he said.

"Takes one to know one," she said.

"I fail to see why you're laying all this anger on *me*, Miss McWorter. After all, I'm only acting on orders, a mere messenger boy. It would be much wiser for you to be friendlier toward me, at least until you were sure I couldn't *help* you in some way."

She had to laugh. "*You* help *me*?"

"I did put the call through to Mr. Bluestern, as you requested, did I not?"

"Yeah, and look at the result."

"I didn't hear you thank me for doing it."

"Look, I'm going to hang up now."

"Perhaps if you were to tell me what it is that you're looking for so urgently, and why you expected Mr. Bluestern to find it, I might have a little more luck than *he* apparently had, you never know."

"What kind of a lamebrain do you take me for? Why would *you* want to help *me*, even if you could?"

"It's no secret, especially to my employer, that I am actively interested in moving out of pots and pans and vacuum cleaners into something more exciting and rewarding. Therefore I make it a rule never to pass up an opportunity to help someone in distress until I find out that the person in question is in no position to help *me*. And inasmuch as I know nothing about you *yet*, Miss McWorter, I am at your service. Shall we have a drink somewhere and talk over your pressing problem?"

"Stanner?"

"Yes, ma'am?"

"I don't trust you."

"Understandable."

"I think you are slightly full of shit."

"Be that as it may, ma'am, do feel free to phone me if you should change your mind."

"You know damn well the number is unlisted."

"Do you have a pencil?"

"Go ahead."

He gave her the number and she wrote it down.

"Naturally," he said, "I am assuming that you won't discuss this conversation with anyone."

"You mean with your boss."

"I shudder at the mere contemplation," he said.

"Get yourself a warmer bathrobe," she said.

"Call me," he said.

"Don't sit by the phone," she said and hung up.

Well, at least I have Bluestern's phone number, she told herself on the way back to the bar. Not that she knew what she'd ever do with it. Certainly she'd not be calling that sly chambermaid, Stanner. *Him* help *her*. Ha.

Just like his boss. The two of them *belonged* together.

First Bluestern cons her at the Polo Lounge, then he does a giant *nothing* for her, and now he tries to freeze her out of his life with a phone call from a hired hand.

"Well, we shall *see* about *that*," she said in a loud voice at the bar of the noisy restaurant and finished her Wild Turkey in one beautiful, endless swallow.

"I'm looking everywhere," the man said, "but I still don't see what it is we shall see about."

She turned to him, the one sitting on the bar stool next to hers. He was so huge, like a mountain, that she hadn't even noticed him. "What's that black patch over your eye for?" she said. "Who do you think you are, the late Moshe Dayan?"

"Did it ever occur to you, young lady, that I might have lost an eye, that I could be a pitiful, single-orbed creature, and that your question could have possibly embarrassed me and hurt me deeply?"

"To tell you the truth, no," she said. "But when you put it that way, I can see what you mean. So what the hell is that patch doing over your eye?"

"I shall tell you, ma'am. But because the story is a long one, as most fascinating stories are, and rather tiring to relate, I think it would be only fair of you to buy me a drink, to encourage me and stimulate me and sustain me during my ordeal."

"I've got a better idea," Diane said. "*Don't* tell me the story. I don't want to hear it. But take the goddam patch off, because you look ridiculous in it, and I'll be happy to buy you any drink you want, within reason."

The man took the patch off and stuffed it in his pocket. He was about thirty, and not bad-looking until he smiled, revealing jagged teeth. He had two eyes, both of them blue, and seemingly without defect. "I feel naked now," he said.

"You look like Peter Ustinov," she said. "Actually, you look like two Peter Ustinovs."

"Give or take a hundred pounds," he said. "Scotch, if you don't mind. Straight Scotch. A triple."

"Wait a minute." She opened her handbag and riffled through a wad of bills. "Yeah, I guess I can handle that."

"You could handle the national debt with that," he said, peering into her handbag with interest.

She snapped the bag shut in his face and said to the bartender, "This gentleman will have a triple Scotch—the cheapest you've got—and I'll have four fingers of Wild Turkey without."

"Without what, ha ha?" the bartender said.

"Without your fingers, for a change." She looked at her newfound friend. He was wearing a thin black turtleneck sweater and soiled white jeans, and his thick blond hair was almost shoulder-length. "Are you sober?" she said to him.

"Only out of economic circumstance," he said.

"Well *I'm* not *really* tanked," she said.

"You'd be more convincing if you chewed on a sprig of parsley now and then," he said.

"My name is Diane," she said, "and you're fresh."

"No," he said. "I'm Bruce Gottesman."

They shook hands.

"What do you do, Bruce?"

"All manner of indispensable things," he said. "During the past two years I've been a part-time captain of a private yacht out of Antibes in the South of France; I've waited tables at Felix's in Cannes; I've chauffeured for Peter O'Toole on location in Swansea, South Wales; I've done a little time in the slammer for assault and battery (she deserved every bloody welt, she did); and I'm here in Southern Cal right now because I fancy myself as having considerable potential as a character actor on the tube."

"You *sound* like an actor. I like your mannered speech. It's so beautifully phony. Just like *you* are, no doubt."

He showed his bad teeth in a smile. "Thank you."

"You're never going to make it with *those* choppers, though."

"I'll never smile again . . ." He sang badly.

"You should see Stanley Vogel," she said.

"Who is Stanley Vogel?"

"My dentist. He could give you a gorgeous mouth. The rest of you is obviously hopeless.''

"Is he expensive?''

"Depends on how much you value a gorgeous mouth.''

He shook his head in despair.

"You could always get a job in a horror flick,'' she said.

Anger flared in his eyes, then faded. "Not funny.''

The bartender brought their drinks, and they dove into them for a while. Then Gottesman glanced at her. "You said something before, to no one in particular. You said, 'We'll see about that.' What, may I ask, was *'that'*?''

Diane looked him over carefully. "Let me answer your question this way,'' she said. "Among your many skills and capabilities, is there any chance that you may have had some experience in managing to go through a door or a window that was not exactly open to the public?''

He looked at her without blinking. "I *have* had occasion to tamper with a lock here and there, if that's what you mean.''

"Lovely,'' she said. "I was wondering whether you might possibly be able to help me to wend my way into my ex-boyfriend's house in Malibu, which is thoroughly locked, I'm sure, but unoccupied as we sit here, and will be for the next hour or three.''

"With what object in mind?''

"Totally harmless,'' she said. "To recover a small item that has no value whatsoever to anyone but me. I just happen to want it very badly, for reasons that are irrelevant right now.''

"Sorry, luv, you're going to have to tell me what that little item is.''

"A tape, Bruce. A cassette.''

"And?''

"And what?''

"What's *on* the tape?''

"Damn you, Bruce.''

He stared at her, waiting.

"My boyfriend and me,'' she said.

"Go on,'' he said.

"Making love,'' she said.

"And?''

"Me saying things, and doing things and . . . oh God . . . things I don't want *anyone* to hear, *ever* . . .''

He stared at her. "Is that it?''

She met his eyes. "Isn't that enough?"

He looked at her for a moment, and she wasn't sure that he believed her. He ran a hand through his long blond hair. "What about a key?"

"I've *got* a key, but I know goddam well it's no good any more. He changed those locks five seconds after I walked out on him."

"How do you know?"

"I know *him*," she said bitterly.

"Who?"

"My boyfriend," she said. "Ex."

"Who?" he repeated.

"For Christsake," she said. "What is this?"

He kept looking at her.

"Teddy Stern," she said. "He's an actor."

"Stern," he said. "Stern. . . . Doesn't he have a twin brother who's—?"

"Yes. Yes. Look, are you going to do it or not? I'll give you two hundred dollars, which is all I've got on me, if you'll get me inside that prick's house right now."

He picked up his glass and downed the remainder of his Scotch and sat there for a few moments, thinking.

She stared at him tensely. "Well?"

"I don't know . . ."

"You can do it, Bruce. It's nothing."

"Shut up a minute, will you?"

She stayed silent, waiting.

He glanced at her. "Two hundred?"

"Yes."

"You got a car?"

"Of course I have a car. What else do you need?"

"A knife. Anything but a butter knife. The sharper the better."

"Wait here." She slid off the stool and started across the crowded room toward the waitresses' station in the rear. Suddenly a hand reached out and grabbed her arm. She turned and looked into the sun-tanned, bearded face of Joey Marzula, Sicily's gift to the California restaurant trade.

"Oh, hi Joey. . . ." Ordinarily she would have been glad to see him.

"Hello, honey." He glanced past her to the bar. "Where's Teddy tonight?"

"Who the fuck cares?" she said.

He frowned. "Oh, it's *that* way."

"In spades." She tried to pull away, but his hand held her tightly as he stared past her at Bruce Gottesman.

"Why don't you let me get you a table? I'll join you. I can have one in a couple of minutes."

"I'm thinking of leaving," she said.

"With him?" He made a head gesture toward the bar.

"If I want to."

"Listen to me," he said, with quiet intensity. "Stay away from that man. He's not for you. Do you dig what I'm saying?"

"Let go of me, Joey."

"Honey, listen to me . . ."

"I *heard* you, Joey." She pulled out of his grasp and walked away from him and went into the ladies' room. She waited for a few moments, then went back out. Joey was nowhere in sight. She hurried over to the service station, glanced about, saw that no one was watching her. Quickly she took one of the steak knives from the metal rack and slipped it into her handbag. Then she made her way back to Bruce Gottesman at the bar.

"Give me about three minutes," she said to him. "I'll be in a red Datsun hatchback."

"Gotcha," he said.

She drained the dregs of her glass, put some money on top of the bar, and walked out into the damp, cooling night.

Joey Marzula was standing on the sidewalk in front of the place, making believe he was just getting some air. Let him. What did *she* care? She was feeling pleasantly stinko now, and very optimistic. What she was going to do was *her* business, not Joey's. He was in the food and liquor business. She was in the housebreaking and tape-stealing business. What was he going to do about *that*?

As she passed him he said, "Diane, I want to talk to you . . ."

She ignored him, went to the parking lot next door and told the attendant which car was hers. Then she turned, and saw that she was not alone.

"Good *night*, Joey," she said.

"Isn't there something I can do?" he said.

"Like leaving me alone?"

"I mean like speak to Teddy . . ."

"He's *your* friend. It's a free country."

She saw the hulking figure of Bruce Gottesman emerging from the restaurant. Marzula turned to her. "Why don't you go home and watch TV or something? I'll tell the guy you aren't feeling well."

"Protecting Teddy's interests?"

"You're a good customer. I'd hate to lose you."

"Touching," she said.

"Am I going to have to call your mother? It's long distance, you know."

"You do and I'll kick you right in the balls."

The attendant pulled up in the Datsun, got out, and let her in. She pulled the door shut, shot out of the parking lot, veered to her right, came to a hard stop before the entrance to the restaurant and opened the passenger door. "Get in," she called out.

Gottesman crossed the sidewalk and worked his body into the front seat, grunting with the effort.

In the rear-view mirror Diane saw Marzula coming after her. She gunned the motor.

"Hey, wait a minute," Gottesman cried, struggling with the open door. The car picked up speed. "Will you *wait?*" Cursing, he managed to get the door closed and turned to her. "What the hell's the matter with you?"

"You're clumsy," she said. "Why don't you get rid of some of that fat?"

"Maybe you better let me drive."

She took her eyes off the rear-view mirror and glanced at him. "What does Joey Marzula know about you that *I* should know?"

"Now listen." His voice had a slight whine to it. "You wanna do business or not? For two hundred dollars, I get you into a house you don't belong in. The story of my life is gonna cost you more money."

"Oh, don't be so fucking uptight," she said.

He eyed her sourly. "Did you get the knife?"

"How do I know you're not Jack the Ripper?"

"You don't," he said.

She shoved her handbag at him. "In there."

He took the bag and found the knife. Then he came out with a slim and ugly brown spray can. "What's this?"

"For God's sake, be careful. Put that back," she said.

"What is it?"

"Worse than Mace. Much more lethal," she said. "A detective I used to date gave it to me. Put it away."

He shoved the can back into her handbag. "With a mouth like yours, you don't need Mace."

She looked at him, but she didn't say a word.

She needed him.

THEY HAD ALREADY seated themselves at Table One, next to each other, ignoring Bea Magnin's loudly announced stricture that neither spouses nor lovers sit side by side, and there was nothing Teddy could do now, or at least *think* of to do, when he saw Jud Fleming, with a heaping dinner plate in one hand and about seven ounces of straight Scotch in the other, walking unsteadily away from the room-length buffet and navigating his way precariously toward the only unoccupied chair at the table, the one facing them.

"Shit," Teddy said under his breath.

"It looks like beef stroganoff to me," Jo Anne said, trying to ease his attention down onto the plate before him.

"Remember me?" the television director said, arriving. "I'm the guy who put his foot in his mouth a little bitty ago."

"Hunger can make a man do almost anything," Teddy muttered, taking up his fork.

"Is this all right, Beatrice?" Fleming called out.

"I don't see why not," Bea Magnin said without enthusiasm from the other end of the table.

"La Magnin yonder has *assured* me," Fleming said to Teddy, as he worked himself into the seat, "that you are truly the real McCoy. Or should I say the real Bluestern?"

"Howard will suffice, Mr. Fleming," Teddy said, without looking at him.

"Thank you. You are a gentleman, sir, which is not a term one gets to use too often in our community, unless one happens to be referring to certain of our young female executives. I apologize for upsetting you *or* your fair lady."

"She seems to be surviving." Teddy turned to Jo Anne. "Or should I speak only for myself?"

Jo Anne glanced at them both, then pointed her knife and fork at her plate. "Why don't we try speaking for no one and find out if Chasen's has done it again?"

"The lady's got a point there, Howard," Jud Fleming said, just before relieving his glass of half its contents. "A little hostile, but a point nevertheless."

They ate in silence for a short while, allowing the crosstalk of the others at the table—Bea Magnin, Rona Barrett, a black fullback turned actor, and an aging movie actress turned real estate agent—to take over. And then Jud Fleming found his tongue again.

"You know who I blame for the whole thing?" he said to Teddy.

Teddy shook his head and took a mouthful of wine.

"That actor brother of yours got me so upset this afternoon that I wound up taking it out on *you*," Fleming said.

"Gone and forgotten," Teddy said quickly.

"Listen," the director went on. "Just because Jimmy Carter never knew how to slip a muzzle on brother Billy doesn't mean *you* have to stand for Teddy Stern trying to exploit *your* good name . . ."

"Being an ostrich in disguise," Teddy said in a controlled voice, "I am happy to say that I don't care to hear another word about it."

"Let me tell you anyway," Fleming persisted. "I want you to have the facts before *he* gives you the manure."

"I can't hear you. My head is under six feet of sand."

"He had the gall today to try to get a role in one of my shows by offering to lean on *you* to get me a feature to direct at your studio . . ."

Teddy felt Jo Anne's hand covering his, as though that could put the lid on what was rising up inside of him, and he heard her saying, "Mr. Fleming, *your* head is *above* the sand and you *still* can't hear."

But the man ignored her. "I'm only telling you for your own good, Howard. He's liable to come to you with some twisted version of what actually went on—"

Fuck it. Fuck *everything*. "You're a liar, Fleming." Teddy spoke very quietly.

The director laughed nervously. "Hey, come on, guy. You have no right—"

"You're accusing my brother of something he didn't do, only to cover your *own* tracks for doing it yourself."

Fleming's face blanched. "Don't tell *me* what happened, Bluestern. I was there."

"You're a dirty goddam fucking liar," Teddy said in a low voice. "You don't belong here tonight. You don't belong anywhere. You got into this world on a pass."

Fleming started to rise to his feet, his face mottled.

Bea Magnin glanced away from Rona Barrett, alarmed. "Howard, darling . . ."

Teddy turned to her. "I want this man thrown out."

Bea Magnin's perfect eyebrows rose. "Poor little Jud?"

"You shouldn't have him in your house. You'll never get rid of the odor."

"You cocksucker." Fleming seized his glass and hurled Scotch at Teddy, missing his face but getting part of his shoulder.

"Oh my God," Rona Barrett chortled.

"Run along, Fleming, before I break you in two," Teddy said, dabbing at his shoulder with a napkin. "Go on. *Scat!*"

"Howard, for heaven's sake. . . ." Bea Magnin was on her feet.

The black fullback and the aging actress stared down at their plates in silent embarrassment.

Jud Fleming glanced around, looking for support, then turned and started away from the table, swaying as he walked.

Jo Anne placed her napkin on the table and said quietly, "Can we go now?"

"Yes," Teddy said, rising.

Bea Magnin was at their side. "Darlings, whatever did I miss?"

"Nothing at all, Bea," Teddy said. "*Less* than nothing. Jo Anne isn't feeling well, so we're going to slip away. Will you forgive us?"

"How can I not, silly? You're Howard Bluestern, and she's my love, didn't you know?"

Teddy waggled his fingers at the others at the table, and Rona Barrett said, "You'll do anything to make my show, you bad man."

Bea Magnin put one arm around Teddy's waist and the other around Jo Anne's and walked them slowly across the room past the crowded tables. "It's my own fault," she said. "I never should have let Blanche bring that nothingburger here. Promise me you'll come again, Howard, and bring this divine girl with you?"

"If you're crazy enough to invite me after this," Teddy said to her.

"People are going to talk. You know that, don't you? I can see heads turning already. Sure you want that? Sure you won't change your minds and stay?"

"Listen, Bea, I know a good exit when I see one. Don't ask me to give this one up." And only after he had said it did he realize that he meant it.

At the front door he took Jo Anne's hand and together they went out into the night, which was filled with stars and parking attendants. There was a deceptive stillness in the air that did not fool him for a moment, nor did Jo Anne's silence disarm him either. Deep in the background, he could hear questions quietly biding their time, and he wasn't at all sure that he hadn't, at long last, finally run out of all the answers . . .

THERE WAS NO PLACE left to look. She knew every square inch of this house and she hadn't missed one. The tape just wasn't here. He must have taken it with him to Mexico. Hard to believe that he would go to such lengths, but what else *could* she believe?

"Bruce," she called out angrily in the dark, "where the hell *are* you?"

"In here," he called back.

"Where's here?"

"The kitchen."

"I already looked in the kitchen," she said.

"Who's looking?" he said.

"Well what *are* you doing?"

No answer.

She made her way through the darkened living room, cursing as she bumped her knee on the edge of the coffee table, and went into the kitchen. He was sitting at the white formica table with an open bottle of J. & B. in his hand, and no glass.

"Goddam it." She moved at him and ripped the bottle from his grasp. "I *told* you I don't want him to know we were here."

He looked up at her with unfocused eyes. "What's he gonna do, count the fluid ounces?"

She capped the bottle and said, "Where did you find this?"

"Under the bar," he said thickly.

"Go put it back, *exactly*."

He struggled to his feet, took the bottle from her, and headed for the living room.

It was hot here in the kitchen. *She* was hot. *Sweating*. She *hated* to perspire, hated ever to be damp. Too much to drink tonight. Too much taking everything out of every drawer and putting it back where it had been. Too much wanting and too much not finding. Two hundred dollars for *this*, for *nothing*. She hadn't given it to him yet, but if she didn't, he'd probably kill her. Or worse.

But what could be worse? Sweating. That's what could be worse, and she was already doing that.

She went over to the door, turned the inside key in the latch, opened the door, and stepped out of the kitchen onto the back porch. The night air, coming through the open screens, made her shiver.

Better. Much better.

Suddenly, in the distance to her right, she saw the first glimmer of approaching headlights at the top of the road, and her heart sank. Surely it was Howard Bluestern, returning early, returning too soon. Quickly she pulled back into the darkest corner of the porch and watched the lights coming closer and closer, and then she realized that the car was a pickup truck, and it was not slowing down at all, and she stepped forward to watch it go by and saw, out of the corner of her eye, an unexpected flash behind her, an unaccustomed glint of something caught in the peripheral sweep of the passing headlights, and she turned her head to look at it, and the porch was dark now, and she stared down at what had caught her attention and she could not make out what it was, so she moved closer and realized that she had not been able to make out what it was only because in all the weeks that she had lived in this house and in all the dozens of times that she had come out to this porch, she had never seen this thing on the freezer, this thing that had caught the lights of the passing pickup truck, this strange shiny lock with the little dials.

She stared at it. She stood there listening to the hum of the very old Frigidaire and stared down at the brand-new lock on its very old lid, and then she heard Bruce Gottesman coming back into the kitchen, calling out, "Diane?"

"Out here," she said.

He appeared in the doorway and looked at her. "Let's get out of here while we're still ahead."

She stared, transfixed, at the humming white box. "Bruce," she said, "do you think a tape would be damaged if it were placed in a freezer?"

"How the hell would I know?" he said.

"Come here a minute," she said.

chapter 13

HE CAME UP out of a deep and dreamless sleep in the darkness before dawn, wondering what had awakened him, for he was in his own bed now and usually slept through until daylight. The rhythmic pounding of the surf outside the bedroom windows was as soothing and hypnotic as it always was, and there were no unusually distracting sounds that he was aware of. Why had he awakened?

Suddenly he remembered Jo Anne and the glorious lovemaking that had started the moment they had returned home from the party, with no questions asked. He allowed himself to think about her for a while, about the two of them together, and then the growing heaviness in his loins told him that he wanted more of her now, there could never be enough, and he turned over in the big bed and reached out for her, and it was then that he began to suspect why he had awakened, because she wasn't there, the bed was empty on her side, and the door leading to the bathroom was open and there was no light on inside, and the bedroom door was open too, and the hallway beyond it was dark, meaning that she was not in the living room either.

He lay on his back for a few moments, trying to think of a plausible reason why she might have slipped out of bed and gotten dressed and eased her car out of the garage and driven home, but before he could come to believe that that was even possible, his eyes, accustomed now to the dark, made out her dress and her pantyhose draped over the chair exactly where she had tossed them hastily in the heat of their hunger, and then he decided that yes, he *was* hearing faint and unidentifiable sounds and they *were* coming from the direction of the kitchen, or was it from the back porch beyond, and now, as he pushed the blankets aside and got out of bed and began to move through the darkened house on silent, unslippered feet, there was no longer any doubt in his mind why he had suddenly come up out of a deep but uneasy slumber . . .

When he arrived at the open kitchen doorway to the back porch, he stood there silently watching her, waiting for her to notice him,

147

and he felt a pang of pity for her when he saw the startled look of embarrassment and fear that came to her lovely face as she glanced up, kneeling there before the unpadlocked, open freezer, with food packages strewn about on the floor on either side of her and her tousled hair, lit by the lone naked light bulb on the ceiling, hanging to her bare shoulders and partially covering her eyes, which were so nakedly vulnerable that he had to look away.

"I used the birth date on your driver's license," she said in a pathetically brave voice. "Open sesame." And then, in a tone of utter resignation, "Oh God, I'm so ashamed, Howard, I could die on the spot."

He raised a hand feebly to silence her humiliation, and she rose slowly, waiting for the storm to strike.

He waited for it too, waited for righteous rage, fury, *something* to well up inside of him, but all he felt was relief, total and unexpected.

Thank God, his terrible aloneness was finally over.

"Finish what you were doing," he said quietly. "Then come back to bed and we'll talk."

"What *am* I doing?" she implored hopelessly.

"You're trying to find out why I was so desperate not to have the lock opened this afternoon. Go on, Jo Anne, keep going."

In answer, she seized the lid of the freezer and brought it down with a crash. Quickly he moved to her side as she slipped the open padlock into the hasp. He pulled her hands away, removed the padlock, raised the lid again and slammed it back up against the catches that would hold it open. "Don't stop," he said. "I don't want you to stop."

"Howard, *please*, I've made an utter fool of myself. Can't we let it go at that?"

"You can, but I can't," he said. "This could destroy us and I'm not going to let it."

"What? Frozen food?" she cried. "I was wrong, the lock meant nothing. I'm sorry, I really am. I don't know what came over me. I despise sneaks as much as you do . . . Howard? . . ."

He wasn't listening to her. He was bending over the freezer working frantically, taking out everything that was left and tossing it on the brick floor, not caring where it landed. She stared at him, bewildered and a little frightened, unable to understand what was happening.

"What have I *done*? I only wanted to see—"

"Come here," he said.

She looked at him without moving.

He straightened up, turned to her. "Come over here."

"Howard, what—?"

He leaned over and took her arm and forced her to the edge of the open freezer and then he looked down into it.

She followed his gaze and stared down, puzzled. The noisily humming box was empty now, except for something plastic on the bottom, all covered with frost, and a zipper; it had a long zipper. She glanced at him. "What is it?"

"What does it look like to you?" he said in a strange voice.

She looked down, and then back at him. Somehow she didn't like this game. "A . . . a suit carrier? . . . A garment bag?"

He nodded slowly.

"I don't understand," she said. "What's . . . in it?"

"Not what," he said. "Who."

She felt herself smiling involuntarily. "Howard, please . . ."

"Please what?"

Please keep my smile alive, please don't say anything that will spoil my smile, say something truly funny. This is getting entirely out of hand, and if you don't say something quickly, if I ever stop smiling . . . "Please, Howard, don't do this to me. I told you—"

"It's my brother," he said quietly.

"—That I was sorry and I *meant* it . . ."

"That's my brother down there, Jo Anne. He's dead."

She tried to laugh but it came out as a little gasp, and then she managed to make it *sound* like a laugh and she put a hand on his arm placatingly. "All right, you win, I'll never do it again. Now let's get this food back in before it thaws out and gets ruined." She kneeled down to busy herself and escape the strange somber look in his eyes and the sound of his voice. "Come on, darling, help me."

"I didn't kill him," he was saying softly. "It was somebody else."

"All right, all right, you didn't kill him, it was somebody else, I heard you, Howard, I heard you. Now will you please—?"

"It's no use, Jo Anne . . ." He reached over her and closed the lid of the freezer.

"I want you to *stop* this," she said, rising.

Gently he took her head in his hands. "Listen to me . . ."

She shrank from his grasp crying, "Why are you doing this to me?"

"I'm trying to tell you the truth because it's too terrible for me to keep to myself any longer and it's going to hurt you, Jo Anne, and you're going to hate me for telling you but I have to, honey, I have to, and you've got to listen to me, please listen to me . . .''

"Stop it, stop it." Her hands covered her ears but she could hear him anyway, he was not going to let her alone, he had caught her and he was going to punish her, he was being cruel, oh so cruel, she had never dreamed he could be such a cruel man. "Howard, please," she implored.

"I'm not Howard," he said gently. "I'm Teddy. And I have been since the night I first took you home and made love to you."

"Don't *do* this to me," she cried.

"I'm Teddy," he said.

Such a cruel man, oh so cruel . . .

"Yes, Jo Anne."

"What a terrible thing to say . . .''

"I'm Teddy," he said. "Do you hear me?"

"Stop *saying* that," she said, shaking her head from side to side in pain. "You are not, you are not . . .''

"Yes, I am," he said.

"No," she cried.

His voice rose to a shout. *"Yes."*

She stared at him wide-eyed. His face was pale under the naked light bulb, his lips were bloodless. She stared at him and waited for his expression to change, she waited for him to say something, anything that would save her from disintegration. She was going fast and she knew it. She could never save herself alone. Every part of her was slipping away, fleeing, escaping, dissolving, dying, she was dying, she couldn't live another moment, she couldn't bear to be alive another moment. He had to save her, he had to smile, he had to say something, he had to rescue her, he had to, he had to, had to . . . "Howard," she pleaded.

"No," he said, in a terrible voice.

"Howard . . . " she moaned.

"Teddy," he said, and started toward her.

"Don't touch me," she shrieked. "Don't touch me . . .'' And he tried to hold her but she tore out of his grasp and ran inside, sobbing, and he called after her but she raced through the kitchen and the hallway and the living room and she heard him coming after her calling out Jo Anne, please, and somehow she managed to get the sliding door unlocked and open and the night wind hit her in the face and the hard wood of the patio was beneath her bare feet and then the sand, the damp, cool sand, and the sea was rough and the crashing waves drowned out the sound of her panting, sobbing, gasping for breath and the crunch of her feet in the sand as she ran as fast as she could into the enveloping darkness, away from the terrible nightmare behind her, away from Howard, away from this man who was making believe he wasn't Howard, away from this man who looked and talked just like Howard only he was demented, wild, crazy, frightening, making her look into a big empty white box that made strange noises and shook violently but was really a coffin, and this man insisting that it was his brother down there lying in the coffin, insisting that this strange terrifying shape concealed in a frost-covered suit carrier was his *brother*, that's what the man who looked like Howard had kept saying over and over again, that his brother was *dead*, that his brother was *Howard*, that Howard was *dead* and that *he* was *Teddy*.

Howard help me, she cried out to the darkness as she ran and ran and ran until finally she could run no more and she fell down in the sand and lay there weeping softly, help me Howard, unheard in the crashing waves, lying there waiting for Howard to catch up with her and find her and hold her gently in his arms and ask her what had happened, had she had a bad dream or something, could he do anything for her, could he help her, did she want to come back to bed now so that he could soothe her back to sleep and keep the bad dream from returning again. . . . Yes, Howard, please do that, yes, Howard, yes, she cried as she heard the sound of his running feet in the sand behind her and his voice calling out to her from the darkness, thank God he had come for her . . .

He carried her back to the house in his arms and he put her to bed and turned out the lights and got into bed beside her and listened to her weeping softly into the pillow, her tear-streaked face hidden from him, her body coiled into itself as though she could escape into herself, be close to him but as far away as she could possibly be. Is it all right if I talk, he kept asking her, and she didn't answer for a long time. Would you rather I wait until morning, he asked her, and she said no, no, and he said can I talk to you now, and she made a sound that was something like yes, so he propped himself up in bed beside her and lit a cigarette and began to tell her everything he could think of that he felt she ought to know and didn't, and he kept glancing down at her and listening to the sounds she was making so that he would know when to pause and when to go on, when to soften his words and circle the truth and close in on it gradually so that he would not give her more than she could possibly endure.

He told her how very much he loved her, respected her, admired her, desired her, worshiped her, needed her. He told her *that* over and over again, hoping it would help her to accept the rest of it, the ugly part of it. He told her he had loved her from the very first moment he had laid eyes on her. He told her how sad he had felt at the realization that she would probably never even have looked at him if it hadn't been for the lucky circumstance of Howard's having asked him to play the role for a night and a day, and if it hadn't been for the horrible unspeakable tragedy that had *kept* him in the role—no, *he* had kept *himself* in the role, he had to face that fact, he couldn't blame it on Diane or on anyone else, certainly not on that vile little man Marvin Gerber, he Teddy Stern, and he alone, had made the decision to go on being Howard, and it was easy enough to say the reason he had made the decision was the ten million dollars of double indemnity insurance that would come to *him*, Teddy Stern, if he successfully pulled off the deception of Howard's accidental death in an off-the-cliff fiery car crash, but she had to believe him, she had to believe that it was equally true, maybe more so than for all the money in the world, that the deep-down genuine honest-to-God reason why he had gone on being Howard was because he knew that he would lose her the moment he became only who he really was, only Teddy Stern, and he hadn't even allowed himself to think of what would happen to the two of them after the final public end of Howard Bluestern when he'd have to *be* Teddy Stern . . .

He looked down at her and saw that she was lying still, not moving, nor making a sound.

"Jo Anne? . . . Sweetheart?" No answer. He put a hand on her gently. She was warm to the touch. "Jo Anne? . . . Darling?"

He heard her measured breathing. She was fast asleep now. Much as he wanted to go on talking to her, thank God she was asleep. He put out his cigarette, slid down under the covers, turned over, and soon was drifting off himself, not once daring to allow himself to believe that, somehow, he had survived, that the worst was over.

When he woke up in the morning, she was gone.

There were no notes, or anything like that. He searched the entire house, but there was nothing.

He had lost her.

chapter 14

GERBER BLAMED IT on the game.

The Dodgers had betrayed him.

Four in the first, three in the second, and a big five in the fifth.

How was he supposed to get involved and lose himself in a laugher like *that*? Fifty-two thousand people were screaming with joy all around him, and *he* was stuck with Howard Bluestern's leukemia, or carcinoma, or whatever the hell it was, or wasn't, unless the Giants could pull a miracle and make a ballgame out of it and take him out of his head, where he didn't want to be. With a runaway like this one was, he and his son could have left the stadium right then and there and beaten the traffic, but naturally Darryl would be insisting on sitting there until the final out.

Gerber was deeply disappointed in the Dodgers for having had it so good today. He hated Sunday games anyway, because they were played in the daytime and he sweated easily. But from the moment he had awakened this morning, much much too early for a nonwork day, he had known that he was going to have to find ways to scramble his mind and distract himself or he'd never make it to Monday morning when he'd be back in his office, where he could at least *do* something about the situation and not just stew over it as he had done all day Saturday, and fret about it and blow up what was probably nothing at all into something really terrible.

He had counted on a tense ballgame and the noise of the crowd and Darryl's usual nonstop commentary to keep him going at least until dinner time, when Helen's chatter would take over and fill up his head, and after that the whole string of sitcoms the networks had lying in wait for him. Then he'd take two Dalmanes instead of one, and maybe a *blue* Valium, and he'd be *through* with this goddam day.

But the Dodgers had crossed him up by busting out with base hits like it was batting practice and he had had too much time to relax and *think* about Bluestern, and so, somewhere around the top of the sixth, because he had had enough of thinking, he had made his decision and

153

determined to stick to it, right or wrong. Yesterday had been lousy, this morning had been lousy, Dodger Stadium had been lousy, and he was not going to suffer through another long and wakeful night in the bargain. And so, the decision.

When he got to his office in the morning, he was going to have his secretary locate the brother—Madeline was good at that sort of thing—and then he was going to mosey around and somehow get into a conversation with this brother and see if he couldn't worm some secrets out of him about Bluestern's health, if there were any to worm, without giving himself away. He had no idea how he was going to do it, and he knew damned well it was strictly non-kosher to be talking to a beneficiary who might not even know he *was* one, but it was all he had been able to come up with in his haste to get the thing out of his mind in the top of the sixth.

He couldn't go to *Bluestern*. You don't go to your customer, the head of a studio, and say, Hey tell me, all kidding aside, are you a liar? And he sure as hell wasn't going to ask questions of that company *doctor*. What could *he* tell him that it wouldn't take a CAT scan, a bone scan, and the whole nuclear medicine department of Cedars Sinai to determine? No, Gerber wasn't going to blow a huge policy and all his commissions by asking questions of *anyone* in the company. Not while there was a chance in the world that there was *absolutely nothing to worry about*. With a little luck, he'd locate this Teddy Stern fellow first thing tomorrow, and sort of drop in on him and maybe catch him off guard. All he needed was for Madeline to find out his whereabouts.

"Absolutely nothing to worry about," Gerber mused.

"But can't we stay till the end?" whined his son.

"Sure," Gerber said. "Why not?"

THE LATE AFTERNOON SUN was warm, but not warm enough to overcome the chilling breeze blowing in from the sea. Teddy sat close to the water's edge, thankful for the running suit he was wearing. For a Sunday, the beach was relatively deserted. He couldn't have taken it any other way. Saturday had been a nightmare, spent indoors staring at a dead telephone and looking into the blackness of his soul. Today he had dared to go outside, sitting there in the sand for hours, waiting for his muddled brain or the rolling surf or a crying seagull to come to him with a clue, to present him with one simple, clean-cut decision about anything at all. Jo Anne's leaving him had tilted everything. Every question, every answer sounded hollow to him, depressing and without meaning. What day to dispose of Howard, Tuesday or Saturday? What difference? Where to do it, Malibu Canyon? Oxnard? Carmel? No matter. More important, did he actually want to go through with it *at all?* Even if he got away with it, of what use would ten million dollars be to someone who couldn't think of one good reason to go on *living?*

How come you're not asking how I feel about all this?

It doesn't concern *you.* You're dead.

So why does my death have to be in vain? Isn't it bad enough that it was you she meant to kill, not me? I just happened to be in the wrong place at the wrong time.

You can't blame me for *that* one, Howard.

No?

No, goddam it, it was *your* idea to switch. It was *always* your idea to switch.

And you were always so ready to oblige, weren't you.

Should I *not* have been? Should I have said *no* to you whenever you needed me badly?

You might have. You could have. But you never did. You never gave up the only way you had of asserting your power over me, right?

Me?

Your superiority . . .

Superiority? *Me?*

Yes, you.

You're crazy.

Not crazy. Dead. So you don't have to try to hide it from yourself any longer. There's no way now that you can make believe I'm the strong one, the superior one. You're alive and I'm dead. I couldn't be more powerless, I couldn't be more inferior. So enough of this shit about how awful it is because some broad walked out on you . . .

What are you driving at, for Christsake? What are you trying to say to me?

Don't start thinking of going seven feet under because I'm six feet under, just to put me on top again. Don't blow it now, schmuck, when you're almost home.

Teddy sprang to his feet. The hell with thinking. Where did it lead to anyway? His joints ached from too much sitting in one position for too long. He looked up and down the beach. The tide was going out, and there was plenty of flat dry sand. He'd do a few miles each way, maybe stretch it to ten. Physical action was good for dispelling anxiety.

He'd read that somewhere, practiced it daily, and succeeded at least once a year. He faced north, did a few limbering-up exercises, and got ready to take off. But he did not run. Instead, he turned and started across the sand toward the house.

There was no use in trying to kid himself. Running would not leave Howard behind. There was only one way to do that, and he was going to do it right now. He should have done it the moment he had first discovered the body. If not then, if he had been too shocked to think clearly then, he should have done it the very next day. The consequences had seemed too terrible then, only because he had never thought them through. Maybe he *hadn't* wasted all those hours on the beach today. Because now he could see that, after the worst was over, the price would seem cheap.

As an actor, he'd lose his reputation at the studios and at the networks, but what kind of reputation was it to begin with? A joke. Fraud had been committed, and he had been an accomplice. But his confession would relieve the insurance company of any financial obligations. Maybe they wouldn't even prosecute him. Willfully concealing a murder for a few days didn't exactly get you life imprisonment. Testifying for the DA against Diane could earn him, at the worst, a suspended sentence. And justice would be done. Diane would probably get no more than a couple of years until parole for her crime of passion. And because the victim was not her intended one, maybe the charge would be reduced to manslaughter. Howard's reputation in the industry? Enhancement, not damage. Genuine sadness and true sympathy . . .

A decent ending, Howard. You deserve it. Forgive me.

Leave me out of this. I don't want to hear about it. You're not doing this for me. You're doing it because you're afraid of trying anything that doesn't come easy. Running away was always your favorite form of exercise. So go ahead. Run.

Good-bye, Howard.

Don't wake me when it's over.

Teddy climbed the steps leading to the patio. In his mind he was already rehearsing the dialogue, because it would be a complicated scene, and he didn't want to go into it unprepared.

My name is Teddy Stern. I'm an actor. I live at ten-seventy Old Malibu Road, and I'm calling to report a murder that took place here several days ago. . . . My brother, Howard Bluestern, the motion picture executive. . . . That's the one, yes, he's my brother, and he's dead. If you'll send the proper people over here, they'll find the body in my freezer, where I've been keeping it ever since he died. . . . I'll explain all that when you get here, okay? . . . No, I didn't do it. It was a young woman named Diane McWorter, and I'll explain that too, including where you can pick her up without any trouble at all. . . . I wish it *were* a practical joke, but if you don't believe me, why don't you send a squad car over right now? I'll be here waiting for you, and so will my brother, who's dead. . . . You're welcome.

What was so hard about that?

The truth was simple. When you tell the truth, you don't even have to pay much attention to what you're saying, you just say it and that's it, because you're not trying to withhold anything, or cover anything up. It's like taking all your clothes off, the wonderful feeling of being naked, telling the naked truth.

He slid the glass door back to enter the living room, because that's where the telephone was, the telephone he'd use to call the police. But he did not call the police, or anyone else.

She was sitting there.

She was seated on *his* sofa in *his* living room, watching his face as he came in, examining him with her wide blue eyes, more to discover her own reaction to seeing him again than to determine his. And she knew immediately that it was not going to happen all at once, there would be a learning period, it would take time for the both of them. But she also knew immediately, at least as far as she was concerned, that there was nothing to worry about, it was going to be all right.

A little cry of gratitude burst from his lips. "Oh my God . . ."

She smiled at him.

He went to her wordlessly and sank down on the sofa beside her and took her in his arms and buried his face in the luxuriant silk of her hair so that she would not see his tears, for he was not ready for her to know that side of him yet.

"Teddy, Teddy," she said gently, calling him by his name for the very first time as she stroked his head.

"Why?" he murmured. "Why? . . . I thought—oh Christ, I'm so glad . . ."

"I don't understand it myself," she said. "All I know is that it's you, whoever you were . . . are . . . it's you I want to be with, for whatever that's going to mean . . ."

"I love you," he cried softly.

"Besides," she said, "you'll never be able to get away with it all by yourself."

He raised his head and looked at her and saw that she was smiling.

chapter
15

THE STUDIO was busy with its Monday-morning busyness, especially up here at the top of the tower where the power was. She sat quietly on the sofa, waiting, wondering how Bruce was doing out at the beach house. He should have been there by now, and on the inside too. She was doing *her* bit here, he should be doing his bit there.

She sat in Howard Bluestern's outer office thumbing through *Time* and *Newsweek* but not reading them really, any more than she was really hoping to get in to see Howard. She was here as a lookout, as Bruce Gottesman's distant early warning system to make sure that Howard was in his office at the studio, and not on his way to Malibu where he could walk in and catch Bruce by surprise. She sat there watching the secretary, Miss Kallen, at her desk, answering the constantly ringing telephones, fending off callers, switching some to the two older women in the adjacent office, putting others on hold, buzzing Howard on the intercom, talking to him in his inaccessible office behind her desk in confidential tones that were too low and private but not completely lost on Diane's acutely sharp hearing.

She admired the way the secretary handled herself, so cool and assured and gentle yet firm. She wasn't exactly beautiful. Some might have thought she wasn't even pretty. Yet there was something exquisitely female about her. Was it the hair? The eyes? The mouth? Diane would have liked to get a look at her legs. She couldn't see them behind the desk from where she was sitting, and she wanted very much to see those legs. Every second, she wanted more and more to see them.

Teddy would have liked this girl. He would have eaten her alive. She shouldn't be thinking about Teddy now, but this girl made her think of Teddy. Whenever Diane had felt stirrings of sexual desire, she had always thought of Teddy, and she would probably go on that way forever. Even yesterday afternoon, and the night before, riding Bruce Gottesman's ramrod and his incredible staying power in a vain attempt to lose herself in meaningless sex, she had almost shouted

158

Teddy's name at the climax, even though he was dead and gone, the poor bastard, even though she had gone to bed with the white-fleshed, repulsive stranger in the hope of *forgetting* Teddy, not remembering him.

She felt a sudden pang of remorse and fear as the image came back to her of Teddy lying dead at the bottom of his own freezer, the way she had seen him Friday night, dead by *her* hands and hidden away by his own brother, who *else* could have answered her frightened phone call that morning after her terrible mistake and made believe that he was Teddy and gotten away with it? How many times he must have done *that* in their twin-brother past? *God* what a sucker she had been, falling for that stale act and actually believing his trumped-up story about a tape that she was now sure had never even *existed*.

She had almost gone to pieces on that back porch in Malibu Friday night, but Bruce had pulled her together with a huge dose of bourbon, and then he had driven her to her apartment and put her to bed and sort of moved in with her, that had been good, that had helped, and by Saturday afternoon she had become sober again, with an awful hangover, but all right, quite all right, surprisingly steady, almost in complete control of herself, filled with a fierce determination to extricate herself somehow from the nightmarish trap she had made for herself with her wild jealousy and that damned fireplace poker and shrewd enough to make Bruce think that Teddy must have been killed by the very person who had hidden his body, his own brother Howard.

This morning, after going to the bank and getting Bruce the thousand dollars he had demanded for expenses before he would agree to do another damn thing for her, she had left the Datsun with him, taken a cab and come here to the studio without an appointment, without even calling Howard's office first, just slipping by the guard at the gate on foot and announcing her presence to Miss Kallen, and then going out to a phone booth and calling Bruce at her apartment to tell him that it was okay to take off for Malibu, Howard was in his office.

She had known that Howard would duck her and pretend to be too busy to see her. That was fine with her. She had no desire to see *him*, no confidence in her own ability to keep from blurting out something that might give away what she knew. Even though she had no idea yet what she was going to do to escape the consequences of the only act of violence she had ever committed in her whole life, she knew that it was vital that Howard Bluestern have no inkling that she had discovered his strange secret in that sudden, shocking, horrible moment

Friday night, after Bruce had picked the lock on the freezer and her groping, searching hands had uncovered the awful evidence that she *had*, after all, smashed the life out of Teddy, that she had merely been *spared* the realization for a day by Howard's tricky, totally inexplicable impersonation of Teddy on the telephone.

What a fool she had been to be taken in so easily by an amateur, a stuffy studio head. It was enough to make you *sick* to realize how dumb you could get from wishful thinking. Who *wouldn't* want to believe that the murder they knew they'd committed had never really happened? And it sickened her even more to think back on her total gullibility at the Polo Lounge, sitting there pouring her heart out to Howard when he had already known that Teddy was dead and that she had probably killed him. (Probably? *Certainly.* How could there have been any doubt at all in his mind after her hysteria over the phone?)

She sat there in Howard's outer office, waiting to warn Bruce in case Howard should leave the studio, and wondered to herself for the thousandth time why Howard had lied to her over the phone and made believe he was Teddy and buried Teddy's body at the bottom of Teddy's freezer and put a goddam *lock* on the box and lied to her that Teddy had gone out of town. Why had he wanted her to think that Teddy was still alive? When you put something on ice, it means that you're keeping it for future use, so why was he saving Teddy?

Why hadn't he called the police when he discovered Teddy's body in the bed where she had left it? Wasn't it *risky* not reporting Teddy's murder? What would the police *say* when he finally *did* call them? And what would *he* say that wouldn't leave *him* open to suspicion? And most important of all, what was he planning to do about *her*, she who had killed his brother and *he knew it*, only *he* knew it, not even Bruce knew it, only Howard. Hadn't she all but *admitted* it to him over the phone that day when he impersonated Teddy? Hadn't she more than *hinted* at it at the Polo Lounge? Was there *any possible chance* on God's earth that he *didn't* know that she had done it? Was it possible that he only *suspected* her and was waiting for her to give herself away? If only she could recall *exactly* what she had said to him over the phone, and at the Polo Lounge . . .

If only she could stop this *dangerous, ridiculous wishful thinking* . . .

He knows you did it, he knows you did it.

Yes, but . . .

Yes but *nothing. He knows you did it.*

Then surely he was planning to turn her in, wasn't he?

Surely he was planning to do *something* to her.

But what? *What?*

And *when?*

Not knowing . . . waiting, and not knowing what she was waiting for . . . was *intolerable*.

And so she had inveigled Bruce into going back to the beach house today to explore every inch of the place in the hope of finding some clue to the mystery of what Howard was up to. She had painted a luridly attractive picture for Bruce in which he would unearth something that would implicate Howard in his brother's murder, leading to all *kinds* of hush money for *them* in return for their silence. That had brought the glint of greed to Bruce's eyes, thank God for his bad teeth. She had filled him with such an obsession to get them capped and gleaming white that he would do anything short of murder now for money, and maybe not even stop there.

Sending him to Malibu was a long shot at best, but there was nothing she would not try, *nothing*, until the inevitable police showed up at her door or she had formulated some kind of plan for staying out of prison for the rest of her life. She would die before she went to prison, yet how was she going to avoid it? Howard was the one who had the whistle in his mouth, and only he could decide when to blow it. Vague thoughts of *getting* something on him (Lord knows he was plotting *something*) and blackmailing him into silence, all the while making Bruce think that she too was after Howard's money, was the best she had been able to come up with so far, but it was a flimsy idea and she knew it. God, how she loathed and detested being this desperate and uncertain, and so dependent on a creep like Bruce.

And now, because she couldn't stand another moment of interminable self-questioning, with never a comforting answer, she was leafing through magazines and pretending to read them and all the while watching the honey-blonde girl with the wide wide eyes and the delicate nose and the luscious mouth, and giving herself over to a perfectly wonderful fantasy that was becoming so real and exciting it frightened her a little. And then suddenly the girl in her arms rose to her feet and walked away from her desk and opened the door to Howard Bluestern's office, and just before she went inside, Diane saw her marvelous legs at last and the curve of her bottom, and she felt an exquisite thrill go through her, and she thought God, how Teddy would have adored this one . . .

Jo Anne closed the door behind her, quietly locked it, and went to the big desk in the deserted office. She sat down behind the desk, swiveled around to the private phone, picked it up, and dialed Teddy's number in Malibu. As soon as she heard Teddy's recorded voice answering on the machine, she hung up, dialed the number again, hung up, and dialed once more. This time, Teddy answered immediately.

"You?"

"She's still outside," Jo Anne said.

"Maybe you should charge her rent or something."

"I just thought you ought to know, in case you decide to come back early for some reason."

"Little chance of that. Gerber hasn't even shown up yet. I'm still waiting."

"I'm dying of curiosity."

"I like you better alive," he said. "How is the studio running in my absence?"

"You'll be sorry to hear that it runs without you very well."

"I'm crushed."

"But you'd be amazed to know how *busy* you've been here this morning."

"Didn't I tell you acting was easy?"

"For you, yes. Especially now, with you playing yourself for Marvin Gerber."

"It happens to be the most difficult role there is in life . . . being yourself."

"You're getting serious, so I better hang up now."

"You do that," he said. "I'll talk to you later. And in the meantime, keep me *very* busy."

He clicked off and glanced at his Seiko digital, which Howard had taken off and placed on the bed table before going to his last sleep. Gerber was late, and the suspense was building. Ever since the insurance agent's secretary had called, Teddy had speculated on the probable reason for the requested meeting. All he was sure of was that it would turn out to have something to do with Howard's policy. But why meet with Teddy Stern, the beneficiary?

Back at the studio, after she had hung up, Jo Anne gathered up some meaningless papers from the desk, went to the door, unlocked it and eased herself out of the office.

The McWorter girl looked up at her questioningly.

Jo Anne answered with a shrug. "I told him again, but he's *inundated*. Sure you wouldn't rather make it tomorrow?"

The dark-haired girl smiled agreeably. "I don't mind waiting."

Quickly, before turning away, Jo Anne swept her with an all-encompassing look and got a flash impression of a fiery, unstable personality, full of nervous energy and sexual appetites and the knowingness to satisfy them. It was not hard to understand how Teddy, or any other man, could have been temporarily captivated by her, especially with those big brown eyes and the perfectly shaped body. But seeing her as a killer? Almost impossible.

As she sat down at her desk, Jo Anne could feel the girl's eyes on her, on every part of her.

BRUCE TRIED shifting his position slightly, but it was useless. There was no way to get comfortable sprawled on your belly under a low-slung bed, especially on *his* belly. How could that McWorter flake have been so inept? True, she had probably not really recovered yet from the shock of finding her ex-boyfriend's body, but one crummy little assignment was all she had taken on, and she had failed completely. He had almost crapped in his pants at the sound of Bluestern's key in the front door lock, with not a word of warning from Diane. And no sooner had he dashed into the bedroom and scrambled under the bed, praying to God that he wouldn't cough or sneeze or let out a fear-inspired fart, when damned if Bluestern hadn't come right into the bedroom and plotzed on the bed and started taking off his clothes, and then changed into some things from the stiff's closet—boots and the bottoms of blue jeans were all that Bruce had been able to see from his cockroach point of view.

The phone conversation he had just overheard, Bluestern's end of it anyway, hadn't told Bruce a damned thing, except that the man had been talking to his office at the studio and was expecting someone here named Gerber. He hoped that Gerber, whoever the hell he was, was coming to take Bluestern away someplace, anyplace, even out on the beach would help, anything to give *him* a chance to slide out from under this bed and make a getaway. It was at times like this that he wondered if he was really *cut out* for some of the things he did to keep his big body and his little soul together, especially this housebreaking and amateur gumshoe work and God knows what else the manic little broad had in mind for him. Eating, boozing, humping, and steering some rich movie producer's hundred-foot yacht through the channel into the harbor at Monte Carlo, *that* he could do, that he could *enjoy*, but *this*? Shit . . . if only if didn't take money to do *anything* in this world, particularly getting your choppers back into shape.

He listened to Bluestern moving around in the living room, heard him dropping ice cubes into a glass, pouring something on the rocks, then dialing the telephone. "Mr. Kramer, please. Teddy Stern calling . . ." There it was, the phony actor-voice, the one Diane had said he had used to fool *her*, or was he imagining it now? He hadn't believed her at first. It had been hard to buy. But hearing the guy actually announcing himself as Teddy Stern gave her story the ring of truth. This Bluestern had chutzpah to spare, and then some. "Hi Ruth, is he available? . . . Yeah, it's me. For the record, I'm back. . . . By 'in a meeting' I assume you mean that he's on the john and doesn't want to be disturbed until he's finished both trades. . . . You're too sensitive, Ruthie baby. . . . No, he needn't. I won't be in. Just called to say hello, and oh yes, one other thing: the answer on Jud Fleming at Universal is, forget it, I'm not interested. . . . That's right. A firm no. Be sure to tell him. . . . Thank you, Ruth."

Bruce heard him hang up, then dial another number and use the same fake voice again, talking to someone named David. He heard Bluestern, pretending that he was the dead guy, Stern, telling this David person that Bluestern had forgotten a pair of women's panties in the bathroom over the weekend and needling the guy on the other end by wondering whether maybe the panties belonged to *him*. He was chuckling as he hung up.

Bruce stirred with discomfort beneath the bed. Maybe *Bluestern* was pleased with his performance, but as far as he was concerned the movie mogul play-acting at being his brother was giving him a pain in the ass, and other parts of his body too. About all that he had overheard that he could take home to little mama was that *she* wasn't the *only* one Bluestern was trying to fool into believing that his brother was still in the land of the live ones. It wasn't exactly the kind of earthshaking news the female was hoping for. She'd give him a bad time if he showed up that empty-handed.

He still couldn't figure her out. From the way she dressed, and the way her apartment in Brentwood was furnished, and the ease with which he had been able to make her cough up a grand this morning, she didn't strike him as being exactly hungry, certainly not needy enough to be so apparently desperate to pin something on Bluestern and separate him from his bankroll. Bruce couldn't quite put his finger on it, but something smelled just a little from herring. Driving out here in her car, and turning things over in his mind, he had come up with an explanation for her strange behavior that shook him a little.

But when he recalled the genuineness of her stunned surprise on discovering the body and the hysteria that had followed, he knew that he was way off and dismissed the idea. Besides, she was hardly the type. Maybe *fuck* a guy's brains out, but that's all.

Wasn't that the doorbell ringing? And Bluestern on his way to the foyer?

The Gerber person . . .

Graham Gerber? . . . Hymie Gerber? . . . Gerber Von Furstenberg?

Whoever, it had better turn out to *be* someone, someone who could make something *happen* around here. He doubted that anything would, but at least he'd have some dialogue to listen to, which was a lot better than thinking about Diane. He inched forward and let out a gentle fart, just to change his luck.

HE HAS SEEN YOU once as Howard. This will be his first shot at you as Teddy Stern. Don't be careless. Don't forget who you are. This is Mutual of Oklahoma you're playing to. This could be for all the marbles.

He went to the door and opened it, and Gerber's expression did not disappoint him. First bewilderment, then confusion, then puzzlement, then understanding, then curiosity, awe, wonder, and finally, acceptance.

Teddy held out his hand, smiling. "Don't tell me, let me guess. You're Marvin Gerber."

"That's me all right." The pudgy man shook Teddy's hand, still staring. "And you're Teddy Stern?" He sounded like he didn't quite believe it.

"What can I do about it? You can't win 'em all," Teddy said. "Come in, come in."

Teddy closed the door and ushered Gerber into the living room. "Can I get you a drink?"

"Nothing, thanks. Nothing."

"Then sit down and suffer while I refuel." He turned away from Gerber's searching gaze, went to the bar, and refilled his glass with Sauza Gold while Gerber sank into the club chair and lit a cigar.

"You don't mind, do you?" Gerber let a grayish-green cloud escape from his lips.

"The cigar? Hell no. Any stink is an improvement on the stink around here." Teddy held up his glass. "*À votre santé*, Marvin."

Gerber held up his cigar. "You too, Teddy."

"So." Teddy smiled at the man. "*Was ist los?*"

The insurance agent looked at him. "If I gave you the bug-eye just now, it's only because your brother neglected to mention that you two were twins."

"Oh, so you've *met* Howard."

"Indeed I have," said Gerber. "Your recording machine didn't leave my secretary time to give you much of a message, and when you called her back, I'm afraid all she was interested in was following my orders and pinning you down for a quick visit."

"And here I am, Mr. Gerber—"

"Marvin . . ."

"—Pinned down. Nailed to the wall. You've *got* me. Only trouble is, what've you got? Nothing."

"Nothing?" Gerber seemed undisturbed.

"You're Mutual of Oklahoma, no?"

"For over twenty years."

"And you're here to sell me some insurance, yes?"

"It's sort of the way I make my living," Gerber said. "But also, I enjoy meeting people, schmoozing."

"Can I save you a lot of time, and myself too?"

"Please do. You're a busy man, I'm sure."

"It's no cigar, Marvin. Blood from a stone. Brokesville, USA. You dig?"

Gerber smiled expansively. "What? You mean all Hollywood actors aren't rolling in cocaine?"

"Don't let this plush beach pad fool you. A gift from my brother . . . a loanout, I should say."

"You're a lucky fellow, Teddy. Not every man has a brother who really cares."

"Come on," Teddy grimaced. "It's a tax writeoff."

"I wasn't referring only to the house," Gerber said.

Teddy could feel the man's eyes studying him carefully for a reaction, so he gave it to him: *no* reaction, meaning Howard Bluestern has not breathed a word to his brother about the policy. "Hey, sure you won't have a drink?"

Gerber shook his head. "For me, alcohol and business don't mix—or should I say *no* business?"

Teddy eyed him and decided to move things along a little bit. "Why do I have this feeling that you didn't come here really to sell me insurance?" He took a deep drag on the tequila. "Something to do with Howard, right?"

Gerber blew a thick smokescreen into the room and ducked behind it. "You really put that stuff away, don't you?"

"The life of a modestly talented actor such as I am, Mr. Gerber . . . Marvin, forgive me . . . is made tolerable only by the ingesting of oceans of tequila. Which may be one of the reasons I live next to the ocean, the other reason being that the beach happens to be where Howard bought a tax shelter—or brother shelter, if you will."

"Not very good for your health." Gerber tapped his chest. "Direct from a man who lives by actuarial tables."

"You're wrong, Marvin. The beach is a twenty-four-hour round-the-clock spa."

"Not the beach, Teddy." Gerber pointed with his cigar. "The booze, the booze."

Teddy gave the man a big grin. "You're a hell of a one to talk. What do you think that *cigar* is doing to *you*?"

"Killing me," Gerber said. "But what's the difference? *I* don't have a brother who just took out a five-million-dollar life insurance policy and made *me* the beneficiary." He watched Teddy's face. "I don't have as much to live for as you, get what I mean?" He let Teddy's stunned expression grow and grow while he blew more smoke into the room.

"Five . . . million . . . dollars?"

Gerber nodded. "With double indemnity yet, which could mean a payout of ten mil."

Teddy stared at him. "Are you shitting me, Gerber?"

"If you tell a soul I mentioned this to you, especially your brother—"

"Then why *did* you?" Teddy sounded angry. "It's none of my fucking business."

"Boasting," Gerber said. "It's one of my weaknesses, like you and the bottle."

Teddy shook his head in wonderment, as though he still couldn't believe it. "You actually sold my brother a five-million-dollar policy and I'm the beneficiary?"

Gerber shrugged. "Would I be boasting about something I never even did?"

Teddy's lips tightened as he stared at the man. "I'm embarrassed. I don't know what I'm supposed to say. Goddam it, give me a straight answer now. What's the real reason you've come here and told me this?"

Gerber examined the cigar in his hand and addressed himself to it. "I thought it might make you feel good to know that your brother, who struck me as being kind of a cool cookie, secretly feels warm about *you* . . ."

"That doesn't sound like a real reason to me," Teddy said sharply. "Why would you care about making me feel good? I don't mean shit to you, and you know it, and I know it."

Gerber's voice remained calm. "I thought it might make you feel good to know something that he might never tell you, namely that you ain't gonna be out on your ass in the cold if he should one of these days God forbid pass on . . ."

"One of these—?" Teddy snorted preposterous laughter. "One of these days pass *on* . . . ?"

The insurance man eyed him. "You don't like the words . . . ?"

"You're still feeding me bullshit, Gerber."

"You'd rather I call it something else . . . ?"

"Bullshit . . ."

"How about leukemia? You like leukemia?"

"Love it," Teddy chortled. "Can't get enough of it."

"Tumor," Gerber said, watching him closely.

Teddy looked at him blankly.

"Tumor," Gerber said.

"I hear you," Teddy said. "Tumor what? What tumor?"

"Malignant," Gerber said.

"What tumor?"

"Your brother's . . ."

Teddy laughed.

"The one we found on the X rays . . ."

For a split second Teddy's heart sank, then quickly rose. *What* X rays? There hadn't *been* any . . .

". . . After the policy was approved."

And then he caught the shrewd, calculating look in Gerber's eyes and it was a dead giveaway, and his own laughter, bursting from his lips now, was genuine.

"You *laugh*. Don't you know that your brother is a dying man?" Gerber's voice flared with anger.

Teddy shook his head slowly, grinning.

"Don't you ever *see* each other?" Gerber said impatiently. "Don't you *talk*?"

"Sure we do." Teddy tried to wipe the grin from his face but it wouldn't go away, and he could see that the insurance man was getting irritated. He was overdoing it, he was getting carried away, he was enjoying the role *too* much. Cool it, Stern. "I gotta tell you, Marvin, you're terrific. I mean, I couldn't have done it better myself, and *I'm* the one who's supposed to be the actor . . ."

Gerber looked away, annoyed.

"You wanted to check out my reactions, right? You wanted to find out if I knew anything terrible about Howard that maybe your doctors had missed. Correct?"

"I'm not saying a word," Gerber muttered to the wall.

"What the hell are you looking so sad about?" Teddy said, with great cheer. "You should be *happy*, Marvin. I've got good news for you, pal. My brother, your client, your what-do-you-call-him, the *insured*, doesn't *believe* in passing on. He won't drink, he won't smoke, I don't think he even *fucks*. All he does is work and exercise, and exercise and work, which is why he's never even *met* the doctors *I've* supported for years. Why do you think I booze so much, Marvin? And *don't* get me started telling you about all the *ladies* I've laid in this town. Twins are strange animals. I'm trying to make up for all the bad health Howard will never have. I'm trying, and succeeding, in raising enough hell for the both of us. *Look* at me, for Christsake . . ."

"I don't have to look at you, I've already seen," Gerber said, turning to him finally. "You don't look so good."

"Howard looks and feels well enough for the two of us . . ."

"Maybe you oughta cut it out," Gerber said solemnly.

"What for? It's a great setup all around." Teddy drained the last of the tequila in his glass. "He's got the kind of life he wants, and I've got the kind I want."

Marvin Gerber stared at him with grave expression. "Maybe that's why your brother decided to say yes to this big policy. Maybe it's his way of . . . of repaying you for what you've done for *him* by . . . what you've done to yourself."

"You know what, Marvin? I think I'm getting a little too pissed to follow you any more. Why don't we continue this some other time?"

"It's pretty deep stuff," Gerber said, rising to his feet and immediately getting eased toward the foyer. "People think I just sell insurance, but actually I'm something of a psychologist, I really am."

"You really are," Teddy said, opening the front door to let him out. "You're a man of multifarious talents, Marvin . . ."

"But an actor I'm not," Gerber said with a wan smile as they shook hands.

"Multifarious," Teddy said and watched him walk down the path toward his car. Everything in the man's manner, the very expression on his face as he turned once to glance back at Teddy in the doorway, bespoke dispelled suspicion, an eased mind, mission accomplished. Marvin Gerber, Teddy told himself, would be driving away convinced that his company had insured the life of a man who had always been, and always would be, unsurpassingly fit. Which was accurate and true up to a point, the point being that right now, unfortunately, the man happened to be dead.

Teddy went to the kitchen and opened the refrigerator and moved some of the bottled beer and containers of orange juice around to make a little more room inside. Then he went out to the back porch, removed the padlock from the humming, rattling freezer and raised the lid. He took out Mrs. Mahoney's strippers, set them temporarily on the brick floor, pushed a few food packages aside, reached down and felt Howard's frozen form, covered him over again, lowered the lid of the freezer, replaced and locked the padlock, took the two strippers into the kitchen and placed them in the refrigerator. Then he wrote a note to Mrs. Mahoney and left it on the kitchen table: "Dear Mrs. M— I'm back (Monday), but won't be here when you come in tomorrow (Tuesday), so I left your strippers in the refrigerator for you. My brother tells me you were upset. I'm sorry. Have a nice day (Tuesday)— Yours, Mr. Teddy.''

Then he went inside to the bedroom, sat down heavily on the bed and began to take his clothes off, so that he could change back into Howard's. He was filled with a sense of the strangeness of the scene he had just played with Marvin Gerber—there had been so much of Howard in the air. As he got dressed now, he found himself with the eerie feeling that his brother was somehow in the room with him. For a moment, sitting there on the bed, he fancied that he could almost hear him breathing.

"MR. BLUESTERN's office."

"I'm leaving now," he said.

She lowered her voice. "How did it go?"

"When I see you. How's the coast?"

Jo Anne looked across the room. "Unclear."

"Clear it," he said.

"Just like that?"

"Just like that." He hung up.

Jo Anne got up from the desk and went over to where Diane McWorter was sitting. "I hate to have to tell you this," she said. "He just went into one of those executive meetings."

Diane's eyes glittered. "That's all right, I'll wait."

Jo Anne smiled ruefully. "I'm afraid he's not coming back, at least not today."

"Back?" Diane's face darkened. "From where?"

"Producers Association. In Hollywood."

"But how could—? I didn't even see—"

"He used his private elevator."

Diane stood up, glared at Jo Anne, then went past her to the closed door to the inner office and pushed it open. She took a few steps inside, glanced around, turned and came out.

"How about tomorrow?" Jo Anne said, watching her.

"How about *forget it*?" Diane snapped as she hurried outside toward the pay phone at the end of the carpeted corridor.

The damned recording machine answered, with Howard Bluestern's rotten impersonation of Teddy, who did he think he was kidding? She hung up and tried again, then finally gave up. Obviously Bruce had left. Either he had left, or had never been there. Never been there? Where had *that* sickening thought come from? Better not be. Better be that he *had* been there and had left, with something vital to tell her.

She was in a terrible mood now as she went down in the elevator to get a cab. Howard Bluestern could do that to her, even without

171

seeing her or talking to her. The mere fact that he had left his office without her knowing it was enough to make her furious. She needed a drink now, a stiff one, to smooth her anger. Also, she needed to celebrate, ahead of time, all the important discoveries that Bruce Gottesman had surely made and was going to tell her about when they met back at her apartment. He'd better . . .

THE LITTLE YELLOW PORSCHE took the coast highway at seventy-five without a murmur. Jo Anne had retrieved it for him from valet parking at LAX the first thing in the morning, and he had loved her for doing it. No one had ever spoiled him like that before. The more he thought about it the faster he drove, because he couldn't wait to get back to her and be spoiled some more. He glanced in the rear-view mirror again. Still no highway patrol on his tail. But the red Datsun hatchback about fifty yards behind him was keeping pace with him no matter how fast he went, and for one crazy instant he had the wild notion that it was Diane following him until he suddenly remembered that she had just been camped outside his office at the studio, and then he saw that a lone *guy* was driving the car and dismissed the idea with a little shake of his head.

When he reached the parking lot on the beach where the Bentley was waiting, he pulled up beside it and locked up the Porsche. And once inside the *big* car, with the gray worsted suit, the Turnbull & Asser˙shirt and the foulard tie back in their natural habitat, he felt whole again, he even felt up to running the big studio he was heading for now. Too bad nepotism had gone out of style in Hollywood. Sound business judgment told him that Howard Bluestern should be urging Casting to give serious consideration to the acting talents and star potential of one Teddy Stern. Purely on the basis of his most recent performance, playing the difficult role of himself, the guy was obviously on the come.

NO NEED to follow him any farther. He had seen all he wanted to see from right here in front of the pizza joint, across the highway from the parking lot. He had seen Bluestern make the switch from the Porsche to the Bentley and drive off. And he had *heard* enough too, back there under the bed. None of it had surprised him. It had all made too much sense to surprise him, especially the stuff about the insurance policy. All he had to figure out now was what to do with his newfound knowledge, and whether to reveal all of it or none of it to Diane.

If he kept the information to himself and played his cards right, he wouldn't have to cut her in, and he'd never need *her* or anyone else ever again. Only trouble was, he really didn't have enough of a stake to go it on his own yet. He still needed her car, he needed her apartment. His furnished room wouldn't do. And the little over a grand in his pocket was only good for openers. Why couldn't anything be easy? The minute you went for anything larger than nickels and dimes, problems.

Suddenly he was hungry, and not just for a big pizza either. He was filled with a ravenous appetite for all the things he had never had, beautiful, elegant, unobtainable women, a sleek, well-cared-for body, a dazzling white smile, fine clothes, a big car. He was going to have them all. A hunger like *he* had *had* to be fed. He went inside the joint, sat down at the counter, and ordered the most expensive pizza in the place and a bottle of beer to go with it. Then he got down to work.

Okay. Number one. No doubt about it any longer, Bluestern was posing as his dead brother.

Two. The guy was halfway home on a five-million-dollar insurance scam. All he had to do was turn his part-time impersonation of Teddy Stern into a lifetime habit and convince the insurance company that the body in question was Howard Bluestern.

Number three was so fucking obvious it was ridiculous. There was going to be an accident, something grotesque and messy where the corpse would be hardly identifiable.

Number four was a question: How was he going to do it? A car crash? Possible, but difficult to pull off. Burn the house to the ground with the body in it? Not bad, not bad.

Number five: When? Good question. No answer. Probability? Bluestern would keep the stiff on ice until his preparations were complete and he was ready to make his move.

Conclusion: Let Bluestern go on thinking that his double life was a big secret and that a freezer with a lock on it was a vault filled with gold. Meanwhile, don't sit there stuffing your face. It could be later than you think. Get moving. There were two options. There was the Gerber guy at the insurance company, and there was Bluestern. Decide which direction to go for the biggest payoff, under the safest conditions, in the least amount of time, and *take* it. If you have to use Diane, use her. If you don't, don't. But get smart, for Christsake. For once in your life, get smart.

He eased his big body off the stool. "Can I have the check, please?"

MARVIN GERBER could have reached his office long ago, but Marvin Gerber was in no hurry. He was busy thinking. He was busy thinking about the swift reversal in his fortunes this day, a day that had started out with typical Gerber bad luck. Now, suddenly, everything had come up sevens and elevens, and it was a phenomenon not to be ignored.

Before calling on Teddy Stern, he had gone into the company's computer room and asked the Medical Information Bureau in Greenwich, Connecticut, to give him whatever they had on one Howard Bluestern, knowing full well that Mutual's medical department had already done that as a matter of course. Gerber had not been at all surprised when MIB had responded on the screen before him with the information that Bluestern was one of about two hundred million Americans about whom the Bureau had no medical records whatsoever.

It figures, Gerber had sourly noted to himself.

Then Gerber had tapped a few more keys and hooked into the Retail Credit Company of Atlanta, Georgia. He hadn't known exactly what he'd been hoping to find out. He knew they'd have *something* on Howard Bluestern. They had something on just about *everybody* who used credit, and after all, who in America didn't use credit? So back had come a nice fat report on Howard Bluestern. Naturally, everything RCC had had to say about him had been favorable, give or take a couple of divorces.

Naturally. The Gerber luck.

And so, as he made the long drive now from Malibu to his office on the Miracle Mile, Gerber had much to think about, and he was giving himself the time in which to do it. Sitting behind the steering wheel of his car with the windows closed, driving nice and slowly in the right-hand lane, he was working on a mathematical problem without the aid of his office calculator. He was trying to figure out what the odds were against Marvin Gerber having anything in his professional life go as perfectly as the meeting with the actor fellow had just gone. He had run every moment of that meeting through his mind over and over again—every word, every inflection, every gesture, every look, every pause, every question, every answer—and nowhere, not once, with the exception of a few momentary ego problems of his own, had he been able to find anything said or done, or unsaid and not done, that had not been pleasing to his cause.

Usually when Gerber embarked on one of his investigatory operations, when he set out to manipulate people by using his private psychological tools to get them to reveal more than they wanted to reveal, he came away with a mixed bag of successes and failures, little wins, big wins, little losses, big losses. But never—and Gerber had been at it almost half his lifetime—never had Gerber come away from such a meeting where the other person had not only said everything that Gerber could have hoped and prayed he would say but had actually given him much much more to be elated about than he could have ever imagined in his wildest dreams.

Gerber was not a man to take uniqueness lightly. Once in a lifetime had not happened many times to Gerber. In fact, it hadn't even happened once. And so, when he had an experience such as he had just had with this Teddy Stern, he wanted to savor it, to examine it, weigh it, analyze it, interpret it, understand it, turn it upside down, downside up, outside in, inside out, just to make sure that it was as perfect as it seemed to be, because sometimes you miss something, or you fool yourself a little, and also he wanted to make sure that it wasn't *better* than perfect, which was another way of saying *too* perfect, which was another way of saying not perfect at all.

Working with the only calculator he had, the one in his head, in a moving car, was not easy, no matter how slowly he drove, no matter how sparse the traffic was, because he still had to give some small part of his attention to not running anyone over or getting himself killed. So the best he finally came up with in the way of odds against Marvin Gerber having that kind of luck was a round number, and a man like Marvin Gerber, who dealt in life to the fourth decimal point, was never completely happy with round numbers, for anything.

However round this number may have been, it *did* have some value nevertheless. For even though he hadn't used the usual multiplier, what Gerber called the T factor—the typical average lifetime percentage of good luck over bad luck, which in Gerber's case was only eleven percent—even without the T factor thrown in, the round-number odds against Marvin Gerber having been fortunate enough to insure the one half of a pair of identical twins who would live to be two hundred, while the other half, his sole beneficiary, would be heading for an early grave, *instead of the other way around*, those odds turned out to be so astronomically high, *for Marvin Gerber*, that there could be only one conclusion to be drawn.

Too perfect.

Gerber let out an audible sigh. Finished business had suddenly gone back into business again. Usually he had warm feelings toward his friend, the calculator in his head. Now he found himself blaming it for the uneasiness that was creeping over him like a damp fog. He'd be glad when he reached the underground garage of the Mutual of Oklahoma building. Too much time alone in a car could be dangerous to your mental health. The Surgeon General should issue a warning.

Walking past his secretary into his office, he saw the policies waiting on his desk, all shiny and new, one for the studio and one for Howard Bluestern. The note from Stigman said: "As per your request, I rushed these through." Next time, don't be so obliging, Gerber muttered to himself. The whole world was in too much of a hurry, including Marvin Gerber.

He picked up the phone and asked Madeline to get him Bluestern's secretary. And when the girl finally came on the line he said, "Would you tell him, please, that I have something for him, to give him in person, that will make him very happy? Five minutes at the most is all I'll need."

She told Gerber to hold on for a moment, then came back to him and said if he could get there in about an hour, she would squeeze him in.

"Thank you, you're very kind," Gerber said. He remembered her blue eyes. She was a nice girl. Attractive. He stuck with the homely ones, like Madeline. He had enough troubles.

His buzzer sounded.

"There's a Bob Gehringer out here to see you," Madeline said. "No appointment. He says it's important."

"Bob Gehringer? Never heard of him."

"I asked him what it was about, but he said he preferred to discuss it with you in private."

"What do you think?"

"Unh uh," Madeline said.

"Send him in," Gerber said. That'll teach her to be homely. "But see that I'm out of here in fifteen minutes."

Gerber didn't like men who were tall *and* fat. He also didn't like men with long blond hair who smelled of sweat. Aside from that, he couldn't find anything else to dislike about his visitor. But that was only in the first second or two.

"Sit down, Mr. Gehringer."

"All right, I will."

Gerber watched the man squeeze his big body into a chair that would have been adequate for anyone else. "What can I do for you?" Gerber said.

"Nothing. It's the other way around, Mr. Gerber."

Gerber eyed the stranger with distaste. "If you're looking for insurance, you've come to the right man. If you're looking for a job, you're wasting your time."

"Actually, sir, I'm not looking for anything." Bruce tried to smile without showing his teeth. "*You're* looking for *me*."

A wisenheimer. "What do I want with *you*? Ask you who does your hair? Find out who your diet counselor is?"

"I figure you're in the market for a private investigator . . ."

"Oh, I see," Gerber said. "Not a public one, a private one, right?"

"Correct," Bruce said. "And now you have found yourself the right one."

"I should be congratulated. This is my lucky day."

"Congratulations, sir."

"Thank you," Gerber said. "Is it all right for me to ask why I'm in the market for a private investigator?"

"Certainly. A private investigator can give you private information that could be tremendously valuable to you and your company."

"And you think I am in need of such information."

"I think you are, sir, and I think you think so too."

Gerber didn't like the feeling that was creeping into the pit of his stomach. He hoped it was indigestion. "What sort of private information are we talking about, Mr. Gehringer?"

"The kind that would save this company from having to pay out five million dollars in the near future, maybe even ten."

It wasn't indigestion.

Gerber stared at the man. "Mutual of Oklahoma prides itself on how much money it disburses every year to its policyholders. What's another five or ten million dollars?"

The big man shrugged. "That's up to you."

"Not just me. It's up to God too," Gerber said.

"Anyway, I thought maybe you'd be interested in saving the five or ten million, but I could be wrong."

Gerber watched him in silence for a moment. "Who *are* you?"

"Me? Nobody, sir."

"Are you by any chance related to *Charley* Gehringer?"

"Who's he?"

"You never heard of Charley Gehringer of the Detroit Tigers, one of the all-time greats?"

"I got a better one than that," Bruce Gottesman said. "I never even heard of Bob Gehringer."

"Oh," Gerber blinked rapidly. "I see." He didn't like this conversation. He was beginning to despise himself for continuing it. "I'm a little on the busy side right now. What do you want?"

"I already told you, it's you who wants, and I've got it . . . for two hundred thousand dollars in cash."

Gerber chuckled mirthlessly. "Would fifty dollars do?"

"Yes or no, Gerber?"

"Yes or no *what*?" His anger with himself was getting the better of him. "I don't know what the hell you're talking about."

"Oh yes you do."

"What kind of fish are you selling? Either tell me or get out and stop bothering me."

"I already told you all I'm going to tell you, and you know fucking well what I'm talking about, and it's going to cost you two hundred grand."

Gerber grabbed the phone and buzzed his secretary. "Would you have the security police sent up here right away?"

"You don't have to, I'm leaving." The big man struggled out of the chair.

"Never mind, Madeline."

"A waste of time. I never should have come here . . ."

"Go get yourself a haircut," Gerber muttered.

"I gave you a chance and you muffed it," Bruce said on his way to the door.

"I muffed it and you bluffed it," Gerber said.

"He made a fool of you this morning, and you're *still* a fool . . ."

Gerber glanced up. "Who did?"

"Fuck you, Gerber."

"Wait a minute. . . . Who did?"

But the big man was already out of the office.

Gerber struggled to his feet and moved on his stiff legs as quickly as he could and went past Madeline's desk out to the corridor. The hallway was empty, the elevator was gone.

He hurried inside to Madeline. "Call downstairs. Tell them to see if they can get the license plate of that man who just left."

"I *told* you not to see him."

"Do as I say!"

He went back to his office and sank down at his desk. His hands were shaking a little, and the back of his shirt was soaked with perspiration. Sure he had acted hastily, but what were you supposed to do? You didn't *do* business with scum like that one. You didn't even let them into the building. Usually their craziness came in the mail or over the phone, crank letters, accusations, tips, squealing on friends and relatives, and anonymous, always anonymous. Never had Gerber had one of them in his office. And it wasn't bad enough that he had had to see him and smell him. Now he was going to have to *think* about him too.

Whatever the man knew or didn't know—probably nothing but wild guesses, stabs in the dark, like all of them—there must have been *some* connection between him and the only person on this earth other than Marvin Gerber who knew that Marvin Gerber had private worries about the Bluestern policy.

Teddy Stern.

He hadn't told another soul of his misgivings, not even his wife. Only Teddy Stern.

The big man who had just left had to be a friend or acquaintance of Teddy Stern's, and he could only have hit so close to home if Stern had told him the gist of the meeting at the beach house, and Stern would have had to have done that almost immediately after Gerber had left.

Or maybe the man had been *in* the house while Gerber was there. Maybe the man had been in the next room, and had overheard their whole conversation, and was trying to make something out of it for himself by throwing this ridiculous scare into Gerber.

Maybe he was a plumber, or an electrician, or a telephone repairman who happened to have been working there at the time.

Or maybe it was actually—no, no, what an awful thing to think. . . . Still, hadn't the actor said Brokesville, USA?

Maybe it was Teddy Stern himself, trying to cash in on Gerber's worries through an intermediary.

Marvin Gerber felt ashamed of himself for having advertised his inner anxieties so blatantly this morning out at the beach. It had left him wide open to the vultures, and made him a laughingstock. The disgusting fat man with the dirty blond hair had treated him with outrageous lack of respect. And if he couldn't stop worrying *now*, the least he could do would be to learn to hide it better in the future.

He would try to make a new beginning for himself when he called Teddy Stern. Like it or not, he *was* going to have to talk to the actor again today.

But not now.

First he had to pay a visit to the other one, the other half of the perfectly matched pair.

He picked up the Howard Bluestern policy from his desk and tucked it in the breast pocket of his suit jacket. It would be good therapy for him to deliver the policy to Bluestern personally, and right now he needed therapy badly. It would give him a chance to feel the grip of the man's vigorous hand, please God, and look him over again. After all, he had laid eyes on the studio head only that one time, the morning of the physical. And besides, it always made Gerber feel good to sit with someone whose life he had insured for a lot of money. At least while you were sitting with him, you knew he was alive.

He heard the buzzer, and picked up the phone.

"He was driving a Datsun hatchback," Madeline said.

"Did they get the number?"

"Yes. It's—"

"Give it to someone in Vehicular and have them call the DMV in Sacramento right away. I want the registration."

"Yes, Mr. Gerber."

He hung up and stared out of the window with unseeing eyes.

Two hundred thousand dollars . . .

For what?

Ridiculous.

Cranks . . . all of them . . .

He hoped.

chapter

17

THE FIRST THING Teddy did when he finally got to the studio was fill Jo Anne in on Marvin Gerber's fishing expedition in Malibu, giving her a short synopsis. He would have given her the longer version, a word-by-word, but they spent too much time on the sofa kissing each other and making other more intimate forms of maddening contact.

"Why can't I keep my hands off you?" he groaned.

"Because you're rude, you've got no manners," she murmured.

"You're coming home to Bel Air with me tonight, do you know that?"

"To do what?"

"Talk, plan, decide how, when, and where. It's going to happen this weekend—I've made up my mind—right after I get back from New York."

She drew back from him slightly. "New York . . ."

He nodded.

"You're actually going?"

"Yes," he said.

She looked away. "And we do it this weekend . . ."

"Yes," he said.

She glanced at him. "Why not tonight, or tomorrow night?"

"We're not prepared."

"Isn't there danger in delay?"

"Yes."

"Doesn't each hour increase the chances of someone finding out?"

"Yes."

"Then why New York, Teddy?"

His eyes met hers. "I've got to go."

"To confront Winthrop Van Slyke and a hostile board?"

"Yes."

"With all the additional risks you'll be taking there playing a role you've never played before?"

"I can handle it," he said.

She studied his face. "Why do you *want* to?"

"I'm not sure," he said slowly. "Frankly, I haven't thought it out, I've just felt it. I think it's because . . . I think maybe for Howard. I think Howard would have wanted to *face* those men, and go down, if he had to, fighting like a *son* of a bitch."

Jo Anne gazed at him for a long time without saying anything. "I'm in this too," she said.

"I couldn't do it without you," he said.

"And if it fails, it fails for me too."

"I know that," he said.

"But you're still going to New York."

"Not if you don't want me to," he said.

She turned away from him sharply. "That's not fair."

"Who said I was fair? You knew that when you came in with me. Would I be in this kind of thing if I were *fair?* And what about you? Would you be?"

"Maybe we should be out of it then," she said in a voice he could hardly hear.

"You don't mean that," he said.

"How do you know I don't?"

"Because I'm just beginning to understand what it's all about . . . for the both of us.".

She turned and looked at him. "I'm not at all sure. I wish I were, Teddy."

"Sure?" He shook his head. "Who's sure? That's asking too much, honey. In the beginning, it sort of *happened* to me, like an accident. At least that's what I told myself. Then, I found myself running with the ball out of sheer fear of being tackled, found out, mostly by you . . ."

"Me?"

"Well of *course* you," he said. "Then I began to believe that being filthy rich was the only way I could ever be secure for the rest of my life. And now . . . well . . . I've come to realize there'll never *be* a game like this one ever again, at least not for me, and just being *in* it, especially with you, is almost as exciting as winning it. Make sense?"

She nodded. "Yes."

"But could be a pile of self-delusion, huh?"

"Could be."

He shrugged. "All I know is, no one walks away from one like this, do they?"

"Not unless a more exciting one comes along," she said, eyeing him shrewdly. "Right, Teddy?"

He looked at her and nodded. "Okay. No argument. Now . . . what about you?"

"Me? I've been assuming it was all because of you . . . help you, protect you, be a part of you, sink or swim with you . . . that simple."

"Come on, honey."

"No?"

"No," he said. "I mean, not just that."

"Then?"

"For one thing," he said, "you've been a good girl all your life . . ."

"You should go to bed with me sometime."

"I'm not talking about that. Everybody's got that. But how many girls with your upbringing ever get a shot at larceny so grand it takes the breath away?"

She looked at him wide-eyed. "How did you *know* that?"

"And for another thing, you know damned well your folks would never be happy in that broken-down little shack you could get for two and a quarter *if* you could afford it and *if* the agent could get the price down from two seventy-five, which she can't, but five hundred, six hundred, seven hundred thousand? Oh what heaven for Mom and Dad."

"I could swear I never even discussed that with you . . . or did I?"

"You don't talk in your sleep, honey, but I do listen to you when you're awake, and sometimes I hear things you don't even say."

She gazed at him, and a smile slowly came to her face. "*Go* to New York, you bastard. I can't beat you."

He grinned. "And you won't jump the team?"

"I don't think so."

"Then we'll win, okay? With a field goal in the final two seconds."

"Take off your face mask and helmet," she said. "I want to kiss you."

And finally he had to kick her out of the office so that he could return Edgar Seligman's call and be ready for Jeff Barnett and Larry Hough when they arrived. And not to forget Marvin Gerber, who was probably already on the way.

He got through to Seligman and said, "What gives, Scotty?"

"Have a nice weekend, Howard?"

"Very restful. Borrowed my brother's beach house and spent two days and two nights reading four thousand scripts."

"You big shots, it serves you right," the lawyer said. "Howard, I've got news, very pleasing, but not surprising. The insurance policy has been approved, and has gone into effect."

"You mean I'm now worth more to the studio dead than alive?"

Seligman chuckled. "I hope not, or I'm selling my stock right now."

"What's the latest on Marty Wallach and Liam O'Toole?" Any conscientious studio head would want to know that.

"Off the lot, thank God. I'll probably hear from their attorneys before the day gives out. You want bulletins?"

"Absolutely not," Teddy said. "That's your shit. I've got my shit over here. And speaking of shit, how come you don't mention Stan Howe?"

"When I kiss someone's ass, I try to forget it," Seligman said. "First thing this morning. Done. But I wouldn't ask him for any favors for at least a couple of weeks if I were you."

"You have my undying gratitude," Teddy said.

"I can't even remember what you're talking about."

"Ciao," Teddy said. He hung up, and got buzzed immediately by Jo Anne.

"Two things," she said. "Barnett and Hough are here, and your machine at the beach got a call from Sam Kramer. He wants you to call him as soon as possible."

"I'll do that myself. Don't send in the clowns yet." He swiveled to the private phone and dialed his agent's private line. "Sammy baby? Teddy. You rang?"

"Don't Sammy baby *me*," Kramer snapped. "Where *are* you?"

"At the beach. What's up?"

"What did you do to Jud Fleming?"

"I didn't like his attitude, so I stuck it up his ass."

"Who told you to do *that?*"

"I don't have to be told, Sam."

"Yeah? Well, he's dumping all over me. He's not gonna use *any* of my clients, not just you, none of them. He's gonna have me barred from the lot. You hear what I'm saying? You wanna turn down a job, you turn down a job, you don't *insult* the man, you don't go to your brother and have him *humiliate* the guy in public. Have you lost your mind if you ever had one . . . ?"

"Hey, wait a minute. Don't you even wanna hear what happened?"

"No, I don't wanna hear what happened. I *know* what happened. I know what *you* told your brother happened, I know what Fleming says *didn't* happen. You fucked me, Teddy, you really fucked me. You and your brother, the pair of you, you're crazy, the two of you, crazy . . ."

"Sam, will you stop it? What do you want me to do? You want me to take the job?"

"You couldn't *get* the job now . . ."

"You want me to apologize to him, is that what you want me to do?"

"Not you, not you . . . *Howard*."

"*Howard* should apologize to Jud Fleming?"

"*Yes*."

"Come on, Sam."

"I mean it. You owe it to me, Teddy. You fucked me good, you and your brother . . ."

"What did Howard do to Fleming?"

"Ask him, just ask him. And then tell him he's gotta apologize . . . for *me*."

"Jesus, Sam."

"I mean it, Teddy. I want you to do this for me, I want you to call Howard—"

"You know how I like to ask him for favors . . ."

"Don't give me any of that, just do it, do it."

"All right, goddam it."

"Now?"

"I'll *call* him now, but I can't guarantee that he'll do it *this minute*. Jesus Christ, Sam."

"I'm gonna hang up now so you can call him."

"Go ahead, hang up."

Kramer hung up. So did Teddy and got to his feet, feeling the sweat rolling down his back.

What did you do to Fleming, Howard? How can you make so much trouble? Don't you know that you're dead? Are you listening to me, Howard? Are you going to do what I say? I want you to call Jud Fleming and make nice with him.

Now?

Yes, right now.

If you say so.

Thank you, Howard. You've become so obliging lately.

Do I have any choice?

Fortunately, Fleming was down on the stage getting ready for a take, so there wasn't much time for anything more than a gritting of the teeth and a getting to the points. Point one: Howard Bluestern had been totally inebriated and on too many painkillers Friday night and deeply regretted anything his errant tongue might have said to Fleming while his head had been out to lunch. Accepted. Point two: Howard Bluestern was mulling over possible directors for an upcoming film called *Legerdemain*. Would Fleming like to come over and have lunch with him sometime next week, or would he still be shooting?

The suspicion was palpable through the phone. "You don't really mean that, Howard, do you?"

"Please, Jud, I do."

"I don't know what to say."

"How about yes . . . unless you're too busy, or not interested?"

"Of course I'm interested, and we finish shooting Friday."

"Then call me sometime next week."

"Jesus, Howard . . . I'm . . . really . . ."

"*Call* me."

"I will, I will. Give Teddy a hello for me, huh?"

"Consider it done," Teddy said and hung up.

Sometime next week?

Howard should live so long.

But right now, he was still on his feet and there could be no letdown, not until the final scene was in the can and it was a wrap.

He went to the door, opened it and said, "Okay, fellows," and backed out of the way to let Howard's executive assistants in out of the jungle.

They flopped down at each end of the sofa, full of bounce and wearing fresh suntans.

"Don't get too comfortable," Teddy said, remaining standing. "This isn't going to take long."

"Who says we're comfortable?" Larry Hough said.

"Oh? Trouble?" They should know what *real* trouble was.

"Wallach and O'Toole," Jeff Barnett said. "They're spreading it around that we stabbed them in the back."

"As though we'd do such a thing." Hough's pudgy face quivered with righteous indignation. "It was right in the belly."

"No, Lawrence," Barnett corrected him. "Just below the rib cage."

They cackled in unison.

"Can I get serious?" Teddy said.

"You think we're not serious?"

"I have to be in New York Thursday."

There was an immediate silence in the room.

"Winthrop Van Slyke and the whole goddam board of American Foods have invited me to come there and get down on my knees and explain why they shouldn't say no to the whole slate I presented for the fall and winter. Six, count 'em, six."

Barnett and Hough exchanged glances, but said nothing.

"What I'd like you both to do is get together immediately, examine the projects in detail, predict every possible attack the board can take against each one, and prepare for me, in writing, a bewilderingly clever and overwhelmingly convincing defense against each and every criticism."

Jeff Barnett looked questioningly at Larry Hough. "You?"

Hough demurred. "You."

"Howard," Barnett adjusted his tinted glasses as he rose to his feet. "We already *have* gotten together, we already *have* examined the packages, in the *greatest* of detail, Saturday at my pool, Sunday at Larry's, and you're going to have to believe me when I say that the fact that *we* had, as you know, nothing whatsoever to do with your choices has nothing to do *now* with how we both feel . . ."

Teddy's lips tightened. "Go ahead, I'm listening."

"One word," Jeff Barnett said. "Indefensible."

Teddy's expression did not change. "All six?"

"Losers," Barnett said.

"All six," Teddy said.

"Total disasters," Barnett said.

Teddy looked down at the chunky assistant on the sofa. "Larry?"

"Total," Hough said with sadness.

Teddy nodded. "You two are terrific," he said quietly, beginning to pace. "I mean it sincerely. I don't deserve you, but thank God I've got you. And here's what *you've* got. You've got two days—three days including today—and I mean, if you have to have Ziggy *barred from the Polo Lounge* in order to get his undivided attention, and Sue Mengers *locked out of Ma Maison*, and Stan Kamen locked *in* his office, I want you to come back to me with six packages, firm deals *closed*, subject to board approval, *six winners*—the property, the director, one or two stars—projects so hot that TWA will be afraid to let me bring them aboard the plane. Am I asking for the impossible?"

Barnett looked at Hough, then back to Teddy. "The difficult we do today, the impossible we do the day before yesterday. Lawrence?"

Larry Hough sprang from the sofa. "Coming, Mother."

"If you need me, holler," Teddy said. "Night and day."

"You are the one," sang Barnett as they hurried out.

Teddy saw Marvin Gerber waiting for him outside.

Jesus, the action. Nonstop, crazy. Crazier yet, he was beginning to like it a little.

He ushered the insurance man in, traded a few insincere pleasantries with him, and immediately felt the full bore of Gerber's probing eyes X-raying him for telltale signs of terminal states. For an instant Teddy felt resentment at the implied criticism of what had been his finest hour as an actor this morning, but he quickly pulled himself together and countered the radiation with the thick lead wall of his own highly visible vitality and keyed-up excitement. Gerber had no place else to go with his X-ray machine, so he turned it off and finally got around to making an effusive presentation of the insurance policy, never for a moment, of course, taking his eyes off Howard Bluestern lest he miss some slight nuance of unhealthiness that could feed his sleepless nights and spoil his days too.

Teddy decided that the least he could do for the man was show him the courtesy of removing the document from its plastic envelope, unfold it, and look it over, and otherwise accord it all the interest and appreciation that any normal, grateful person would display upon realizing that, in his hands, he was holding his first ten million—which, they say, is the hardest. But not to overdo it, Teddy tossed the policy aside into the general mess on his desk and flashed a little smile at the watching Gerber. "So much for that," he said.

"You make the pictures, that's *my* production," Gerber said proudly.

"Except movies are a crapshoot," Teddy said. "Whoever heard of an insurance company losing money?"

Gerber leaned forward and knocked wood on the desktop.

Teddy glanced at his wristwatch.

Gerber let the gesture pass and remained seated. "By the way, I had the pleasure of meeting your brother," he said casually, and Teddy could feel watchful eyes on him waiting for a reaction.

"Teddy?" *He* could be even more casual.

"Yes."

"When was that?"

"As a matter of fact, this morning."

"This morning? Impossible. He's out of town."

"No he isn't, Mr. Bluestern. He's at his house out in Malibu."

"Not that I doubt your word, Mr. Gerber. Excuse me a moment." He picked up the phone. "Jo Anne, would you get me my brother please?" He heard her astonished silence. "Yes, at the house." He hung up and turned to Gerber. "What did he *want* with you?"

"He didn't call me, I called *him*," Gerber explained. "I went out there to see if maybe I couldn't sell my wares to him too, sort of cover both sides of the family coin."

The man was not a bad liar. A little careless, but pretty slick. "What am I, heads or tails?"

"Definitely heads, Mr. Bluestern. You bought."

The buzzer sounded. Teddy picked up the phone and heard Jo Anne say, "Do you want him to be in?"

"Yes," he said. Then, jovially: "Teddy? When did you get back? . . . Oh, I see. How did it go? . . . Good, good. . . . No, I just—I didn't know you were back, that's all. I'm sitting here with Mr. Marvin Gerber. . . . Exactly. . . . The brother is always the last one to know . . ."

Gerber raised his hand. "Can I interrupt?"

"Hold it, Teddy." He turned to Gerber.

"Could you ask him how long he's going to be there? I'd like to speak to him."

Okay, so you're going to talk to Teddy Stern again. I don't give a shit. If Howard Bluestern can handle you, so can his brother, *four* times a day if necessary.

"Teddy, Mr. Gerber is going to call you. Will you be there? . . . Uh huh . . . Uh huh . . . I'll ask him. . . ." To Gerber: "He was just going out the door. Will you be in your office this afternoon?"

"Until six," Gerber said.

"Until six," Teddy said to Jo Anne, who was listening silently. "Okay, kiddo. Glad you're back. Gotta run. . . . You too." He hung up and said to Gerber, "He'll phone you."

"Thank you," the insurance man said. A frown came to his face. "Mr. Bluestern, I'm afraid I . . . uh . . . owe you an apology . . ."

"Really?"

"With your brother . . . I don't know exactly how it happened. . . . It just sort of slipped out in the conversation."

Teddy gave him a look and held it for a couple of beats. "You mean about the policy?"

Gerber nodded, shamefaced.

"I would have told him eventually anyway," Teddy said easily.

"Which should have been your prerogative. I'm really embarrassed . . ."

"Will you stop it?"

"For what it's worth to you, I've got to tell you he was touched, really touched. He thinks the world of you."

"Well, I think the world of *him*, even if I don't always wear it on my sleeve." He knew Gerber was leading to *something*. All he could do was wait for the cue.

"Pity he doesn't follow your example," Gerber said.

"Teddy? He doesn't want to be a deskbound executive like me."

"I mean healthwise," Gerber shook his head sadly. "You could do him a favor, if you'll pardon my saying so."

"How?"

"Send him to your personal physician."

"I don't *have* a personal physician." There . . . you like?

"Not even one?"

"Not even one," Teddy said.

"Then how about a former one?"

"No got," Teddy said. "Sorry."

"Which proves my point," Gerber said, feeling the pleasant glow he had been hoping for. "If you could get him to live more like *you* live . . ."

"I've tried," Teddy said, and shrugged. "It's his life though. As for me," he glanced at his wristwatch again. "I don't know what's so healthy about being as busy as *I* am today." He took the life insurance policy from the desk and held it up. "Sure you don't want this back?"

Gerber smiled. "Not me. I like to live dangerously, betting on Type A high risks like you. Why do you think I got *into* this business?"

"So *that's* it." Teddy rose to his feet.

Gerber got up too, glad to be quitting while he was ahead, and he definitely was. He felt so much better now than when he had arrived. Somehow Bluestern aroused more confidence than his actor brother had, particularly in corroborating the stuff about no doctors. Stern had made it sound like a pitch, like he had been *selling* it to Gerber. Here, Bluestern had been totally unimpressed with his own unique health record. Remarkable how much the two could look alike and yet be so different in so many ways.

They shook hands at the door. "Again, many thanks, Mr. Bluestern."

"And thank *you*," Teddy gestured with a thumb over his shoulder, "for you know what."

"Wear it in good health," Gerber said, smiling.

Teddy closed the door and walked back to his desk wondering if the man would ever give up. Would he never get tired of playing his circuitous little games? Teddy had given him his best shot twice today, first as himself, and now as Howard, and it still hadn't been enough. He was still going to have to come through with a call to Gerber's office later in the afternoon and be ready to ad lib his way through whatever the scene called for.

When it came to men you could cheat and defraud easily, Marvin Gerber, it struck him, was not as reliable as one could wish for.

The door opened and Jo Anne came in. "What was *that* little phone game about?"

He told her.

She saw his troubled expression and tried to brush it away with her lips, but it didn't work. "Darling, we have larger problems ahead of us than Mr. Gerber, believe me."

He looked up at her. "How do you mean?"

"Some material the research department dug up for me—for that new crime series, of course, the one you're considering for next season? . . ."

"Of course."

"A book called Gradwohl's *Legal Medicine* . . ."

"It'll never make a musical."

". . . And a whole file on Brancusi."

"The sculptor?"

"Anthony J.," she said. "Chief Coroner of Los Angeles County."

He grimaced. "And you've been reading this?"

"Browsing through it, while *you've* been wasting your time running this company."

"Somebody's got to," he said.

"Why?" she said sharply. "This studio is going to die for you forever in a few days."

He looked away. "I'm just trying to be a credible Howard, that's all."

She didn't say anything, but her silence did.

"Lay off me, will you, honey?" he said. "Not now."

She came closer and held him. "You and I are going to have to do some homework tonight, darling."

"What do you think I've been thinking about all afternoon?"

"I mean the research," she said. "You're going to have to play catch up and do a quick study. Then I'll test you."

"That's not exactly what I had in mind."

"I know what you had in mind." She gave him a squeeze. "I did too, and I still do. If you leave now and get to work, there'll be time for everything."

He smiled at her. "Trying to get rid of me?"

"Uh huh. Go home. I'll join you later."

"I'll tell David to take the night off, and we'll raid the icebox."

"I've already told him," she said.

"You've got a hell of a nerve," he said.

"So do you, darling. Wait'll you read the research."

chapter

18

WHERE in the name of God *was* he?

She tried to feel anger, but she was too tired for that. She was way past anger now.

She had felt so *terrific* when she had gotten back to the apartment, not even *remembering* the foul mood Howard had put her in, feeling so *great* after a few drinks, looking *forward* to seeing Bruce, *knowing* that he had uncovered something *lifesaving*, *knowing* that he wouldn't let her down, how *could* he, for God's sake, when she needed a *miracle*, who *else* was she going to turn to to help her out of the mess she was in? If he knew how serious it was for her. . . . But she didn't *trust* him to know. How could she? It was bad enough that she had to *lean* on a man like that, a scavenger, a loser, but to tell him that she had killed Teddy? Never . . .

Where the hell could he *be?*

The interminable wait had all but destroyed her. The edge had worn off. She had been alone for too many hours. She had had too much time to think. Too many times the true hopelessness of her plight had come through to her in sudden unwanted flashes of insight, and the drinking wasn't working any longer, it wasn't doing anything to make the truth go away, it was just making her more and more tired, until finally there was nothing more she could do than go into the bedroom and lie down on the bed and hope that she would fall asleep, or better yet, die . . .

THE SUIT CARRIER had been easy. He had quickly found a big chocolate-brown vinyl one at Sears Roebuck with red, green, and tan stripes on it, large enough for three suits or one frozen body, depending on what kind of trip you had in mind. The portable ice carriers had been easy to find too. He had bought six of those. But the freezer had been another matter, not so simple.

Sears had a large walk-in Kelvinator that would have been perfect, but it was a floor model, for display only, with a ten-day delivery date. The hundred-dollar bill he had flashed at the salesman had gotten him nothing more than a polite suggestion that he try Carlson's, only a few blocks away on 5th Street. So he had gone to Carlson's.

They didn't have the walk-in Kelvinator. However, they did have an immense horizontal GE on sale, four by eight and plenty deep, with no trays or anything else to get in the way of the body. Best of all, they had been willing to guarantee turning it over to a shipper for delivery by noon the next day. He had paid for it in cash out of Diane's thousand, and now he was on his way back to the apartment, with the vinyl suit carrier and the portable ice buckets in the back of the car. He'd wait until the freezer was installed before he bought the dry ice or made the trip down to the Majestie Meat Company on South Robertson in LA.

Diane was going to be pissed off at his lateness, he knew that. But what had to be done had had to be done. And how could he have known that the insurance guy was going to turn out to be such a total bust? It had seemed like a smart move, quick, clean, and without the need to cut Diane in. Even now he didn't regret it, because if he hadn't even made a stab at Gerber, how would he ever have known what might have been? Now he knew, and the answer was nothing. And with that out of the way, now he was moving in the *right* direction.

Before Howard Bluestern could successfully go through with his scam, he'd have to be coming across with a huge ransom to Bruce Gottesman first. That's what Bruce reminded himself to psych himself for Diane as he pulled her car into her underground parking space. He hoped she wouldn't be too unmanageable now. He was going to try not to tell her any more than he had to. He wanted no arguments, no conflicts. His own mind was made up. Why stir up trouble with her now, before it was really necessary? She'd know everything soon enough, when the big stuff arrived at her apartment tomorrow. By then he'd know how to handle her. She wasn't easy.

He placed the vinyl suit carrier and the portable ice buckets in the storage cabinet near her parking area. Then he went up in the elevator and rang the front-door buzzer, pushing aside the flicker of anger at her for not letting him have his own key. There was no answer, so he held the button again for a long one this time.

Finally he heard the chain and then he heard the lock and then the door opened and he saw her standing there, staring at him. She was in a blouse and skirt and no shoes, and her face looked all rumpled and mascara-stained, as though she'd been crying or something. He waited for her to yell at him. Instead she said quietly in a dull, flat voice, "Oh, it's you."

"Did you think I got lost?" he said lamely as he went inside.

"I thought maybe you stole my car. I wouldn't put it past you." Her voice sounded weary.

He decided to put her on the defensive. She deserved it anyway. "Why didn't you warn me that he was coming?" he said testily. "I don't know *how* I escaped getting caught. You were supposed to warn me."

"So he went there," she said, without interest.

"Yes. What happened?"

"He was smarter than I was. It's a boring story." She walked away from him to the living room.

"Where are you going?"

"Get another drink."

He followed her inside. "Have you been doing a lot of drinking?"

"What do you *think* I've been doing here waiting for you . . . baking a cake?"

He watched her pour a lot of bourbon into a highball glass and her hand wasn't steady. He didn't like the way she sounded. He'd have to be careful. She could give him big trouble. And be a weak link too. He didn't like that.

"I don't want anything," he said, though she hadn't offered him anything.

"You know where it is," she said. She took her drink over to the sofa and sat down and looked at him. "All right, I'm waiting."

"Look, you're not being very friendly," he said.

"Who said we're friends?" she said. "Friends don't take two hundred dollars before they'll do a friend a favor and then insist on another thousand in expenses before they'll do another. We're not friends. We've got a business arrangement. So tell me. How's business?"

"Jesus, you must've gotten out of the wrong side of the bed . . ."

"Better than getting *into* bed, if you know what I mean."

"What are you complaining about? You came twice. I didn't get off once."

"You want a refund?"

He sat down on the sofa next to her and put his feet on the coffee table.

"Take your feet off my furniture. Do you mind?"

Shaking his head slowly, he removed his feet.

She looked at him. "Well?"

"What do you want to know first?" he said.

"Did you find out anything?"

He swallowed. "No."

"Nothing?"

"Nothing."

She looked away for a while, then turned her gaze back to him. Her lips quivered. He thought maybe she was going to cry, but she didn't. "Where have you been all day?" she said.

"Most of the time out at the beach house," he said. "Where did you think I was?"

"Then what?" She stared at him with her tired, piercing brown eyes.

"There's a hell of a lot of traffic on the highway, you know . . ."

"So?"

"And I had to have lunch. Everything takes time . . ."

"This is taking time too . . . too much. And after lunch . . . ?"

"I had to do some shopping."

"Shopping?"

"In Santa Monica . . ."

"For what?"

"Some things we're going to need." He squirmed in his own sweat. "You'll know all about it in due time. Just don't worry, I've got everything under control. I've got some ideas."

"I'll bet you do, and they're all going to cost me money, right?"

"Jesus, I'm all sweaty . . ."

She took a long pull on her bourbon, then looked into her glass. "Where else did you go?"

"Where else did I go?"

"That's right. Where else?"

"Oh yeah, I forgot. I stopped off at a pizza place on the highway."

"That was your lunch?"

"No, no. That was before lunch." He got to his feet abruptly.

"What are you doing?"

"I've gotta take a shower," he said.

"You don't smell any worse than usual," she said.

"Anyway, you're being a bit of a cunt, Diane."

"Sit down. It's my dime. A thousand dollars' worth."

He sank back onto the sofa again.

She took another swallow of whiskey. "So you found out nothing, huh? All that time out at the beach and you came up with nothing."

He averted his eyes. "Not a goddam thing."

She turned her head and stared at him.

He waited for her to say something, but she remained silent, just looking at him. Finally he couldn't take it any longer. "Well what did you *expect* me to find?" he cried. "You send me looking for clues and you don't even know for what, you don't even know what I'm supposed to be *looking* for. Isn't that true? Isn't it?"

"Yes," she said quietly, still watching him.

"Why should there be any clues *there*? It isn't even *his house*. Why aren't we looking in *his* house, *Bluestern's* house? Wouldn't that make more sense?" The minute he said it he knew he shouldn't have.

"All right," she said tersely. "We'll go there . . . tonight."

He jumped to his feet. "Jesus, isn't that going to be dangerous?" He tried not to sound whiney, but that's the way his voice came out.

"You want to be safe, go back to pumping gas or whatever it was you were doing before I met you at Joey's, my lucky night."

"Okay, so we go there tonight," he muttered, starting for the bathroom to get away from her. It was his own goddam fault. He had brought it up. He already knew everything he had to know. What could he hope to find out at Bluestern's except possibly how soon the man was planning to make his move and how he was going to do it? That could be helpful, but was it worth the risk? Christ, it would be so dangerous. But how could he say no to her without tipping off how much he knew? Besides, he still needed her car, and her apartment, and maybe he'd even need more money. After it was over, he'd be able to say no to her all he wanted. Maybe he'd give her a no that was so definite she'd never hear yes for an answer ever again.

"Bruce . . . ?"

He stopped in the bedroom doorway and turned to her.

"You know, of course, that you're a big fucking liar," she said evenly.

He smiled feebly. "Come on, luv."

"You're holding out on me, aren't you?" she said.

"Finish your drink, will you?"

"That's all right. Howard Bluestern is a big fucking liar too. Some of my best friends are big fucking liars. Even my mother is. You're just *bigger* than all of them."

He turned away with a pitying shake of the head and went inside to the bathroom to take his shower.

She sat there on the sofa, sipping the dregs of her drink, staring into the glass, into her future. One of the compensations you got from depending on vermin like Bruce was that you expected nothing but the worst from them, and they rarely disappointed you.

But something good would happen, she reassured herself.

She didn't know what, but there was always a chance. She was still free, wasn't she?

Maybe she'd think of something herself.

One thing she knew, she'd never let them put her in prison.

It would be another half hour before she would suddenly remember David Stanner.

A WATCHED TELEPHONE never boils, Gerber reminded himself as he sat in his office fretting. It was only twenty to five; what was he getting so antsy about? Teddy Stern was a busy man. Right now he was probably very busy mixing a drink, or busy drinking a drink, or busy finishing a drink. Whatever he was busy doing, he obviously preferred doing it to calling Marvin Gerber, that was for sure.

At twelve minutes to five the alcohol must have run out.

"On two," Madeline said. Gerber punched the button and said to the phone, "Don't worry, I'm not selling anything."

"Don't worry, I'm not buying," the actor said. "What can I do for you?" He sounded a little irritable. Gerber took note.

"Look, I won't keep you," he said. "I just thought maybe you should know that your brother asked me point-blank today whether I told you about the policy, and I had to give him an honest answer and say yes. He was very gracious about it and accepted my apologies. I thought you should know this."

"Fine. No sweat, Marvin. Much ado, and all that."

'No, it's a little more than that, Teddy. After all, your brother is a client, and what goes on between him and me is supposed to be highly confidential, and I shouldn't have violated that confidence."

"Okay, so you apologized and he accepted. Isn't that enough?"

"For me, yes, but I don't have any control over other people."

"What other people?"

"Like you, for example. You remember I asked you not to breathe a word—"

"And I haven't, not to a soul."

"Nobody?"

"Of course not."

"Was there someone else in your house this morning while I was there?"

"Absolutely not."

"No workmen, no repairmen or anything?"

"I already told you no. Look, what is this all about, Gerber?"

"Nothing, nothing. I shouldn't've brought it up. I'm a nervous man. I see things, I imagine things." Gerber abhorred liars. He preferred to think of himself as an occasional bender of the truth. "I'm driving away from your house, I could've sworn I saw this man coming out of the back entrance or the side entrance or whatever it was . . ."

"You're crazy. There *was* no one. What did he look like?"

"A great big guy, well over six feet, very fat and blubbery, must've been over two hundred and fifty pounds, I wouldn't insure him for ten dollars, pasty face, long blond hair . . ."

"You've got a terrific imagination, Marvin."

"Didn't I tell you?" Gerber said. He was feeling greatly relieved. The big man in his office had been sheer bluff and a mile wide. "Anyway, I'm happy for *you* Teddy, because even if such a man was in your house, which he wasn't, obviously all he took with him was words, some conversation, or you would've noticed, right?"

"So if I'm not worried, what's *your* excuse? You're not even a drinking man, you have no right to be seeing things. Which reminds me, it's almost the happy hour . . ."

"And you want to run, huh?"

"May I?"

"Of course." Gerber felt so relieved that he almost didn't bother with the slip of paper in his hand, the one on which Madeline had taken down the report from the Department of Motor Vehicles in Sacramento. But it was not in his nature to feel *too* relieved for too long, so he took a final shot in the dark anyway and said, "By the way, Teddy, you don't happen to know a woman by the name of Diane McWorter, do you?"

The length of the pause could have been a figment of Gerber's imagination. "Why do you ask?" the actor said.

Gerber's practiced mind moved nimbly. "Well, I sold her this policy; that is, one of my agents sold her some automobile insurance today, for a Toyota or a Datsun I think, and am I wrong, or is it possible that she could have given your name as a credit reference, or maybe it was your brother's, or is maybe my lousy memory making the whole thing up?"

"I guess *you'd* know the answer to that one," the Stern fellow replied evenly.

Gerber nodded to himself. "But you do know a Diane McWorter."

Again Gerber's imagination manufactured a pause. "I did . . . once . . . yes," the actor said.

"Ah, so I *didn't* make it up," Gerber said cheerfully. "Any way you look at it, a coincidence, no?"

"Life is full of them," the other man said.

"That's why I brought it up," Gerber said. "Okay, you want to run, I'll let you go now. Take good care of yourself, young man."

"You too, Marvin."

Gerber felt perverse pleasure as he hung up the phone. He would not have to go to bed tonight with absolutely *nothing* on his mind. The overweight, long-haired man who was a bluff had been driving a car owned by a woman who had once been a friend of Teddy Stern's, for which, if it was not a coincidence, there would have to be a new word invented. And if Gerber should ever want to call the man's bluff by offering him maybe ten dollars, instead of two hundred thou, he could always find out who the man was, and where he could be reached, by locating this woman, this former friend of Teddy Stern's.

The world, Gerber decided, was getting smaller and smaller.

And more unsafe every day.

And as Teddy Stern stared at the phone on *his* desk, he felt the walls of Howard's office closing in on him. Diane McWorter trying to get her hands on a tape was one thing. Diane McWorter suddenly showing up in the life of Marvin Gerber was another, and too much of a coincidence to be a coincidence. Either the ferret Gerber had been lying to him or Diane was onto something, and the warning lights in Teddy's head had already started flashing red for danger.

He got to his feet and gathered up all the material Jo Anne had given him to take home tonight for their study session. It was going to be a beautiful night for the both of them, and he was not going to ruin it by mentioning anything to her about this conversation with Gerber. Especially he was not going to mention the heavy-set stranger Gerber had conjured up out at the beach house. He was thinking about Howard now, thinking about Howard being in the Malibu bedroom with him this morning, thinking about imagining that he had almost heard Howard breathing. And he knew now that it hadn't been Howard, and that he hadn't imagined it, because Howard wasn't breathing any longer, Howard was dead, and Howard didn't have long blond hair . . .

HE SPRAYED HIS ARMPITS with Pierre Cardin antiperspirant, then doused his body with Jovan musk oil cologne, and used the big white powder puff to dust his crotch with Coty's Emeraud. Let no man say that David Stanner did not smell sweet and taste lovely, even if his heart was not between his legs tonight. He would give it his best, though he felt oddly at sixes and sevens about having the night off.

One part of him, lusting and insatiable, was already doing its anticipatory cockstand about what the evening would bring him, he'd see to that. But another part of him, the impossible dreamer, wanted to stay home and be with *them*, even if they didn't want him, even if all he'd get out of it would be the sweet ache in his balls and the longing for release that would come from knowing that he was under the same roof with them while they were in the bedroom together.

He thought about darling Jo Anne—that's what he called her in his thoughts—and how she had sounded on the telephone this afternoon when she had called with Bluestern's instructions, and how she had sounded that night in bed in the throes of her orgasm, and thinking about her, he decided to put on his blue boxer shorts rather than the tight-fitting jockey shorts he usually wore, because if there was one thing he did not want at this moment, or for the rest of the evening for that matter, it was anything that would confine and restrict him and keep him from pointing boldly in whatever direction he wanted to go. And it did not seem to worry him in the least that he seemed to be wanting to go in the direction of pussycat whenever Jo Anne was on his mind.

He was teasing himself, that was all, arousing himself with irresponsible fantasies, secure in the knowledge that he knew his own true love and always would, and would find it tonight in the hot-blooded grasp of some as yet unmet, brand-new stranger.

Toilette completed, Stanner laid out his ice-cream slacks, a blue Madras shirt slit to the navel, cordovan loafers, and a few gold chains for his neck. Then he gave a final touch-up to his coif, slipped off his robe, and surveyed himself in his boxer shorts before the full-length mirror on the door of his inadequate little closet.

No two ways about it, luv. Bloody irresistible.

His private affair was interrupted by the sound of the ringing telephone.

For a moment he considered letting the service pick it up, then decided to earn his salary, pittance though it was, and picked up the extension beside his bed.

"Mr. Bluestern's residence."

"Is that you, David?"

For a split second he thought it was the Kallen girl again, then realized immediately that the familiar voice was, alas, not hers. "Speaking," he said.

"I wonder if you remember me? Diane McWorter."

His nostrils flared. "How could I not remember you, Miss McWorter? He's not in yet."

"I'm not calling *him*, David. I'm calling you, as you suggested. Do you have a moment?"

"I think I do," he said warily. Could it be? He had given up all hope of hearing from her.

"Look, I'm not exactly alone," she said, lowering her voice, "and I'll have to talk rather fast . . ."

"My ears are quick, ma'am . . ."

"Cut out the ma'am shit and call me Diane, will you please?"

"Yes, Diane."

"The other night when you offered to help me with some personal difficulties I was having, and you suggested that we meet for a drink or something . . . ?"

"Yes?"

"Let me ask you something, David, and please try to understand what I'm saying." She measured her words carefully now. "If you and I were to meet someplace, and I were to ask you whether you thought Mr. Bluestern was up to something *peculiar . . . mysterious . . .* these days, would you say to me, 'I don't know what you're talking about'?"

Stanner sniffed, and liked what he smelled. "No, I certainly would *not* give you that kind of reply," he said, thinking as fast as he could. "I would be more inclined to say that I myself have some interesting observations which tend to substantiate the same conclusion."

"You really do?"

The excitement in her voice startled him. He had baited the hook with such a tiny, nebulous worm. "Indeed I do," he said.

"Then I would *not* be wasting your time if we got together and talked?"

He started pulling in the line gently. "I seem to recall that when I first made that suggestion to you, Diane, I received a fairly strong negative response."

"Oh, come on, David, I can be very rude at times, you know that. I think it's time we met, and the sooner the better. When do you get off?"

"As a matter of fact, tonight I'm being turned loose before dinner—"

"Wonderful. Do you think we can—?"

"Oh, damn, hold on," he said suddenly.

The doorbell was ringing.

"David . . . ?"

"Can you hold it a minute?"

"What's wrong?"

"The front door. Somebody's at the door. I'll put you on hold."

More ringing.

"But David—"

"Right back."

Who the devil could it be? He hadn't even heard a car.

He set the phone down, slipped on his robe, and hurried through the house toward the foyer.

The doorbell rang again.

He crossed the foyer, undid the chain on the front door, and pulled it open.

Bluestern.

At this hour?

His arms were loaded with books and files as he pushed past him saying, "Where the hell *were* you?"

"On the phone, sir. I'll get right off. Take those for you?"

"No, that's all right, I'll manage."

Stanner went quickly to the study and picked up the extension, his hand shaking a little. "Honey, I'll have to get back to you." He hoped his voice was low enough.

"Wait a minute. When?" She sounded frantic.

"As soon as I can."

"But I thought you and I—"

"Have to hang up."

"I'll wait here. I'm in the book. Brentwood."

He hung up hastily, pulled himself together, and went out to the foyer, where he saw Bluestern still looking around distractedly for a place to deposit the books and files.

"Welcome home, sir. Here, give me all that." He reached out, but Bluestern pulled back reflexively.

What was the big deal? He was only trying to help.

He watched him go into the den, leaving behind an impression of weariness and strain, a difficult Friday at the studio perhaps, followed by a possibly unrelaxing weekend at the beach, and a troublesome Monday that was not yet over? It was more like the old Howard

Bluestern, the one he'd been wondering about, yet the man was not quite the same. What *was* the difference?

He was emerging from the den now empty-handed. Apparently he'd found some private niche for all that stuff he'd brought home, and Stanner felt vaguely insulted, as though he or anyone else were about to poke around in Bluestern's private papers. More untypical Bluestern behavior to add to the grist that was already in his mill. He couldn't *wait* to hear what the McWorter girl had to offer . . .

"Who were you on the phone with just now, David?" Christ, the man must have been reading his mind, looking at him now with eyes that were uncomfortably piercing.

"A friend," Stanner said quickly, then smiled. "I was sort of expecting Miss Kallen to be with you, sir, not that I'm not happy to see *you* after the long weekend."

"She'll be here," he said, still looking at him.

"Your brother called," Stanner offered. "He's back."

"Yes, I know."

"He wanted you to know that he found a pair of female undies in the bathroom."

"David, would you sit down a moment, please?"

"Me, sir?"

"Yes."

He didn't like the sound of Bluestern's voice. Much too serious. What now, for heaven's sake? He sat down in the cane-back chair right there in the foyer and looked up questioningly.

"Now give me a straight answer this time," Bluestern said to him. "Don't duck your head, don't look away and don't change the subject. Okay?"

"As you wish, Mr. Bluestern." On the bloody witness stand, that's where he was.

"Some of these friends of yours. . . . Have any of them been prying into my affairs lately?"

"Which friends, sir?"

"Your friends. People you meet in those bars you go to. People you talk to on the telephone, like just now . . ."

"You mean men, sir, don't you?"

"Not necessarily."

"Women?"

"Yes, women."

"Mr. Bluestern, I really don't have any women friends . . ."

"I know goddam well you don't. So who were you just talking to?"

"I don't understand, sir."

"Then let me put it this way—*look at me, damn it . . .*"

"Sorry."

"Who was the woman you were just talking to?"

"Woman?"

"The one you just addressed as honey. Did you think I was deaf, for Christsake?"

Stanner was about to explain to him that he called many *men* honey, *some* of them *darling*, and a chosen few dearest, but something in Bluestern's cold blue eyes, the expression on his face, told Stanner that this was not quite the right moment to fuck around with the man. "I was hoping to spare you, sir, really I was. I wanted *so* not to have to burden you with problems that you told me to take care of myself, and that's what I've been doing, and I still am, and I don't want you to give her another *thought*. Just let me take care of everything, all right? Promise?"

"Diane McWorter," Bluestern said, making it sound oh so heavy.

"Yes, sir," Stanner said. "But will you *please forget* her? She's completely under control. Each time she calls, I give her the same message . . . you found nothing, there's nothing more that you can do, nothing more you *will* do. I keep telling her don't waste your time, honey, just stop calling, and she's *getting* the *message*, she really is. She'll stop. You can count on it. I could *kick* myself that this even came *up*. Can I get you a drink, sir?"

He got up from the cane-back chair only to find Bluestern's finger practically in his *face*, pointing at him. "I don't want my personal affairs, or my brother's affairs, discussed with *anyone*, is that understood?"

"Your *brother's* affairs . . . ?"

"Is that understood?"

"But it always *has* been understood, sir."

"And that goes for all those guys you meet on streetcorners too."

"What guys?"

"How do *I* know who they are?"

"I don't know what you're talking about, sir."

"I'm talking about I don't want you having *any further conversations* with that McWorter dame. Hang up the fucking phone if she calls again. Is that clear?"

Stanner blinked as though struck. "I don't know why you feel you have to say things like this to me, Mr. Bluestern . . ."

"If I feel I have reasons, that's reason enough for me and it should be reason enough for you too."

"If you're worried that I'm *indiscreet* or something . . ."

"I didn't say you were indiscreet."

". . . Or that I go blabbing to strangers . . ."

"Who said you go blabbing to strangers?"

"Well, you implied it."

"I didn't imply anything of the kind."

"Then why am I feeling so . . . under attack . . . embarrassed?"

"If you feel guilty about something, that's *your* problem."

"See what I mean, sir?"

"Never mind." Snapping at him. Unpleasant. "Just remember what I told you."

"I think maybe I'd better go get dressed now and take off for the evening." Stanner could hear his own voice tremble with injury. Suddenly he was *so depressed*.

Less than thirty minutes ago he'd been dreaming a lovely, lascivious dream of watching and listening to the two of them together, the blonde-haired darling and this very man, his employer. And less than ten minutes ago he'd had an equally exciting vision of getting together with the other one, the dark-eyed McWorter female, and squeezing out every drop of poison that she had in her about Bluestern, so that he could eventually climb out of his squalid station in life and piss on all of them. And then, without warning, the bloody bastard suddenly turns on him and plunges him cruelly into the depths by suggesting that he, David Stanner, was without discretion and nothing more than a loose-tongued traitor who would spill the private secrets of Bluestern and his brother to anyone who bared his ass to him.

Well, he was no such thing and he'd *do* no such thing. *Threaten* to do it, of course, and be paid handsomely not to, but *do* it? Never.

And now his hopes had been dashed.

He would never dare to meet with Diane McWorter, not after *this* tongue-lashing. He would never even dare to call her back. Christ, but Bluestern had been livid. He had never seen or heard him that way. Something was *really* under the man's skin. Something was really going on, and it had to do with the McWorter girl too, that was obvious.

If only he could have been able to get to her . . .

"By the way," his employer was saying, much cooled down now.

"I'll be leaving for New York Wednesday for a board meeting. I'll be back Friday."

"Very well, sir."

Three thousand miles away? For at least two nights?

Stop it, David Stanner, stop it.

"And you, David, are you staying out overnight tonight?"

Stanner's lips trembled a little. "Do you want me to?"

"I didn't say I wanted you to. I merely asked you."

"When would you *like* me to return, sir?"

"Whenever you want. Noon tomorrow would be all right."

"I see," Stanner said tightly.

"Whatever suits you."

"Yes, well, I don't know. It depends on . . . I don't know."

"Have a nice time," his employer said, without any feeling at all, and walked away to the bedroom.

"You too," Stanner said morosely.

Presently he heard him in the shower.

Alone.

He felt miserable.

Suddenly the phone rang.

Quickly he snatched it up on the first ring and held the receiver to his ear, waiting.

"Hello . . . ? Hello, David? Is that you . . . ?"

"Don't you *ever* call here again," he said harshly.

"But I thought—"

"Never," he shouted at her and slammed the phone down.

Then he started for his own pitiful little bedroom, to get ready for the evening.

Oh God, did he ever need a good dry cleaning tonight.

THEY SAT in the front seat of the red Datsun, parked about fifty feet to the east of Bluestern's house on the other side of the street, giving them a good view of the house, the driveway and the garage, without their presence being too conspicuous. The huge garage door was raised, and they could see Bluestern's gray Bentley inside on the left and, parked next to it, a black Volkswagen. There were no lights on in the house yet, because it wasn't dark enough, and it was impossible to see any activity inside through the curtained windows.

"We're wasting our time here," Bruce said. "I don't know why you had to race over here like maybe the house was gonna run away."

"What have *you* got to do that's so much more important?" Diane had her elbows propped on the steering wheel as she peered at the house through small binoculars.

"We could always go somewhere and have a good steak," Bruce sighed.

She lowered the binoculars and gave him a withering look.

"What's that supposed to mean?" he said.

"Read anything you want into it and you'll be right," she said.

He didn't know what the hell had made her so feisty. Ever since *he* had taken a shower, *she* had seemed refreshed. Maybe it was because she had sobered up. He had noticed that when she was sober, like now, she was much harder to handle. Or maybe it was that quick phone call she had made before. She had said it was her mother, but since when did a mother make you feel better and cheer you up? Of course, how would he know? He didn't even know who his mother was. *Or* his father. Maybe that was why he was always so cheerful.

Except now he wasn't.

"Two things I'm not gonna do," he grumbled, watching her peering through the glasses. "I'm not gonna go without dinner, and I ain't going into that house while anyone's in it."

Diane didn't say anything.

"Did you hear what I said?"

"I don't know which is worse," she said, "turning on the news or listening to you."

"Pretty soon you're gonna be hearing my stomach."

"Up ahead," she said sharply.

He looked out.

A car was coming around the curve and slowing down, a brown Toyota. It slowed down even more, turned into Bluestern's driveway and braked to a stop. A young woman with honey-colored hair got out.

Diane leaned forward, watching through the glasses.

"I know her. That's his secretary, Miss Kallen," she said.

"Delivering something?"

"Probably herself. She's going inside."

"Full house. Beats my flush," Bruce said. "Let's get out of here."

Diane shifted the binoculars slightly. "Someone's coming out."

Bruce saw a figure appear from behind the house and go into the garage. "Bluestern?"

"His servant, David Stanner, the son of a bitch," she muttered.

They heard the sound of the Volkswagen being started. Then the small black car slowly backed out of the garage. It came to a stop alongside the parked Toyota. David Stanner got out, climbed into the Toyota, started the motor and drove into the garage. Then he came back out on foot, pressed a button on the outside of the garage, and the huge door started down slowly, closing with a rumbling crash.

"That's David the fag all right," Diane said, looking through the glasses. "All dolled up and ready for love."

"You can bet Bluestern and that girl aren't gonna budge tonight," Bruce said. "She and her car are in for the duration."

David Stanner was back in the Volkswagen, making a U-turn. The little black car moved out of the driveway into the street, then turned right and drove off, gathering speed.

Diane dropped the binoculars on the seat, turned the key in the ignition, and the Datsun shot forward.

Bruce glanced at her and saw the excitement on her face. "What are you doing?"

"Following him. What does it look like?"

"What for?"

"To see where he's going." She turned left on Beverly Drive.

"What the hell do we care where he's going?"

"Where he goes, you go," she said.

"What are you talking about?"

"You've been saying breaking into Howard's house was going to be too dangerous for you, so stop complaining. You're getting your wish."

"Pull over, goddam it."

She drove faster, trying to beat the light.

He put a hand on the wheel.

"Stop that, you want to get us killed?" she cried.

"I want to know what's going on," Bruce demanded.

"So do I, and that's what I'm finally going to find out." The light at Sunset turned red on her. "David Stanner happens to know something, probably a lot, about Howard, and what he's up to . . ."

"How do *you* know?"

"I just talked to him on the phone . . ."

"I thought you said it was your mother."

"What's the difference what I *said*? It was him. He knows something, but he won't talk to *me* at *all*. Maybe he'll talk to a stranger, if the stranger gets to know him real well. That's you, Bruce. . . ." She headed east on Sunset.

He looked at her and frowned. "I don't *go* the fag route."

"It won't kill you," she said.

"You're out of your mind," he said sullenly.

"Am I?"

"Yes."

But maybe she wasn't. At least it wouldn't be *dangerous*. He hated her when she was right.

"Why didn't you tell me any of this before?" he grumbled.

"You mean like *you* tell *me* everything?"

"I don't see why *you* can't meet with him if it's you he knows." He heard the whine in his voice again.

"I *told* you. . . . He won't come near me. I don't know why, maybe he's afraid to. . . . And be sure not to mention my name. You never even *heard* of me."

"I should be so lucky," he muttered.

They followed the Volkswagen to Hollywood, trailed it along the Strip, then through Holloway Drive to Santa Monica Boulevard. Finally they saw the little black car pull into a parking lot next to a nondescript-looking disco bar called The Plumbers Union. Diane stopped the Datsun at the curb and they watched as Stanner locked his car, took a parking ticket from the attendant, sauntered to the entrance to the bar, glanced up and down the boulevard, and went inside.

"Go ahead," Diane said, turning. "Be charming. Get picked up. Like you did with me."

Bruce squirmed. "Shit." Who *needed* this?

"Who knows, he might even ask you back to his bedroom. That's *one* way of getting inside Howard's house."

"Goddam it." He looked around, as though for escape. "What are *you* gonna be doing?"

"I'll wait right here. If you're not out in ten minutes, I'll know you're making progress, and I'll go home, get in bed, and watch television."

He glanced toward the entrance to the bar with an anxious expression. It would be far less risky than breaking and entering, but still . . . "How am I gonna get back home?"

"He's got a car. Maybe he'll like you so much he'll give it to you afterward, out of gratitude."

He looked at her. "Once a cunt, always a cunt."

"Makes a nice fit with what you are," she said. She reached across him and opened his door. "Now *do* something, for Christsake. You haven't accomplished a thing all day."

He had half a mind to tell her. But then he thought better of it and squeezed his huge body out of the car.

"And don't enjoy yourself *too* much," she said.

He slammed the door in her face, walked quickly to The Plumbers Union, and went inside.

chapter

19

SOMETIMES you could look back on your life and say *there*, that was the moment, that was the decision, that was the turning point.

And the moment could have been so insignificant when it took place that it could have slipped by unnoticed, with no hint that lives would be unalterably changed for better or for worse or that some lives would actually come to a premature end because of that one unremarkable moment.

Teddy would look back on one such as that for years to come, and always he would arrive at the same conclusion. His life would have been different, Jo Anne's life would have been different, and the dead would have gone on living out their lives if he had made just one small decision another way, if he had decided to return a phone call from Joey Marzula as soon as he had heard about it instead of putting it off.

When Jo Anne had arrived at the house in Bel Air that fateful night—fateful only in retrospect; God knows it had been more beautiful and rapturous than fateful while they were living it—she had given Teddy a rundown on the business calls that had come into the office after he'd left the studio, and then verbatim the one message that she had picked up from his own answering machine at the Malibu house: "Teddy boy, this is Joey boy, Joey Marzula. Call me, will you? It's kind of important. Better yet, drop in. I could use the business."

Teddy nodded. "Got it."

"Who is he, your bookie?"

"Good guy. Good friend. Owns Pal Joey's, the restaurant. You may be the only woman I've ever known who has never been there with me."

She pouted. "Thanks a heap."

He kissed her pouting lips and put his arms around her waist and felt the hunger swelling in him.

"Aren't you going to call him back?" she said.

"He probably wants a game of handball with me at the Y. It can wait."

212

Just like that.

He had wanted her too much. Nothing else could have seemed important to him, not then it couldn't. Mostly it had been her, and partly it had been his relief at knowing that he'd be free now, at least for tonight, of having to think about Stanner, or Gerber, or Diane, or mysterious ghosts that weighed two hundred and fifty pounds. There'd be only her, only Jo Anne . . .

The moment she had stepped into the house, all freshened up for him, and lovely for him, and sweet smelling for him, and after David had left and they were alone in the house together, in Howard's house together, with the darkness of night coming down outside like a screen to protect them, and no one to intrude on them inside here where they could do and be anything they wanted, he had felt his desire for her growing wild and lawless, pent-up all day, waiting for her all day, insane now, Christ, this strange erotic feeling from a childhood long gone that they'd be doing something wicked and forbidden and therefore hopelessly exciting because it wasn't what they were supposed to be doing, not yet it wasn't, not until after they had done the serious thing, the important thing, examined the ways and means of carrying Howard to his public death and fortified themselves against the pitfalls and dangers, only then would they be allowed to do this, which he could hardly bear for wanting it so much, holding her now, his hands and lips all over the warmth and the softness of her body as she teased him with her reluctance and tantalized him with her unwillingness to allow him to have her until after they had first gotten past the evening's grim purpose, contained in the books and the files he had brought home for them to study.

"We can do that later," he murmured. "Of course we will, later. We've got the whole night for that . . ."

"Oh God, darling, you're so impossible . . ."

"Worse than that . . . much worse than that . . ."

How he loved the earnestness of her expression and the sweet reasonableness of her arguments as he led her away, she was so right and he was so wrong, it was so wrong what he was doing to her, so wrong to be taking her to Howard's bedroom this way, this beautiful, sensible, intelligent woman, listening to all her rightness and her thoughtful murmurs of protest as he undressed her in the semidarkness of the fading light and took off his own clothing and gently captured her nakedness with his hands and his mouth and took command of her intelligence and her common sense and her sweet parted lips and slowly, slowly began to seduce her, how he loved her for letting him seduce her this way, moaning softly in his ear, sighing helplessly as he brought her down on the bed with him and gazed into her eyes and saw the look on her face, all flushed with desire, and knew then that he had brought her finally to his own special wrongness, and now he was no longer seducing her, for she had become an equal partner with him in this wicked and forbidden and unbearably exciting act of love, uncoiling her long, tawny legs and opening herself wide to him and attaching her open mouth to his and inviting him, guiding him, urging him inside her . . .

"Oh my God," she cried. "Oh my God, my darling . . ."

As he entered her and began to take her the way he had dreamed all day of taking her, slowly and surely with inexorable, undeniable, loving thrusts, groaning in sweet agony, feeling her thighs and her legs enfolding him and tightening on him and her hands all over him, clawing and grasping and stinging his back and her teeth on his neck and her hips moving beneath him, meeting his rhythm with her own loving answers and finally easing him, easing him until he knew what she wanted and allowed her to have it, to come over him and master him and possess him from above with the quickening passion of her tight wet love and her full breasts in the suckle of his mouth and her golden hair brushing his face and her voice in his ear moaning darling I want you oh yes I'm going to take you oh yes I'm going to come oh God I'm going to come oh God I'm going to come and her shouts of joy as her womb began to throb and bathe with her juices the stiff and swollen maleness that she held in loving clasp, pulsing, spending, crying out, crying out, and he gasped as suddenly she gave him back to the cool night air for an agonizing moment before she took him in her hand and kneeled beside him and kissed his mouth deeply and said to his ear I want to taste your love, darling, all of it, all of it, and he groaned with voluptuous delight as he felt her warm mouth coming over and down on him widely and closely to take possession of him and feast on him, and his hands went to his face and he clasped his mouth and did everything he could to stifle his gasps of pleasure but he was no match for her loving tongue and the sucking kiss of her lips, and soon he knew that she was winning and he didn't want her to win, not yet, he wanted it to go on forever but that couldn't be because she was too much for him, too much for him, she wanted it all from him and she was going to get it and there was no way he could stop her and then suddenly he knew that there was nothing on earth that could stop her now and when he knew that, he cried out, and his body arched upward to meet her and be enveloped by her and held by her, higher and higher he rose to his heavenly captor, shouting, shouting, and for one final moment went as high as he would ever go and let out a great gasping cry as his love suddenly burst and spilled over and began to pour into her and she took it from him hungrily and made him give her more and more and more until he begged for mercy but she would not show it, she took him and took him and took him until she had what she wanted which was all of him, she had all of the love that was in him to give, and then she went up to his lips and they lay there mouth to mouth in each other's arms and continued to love each other with their tongues forever, it seemed, dreaming of the wonder of it all and the beauty of it all, but it wasn't forever, it only seemed to be, which was lucky for the both of them because there was so much to do tonight of grim and important purpose, they would have to let go of each other soon, they would really have to, and it was the last thing they told each other before they slipped off into slumber to replenish the love and the energy that had been drained from the both of them.

DIANE HAD NO CLEAR IDEA why she was doing this. After leaving Bruce she had intended to drive straight to the apartment. But then, the thought of being alone with herself began to make her uneasy. She knew she could drown the feeling in liquor, but apparently that was not what she wanted, and at first, when she drove past her turnoff in Brentwood and then veered south toward the airport, she thought that she'd just be taking the Cessna up for one of her aimless, soothing flights up the coast or over the Valley. And then somewhere along the way to the plane, it came to her that she wanted to see her mother, which made no sense at all, because what could her mother do for her except aggravate her and irritate her and make her feel worse about herself than she already did? Still, she wanted to see her mother.

The night was clear and the stars were as bright as the lights below as she flew southeast at fifty-five hundred feet and pretended to herself that she could already see Palm Springs up ahead. She'd easily be able to make it back to Santa Monica before the airport shut down for the night and would probably be back in her apartment before Bruce returned from whatever it was that was happening to him, or he was making happen, she didn't know which and she didn't want to think about it now, she just wanted to see her mother. Maybe Mommy would put her arms around her and make everything bad go away, fat chance.

The desert night was unbelievably hot when she landed a short time later. No matter how many times Diane had stepped out of her plane in the Springs, she had always experienced the same momentary heat shock and then quickly adjusted to it. As she walked across the field to the cab station, she felt a sense of temporary escape. Her troubles had ceased to exist. They were all back there around the bend, behind the purple mountains that rose to meet the stars and protected those who lived here from the evil that lurked back in Los Angeles.

She took a cab to her mother's house on Palmetto Drive, and when she saw that the house was in darkness, she had the driver turn around. She was not upset. She knew her mother would be at the club.

She found her sitting at the bar, all by herself, nursing a Scotch on the rocks and forcing small talk on the patient young Mexican bartender. She was all in white, bare-shouldered and bare-armed, her skirt slit to the waist on both sides to show her deeply tanned thighs. Diane never failed to be surprised when she came upon her mother's rampant sexuality, as though it were something unexpected and inappropriate in a woman of fifty-five. And each time that she saw her, she became certain all over again that her mother was fornicating with any number of men who lived down here in the Springs, who played golf and gin rummy all day and drank too much at night and thought constantly of how to work up their lust and then get it off. Long ago Diane had sensed that her mother gave off the musky scent of availability and knew how to smell desire in men from a hundred yards away. She had envied her, and still did, for all those wonderful times in bed, undistracted by any real love for her husband, now dead, or by undue affection for her only child, her daughter.

Diane saw the coppery face beneath the streaked blonde hair come alive now with surprise and a hint of dismay. "Di, baby, for heaven's sake . . ." They kissed, and Diane smelled the liquor on her breath and it made her think of Teddy, and she felt inexpressibly sad. "I love the way you drop in like this. Why didn't you call me and tell me you were coming?"

"Spur of the moment, Mother." She took the stool beside her. "I just flew down for a quick hello to see how you were."

"Me? You know me. Did you ever know me when I wasn't fine?" Her smile showed a gleaming white set of caps.

"How come you're alone tonight?" Diane said.

Her mother's glance shifted past Diane to the entrance, then back to Diane. "Is everything all right with you, honey?"

"Of course. Why?"

"I mean, what are you doing down here when you could be with Teddy?"

"Teddy and I have split," Diane said.

Her mother looked at her, then took a sip of her Scotch and said to the bartender, "Manuel, you know my daughter, Diane, don't you?"

The Mexican smiled. "Good evening, miss."

"Hi."

"What would you like?" her mother said to her.

"No, I can't. I'm flying," Diane said.

"Then . . . you're not going to spend the night here . . ."

"No," Diane said. "I have to get back."

"For what?"

"I just do," Diane said.

"I see." She turned to the bartender. "Manuel, give my daughter a Perrier or something." Then back to Diane. "You don't look so good, honey."

"I know," Diane said.

"You should come down sometime. The air conditioning at the house is beautiful. Your room is waiting. A couple of days might do you good."

"Soon. Real soon," Diane said.

The bartender set a glass of Perrier water before Diane. She let it sit there. What the hell could Perrier water do for her? She watched her mother work on the Scotch and nod her head several times as though she were agreeing with her own unvoiced thoughts. "You don't want to *tell* me about Teddy . . ."

Sure I do, she said, silently to herself. He's dead. I murdered him. Your daughter is a killer. Do you realize what a disaster that is? No man may want to sleep with you any more.

"Suit yourself," her mother said to her silence.

"There isn't much to tell," Diane said. "He hasn't the faintest interest in a permanent relationship."

"You mean marriage?"

"Among other things."

"I could have told you that, Diane."

"What do you mean, you *could* have? That's all you ever *did* tell me about him, over and over again . . ."

"Was I wrong?"

"I never heard you say anything *nice* about him."

"So now you two have broken up, is that it?"

"I'm not broken up but *he's* plenty broken up, I'll tell you that."

"Well, I never did think much of his future. If he hasn't made it by now—"

"Who's your lawyer in Los Angeles?" Diane said abruptly.

Her mother glanced at her sharply. "Lawyer? I have Paul Schreier down here. I don't have anyone back in LA any more. Why would I be needing a lawyer now? All that's behind me."

"Would this Mr. Schreier have connections with anyone in Los Angeles?"

"I don't know. I could ask him. You aren't thinking of suing Teddy, are you?"

"No," Diane said.

Her mother stared at her. "You're not pregnant, are you?"

"No."

"You can tell me."

"I just did."

"Is there a chance that you two will be getting together again?"

"Impossible," Diane said.

"That bad," her mother said.

"Worse," Diane said. She turned to the bartender and held out her glass of Perrier. "Put a shot of bourbon in this, will you please?"

The Mexican took the glass and turned away.

"Do you think that's wise, Diane?"

"No," Diane said. "It's necessary."

She watched her mother take a small address book from her handbag and consult it. Then she put it away and got off the barstool.

"I'll be right back," she said.

"What are you doing?" Diane said.

"I'm going to call Paul Schreier. He may be home."

"Wait a minute. What are you going to tell him?"

"I'm going to tell him that my daughter is in trouble and needs a good lawyer to whom maybe she'll tell what the trouble is. You wait here." She left Diane and walked toward the powder room, where the pay telephone was located.

Diane signaled the bartender. "Put an extra shot in there."

"A double?"

"Yes, and also give me a double shot on the *side*."

"Very well, Miss."

Diane heard the ring of her mother's coin being dropped into the pay telephone. Suddenly she found herself wondering how Bruce was doing and wondering what the hell she was doing here. When the Mexican brought her the highball and the large shot glass, she downed the whiskey quickly and returned the shot glass to him saying, "Would you call a cab for me, please?"

He used the phone behind him to call the desk.

Out in the powder room, Diane heard another call being made on the pay telephone. She took several gulps of her bourbon and Perrier, and then saw her mother coming from the powder room back toward the bar. She still had a good figure, the kind men would want to get into.

"Mr. Schreier wasn't home," she said to Diane, perching on her stool again. "I'll get him tomorrow. You're at your apartment?"

"Yes," Diane said. She saw her mother's eyes shifting nervously toward the entrance. "Are you expecting someone?"

Her mother looked at her. "What do you mean?"

"Are you meeting someone here tonight?" Diane said.

"Well . . . yes," her mother said.

"Who?"

"An old friend."

"What old friend?"

"Jack Sobel," her mother said. "I don't think you know him. He lives at Tamarisk."

"Is he married?"

"I didn't ask him."

"Is that who you just called, to tell him not to come here until you got rid of me?"

"Don't be ridiculous, Diane."

"Are you going back to the house with him?"

"Look, I can always get out of the evening. It can end right here, if you want to stay over."

"No," Diane said. "I was just curious."

"Is that why you flew down here?" her mother said. "To see if I'm going with the right kind of men? Don't worry, I know what I'm doing . . ."

"I'll bet you do."

". . . I wish I could say the same for you . . ."

"You wouldn't even if you could," Diane said.

"How do you think I feel seeing my own daughter looking like you look tonight, barging in on me with no warning and then making no communication with me whatsoever? Do you think this makes me happy, Diane, or gives me any peace of mind?''

Diane looked at her. ''I hate to go,'' she said. ''I would have loved to watch you and Jack Sobel fucking. I'll bet you're a terrific lay. Does he come inside you, or do you take it in your mouth?''

''You horrible person, you.'' Her mother's voice was hoarse.

''Did you let Daddy watch you fucking all those other men, or did he have to find out for himself?''

Her mother got off the barstool and hurried away toward the dining room, her lewd hips twitching as she walked.

Diane looked toward the bartender, who was trying to sink through the floor at the other end of the bar. ''Does she take you in her mouth too?''

The Mexican pretended not to hear her.

She got up and left.

The cab was out front waiting for her when she got there.

Riding back to the airport, she knew why she had come. She just didn't understand why she had waited so long.

chapter 20

SHY WASN'T the word. How could anyone that huge be shy? Elusive wasn't the word either. Could an elephant be considered elusive? He was reticent, that's what he was. *Reserved*, if you will.

"Are you reserved, Bruce?" Stanner asked him above the din of the place, through the sweat and the smoke of the place, as they moved face-to-face to the relentless beat of electrified noise.

"For you, David. Reserved only for you," Bruce shouted.

Stanner peered into the eyes of the big creature who was dipping and swaying and slithering before him with more sensuous grace than he would have imagined possible in a body so gross and seemingly awkward. "I appreciate the exclusivity of my possession, don't get me wrong, luv. But I was using the word in the sense of meaning held back, restrained, perhaps a little *unsure* that one is *comfortable* in this kind of unified, singular, homogeneous environment."

The face before Stanner broke into a slow, heavy-lidded smile. "It's the rhythm of the music that keeps you from saying what you really mean, isn't it, David?"

"How's that, luv?" Stanner did a fast turn and came back to face his partner in time for the reply.

"You're finding it difficult to use any words that don't scan. Therefore the horseshit."

"May I remind you, vulgarity breeds contempt?"

"Why don't we wait until the music stops?"

"It never stops here," Stanner said.

"Then I'll say it *for* you," Bruce said, shaking his arms and snapping his fingers and rolling his huge hips as if they were weightless. "Is it true—you are trying to ask me—that inside of every fat queen there's a thin straight screaming to get out? Am I close, David, am I close?"

Stanner glided nearer and put his hands on the big man's hips and felt the roll of them and let the feeling travel through his arms to his own slim hips, which began to move with the same rhythm. "You're very close, luv," he said to the puffy lips and the moist and fatty face. "But you can never be *too* close, as far as I'm concerned, not ever."

"Thank you," Bruce sighed. "I do hope you mean that."

"I intend to show you how much I mean it, if you'll let me," Stanner murmured, and took the soft face in his hands and felt the big man flinch as he eased the moist mouth open with his own and their bodies swayed to the beat as their tongues began to do a dance of their own and they stayed that way, glued together, tasting on each other's breath the whiskey they had been pouring into themselves, moving together now, oblivious to the sweating, blue-jeaned, leather-vested, hairy, sex-smelling bodies packed in on all sides of them on the tiny dance floor, until finally Stanner came up for air and said, "You never really answered my question, luv, the one that you expressed for me so deliciously well."

"That is true," Bruce said, hesitating while he gathered his thoughts together, putting aside for the moment further attempts to figure out why he was not disliking himself more than he was. The fact that he had a purpose, a mission, the fact that he was oiled to the eyeballs didn't seem to be enough of an explanation. "I will do so now. And the answer is yes. Inside of every fat queen there is a straight prick screaming to get out after screaming to get in, and then screaming to get in again and out again and in again. Oh it's a scream, David, a wonderful scream, and I can't wait to hear it, can you?"

Stanner's eyes glittered. "Let's sit down and have one more before we scream."

"My God, haven't you had enough?"

Stanner took him by the hand and led him off the floor to their little table in the corner, and when the bare-chested boy came over to take their order, Stanner asked for another round of double Scotches, and they came almost immediately and started disappearing even faster.

"How are you going to drive?" Bruce said thickly.

"Oh, am *I* going to drive?" Stanner's voice slurred.

"I'm a footsoldier," Bruce said.

"Better question yet. *Where* am I going to drive?" Stanner said woozily.

"Don't look at *me*, darling," Bruce said. "Because when you look at *me*, you look at a nephew whose *uncle* is letting him use his son's *sleeping* bag on the living room *floor*, which would be horrible enough *without* the three cats and the slobbering dog on the premises."

"Oh, Bruce, Bruce," Stanner cried softly, shaking his head.

"And you, David?"

"The maid's room," Stanner wailed.

"The *maid's* room? Who's the maid?"

"I am," Stanner exclaimed.

"My God, you *are*?"

"Yes."

"And where's your mistress?"

"I don't *have* a mistress. I've got a master."

"You certainly do, and it's me," Bruce said. "It is I."

"It is Howard Bluestern," Stanner said.

"And where is Howard Blueballs right now?" Bruce asked.

"At home, in bed, fucking his mistress, no doubt."

"So *he's* got a mistress and you've got two masters."

"Exactly."

"Well why can't *you* be fucking *one* of them while *he's* fucking his mistress?"

"Is that an invitation, loveboat?"

"To the maid's room, darling."

"Suppose he hears us?" Stanner said.

"Suppose *we* hear *him*?" Bruce said, and he wasn't too drunk to realize that that could be what could make all this worthwhile, not that he was minding it that much, or at least, if he was minding it, apparently his rod didn't know it, because he could feel it straining to get out and go.

"No," Stanner waggled a finger at his partner. "Hearing *him* is nothing, but wait until you hear *them*. Oh glory, glory, *them together*, particularly *her*, I could get off just *thinking* about it, and *have*, I daresay, and have . . ."

"Stop it, David, don't do this to me. You're toying with me and I can't stand it."

"Aw, Brucie . . ."

"You don't believe me?" He took Stanner's hand and placed it on him.

"Oh yes, I believe you. You are telling the *truth*, luv, and I want it. I want nothing but the truth."

"In the maid's room, you shall have it," Bruce said.

"And you'll be very quiet?"

"So that we can hear your master and his mistress?"

"I want you to hear them," Stanner said with emotion. "I want to hear *you* while you're hearing them."

Bruce struggled to his feet and helped Stanner up, and they both put some money on the table for the bare-chested waiter and made their way through the bodies on the dance floor and the fresh bodies coming in through the entrance, and found themselves outside on the sidewalk in the cool night air.

"Where's the Rolls?" Bruce said.

Stanner led him uncertainly to the parking lot saying, "It's a Volkswagen, luv. You'll have to leave part of your body here."

"Which part?" Bruce said.

"Let's see if we can make it." Stanner paid the attendant, unlocked the driver's door of the little black car, got in behind the wheel and opened the other door from the inside.

Bruce struggled to squeeze his hulk through the opening. "I can't," he wheezed.

"It's that cockstand of yours," Stanner said. "Get rid of it."

"I don't see any cockstand around here. You're crazy."

Stanner clambered out of the car, went around behind Bruce and leaned on him and pushed him and shoved him until finally he got him inside the car. Then he forced the door closed, went back to his own side and managed to squeeze himself into the space that was left behind part of the steering wheel.

"Drive slowly," Bruce said.

"I haven't even started the car yet," Stanner said.

"The safest way to drive," Bruce said. "Where are we going?"

"To the Blueballs residence."

"And where is that?" Bruce inquired.

"In Blue Air," Stanner replied.

"Oh yes, I seem to remember being there once." Only a few hours ago? Jesus Christ, Diane, what the fuck have you done to me?

Stanner started the car and they drove away, and somehow managed to make it to the Blueballs residence in Blue Air, where David Stanner quietly eased the Volkswagen into the driveway and left it standing there, and shushing Bruce Gottesman all the way, led him to the servant's entrance and inside the silent house, tiptoeing down the narrow hallway to the pitifully small maid's room with its narrow bed on which, in no time at all, they lay naked and swollen with lust and alcohol, their throbbing phalluses straining to touch each other and move upon each other, and when the great shouts began to well up in their throats, they knew instinctively that there was only one way to silence themselves, and so, as one, as though choreographed, they moved quickly on each other and quieted their mouths.

TEDDY WOKE UP abruptly in the darkness. He wasn't certain, but he thought he had heard car doors opening and voices outside the house, perhaps on the neighboring property. Jo Anne had turned in her sleep and lay now with her back to him. He had an urge to kiss her shoulder and the back of her neck, but he was reluctant to awaken her. He reached out for the small quartz clock on the night table and brought it into bed and read the semiluminous dial, and when he saw that it was twenty after nine already, he immediately turned on the lamp next to him and got out of bed.

He went into the bathroom, showered briefly, toweled himself dry, and put on one of Howard's blue silk robes and a pair of slippers. Jo Anne was awake when he returned to the bedroom, stretching her body and making sounds of deep satisfaction. He smiled down at her.

"I suppose you know it's nine-thirty," he said.

"Give me a kiss," she said.

He leaned down and kissed her gently on the lips.

"I took advantage of you," he said.

"You certainly did."

"I took liberties with you."

"Many," she said.

"What are you going to do about it?"

"Now?"

"Yes."

"I'm going to lie here," she said, "and think lovely thoughts and wait for you while you go to the kitchen and find something scrumptious and bring it to me here in bed, and as further punishment, I'm going to make you join me in this repast."

"Cruel and heartless woman."

He left her and went to the kitchen, turning on lights on the way. He had never spent much time in this kitchen while Howard was alive, and wasn't too good at knowing exactly where to find certain dishes and eating utensils, but the refrigerator itself was an uncomplicated embarrassment of riches; David had seen to that. Puttering around, using his fingers to taste this and that, he thought he heard strange sounds in the house, then realized that Jo Anne must be in the bathroom by now.

It was on his way back to the bedroom with the large tray in his hands that he saw the black Volkswagen parked in the driveway. For an instant he felt dismay and anger, then quickly resolved not to let David's unexpected return and unwanted presence in the house annoy him enough to spoil the evening. If it was all that important, he should have ordered him not to come home under any circumstances, and he hadn't. You gets what you deserves, he told himself, and even managed to feel secret pleasure at the thought that the arrogant little bastard had apparently failed to score.

He decided not to say anything to Jo Anne.

She was propped up in bed, wearing her eyeglasses and a green silk robe. The reading lights were on, and the bed was strewn with books and clippings which she had brought in from the study. Her expression of serious concentration turned to delight as Teddy came in, and she quickly made room on the bed for the supper he brought with him.

"Vichyssoise, cold roast chicken, purée of cranberries and apples, potato salad, cole slaw, and a Tartuffo direct from Tre Scalini in Rome by way of West Hollywood," he announced.

"Heaven," she exclaimed.

"Some wine with it?"

"Better let's not, darling."

Teddy grimaced. "You're going to ruin me with sobriety."

He sat up in bed beside her, with plenty of napkins spread out to protect them both, and they began to eat with ravenous hunger, talking constantly and trying desperately not to let what they talked about interrupt the flow of their gustatory pleasure as they covered such diverse and not truly enjoyable topics as the incontestability clause in short-term life insurance policies written by Mutual of Oklahoma and the necessity, in double indemnity payoffs, of being able to face relentless investigative efforts on the part of the insurer to determine whether the departed might have contributed to his own accidental death through negligence, design, or too much alcohol.

Also discussed—actually, Jo Anne did a major part of the talking and Teddy did more than his share of agonized listening—was the possibility that an extremely fussy medical examiner from the coroner's office could use the subtle distinctions in various types of injuries to the brain to differentiate between death allegedly caused by a moving head being arrested by sudden impact with the interior of a car going off a cliff to the rocks below, for example, as compared to the head being struck by a blunt rounded instrument such as a fireplace poker while the head was stationary or fixed, like while resting on a pillow in bed.

When it became clear to the both of them, though Jo Anne had sensed the inevitability of it long before Teddy was ready to face it—when there was no longer any doubt in their minds that there would have to be an autopsy and postmortem examination of Howard before they could pull off the fast shuffle of cremation, Teddy insisted that they finish supper before talking any further, and he didn't even tell Jo Anne that he was going to have a stiff drink. He just went inside to the bar and dealt himself a highball glass full of tequila and ice, and returned to bed and to Jo Anne, and pretended to make a great fuss over the chocolate thrills of the Tartuffo.

Afterward, he brought everything back to the kitchen and killed off the tequila that remained in his glass and then they got down to business again, and it was the tequila that made it possible for him to think, if not clearly, at least without quailing, of the kind of scenario they would have to contrive for the accident. He would not let Jo Anne use Howard's name. Secretly, he made believe they were discussing a hypothetical case and fooled no one but himself. She tried to make it bearable for him by wiping all feeling from her voice, making of it a game, a rehearsal, a cramming for an exam.

"Ready?" she said.

"Go ahead," he said.

"The body is frozen. It has to be thawed out."

"Naturally."

"How?"

"Heat."

"How?"

"A hot tub."

"Good," she said. "What's he wearing, forgive me, right now."

"Nothing," he said, hating her for the question.

"He'll have to be dressed."

"In something from that wardrobe right over there."

"Who's going to do it?" she said.

"You?"

"No."

"Us?"

"*Can* you?"

"I don't know," he said.

"All right, *we're* going to do it," she said. "What about the bubbles."

"What bubbles?" he said.

"That form in the cells of a body that's been frozen."

"Christ, *I* don't know," he said. "Why would a pathologist look for *that?*"

"Suppose he had nothing better to do with his time that day? Suppose the coroner tells him to?"

"Okay," he said finally. "Then there's got to be practically no body left, nothing much of anything left, like in a big airliner crash. One hell of a fire, with the Bentley a crematorium."

"Did he die in the fire?"

"Yes," he said.

"Wrong," she said. "Carbon monoxide is always present in the blood in a death by fire. In this case, the death occurred before the fire, therefore there's no carbon monoxide present."

"Suppose there's no *blood* present?"

"They've developed a technique for splitting a bone and using the marrow for a gas analysis for carbon monoxide, specifically for cases where no blood or tissue is left."

"Who says so?"

"Do you want to read the paragraph?"

"No. I'll take your word for it."

"So he died instantly from impact in the crash," she said. "The fire hit him immediately after. That's why no carbon monoxide was taken in."

"Makes sense, but doesn't that leave us with the wrong kind of brain injury to worry about?"

"Not if the heat is intense enough and lasts long enough." She hesitated. "Don't make me use the word."

"Say it," he said.

"Shrinkage," she said.

"Of the brain?"

"Correct."

"The Bentley's tank holds twenty-five gallons," he said. "We'll soak the body and the interior with another ten."

"Suppose the car doesn't catch on fire?"

"The engine will be hot, and the smog burner will be hotter."

"But suppose the car doesn't—?"

"Christ, I'll *light* it first like a firecracker, okay?"

"Suppose the body falls out?"

"Not with the kind of shoulder harness in *that* Bentley."

"Who's going to set the car in motion and jump?" she said.

"I've got to be good for *something*," he said.

"And where does all this happen?"

"I'll show you the spot in Oxnard," he said.

"When?"

"Tomorrow. It's just off the highway but concealed from passing cars. Totally treacherous under the best of conditions."

"Why does a driver go off the road?"

"Poorly lighted, lost in the dark."

"To avoid an animal."

"Or he falls asleep."

"Or another car causes a near miss, then speeds away."

"The glare of headlights on high beam."

"Which way is the Bentley traveling?" she said.

"South," he said.

"Coming from where?"

"Santa Barbara, late at night."

"What night?"

"Saturday."

"Saturday?"

"Saturday," he said, with finality.

"How do you know he didn't have too much to drink the night he . . . *you* know?"

He shook his head. "Forget it."

"But *could* he have had a few that night?"

"I don't know for sure," he said.

"If he did have, it would be foolhardy to claim accidental death," she said. "You'd never collect double indemnity, but you *would* stir up an investigation."

"Then I'll have to find out," he said, frowning.

"How?"

"By talking to the one person who would know, if she can still remember . . . the girl who was with him that night."

"Oh, of course. But . . . would that be safe?"

"I can be as casual as hell when I go shopping at Holman-Meyer."

"Why do you look so worried?"

"I'm thinking about Marvin Gerber," he said.

"Right now that's wasted worry," she said. "He won't make a move until the beneficiary makes a claim. And you won't do *that*, will you, until the period of contestability ends, which in this case is a year?"

"Okay, then I won't bother worrying about Gerber *yet*," he said.

"Save your worrying for Anthony J. Brancusi."

"Brancusi the sculptor?"

"That's right, Brancusi the sculptor. He could carve out your future."

"And yours too, lady."

"I'm well aware," she said. Suddenly her head turned. "What was that?"

"What?"

"That noise."

"What noise?"

"At the bedroom door. I thought I heard someone."

"I didn't hear anything."

"Your head turned."

"Wait a minute." Could it have been David? He got out of bed quickly, went to the door and flung it open just in time to see a large shadowy figure disappearing through a doorway in the darkness at the far end of the hall.

Teddy moved forward quickly, hurried down the hall and called out softly, "David?"

But it couldn't have been David. The figure had been too large.

He went through the kitchen to Stanner's bedroom. The door was closed. Quietly, he opened it. The room was in darkness. It smelled of body sweat and whiskey. He heard the sound of heavy snoring and snapped on the ceiling light. Stanner lay on top of the covers on his stomach. He was naked, in a deep and drunken stupor.

Suddenly Teddy wheeled about as he heard quick footsteps and a door opening and closing at the other end of the house. He ran to the living room, stopped, glanced about, went swiftly to the big window and peered out. Something, *someone*, was darting across the front lawn beyond the driveway and hugging the shadows before disappearing from view. For an instant Teddy felt a sickening clutch of fear as his brain registered a fleeting impression of a tall bulky figure with long blond hair. Then, just as quickly, the fear turned to anger, at himself, for filling in details that hadn't even been there, and anger at the tequila for what it could do to the imagination. Whoever the man had been, whatever his reasons for fleeing so precipitously and furtively, there was no cause for panic, not yet there wasn't. But no cause for rejoicing either.

Either way, he'd have to have another one of those embarrassing damned talks with Stanner in the morning.

He went back to Howard's bedroom, hoping his face wouldn't give him away.

Jo Anne looked up with concern in her eyes. "What was it?"

"Nothing," he said. "David Stanner came home and went to bed. You must have heard him in the kitchen or something."

"That's all? Are you sure?"

"Yes," he said.

She continued to stare at him.

He got back into bed and busied himself examining some of the clippings in the cardboard files. Eventually Jo Anne joined in, and they started reviewing the plan all over again. But this time, for no openly stated reason, they both kept their voices much lower.

But they needn't have.

Bruce Gottesman was a good mile away by then, huffing and puffing as he ran through the darkness toward the taxi stand on Sunset, trying to burn into his memory what he feared his befogged and swooning brain would fail to hold onto when the Scotch finally caught up with him and zapped him unconscious . . .

Saturday night . . . Bluestern and the girl were going to go for broke on Saturday night . . .

That's what *they* thought.

And he had to remember. . . . What else was it he had to remember? . . . He had to remember what David had gurgled into his ear before passing out. . . . Save yourself, luv, save it for *me*, 'cause he'll be in New York Wednesday and Thursday night, and we'll have the whole bloody place to ourselves, won't it be beautiful, luv?

Better than that, much better than that, Bruce panted to himself as he ran.

With Bluestern back East, the Malibu beach house would be free and clear, nobody in it, nobody around. He'd be able to take his own sweet time and do it right, and give Bluestern and the girl the shock of their lives. . . . If only Diane would be fast asleep now when he got to the apartment. He wouldn't have to tell her a goddam thing until tomorrow, when the freezer was delivered. . . . All he wanted to do now was sleep, and remember what he had heard tonight, and forget what he had done in order to be able to hear it . . .

chapter 21

JO ANNE WOKE UP at dawn, feeling unlawfully contented but thirsty. She slipped out of bed without disturbing Teddy, and went inside to the kitchen to get some orange juice. On the way back to the bedroom she saw the black Volkswagen standing in the driveway, recalled suddenly that David Stanner had come home during the night, and immediately decided to get dressed and leave before breakfast. She would feel awkward in David's presence, and besides, she wanted to stop off at her own apartment before going to the studio, to change her clothes for the drive to Oxnard. She and Teddy had agreed that they'd go up there right after lunch.

In the bedroom, she got dressed as quietly as she could, but Teddy stirred and came awake anyway, long enough to ask her to take the medical books and the newspaper clippings back to the office with her. After she left, he fell back to sleep again and didn't get up until nine.

He waited until he was almost finished with breakfast before he ventured to ask Stanner, as casually as he could, what sort of night he had had.

"A trifle debauched, I'm afraid," the houseman said, pouring more coffee into Teddy's cup.

"You came in so quietly I didn't even know you were home."

"Special effort, sir."

"Alone?"

"Sir?"

"Did you come home alone?" Teddy said, very distinctly.

"Indeed," Stanner said.

Teddy wiped his lips with the napkin. "Why do you lie to me, David?"

The houseman didn't even blink. "Because I have a headache of such magnitude this morning I don't think I could weather the storm of your disapproval, Mr. Bluestern."

232

"You knew I was home last night . . ."

"Yes."

"You knew I was not alone . . ."

"Yes."

"Then why did you do it?"

"I was helpless, sir, and more than a little shitfaced. He swept me off my loafers."

"Who? Don Juan? Casanova? Who?"

"Bruce."

"Bruce who?"

"I haven't the foggiest. He picked me up at The Plumbers Union, a delightful little den of degradation in Hollywood."

"You didn't pick *him* up, he picked *you* up."

"I won't pretend that he carried me off kicking and screaming," Stanner said.

"But he did single *you* out," Teddy persisted.

The houseman stared at him. "Is that such an impossibility, sir, that somewhere on this planet there should exist a person who finds me attractive?"

"What did he look like?" Teddy said, not wanting to hear the answer.

"Very tall, dreadfully overweight, with long, pale yellow hair. If you want a more intimate description, I can furnish that too."

Teddy stared down at his empty coffee cup and tried to keep his voice flat and calm. "I want to know every single thing you know about him. Who is he, what is he, where does he come from, where does he live, could he be a private investigator? Anything and everything."

Stanner licked his lips, taken aback by the tension that was so poorly hidden in his employer's voice. "You've got to believe me now, Mr. Bluestern. I don't know a bloody goddam thing about him. I never saw him before in my whole bloody life. Street trade. Drop-in trade, that's all. Frankly, if you want to know the Lord's living truth, I had the feeling that he doesn't *work* my side of the boulevard, that he was, well, *forcing* himself a little."

Teddy looked up at him. "Did he ask any questions?"

"About what, sir?"

"About me, or about my brother?"

"Never, never, never," Stanner said. "My word of honor, which is sometimes good, and this happens to be one of those times."

"And did you tell him anything that perhaps you shouldn't have told him? Think hard now."

Stanner went into a reflective mode and finally said, "I'm afraid so, sir."

"What was it?"

"I inadvertently let slip that you had feelings that were somewhat more than friendly toward Miss Kallen."

Teddy stared at him. "That's all?"

"Isn't that bad enough? What's the use of apologizing? I'm hopeless, sir."

Teddy's lips tightened. He got up from the table abruptly. "Can you manage to get with him again?"

The houseman eyed him nervously. "Do you really want me to?"

"Can you?"

"I think so."

"How soon?"

"Tomorrow night."

"I'll be in New York tomorrow night."

"I know," Stanner said.

Teddy looked at him. "You're bringing him here?"

"I'm going to The Plumbers Union. He'll probably meet me there. If he doesn't show up, there's nothing I can do."

"Bring him here," Teddy said. "Find out who he is, what he is, where he lives, where he can be reached, phone number, everything. But don't press."

"Leave it to me, sir."

"I'll call you from New York. Or, wait a minute, if *I* don't, my secretary will."

"Miss Kallen?"

"Yes."

"Very well, Mr. Bluestern."

"You know, of course, that I'm pulling all kinds of strings at the studio to get you an interesting job."

"You don't have to, sir. I'm perfectly—"

"I know I don't have to, but I'm doing it, and I'll succeed, very soon. I just wanted you to know."

"That's very kind of you, sir."

Teddy left for the studio, hating himself for having to pander to David Stanner.

He was going to tell Jo Anne the whole story.

He had no idea how much the man named Bruce had heard through the closed bedroom door. Possibly nothing. Probably everything. Either way, Teddy was going to dump all of last night's little withhold into Jo Anne's lap, where it had belonged in the first place. He'd be goddamned if he was going to live alone with *this* one any longer.

DIANE SAT THERE in an empty pew, off by herself, listening to the silver-haired priest mumbling at the altar. She couldn't understand a word he was saying, and even if she could, what difference would it make? What the hell did he know about life? All he knew about was God and death.

She turned her head and saw an old man coming out of the confessional. He looked gray-faced and shaken. He probably felt worse now than when he had gone in. That's what they did to you. They lured you into that booth with promises, and once they got you in there they slipped you a whole new set of miseries in exchange for the old ones. What was so terrible about sin anyway? Who *said* you had to talk about it? Stupid beliefs and empty rituals. She knew more about sin than the priests did. Why should she talk to *them*? They should be talking to *her*. She was the expert. She had lived with sin for years.

She should have stayed home this morning and waited for Bruce to wake up. The noise of his open-mouthed snoring and the reek of his Scotch breath filling her bedroom were no worse than sitting here watching fearful people kneeling on the floor and lighting candles and listening to Latin mumbo jumbo. Church had never done anything for her. She gave it a tumble a few times a year just to keep her hand in, keep the franchise, in case they ever came up with some magic that worked, like how to be happy for one day in a row, or how to keep off the sauce for two.

Bruce had already crashed, dead to the world, positively *stinking*, when she'd gotten in from the airfield last night. So she hadn't even had *him* to talk to, not that he would have given a good goddam about anything that was eating *her*. Waking early, with him still out of it, she had had a fairly sizable belt of mouthwash to open her eyes a little and had come here to the church in Westwood, one of the dumber moves of a dum-dum life. Any port in a storm, Diane. One ear was as good as another, or just as useless.

She glanced to her right again. No one else had gone in. The confessional was empty. In her head, she tossed a coin, called heads, and came up what she'd always be, a loser. She got up, walked over to the booth, went inside and sat down and waited until she heard breathing on the other side of the screen.

"Good morning, father," she said.

"Good morning, my child." It was the gloomiest voice she had ever heard. Who needed that? Maybe she should say something to cheer him up, so that his voice wouldn't depress her so. She hadn't come here for a downhill slide, for Christsake. She wondered if his feelings would be hurt if she got up and walked out. It was too dark in here anyway. It needed better lighting, and a more cheerful decor too.

"What is it, my child?" the priest's voice said.

"I have sinned," Diane said.

"Tell me about it," the priest said.

"I destroyed my mother last night . . ."

"In what way?"

"I let her know that I know she's a whore . . . I let her know that I know she cheated on my father when he was alive, God rest his soul. . . . The only thing my mother had left in this life was the illusion that I didn't know what kind of woman she was. I took that away from her. I destroyed her . . . "

"And what was the sin, my child?"

"I'm glad I did it," she said.

There was only silence from behind the screen.

"Did you hear what I said?"

"I heard you," he said.

"Well?"

"Is there anything else?"

"I'm a hypocrite," she said. "Is that a sin?"

"Do you think it is?" the voice asked her.

"Yes, I think it is," she said.

Silence. This priest was very big on silence. On silence alone he could become pope someday.

"I'm no better than she is," Diane said. "In fact, I think I'm much worse. She isn't an alcoholic, she isn't schitzy, and she never murdered a man while he was sleeping. So I think I behaved in a very hypocritical manner with her, and that is my sin, father."

"Is that all you have to say to me, my child?"

"Isn't that enough?"

"I don't think you're ready for me," the priest said.

"What do you mean, not ready? I'm as ready as I'll ever be. I've got hypocrisy written all over me, and I'm asking you to do something about it, and you tell me I'm not ready. I don't understand you people at all. No wonder I never come here any more."

"Come back when you are ready, my child."

"I've confessed my sins and I'm asking you for absolution, father."

"Come back when you are ready."

"Are you suggesting that I leave?"

"I will be here waiting for you," the priest said.

"Don't hold your breath," Diane said, and got up and left.

On the way home she stopped off at Club 77 and had a few. Bruce probably wasn't up yet anyway.

MARVIN GERBER sat at his desk returning telephone calls. They were all business-related and did nothing to assuage his gnawing, indefinable psychic discomfort. After completing the last call, he summoned Madeline and dictated replies to several letters he had allowed to linger on his desk too long. When he was alone again, he felt the hollowness almost instantly and decided that he hadn't been putting sufficient effort into dealing with his list of potential new customers. He opened the top drawer of his desk and drew out the list. It was sizable. He picked a name at random. Paul Ziffren, a prominent attorney. The chances that a man of Ziffren's importance would be careless enough to have unfilled insurance needs were slim indeed, but Gerber had met him at a fund-raising dinner and did not believe in letting the stones of opportunity go unturned.

He called Paul Ziffren's office. The attorney was not only not in, he was not even in the country. Gerber called three other names on the list and received the brushoff he deserved. It did not bother him in the least. Any insurance salesman who was sensitive to brushoffs did not belong in the business. On the next try, he landed a luncheon date with a rising nightclub and television comedian named Danny Tolan. Tolan had been rising for fifteen years. Gerber wanted to catch him before he discovered that it was never going to happen.

Gerber looked at his wristwatch. He had a long way to go before lunch. His desktop was clean. The phone was silent. His doorway was open, but no one was coming in. He felt empty. There was something missing in his life, and he knew damned well what it was. Early that morning—while brushing his teeth—he had decided that he would have to make a certain phone call. And it was the one call he had not made. And he had run out of excuses for not making it.

He reached behind him and removed the West Los Angeles telephone directory from the bookcase. There was no Diane McWorter listed, but there was a D. McWorter, with a number and no address. He wrote the number down on a slip of paper, replaced the directory, got to his feet, and closed the door to his office. This was none of Madeline's business.

He called the number himself. It rang at least ten times; he wasn't counting. Obviously no one was there. He was about to hang up when he heard the phone clattering at the other end, and a man's voice answered. The voice sounded half asleep. Gerber was certain he had awakened the man. He was equally certain that the man he had awakened was his miserable-smelling visitor of the previous day.

"Is this the McWorter residence?" Gerber asked.

"She's not here," the man mumbled.

"Are we talking about Diane McWorter?" Gerber said.

"I just told you, she's not here."

"And who am I talking to, sir?"

"A friend," the man muttered.

"I'm sorry, I didn't get the name," Gerber said.

"Who *is* this?" the man demanded.

"Don't you recognize your friend, Marvin Gerber of Mutual of Oklahoma?"

"You must have the wrong number, mister."

"No I don't," Gerber said. "I just wanted to tell you that I spoke to my superiors here about your business proposition—"

"I don't know what the hell you're—"

"—And they were unanimous in feeling that I dismissed your suggestion too hastily—"

"You've got the wrong number."

"—So if you'd like to drop in and have another talk with me—"

"Don't call here again, do you hear me?"

Gerber heard the clatter of the phone, and the connection was broken.

He hung up slowly, assessing his feelings. He felt better now. Not terrific, but better. At least he had made the call. He had done what had to be done. Getting or not getting the man's name was not important. Reassuring himself that the man obviously had nothing to sell *was*. The man hadn't even wanted to hear him out. Not interested.

Good enough. No complaints.

Soon Gerber found his thoughts wandering back to the comedian, Danny Tolan. He had an idea he was going to enjoy having lunch with him. Even if he couldn't interest him in a policy, he'd get some laughs out of him anyway. Which was more than you could say about Howard Bluestern.

*   *   *

HE WAS THANKFUL that Jo Anne was on the other side of the closed office door where she couldn't see him or hear him now. He'd never be able to look her in the eye, and she'd be right too. Teddy Stern was getting lost in Howard Bluestern's shuffle, and it wasn't getting better, it was getting worse. He was beginning to sound more like Howard than Howard himself, and as for Teddy Stern, who the hell had time to be *him* right now? There was a *studio* to be run, and trouble here with two young punks who couldn't understand a simple word like no . . .

"Forget it," Teddy shouted.

"Look, we're all on the same side, Howard. We're with *you*," Larry Hough insisted.

"Then stop trying to ram something down my throat."

"Nobody's ramming anything down your throat."

"All right, then stop twisting my arm," Teddy said. "A no is a no, just like the five yeses I gave you are five yeses. I've *told* you fellows, you've pulled off a miracle and I'm tremendously grateful. So don't give me a hard time just because you're not batting a thousand."

"But, Howard—"

"I said no!"

Between Larry Hough's rasping doggedness and Jeff Barnett's wounded silence, he was slowly losing his already overcrowded mind, slowly losing his grasp on what was important in his life and what wasn't. Should he be caring *this* much that they had brought him one bad project out of six? Would Howard have to be one hundred percent right about *everything* he did and said before that board of directors in New York? Couldn't Howard be like everybody else and make mistakes? How could *he* be giving his time and his energy, his very *life's blood*, it seemed, to battling with a couple of executive assistants over one goddam film package when he should have been thinking about nothing else now but how to stage Howard's death and get away with it even though a mysterious man was dogging his trail?

"I want a replacement," Teddy said, very quietly. "Go out and find me another one. And don't make me say please."

"Are we to assume then that there is no hope at this studio for quality pictures?"

"There is no hope at this studio for quality pictures that also happen to be guaranteed commercial calamities."

"With *that* cast?" Hough cried.

"With that cast," Teddy said.

"What about the director's track record?"

"I don't care if he won the Triple Crown," Teddy said.

Hough turned to Barnett sitting on the sofa, hiding behind tinted glasses. "Jeff, for Christsake, will you say something?"

"Don't bother," Teddy said quickly. "Under no circumstances am I going to present to that board, which is loaded for bear, a twelve-million-dollar picture that takes place in a home for the aged."

"You're the head of the studio," Barnett muttered. "I guess you have a right to be wrong."

"If I had the time, I'd tell you what I think of that remark. Now, are you fellows going to go out and find me another one or not?"

Larry Hough turned away.

Teddy looked down at the other man. "Jeff?"

Barnett fussed with his glasses. "Question."

"Go ahead," Teddy said.

"What time does your plane leave tomorrow?"

Teddy stepped to the desk, leaned over and flipped the intercom switch. "Jo Anne, what time is my plane?"

"Twelve noon," she said.

Barnett shook his head slowly. "No way."

"You've got practically all day today," Teddy said.

"Still impossible," Barnett said.

Teddy frowned. "Tell you what. If you strike out today, I'll change the reservation and take a night flight, like eight or nine. That'll give you all of tomorrow too."

Barnett rubbed his chin, then shrugged and rose slowly from the sofa. "Ours is not to reason why, ours is just to try and try." He glanced at Hough, whose back was to him. "Larry?"

The pudgy man turned to Teddy, his lips quivering. "I made a *deal*, Howard. I followed *your instructions*. How the hell am I going to go back to those agents at IFA and tell them it's no cigar, the deal is off, if you won't even present it to the board and let *them* turn it down to get me off the hook?"

Teddy looked at him with serious expression. "You're right, Larry, and I'm really sorry to do this to you. But it's just not in my philosophy to be turned down by that board if I can help it."

Hough's voice trembled. "Well it's not in *my* philosophy to be double-crossed and have my credibility destroyed. I quit."

Teddy put an arm around his shoulders. "I won't let you, Larry. You're too good a man. I need you very much."

Hough blinked back tears and averted his face. "Please tell me what to say to IFA."

"Certainly," Teddy said. "Howard Bluestern is typical of the new breed of film-company executives. He is without ethics, without scruples, without honor. He is a liar, a cheat, a double-dealer, and not to be trusted."

Larry Hough nodded. "Thank you," he said softly, and followed Jeff Barnett out.

Also, Teddy reminded himself, you can tell IFA that Howard Bluestern is going to go out in style in New York with a big win and be remembered in Hollywood for the string of successes he left behind. *Bet* on it.

BRUCE WAS AWAKE. She could hear his voice through the door even before she got her key in the lock. She could hear other voices too, men's voices, and she couldn't imagine who they were. And then she opened the door and walked in and stood there for a moment, bewildered, because she had more than a few in her, and it took her a while to understand what the hell it was exactly that she was seeing.

Bruce was on his hands and knees on the living-room carpet helping two burly, sweating, T-shirted men shove casters up into the stubby feet of a huge, white-enameled box at the far end of the room. At first glance she thought maybe the box was a piece of modern furniture, and then she noticed how shiny it was and a crazy idea went through her head that was too unacceptable, so she let the thought keep on going, over and out, and she advanced into the room, feeling a nameless rage building up inside her.

"What the hell is that?" she demanded.

Bruce didn't even look up. "What does it look like?"

"Goddam it, answer me."

One of the men, gap-toothed and unshaven, turned his head. "It's only a freezer, miss."

Christ, she had been *right*. "In my living room? On my carpet?" The rage came into focus. She felt invaded, humiliated. "Get it out of here," she said harshly.

"This is where he told us to put it," the other man said, looking at Bruce.

She moved forward angrily. "Take the fucking thing out of here this minute."

"Now come on, Diane," Bruce whined, struggling to his feet.
"Don't tell me come on . . ."

"This is the only room it'll fit in."

"Out of the *apartment*," she shouted. "I want this thing out of
here *completely*. This is *my home*, not yours." She turned on the men,
who had straightened up to stare at her with frightened eyes. "Who
are you two?"

"Acme Movers," the sandy-haired one said. "We're only doin'
a job of deliverin'."

"Well you just get this thing the hell right back where it came
from."

"We don't have no work order for that."

"I don't give a damn *what* you've got—"

"Don't pay any attention to her," Bruce said.

"*How* . . . *dare* . . . ?" She whirled and slammed her fist into
his soft belly.

He cried out with pain and seized her wrist with one of his huge
hands, and when she tried to smash her handbag into his face, he grabbed
the other wrist, too. "Drinking again. Jesus, you *stink* of it . . ."

"Son of a *bitch* . . ." She kicked at his shins and he twisted her
wrist sharply. "Oh . . . *don't* . . ."

"You gonna cut it out?" he cried hoarsely.

The two men scurried toward the door. "We're leavin'. You can
read the instructions."

"Okay, okay," Bruce panted, struggling to subdue Diane. He
dragged her over to the sofa and threw her down on it. "Is that *it* for
now, or is there gonna be more?"

"Treacherous bastard." She looked past him at the freezer. "Why
didn't you tell me?"

"I *told* you I did some shopping yesterday."

"You call that shopping? And with my money?"

"It's an investment. You're gonna get rich from it."

"I don't want to hear about it," she cried fiercely.

She didn't need an explanation. She knew damned well what he
was planning to do, that was obvious. He was going to kidnap the
body and hold it for ransom, to be paid by Howard. He was going to
bring her poor dead Teddy into *her* home, into her living room . . .

Like hell he was.

She sprang to her feet. "Look, I want you out of here . . ."

Bruce's eyes widened. "What kind of shit is that?"

"I want you out of my *sight*, out of my *life*, so pick yourself up and get the hell out of here. I mean it. We're through."

He stood his ground. "Come on, luv, you don't mean that. You're just saying things because you're angry . . ."

"I'm goddam more than angry . . ."

"You haven't even given me a chance to tell you what I found out last night, what this is all about . . ."

"I don't *have* to know, I can *tell* what you're going to do . . ."

"Sit down, baby. Come on now, sit down and I'll tell you what." He spoke softly, easing her back toward the sofa. "You hear me out, just listen to me, and if you still want me to go, I'll go. I promise. Okay? Will you listen?"

She stared at him for a moment, fatigued by the very bulk of him. Anything to get rid of him, she decided. Anything to be done with him. "Go ahead," she said wearily, hating herself for saying it. She sank down on the sofa again and looked up at him. "Well, go on."

She sat there and watched him as he started to pace back and forth and tell her all the crap he claimed he had picked up the night before when he had gone back to Howard's house with David . . . stuff about a life insurance policy, and an upcoming trip to New York by Howard, and Howard's plot to steal ten million dollars from the insurance company by using Teddy's body, and how *they* would be able to hold him up and call all the shots once *they* had control of the body . . . and she could tell from the way Bruce avoided certain details that he was hiding something from her about him and David, as though she gave a damn, and it never even occurred to him, or maybe he didn't care, that she would know he had found out some of this much earlier than last night or why would he have ordered the freezer *yesterday*?

Diane listened closely and watched his face as he talked, particularly his eyes, shifty, avoiding hers, the eyes of a liar. He was lying to her. And he wasn't even a *good* liar. He probably thought that she was too drunk or too stupid to notice, so why waste the effort? And he was right in a way, because she didn't *care* which were the lies and which were the truths. All she kept hearing was the one thing that was important for her to know: he was going to give Teddy *back* as soon as he got paid off.

Of course if he weren't such a two-faced, untrustworthy monster, she could have told him right then and there that *she* had been the killer and pleaded with him that nothing he was planning had anything to do with rescuing *her* from her horrible predicament. But how could she dare confess to anyone as subhuman as Bruce Gottesman? He wouldn't even *care*. All *he* was interested in was the money . . . so obsessed with it, in fact, that she knew how useless it would be to try to convince him of the obvious: Howard would abandon his scheme immediately and go right to the police the moment he realized that someone was on to him. There would *be* no money.

Well, all *she* was interested in was her own survival.

She had *herself* to think about, and that was exactly what she was doing. Even as Bruce went on talking to her and lying to her and taking her for a fool, she was thinking about nothing except what she could possibly do to save herself now that she knew what he had in mind for *himself*. And it dawned on her gradually that the one big threat to her existence, the *real* threat, was the evidence of murder. Without that evidence, what was there that could convict her beyond the shadow of a doubt? Certainly not the words of guilty liars and conspirators like Howard Bluestern and Bruce Gottesman.

The only overwhelming threat to Diane McWorter was the body of Teddy Stern.

And long before Bruce had finished his windy, whining, lying explanations, Diane had known what she was going to have to do.

Impulsively, she got up from the sofa. "All right, enough," she said to him.

He studied her face tensely. "What does that mean? Are you with it?"

"What are we waiting for? Let's get it over with," she said tersely.

Bruce's relief gave way to a frown. "We're not doing a thing until Bluestern leaves town tomorrow."

"What time?"

"Twelve noon. I checked the airlines. But we're not going in until after dark, when he's three thousand miles away. I don't want any more surprises."

That's too bad, she thought, because you're going to get one, Bruce.

Her eyes went to the freezer, standing there in her living room. It hadn't been plugged into the wall outlet yet, it hadn't been turned on, it hadn't begun to hum.

To Diane, as she stared at the freezer now, it was as silent as a grave.

chapter 22

THE AFTERNOON SKY was blue and cloudless, and the hills of Calabasas on either side of the Ventura Freeway glowed green and gold in the warm sunshine, but inside the car the weather felt decidedly chilly to Teddy. His face was set in a deep frown as he gripped the wheel of the Bentley and peered at the road ahead. The silence was getting to him. Not just Jo Anne's, but his own too. Traffic was sparse on the multilane thoroughfare leading north to Oxnard. There were no high dramas here, no dangers, no near misses to relieve the strained atmosphere inside a moving vehicle, and right now Teddy needed all the help he could get.

He never should have told Jo Anne about the man who called himself Bruce. What purpose had it served other than to relieve *him* of a small portion of his anxiety? What was *she* supposed to be able to do about a phantom he could do nothing about himself? And he should have thought twice before admitting to her that he had twisted the truth about the man's presence in Howard's house last night. All *that* had done, he was certain, was restimulate her carefully buried feelings about the terrible lies he had perpetrated on her during the earliest days of their relationship. She had taken his confession in what, to him, had been the worst possible way . . . utterly coolly, without a trace of visible reaction. It had been damned unnerving. And then the silence on this drive, not even small talk, eating him alive now. He had had just about enough.

"Okay, you're really pissed off at me, aren't you?"

"Not at all," she said, looking straight ahead.

"No?"

"Disappointed," she said.

"You may not believe it," he said, "but I think what I was *trying* to do was spare you unnecessary worry."

She turned to him, and he could see in her eyes that she *was* angry, whether she knew it or not. "Not unnecessary. *Necessary*," she said hotly. "If there's any danger to us at all, anywhere, anytime, *I* have to know about it as well as you. With me, this is a full-time job."

He glanced at her sharply. "What's that supposed to mean?"

"Think about it," she said.

"For *me* a *part-time* job?"

"You're getting warm," she said.

"Back to the two slices . . ." He shook his head slowly.

"Frankly, I'm scared," she said, "and I wish you would be too, all the time. The two of you are trying to juggle so many problems, you're too *busy* and too *preoccupied* to be scared."

"Hey, wait a minute, I'm Teddy," he said.

"Are you *that* sure you know who you are at any given moment? I don't mean just with me."

"When it's important to know, *yes.*"

"How about this morning?"

"Howard," he said. "I was goddamned concerned about Larry and Jeff . . ."

"And you still are, *Howard.*"

"Look, it's not going to be easy to put a whole project together before this day ends."

"Are you talking about Oxnard?"

"Of course not . . . I meant . . ." He faltered to a stop. "I love you, honey, but fuck you."

She smiled in spite of herself.

Thank God, he thought. She still has one in her.

"Tell you what, Mr. Bluestern," she said. "If we don't get back in time, I promise to remind you to call your two eager beavers before six. Okay?"

"And don't you forget it, Miss Kallen."

"Now, inasmuch as there isn't a *thing* you can do about it until then, will you stop being the wrong brother?"

He put an arm around her shoulders and brought her closer to him. "Is this any better?"

"Much," she said.

Up ahead, he saw the green turnoff sign with white letters that spelled out MALIBU CANYON RD. A few miles away, at the western end of that road, lay the beach house. But they were headed in a northerly direction now.

He glanced at Jo Anne. "You know, timewise we're in very good shape. If it's all right with you, I'd like to take Malibu Canyon to the ocean, grab a quick peek at the house, and then shoot up the coast highway to Oxnard."

"Can I ask why the quick peek?"

"A little reassurance, that's all," he said. "Contrary to public opinion, I *am* scared of any guy who can be in my house, we *think*, in the morning, and in Howard's house the same night, without our even knowing who or why. All I know is I wish we had Saturday behind us already."

She looked at him, and she didn't have to say a word. Her eyes said it all.

If only he weren't going to New York . . .

He turned off the freeway onto Malibu Canyon Road, and tried to empty his head of problems large and small, while Jo Anne turned the car radio on and let some of George Shearing's soft jazz substitute for conversation. The winding road was relatively deserted now, free of the long lines of slow-moving cars that usually impeded the single narrow lane in each direction. Halfway to the ocean the terrain changed dramatically. Gentle curves through soft green hills became sharp and perilous turns through red-clay mountains, their sheared-off sides on the Bentley's right. To the left, beyond the narrow opposing lane, steep cliffs, some fenced, some unprotected, dropped off into the canyon floor hundreds of feet below. At carefully spaced intervals, turnouts had been fashioned on the edges of the cliffs so that slow-moving cars could pull off the road and allow impatient drivers in the rear to go through.

But death does not always give fair warning. Sometimes one's thoughts are inappropriate to the occasion. Teddy was wondering whether Jo Anne would resent it if he asked her to visit a few auto supply stores while he was in New York and pick up some five-gallon gasoline cans. She in turn was idly speculating on the probable reactions of her mother and father if she were ever to tell them the whole true story of Teddy and herself, and it almost brought a smile to her face.

The Bentley was taking the sharp turns with a smoothness that was deceptively reassuring, and the turns were coming up with a regularity that was almost hypnotic. Lost in thought, lulled by the radio, Teddy suddenly heard a terrible scream, and it was a moment before he realized it was Jo Anne, and she had grabbed the wheel, and then he was fighting her instinctively even as he saw the huge boulder in the road directly in their path, and he pulled sharply to the left to escape the unavoidable crash and jammed on the brakes and felt the big Bentley careening across the opposing lane and hurtling them swiftly toward the death that lay beyond the unprotected edge of the cliff, and he heard her shout "Teddy!" and he cried out hoarsely and twisted the wheel desperately to the right and there was a terrible skidding and the screeching of rubber and the rear of the Bentley swung around and hit the rocks at the edge of the precipice and suddenly they came from certain death back to life as the car slammed to a halt in a cloud of dust and Teddy leaned his head against the wheel with a strangled cry and heard Jo Anne moaning "Oh God" through the hands that were covering her face . . .

"Are you all right?"

"No," she said in a muffled voice. "Yes . . ."

"I'm . . . I'm sorry . . . I . . ."

She shook her head, silencing him.

They sat there for a few moments, waiting for the pounding of their hearts to subside and the fright and the sickness to let go of them. Then Teddy started the car again and moved it forward slowly and made a cautious U-turn and pulled into the nearby turnout and shut off the motor.

"Come on, honey," he said to her. She took her hands from her face. He saw tears in her eyes. He kissed her on the cheek. "Let's get out," he said.

She opened her door. He opened his. They met on the edge of the rim, and he held her hand as they looked down at the canyon floor a thousand feet below. In their haunted eyes they saw a terrible funeral pyre, they saw their bodies vanishing in searing flames, and they shuddered.

And Teddy saw something else.

"We don't have to go to Oxnard," he said quietly. "This is where it's going to happen . . ."

Jo Anne looked at him, her eyes stricken.

"Right here," he said. "On his way from the Valley to my house."

She buried her face in his shoulder, and he held her silently.

After a while they got back in the car and continued on. Neither of them felt like talking.

A dark bank of sea fog hovered offshore, waiting to move in and swallow up the still-bright sun, when the Bentley finally reached the coast highway and Teddy crossed over toward Old Malibu Road. The silent ride had helped them both to recover somewhat from their deeply felt primal fear, but they were not ready yet to trust their feelings completely.

As the car pulled up before the beach house, Teddy realized that he had forgotten completely that this was one of Mrs. Mahoney's days. "In case she shows up early, what's Howard doing here anyway?"

"Simple," Jo Anne said, as they got out of the car. "He's picking up something he left behind over the weekend."

"You're so smart," he said, trying to feel as light as he sounded. "Twice a year," she said, meeting his attempt.

He took out his key and let them in, and the first thing he did was double-check every room and closet in the house. On the back porch, Jo Anne watched him stand before the freezer, staring down at Howard's white coffin fixedly, hardly moving a muscle. She waited for him to open the lock and raise the lid. Instead, he merely tried the lock to make sure it was secure, patted the lid of the freezer twice in case Howard was listening, then turned away quickly and walked past her into the house. She was not surprised.

She found him in the kitchen, adding a postscript to the message he had left for Mrs. Mahoney: "Please leave *all* the lights *on*, and the *radio on too*, exactly as I've set it."

Reading over his shoulder, Jo Anne said, "Occasionally *you're* smart too."

"It'll scare away exactly one moth," Teddy said bleakly.

"Every little moth helps," she said, knowing full well that she could have suggested he spend the night here himself as his own best housesitter. But having seen him at the freezer, she had no wish to subject him now to explaining why he couldn't. Besides, what good would one night of security be when there would be unguarded days for evil to slip in here undetected?

In the living room, he turned on the stereo FM radio to KJOI, "music all the time," and set the volume moderately high. Then together they turned on every light inside and outside the house, and just before leaving, he took her by surprise, and she found herself turning unexpectedly right into his waiting arms. "Hello again," he said, and kissed her tenderly.

"Hello," she whispered, and gave him a gentle, lingering kiss in return, and it was at that moment that they both admitted to themselves that they were indeed feeling better again, especially about each other.

Outside, as they walked to the Bentley, Teddy saw a car approaching in the distance, and his heart did a little dip until he saw that it was not Mrs. Mahoney's battered old Chevrolet, and it was not slowing down.

They got into the big gray car and Teddy quickly pulled away.

He felt Jo Anne's eyes on him. "Back to the studio?" he said.
"Must we?" she said quietly.

He heard something in her voice, and looked at her, and saw it in her eyes. "Not right away," he said.

She moved close to him, held onto him, got as close to him as she possibly could, and tried to get even closer.

"I want to make love to you now until I die from it," she said.

"Yes," he said. "Yes." And his hand moved down and covered hers with a fierce grip, and he held her that way, never letting go, looking into her eyes occasionally but never letting go of her, until he pulled the car into the parking lot of Highcliff Manor overlooking the sea ten miles north of Malibu, and he held onto her hand again as they went into the lobby and up to the desk, and he held her close to him on the way up to their room, a warmly decorated room with a terrace facing the water, and a large bed from which they could see out to the edge of the distant fog bank as they lay down together in loving, intimate nakedness and joined themselves to each other, committed by unspoken agreement, born of their instinctive understanding of each other's needs and desires, to lie this way, joined together, allowing their love to flow from one to the other through their mouths and their tongues and their wordless sighs and their hands gently upon each other and his sex deep and secure in the wetness of her embrace and their eyes opening occasionally to adore each other until love became unbearable and had to be taken from view and he would speak to her in the innermost recesses of her soul without words and she would answer him back with the clasp of her love for him, and they lay that way forever and ever, restfully, peacefully, lovingly, wordlessly, there was no need to say anything, their love went back and forth from one to the other and fed upon itself and grew greater and greater and they became more and more filled with adoration for each other and yearning for each other, lying there joined together in each other's arms, kissing each other deeply and gazing into each other's eyes and listening to each other's sighs and feeling the hunger in each other's mouth and the ache and the longing at the depths of their union, speaking to each other there in the urgent tones of expansion and the answering grip of passion, and she knew from the feel of him, the heat and the stiffness and the throbbingness of him, that she had given him as much of her love as he could hold, and he heard her sighs, he felt the hardness of her against his chest, he felt the gentle heave of her bosom growing deeper and needier, she needed more room inside her, there was too much of his love inside her, she had no place left for it, and too much of her love for him, she was going to have to let go of it, she couldn't hold her love for him any longer, she couldn't handle it any longer, she loved him too much, too much, too much, she let out a cry as she knew that her love was more than she could bear and she cried out again at the beautiful agony of knowing finally that she was about to give it up and now she was giving it up and crying out and giving it, giving it, giving it, and he heard her and felt her and loved her all the more, too much, too much, for what she was giving him, and he began to answer her cries with cries of his own because he no longer knew what to do with all this love for her, he couldn't hold it any longer, couldn't contain it, endure it, withstand it, he couldn't bear it any longer, couldn't bear it, he was going to burst with it, he burst with it, he gave it, he was giving it and giving it and crying out from the excruciating ecstasy of giving his love to her, and they kept on giving their love to each other and crying out with the immensity of their feeling for each other, and they bathed each other with their love and moistened each other and anointed each other with it and joined their mouths together and never let go, never, not ever, never, never, never, and the fog finally came in from the sea and covered the sun and the room grew darker and they lay there together as man and woman in love . . .

Propped up in the marvelous big bed wearing nothing but the sheet that covered her, Jo Anne gazed out through the French windows at the fog swirling outside beyond the terrace and wondered to herself how many lovelier sounds there were in the whole world than the sound of a man whistling in the shower after he has just been to heaven and back with you. She reached out lazily, brought the telephone into the bed, direct-dialed her own number at the studio, and asked Grace Fahnsworth, her alter ego, if Mr. Bluestern had returned to the office yet. Mrs. Fahnsworth answered in the negative, whereupon Jo Anne inquired if there had been any calls, visits or interoffice memos from either Mr. Hough or Mr. Barnett.

No. There had been none.

Jo Anne requested the direct telephone numbers of the two men in question and informed the elderly secretary that she would be back at her desk just as soon as the dentist unchained her from the chair, and suggested that Mr. Bluestern be apprised of this fact when he returned.

Jo Anne then called Larry Hough. His secretary said that he was in a meeting in Jeff Barnett's office. Jo Anne called Barnett, whose secretary stated that he was in a meeting and could not be disturbed. Jo Anne characterized this statement as being a little pompous and told the young lady to convey a simple question from Mr. Bluestern to Messrs. Hough and Barnett while Jo Anne held the phone.

The question was Shall I take a later plane tomorrow?

The reply, when it came back, was brief.

Unfortunately, Yes.

Jo Anne then called Mr. Robin Jacoby in the Transportation Department and instructed him to take Mr. Bluestern off TWA at noon and place him on Eastern at eight P.M., which Mr. Jacoby successfully accomplished while she waited on the line.

Along about this time, a rather handsome young man smelling soapy-clean and wearing not very much emerged from the bathroom to be told by his secretary that he had not returned to his office yet, that his executive assistants were working, at the moment much harder than he was, and would continue to do so, and that he would therefore be departing for New York on the morrow eight hours later than had previously been scheduled.

The handsome young man took the news, which was not catastrophic but still nothing to cheer about, with unusual equanimity and good spirits, and his only immediate comment was that what he really felt like having now more than anything else he could think of was a bowl of good New England clam chowder.

Jo Anne thought that was a wonderful idea and asked if she could go as she was, and when her employer asked her what she meant by that, she showed him, and that led to all sorts of delays. But finally they had their clam chowder, the two of them, at a place on the water called the Sea Lion, and then, reluctantly, they entered the real world again.

chapter 23

WEDNESDAY in the Los Angeles Basin began with a cloud over its head, low and gray and dismal to the eye. But only a few were fooled by it. Most of the natives went to their places of work or play dressed for the hot sunny day that Wednesday was destined to become.

Marvin Gerber wore a white, short-sleeved cotton shirt, open at the neck, with his featherweight cocoa-brown suit, and spent a good part of the day at the Beverly Hills branch of E. F. Hutton & Company, a prominent brokerage house, where he amused himself buying and selling a number of medium-priced common stocks in transactions of anywhere from one-hundred- to five-hundred-share lots.

The pleasant increase in Gerber's income over the next five years, stemming from the quick and easy sale of the Bluestem policy, was going to provide him with plenty of playing-around money, and he knew it, and had decided the night before that dabbling in the stock market would be the ideal kind of playing around for him. It would provide him with day-to-day worries, day-to-day suspense, with nothing serious at stake, only a little money, all in all marvelous medicine for a man with Gerber's Disease, as he called it, the way some people called their illnesses Addison's Disease or Multiple Sclerosis. On this particular day, Gerber bought and sold a combined total of one hundred and eighty-two thousand dollars' worth of shares on the New York and American Stock Exchanges and made a net profit of three hundred and ten dollars for his efforts, which was nothing to write home about (because his wife would have been annoyed with him), but wasn't all that bad either. However, Gerber would have gained more enjoyment from his day's activities if he could have succeeded in thinking of his net profit as something other than merely the amount that would have had to be added to one hundred ninety-nine thousand six hundred and ninety dollars if he had been impulsive enough to have accepted the deal proferred to him by the blond-haired man who had lied his way into his office under the name of Gehringer, and from whom Gerber,

253

of course, had not heard a word since their abruptly terminated telephone conversation.

It would be at least another day before Marvin Gerber would know, with utter certainty, that such word, whatever it might or might not have been, would never come.

FATHER DINEEN MORAN of St. Mary's, Westwood, sat in his shirt-sleeves in the refectory while partaking of his morning bacon and eggs and toast and coffee, and felt considerable regret that he could not remain thus clothed—or, more accurately, unclothed—the whole day through, for the robes that he would soon put on would cause him to perspire grievously and were truly for no one's benefit, not even the Lord's, and yet he would wear them in the confessional booth just the same, just as he had worn them the day before, and countless days before that.

Buttering his toast now, he lapsed into thinking of the girl's voice again, as he had thought of it for a good part of the night, and he found himself hoping against hope that he would not hear that voice today, for he was tired after a poor night's sleep, and he did not want to face the burdens of conscience that would be placed on him were she to return to him today in the state of readiness that he had suggested to her.

If hope could be considered prayer, Father Moran's prayers would be answered. Ready or not, the girl would never return.

DAVID STANNER wore only his jockey shorts and a pair of sandals as he hummed Cole Porter tunes about the Bluestern residence this day, looking for things to straighten up that actually didn't need straightening. His employer had dined alone and slept alone the night before, and had left for the studio early this morning after having spent the previous evening studying what had appeared to be movie scripts, treatments and synopses, preparatory, Stanner supposed, to the trip to New York this very evening. There was little for Stanner to do right now but set out what he *thought* his employer might want to pack for the Eastern trip. After doing that, Stanner went outside and lay in the sun in the well-screened private area beside the pool, first taking off his jockey shorts and his sandals to expose the more popular parts of his body to the tanning rays.

He tried not to think about his hoped-for rendezvous tonight with the man called Bruce, for it would remind him of the heavy fact-finding responsibilities that his employer had laid on his shoulders, and David Stanner did not relish this task. And while he was unable to keep Bruce out of his mind entirely as he lay there in the sun, he did manage to confine his thoughts only to mental image pictures of some of the more pleasurable scenes the two of them would hopefully be enacting tonight, scenes having nothing at all to do with inquisitorial responsibility, scenes that would be taking place in any room or rooms he and Bruce chose, for the house would be theirs tonight, the whole night would be theirs.

And before long, as he lay there, David Stanner had something on his hands that he had not bargained for, which would not go away, it was quite insistent. And so he got up and took it inside the house, well-screened pool area notwithstanding, and it would be the last time he would utter Bruce's name quite that way ever again.

JERRY DANZIGER of the William Morris Agency had little interest in weather, good or bad, hot or cold. Always he dressed the same, tastefully and impeccably, in one of his variously shaded, variously patterned, lightweight worsted Dick Carroll suits, accessorized with Yves St. Laurent shirts, narrow knitted ties, and cordovan or black oxfords from Bally of Switzerland. While it gave him personal satisfaction to be more conservatively attired than was customary in the somewhat informal community of filmdom, vanity had little to do with it. He felt that his sartorial style added credibility and persuasiveness to his soft-spoken, low-key method of salesmanship in putting over those occasional deals that were of questionable merit. The hot packages needed no help.

Danziger also believed in conducting business in *his* office, in the newly remodeled building on El Camino Drive in Beverly Hills, rather than in the studio office of the producer or executive with whom he was dealing. He was a staunch advocate of the home-court advantage, of the mountain coming to Mohammed, and possessed a vast arsenal of excuses he used on each prospective buyer or seller in order to insure that the negotiation took place within walking distance of *his* men's room rather than someone else's.

It is immaterial whether Jeff Barnett and Larry Hough would have requested that Danziger travel to their studio if Danziger had not declared that he was expecting several crucially important overseas conference calls and could not budge from his office. It is immaterial whether the deal would have turned out differently if Danziger had worn a sport shirt, blue jeans, and Adidas running shoes instead of the gray worsted single-breasted, the pink Madras button-down, the slim maroon knit, and the black oxford wingtips that he wore that day. More important to the outcome of the proceedings, which lasted for two hours, was a factor that was totally unknown to Jerry Danziger. Barnett and Hough were desperate, and running out of time. Danziger could have worn only his underwear. The results would have been the same.

When the negotiations were over and the deal concluded, Danziger had obtained combined fees of two million dollars plus points for his two actors, six hundred thousand plus points for the director, three hundred thousand plus points for the original screenplay, and a guarantee that the budget would be no less than eleven million, with an additional guarantee of four million for advertising.

After Hough and Barnett departed, Jerry Danziger congratulated himself, and Yves St. Laurent, and Bally of Switzerland, and the entire staff of Carroll and Company, where he bought his suits. Hough and Barnett, in turn, congratulated their own dumb luck. While the project they had wrapped up was, in their considered estimation, sheer shit (Jeff had suggested that the title be changed to *Sheer Shit*), they knew that Howard Bluestern would see immediately the ease with which he'd be able to sell the project to the board of directors of American Foods. Not only was the film youth-oriented, it was a romantic comedy about a new breakfast cereal.

What Hough and Barnett did not know on this day, nor did Jerry Danziger, or he wouldn't have been so quick with self-congratulation or the pats on the back to Yves St. Laurent, Bally, and Dick Carroll, was that the package was worth three times what the deal called for. For such are the vagaries of show business and the tastes of the moviegoing public that *Sheer Shit* was to turn out to be the highest-grossing film in the history of the studio and would redound to the glory of the Bluestern regime for years to come.

THOUGH HE HAD MOVED out of his wretched furnished room in Venice and had transported his meager wardrobe to Diane's apartment in Brentwood, Bruce Gottesman insisted on wearing the same white (not so white) trousers and the same black turtleneck sweater today, even though the weather, and the olfactory sensibilities of others, dictated a change of clothing. Diane, who wore a smart gray poplin jumpsuit, white blouse with collar, and black lace-up flats, wondered to herself in a fit of pique if Bruce would be *buried* in the same damn outfit.

Actually, he would not be.

She drove him to the Majestie Meat Company on South Robertson Boulevard in Los Angeles, and watched him as he picked out a side of beef and a side of veal weighing a total of one hundred and eighty pounds. By the time the butcher had cut and trimmed the huge pieces of meat according to his customer's directions, which were inner-dictated by a need to simulate a certain physical shape, the total weight came to a hundred and sixty-one pounds.

Bruce paid for the purchase with some of Diane's money, and allowed her to drive him back to the apartment. Diane watched him place the meat in the new freezer and noted that there was plenty of room to spare. Bruce then invited her to drive him to the Barrington Ice Company in West Los Angeles, where he intended to pick up some dry ice, but Diane begged off and Bruce made the journey alone.

While he was gone, Diane seized the opportunity to make several telephone calls, the first call to Harry Blitzer, who was manning the desk in the airfield Security Office at the time. She inquired who would be on the gate that night from six to ten, and when Blitzer told her Lou Poliano, she cajoled Blitzer into giving her Lou's home telephone number, which she probably had somewhere around the apartment anyway.

Lou Poliano was audibly thrilled to receive a call at home from Diane McWorter, whom he always called honey, as in how's my honey today? He always loved to chat with her whenever she came through the gate, she was so high-spirited and full of fun. If he could have had another daughter (or did he mean a second wife?), he had always wished it could have been someone like Diane. Many times he had had that thought, and banished it instantly. She asked him for a favor now. Anytime, honey. Would he help her load something kind of heavy when she came through later? He said he'd be delighted to, honey, and Diane thanked him effusively.

Lou Poliano thought about that phone call all afternoon. He thought about that phone call so much he could hardly wait to go on duty. He had no idea he'd be thinking about that phone call for the rest of his life.

TEDDY WORE tan gabardine slacks, a pale yellow sport shirt, and a navy blue blazer early in the day. He would change to one of Howard's sleek, Dorso-styled business suits later on, when he returned to the house in Bel Air to get ready for the studio limousine that would pick him up and take him to the airport. Jo Anne had offered to go along for the ride, just to keep him company and be able to say that she had once held hands with him in the back seat of a limousine, but he had turned down her self-sacrifice with a smile, claiming that he didn't know if he could stand anything that sexually exciting.

They sat together in the office now, sharing a light lunch and equally light conversation, he at his desk, she on the sofa, with her steno pad and pencil placed conspicuously at her side for the benefit of the waiter who had brought their trays. Outside, beyond the closed office door, Grace Fahnsworth had been instructed to hold all calls. Jo Anne wore a pale green cotton dress, no stockings, and high-heeled bone-color shoes, and her honey hair, freshly shampooed and blown, made Teddy's heart grow faint every time he looked at her, which was constantly. They did far less talking than they might have, preferring to gaze at each other and luxuriate in the unstated longings and sweet sadnesses of a separation that hadn't even started yet.

Briefly they discussed the dossiers Jo Anne had prepared on each member of the board for Teddy to study on the plane. Then she told him of her plans to take her mother and father out to dinner on the nights that he would be away and promised him that she would not call him at the Regency in New York, though it was understood that she would never speak to him again if *he* didn't call *her* just as soon as the board meeting was over, regardless of whether the news was good or bad. Also she warned him that she intended to meet his plane on Friday whether he liked it or not. That was the closest they came to talking about the future. Friday. Saturday would be with them soon enough. Why rush it?

When Mrs. Fahnsworth's voice came through on the intercom announcing that Mr. Bluestern's two executive assistants had successfully completed their mission and were on their way back to the studio, Teddy and Jo Anne were already past lunch, and already aware that, in a way, it was time to say a kind of good-bye that neither could quite define, though they both felt it strongly. It was in their eyes and in the gentleness and tenderness with which they held each other and kissed each other as they stood in the center of the room murmuring words of endearment.

They clung to each other and resisted the passionate urges that had quickly risen in both of them, for passion was not what they wanted to express now, and neither of them could understand why there were tears in their eyes, for they were truly happy about each other, and yet there were tears in their eyes, so it must have been something of sadness they were feeling too, perhaps for all that had not happened yet, much of which was planned and known to them and was by its very nature unhappy, and for all that they could not know about, for it had not been planned and had not happened yet, but would happen, as it often did when two people dared to be too happy together.

This then was their good-bye, even though Teddy did not leave the office until shortly after four, after the meeting with Hough and Barnett. He had quickly read a synopsis of the new screenplay, the sixth and final project, and had known after the first page that it was exactly what he wanted. He'd start reading the screenplay itself in the limousine and finish it on the plane. His attaché case was full, his battle plan complete. He walked out of Howard's office with no last looks around. Without knowing that he did, he already knew something.

EVEN THOUGH it was almost five-thirty and much of the desert was in shadow, the outside air temperature in Palm Springs was 120 degrees Fahrenheit. Inside her house on Palmetto Drive, Millie McWorter had the air conditioning adjusted to an unusually conservative 80 degrees. She did not like the place to be too chilly when she had no clothes on. Besides, Phil liked things on the warm side when he came over. He claimed that he always had a better chance for an orgasm when he was too hot, rather than too cold. That was why he had moved to Palm Springs from Detroit in the first place, only to discover that it was warm on the outside but freezing on the inside. The two things he liked best about Millie McWorter, aside from her voluptuous body, were her willingness always to be naked when she greeted him at the front door and her preference for a warm bedroom when they got down to it.

Phil was late now, but Millie McWorter was not displeased. In fact, she wished he would call and say he wasn't going to be able to make it at all, that his wife was coming down from LA or something, or that he couldn't get away from the office—anything. She was in no mood right now for his frantic efforts to capture the ultimate pleasure. Whenever she had something on her mind, he could sense it immediately, and it invariably added to his difficulties. It could take him two hours tonight. Maybe he wouldn't get off at all.

She sat down on the side of the bed, placed the phone on her naked thighs, and dialed Diane's number again. When she got no answer, she dialed the operator and asked *her* to try it. Still no answer. Obviously Diane was not home. She wouldn't just *not answer*. Millie McWorter thanked the operator, hung up, went inside to the living room, and poured herself some straight Scotch.

For many years of her life she had secretly hoped that someday, impossible as it might have seemed, her daughter, her only child, her Diane, would become her friend (she had never dared, not even to herself, to hope for *love*). Last night Diane's visit, her horrible words, had been a crushing blow, but bad as it had been, it had not been entirely unexpected. Today's phone call from Diane had been infinitely more upsetting. And if anyone had told Millie McWorter that someday her daughter would tell her that she loved her, and that when she did, it would shock Millie and fill her with dread, Millie would have told them they were crazy.

Maybe it was the tears. She had never liked to hear Diane crying, even when she was a little girl. Maybe it was the way Diane had kept apologizing for her whole life, and saying too many times how sorry she was for having done things that Millie couldn't even remember, and all those other things she had said about making some kind of dangerous trip tonight, Millie hadn't understood half of it, probably the poor child had been drinking again, but obviously she was in some kind of trouble, even last night she had hinted at *that*, and now she was going to get into even more trouble, dangerous trouble, to hear her tell it. So it wasn't that Millie was being ungrateful for her daughter trying to make up with her. Millie was *frightened*, and had good reason to be, and she would keep on *being* frightened until she managed to get through to Diane on the telephone and speak to her and reassure herself that nothing serious was going to happen to her. She hadn't liked the sound of her voice and the ominous tone of her cryptic words, and if Millie didn't succeed in getting through to her soon she was going to put something cool on and get in the Eldorado and turn on the air conditioning and try to get across the sweltering desert and back to Los Angeles in a couple of hours and maybe *find* Diane someplace before anything happened.

She'd keep trying her on the phone, as she had been doing now for over an hour, and if that didn't work, she'd give up and make the long trip, inconvenient as it would be. She didn't know for sure that Phil was going to show up, he was so late, but if he did, she'd have to do her best to drive him crazy into a quick orgasm before he got a chance to worry about himself and ruin everything. She thought of a few things she could do to him and soon realized that there were a few advantages to his showing up. At least the desert would have cooled off a bit by the time he left, and there'd be less traffic on the freeway for her. She'd try the phone again in a few minutes. Right now she was going to have another Scotch first.

She poured a good stiff belt into her glass and turned the hi-fi on and got some good slow jazz. The sun had long since disappeared behind the mountains and dusk was coming and the house was getting shadowy and mysterious and alluring, and she liked the way she felt as the Scotch warmed her blood, and she liked the way she looked to herself in the mirrors on either side of the fireplace as she undulated back and forth and imagined Sam or Jack or Phil seeing her this way, and then she heard the front door chimes sounding, and her heart leaped a little, and she felt the moist hunger beginning between her legs as she went to the front door and opened it and let Phil in, and she loved the way he looked her over with his pleased and greedy eyes, and by the time they had had a couple of drinks and gone into the bedroom, she couldn't quite remember why she had been hoping that he wouldn't show up, and when he mounted her, she raised her knees and spread her tan thighs and brought him deeply into her, and after that she didn't care how long he took, she hoped he would take forever.

THE LIMOUSINE came too early, and Teddy was not surprised. Studio drivers always played it on the safe side. Even on those rare occasions as an actor when he had had the luxury of a limousine pickup and a ride to a location, his driver had shown up before Teddy was even awake. He could have imagined then how safe they'd play it for a studio head with a plane to catch. After tonight, he wouldn't have to imagine it. He now knew.

David Stanner placed Teddy's one small piece of luggage on the rear seat and Teddy carried the attaché case himself. They shook hands when they said good-bye in the driveway, and neither of them mentioned the man called Bruce. That subject had been thoroughly covered the day before and needed no further discussion. When the black Lincoln pulled away, Stanner went back inside the house and began immediately to anoint himself for the night's adventure.

The studio driver, whose name was Schultz, took Sunset Boulevard west to the San Diego Freeway and headed south. Traffic was bumper-to-bumper in the other direction, but only moderately heavy going south, and Teddy found it easy to concentrate on the original screenplay that Jerry Danziger had dealt to Hough and Barnett for far less than it would prove to be worth. By the time the limousine reached Los Angeles International Airport and pulled up before the terminal, Teddy had read rapidly almost half of the script, and had actually laughed out loud many times, astonishing himself with the unfamiliar sound of his own laughter.

The screenplay had had another effect on him. Its breezy, silly good humor had served to let some of the tension of the last few days leak out of him. He felt almost too relaxed as he stepped out of the limousine. He tipped the driver Schultz too heavily, did the same with the redcap who took his bag and checked it through, and even found it difficult to feel more than mildly irritated when he looked up at the flight board once he was inside the terminal and saw that his plane would be thirty minutes late in departing.

He heard a woman's voice call out "Hi, Teddy," and he started to turn, then caught himself and slowed the turn considerably, so that when he found himself facing a heavily made-up Mexican girl he did not recognize, he was able to smile at her easily and say, "I'm not Teddy, but you're very close." The girl laughed with embarrassment and said, "Oh, excuse me, Mr. Bluestern," and he said, "Quite all right," and walked on through the crowded ticket counter area.

Obviously she was an actress, or a hairdresser, or a wardrobe lady, something like that. He had such a lousy memory for names and faces. On his way to the lounge he kept trying to place her, and in running down the list of some of the shows he'd done, he was an actor for a moment, back on the sound stages again, and just like that it flashed on him suddenly that he had forgotten completely to tell Sam Kramer how he had straightened out the Jud Fleming situation. It was a base he had failed to touch.

He glanced at his wristwatch. Plenty of time to kill. Too much, in fact. And there was an outside chance that he might still find Kramer in the office. That place rarely closed if there was still a buck to be made. He went to the telephone booths along the wall, put on his Teddy Stern hat, and gave it a try.

"He's gone, Mr. Stern," Ruth said in her melancholy voice.

"Don't *you* ever go home?" he said.

"What for?" she said, and she had a good point there.

"Do me a favor, will you? Tell him I got my brother to apologize to Jud Fleming. Everything is now buddy-buddy, and Howard is having lunch with Fleming next week."

"That's wonderful, Mr. Stern. I think Mr. Kramer will be very happy to hear that," she said.

"Anything that makes him happy makes me happy," he said.

"By the way, Mr. Stern, a Mr. Marzula, Joey Marzula, has been calling here several times to see if we knew where you could be reached. He's been trying to get in touch with you . . ."

"Yes, I know . . ."

"I have his number here—"

"No, that's all right, I—"

"Four five one, two two hundred."

"Thanks, Ruth."

"Did you get it? Four five one, two two hundred."

"Yes, I got it. Four five one, two two hundred. Go home, Ruth."

"Maybe I will," she said.

He hung up and started out of the booth, and then decided to get it over with, and went back in and put another dime in and called the restaurant. It was a little too early for the dinner crowd, but he could hear the action at the bar in the background when a girl whose voice he didn't recognize answered, and he asked for Joey.

"Is this for a reservation?" she asked.

"No," he said. "Let me have Joey."

"Hold on a minute."

Why *not* hold on a minute? He had no place else to go. If that driver hadn't come so damned early, and his plane weren't taking off late, he'd have less time to fritter away now. He could kill the time with a couple of margaritas at the bar, but he didn't want to drink if he could help it. He wanted his head reasonably clear until he had finished the screenplay on the plane. His consumption of alcohol had dropped alarmingly in the last few days. Being Howard had given him some bad habits.

He fingered the attaché case in his lap, and was reminded of the dossiers on the members of the board. *More* homework at thirty-nine thousand feet. You lead a hard life, Bluestern. Soon he'd be back on the beach and at the Y, playing handball with Joey Marzula again. But first Howard had to slay a few dragons in New York. He sat in the booth waiting, watching the crowds hurrying by on their way to the boarding gates upstairs. Then he heard Joey Marzula approaching the phone. It was good to hear Joey's voice. He realized how much he had missed it. He heard Joey pick up the receiver.

"Hello?"

"No, I will *not* take a job as a busboy," Teddy said, with a smile on his face. "There are limits."

"*Hey . . . Teddy . . .*"

"Hey . . . Joey . . ."

"You know how many times I called you?"

"I only got one message," Teddy said.

"That's because I stopped leaving my name on that fucking machine of yours," Marzula said. "I figured you'd be dropping in Sunday night."

"I was out of town," Teddy said.

"How's Diane?" Marzula said.

"Why do you ask?"

"Why not?"

"She's okay," Teddy said.

"Are you sure?"

After a moment, Teddy said, "All right, Joey, what is it?"

"I know you two have split," the restaurant man said.

"Good news travels fast," Teddy said. "Who told you?"

"She did."

"You want her, you got her."

"That's not funny, Teddy."

"I know. I'm sorry."

The operator broke in and told Teddy his time was up.

"Where are you?" Marzula asked.

"A phone booth," Teddy said. He was going to say good-bye and hang up. Instead, he dropped a quarter into the slot, because he liked the sound of the chimes.

"Look, I know this is none of my business," Marzula was saying through the bong-bong-bong. "I got no idea what has or hasn't gone down between you two, or whether the trouble is just a temporary thing . . ."

"It's not just temporary," Teddy said.

"Still, I wouldn't rest easy if I didn't tell you things you probably already know . . ."

"Like what?"

"This guy she met at my bar Friday night, and went off with. Have you seen her since Friday?"

"No, I haven't," Teddy said. "What guy?"

"Have you talked to her?"

"No."

"I warned her, Teddy. I tried to stop her, but she left with him anyway. I mean, how do *I* know if you still care?"

"Who's the guy?"

"Very bad news," Marzula said. "Manny Clinko, you know Manny
. . . Well, Manny says the talk is that this guy is really an ex-con
passing himself off as an actor . . . assault and battery, car theft,
housebreaking, and that kind of shit . . ."

"Doesn't sound like Diane's type," Teddy said, not yet certain
why his mouth was going dry.

"Her *type?*" Marzula exclaimed. "You know how fussy *she* is,
for Christsake . . . *finicky*. And this guy is the biggest, fattest, fuckin'
mountain of flab you ever saw. This guy, I'm telling you . . ."

Teddy pulled open the door of the booth. He needed the noise of
the crowds hurrying by. He wanted the sound of laughter and the click
of heels on the stone corridors and the babel of voices in meaningless
chatter, not Joey Marzula, who wouldn't shut up.

" . . . Claims he's an actor, but who the fuck knows *what* he is.
SAG never even *heard* of no Bruce Gottesman . . ."

"Who?"

"Bruce Gottesman he calls himself."

Oh God . . .

"Listen, Joey, I gotta run—"

"I just don't understand that girl . . ."

"Gotta go now." He had to get off the phone before panic set in.
It was in his voice already . . .

"So when'll I see you, Teddy?"

"I have to *go*, Joey. I'll call you. Okay?"

"Okay but—"

Teddy quickly hung up and stared at the phone, his face ashen.
It had been Diane all along . . .

With someone called Bruce Gottesman . . .

She had teamed up with an ex-con, a thief, a housebreaker, who
had invaded *his* house and *Howard's* house and could do it again,
would do it again. What was there to stop them? No secret was safe.
Nothing was safe. Was there anything Diane wanted to know that she
couldn't find out? How much had the man already found out for her?

What was it she wanted?

Questions flooded in on Teddy, overwhelming him.

Why had Diane suddenly taken up with the kind of man she ordinarily
loathed and detested?

What were she and the ex-con *after?*

Why had she been waiting outside Howard's office for a whole
morning while her accomplice was lurking around the beach house?

Why had the man called Bruce deliberately picked up David Stanner and infiltrated Howard's house, and what had he been listening for outside the bedroom door?

Why had Diane suddenly appeared in the world of Marvin Gerber?

Why had she suddenly melted into the background, gone strangely silent, biding her time . . . waiting . . . ?

She was *waiting*.

For *what*?

She and a housebreaking, car-stealing thief were waiting for *what*?

For him to leave town?

For him to leave the beach house unguarded?

For him to leave *Howard*?

No. Impossible. They knew *nothing* about Howard.

Or *did* they?

Hadn't the man been listening outside the bedroom door the night he and Jo Anne—?

Teddy's heart sank.

Suddenly he recalled every jealous, vengeful moment that Diane had ever inflicted on him.

What was the *biggest secret* that he, Teddy Stern, her former lover, now involved with another woman, was trying to hide?

What was the *worst single act* that Diane McWorter could carry out now, short of murder, that would ruin the lives of both the man who had jilted her and his newfound lover?

Scandal.

Exposure.

Incrimination.

Criminal disaster.

The end of everything.

Diane McWorter had found him out, right? Or if she hadn't, she was about to, no? She and her accomplice were doing everything they could to destroy him, and by association, Jo Anne too. What *else* could they be up to? *That was it.*

And what better time to do it than when he was out of town, when they would have free rein, the run of both houses?

Good God, he had told David to bring the man to Howard's house tonight, and it was too late to reach David now. What *was* that place he had gone to? But what was the difference? It was too late.

And who would guard the beach house?

If only he could reach Jo Anne, but she was gone for the evening . . .

Fear raced through his body. His brain couldn't comprehend it all yet, it was too soon, but his body sensed the threat, his body knew that their whole future, more than *that* if there could *be* more than that, was in mortal danger, could be blown apart.

His heart was pounding as he rushed from the booth and began to run through the terminal, against the human tide, crashing into people without apology, pushing them aside, shoving his way through the crowded entrance and out into the night, shouting hoarsely and looking about wildly for a taxi.

Whatever Diane and the man called Bruce were planning to do, it could be nothing but disaster for him and Jo Anne. He *had* to find out what it was.

He had to *stop* them.

chapter 24

IF ONLY she could have done what she was about to do tonight without having to use Bruce. But she needed his strength, his physical strength, the only kind of strength he had. She sat in the Datsun, parked in the darkness across the road from the beach house, waiting for him to complete the transfer inside. He didn't really need her out here as a lookout. Nobody was going to barge in on him. Howard was in far-off New York by now. Still, it was just as well that she was out here, not in there with Bruce. She wouldn't have been able to take it. Only someone like Bruce could have handled that frozen, naked, broken body and place it in its new shroud without getting sick, without feeling anything. Bruce had no feelings. He was a monster. It was important that she remember that. A monster.

She reached across to the glove compartment, opened it and took out a small bottle of Wild Turkey. Uncapping it, she took a deep swig, then put the bottle back, even though she could have used more. She couldn't afford to lose her concentration, not tonight she couldn't. She felt strangely calm but didn't trust it. Did calmness mean that she had managed to work up the necessary courage, or was it the numbness of fear?

She glanced up as she saw a glint of light in the rear-view mirror. Far behind her, a car had turned into Old Malibu Road and was rapidly approaching. The headlights grew larger and brighter. She held her breath for a moment. Then the glare swept by and became the red tail lights of a car disappearing into the darkness up ahead. Suddenly her peripheral vision caught another gleam of light, and she turned her head sharply. From inside the house, Bruce had opened the door cautiously and was signaling to her.

He was ready.

She wasn't.

She'd never be.

Fear clutched her heart for an instant, then let go.

She got out of the car, went to the rear and raised the hatchback door. Crossing the road to the house, she sensed terror lurking beneath her calm, waiting to pounce. She drew several deep breaths, cursing herself silently for her gutlessness. What was she afraid of? This wasn't the ultimate moment. There was only Teddy to face now, and he was dead.

Inside the house, on the back porch, she stared down at him without having to see him. He was inside the brown plastic garment bag from Sears, the one with the colored stripes, stretched out on the brick floor. The dry ice surrounding his body made the suit carrier bulge unnaturally, and she thought she was going to be sick, but after the first wave of nausea she got control of herself and looked up at Bruce, who was watching her. She hated the loud music that was playing in the house. It unnerved her.

"Well, come on, do something," Bruce said impatiently.

She looked at him blankly.

"Go into the bedroom and get a pair of his slacks and a shirt and some socks and shoes.

"Must I?" She heard the tremble in her voice.

"Yes."

"Why?"

"In case we need them. You never know. Now go on."

She went to the bedroom and got in and out as fast as she could, returning with some blue jeans and the other stuff.

Bruce pointed to the empty dry-ice containers on the floor. "Put those in the back of the car with the clothing and come right back."

On her way out she saw him replacing the frozen food packages in the freezer, and when she came back into the house, the freezer lid was closed and the padlock was in place, and he was standing over the chocolate-brown plastic thing on the floor.

"All right, you take one end and I'll take the other," he said. "And be careful."

She stared down, unmoving.

"Go ahead. He won't bite you," Bruce snapped.

He let her take the end with the feet, probably without even thinking, certainly not out of any feeling for her. The body felt much lighter than she had thought it would. For a moment she wondered whether she might have been able to manage it alone, but that was beside the point now. It was too late for that. They carried the body outside, set it down on the walkway, and then Bruce went back into the house to make sure he hadn't forgotten anything. Diane did not like standing alone with Teddy lying at her feet, but she knew that the sooner she got used to it, the better it would be for her later on. If she had had the small bottle of Wild Turkey on her now, she really would have tilted her head back.

Presently Bruce emerged from the house and closed the door behind him, leaving the lights blazing the way he had found them. Then together they picked up the body again and carried it across the road to the open rear end of the red Datsun, and now Diane stopped making believe to herself that she was calm. The tightness in her chest, the coldness of her hands, and the unbearable pounding of her heart made the lie impossible.

She helped him set the ice-packed body down carefully in the back of the car. Then she turned away slowly and started walking toward the front door on the driver's side.

"Wait a minute, help me with this," he called out.

She stopped and turned and saw him unfolding a large blanket. She hesitated.

"Come on. Hurry."

She walked back to his side, took one end of the blanket, and together they wrapped it around the freezing plastic carrier with the body inside it.

He reached up to close the hatchback door.

Suddenly she wheeled and ran, her heart in her throat.

It was only a few strides to the front of the car but it took her forever. She heard the hatchback door slamming shut as she slid behind the wheel. The starter was already turning over as she saw Bruce lumber forward. The engine missed on the first turn. *And* the second. *Christ!* It fired up on the third. *Go!* She wrenched the lever into Drive. Bruce's door flew open. The car leaped forward.

"Hey, wait a minute!"

He was halfway in.

He was in the car.

The open door was swinging shut with the forward lurch of the car and he was inside now.

"What the hell do you think you're doing?" he cried.

"I . . . I thought I saw someone coming," she said in a strangled voice.

"Goddam fool, you almost killed me," he muttered, eyeing her strangely.

"Almost," she said to herself bitterly.

She drove on into the darkness, weeping silent tears of self-hatred and disgust.

But not for long.

She couldn't afford the luxury of self-pity now.

There wasn't enough time.

Driving through the darkness, feeling his suspicious eyes on her, she began to think about her alternate plan, the one she had been hoping against hope that she could avoid.

CHRIST, the *traffic!*

"Where the hell is everybody *going*?" Teddy cried with exasperation. "It's not even the rush hour."

"Every hour's rush hour, mister," the cabbie said.

"Can't you do something?"

"Whaddaya want me to do, fly over them?"

"How about getting off the freeway?"

"That ain't gonna accomplish nothing. Besides, we're practically to the coast highway anyway."

"*Shit.*"

"I agree with you," the cabbie said. "This whole damn city is shit."

Teddy peeled off his jacket, loosened his tie, and fell back on the seat again, feeling his shirt clinging wetly to his body. He looked at the attaché case in his lap and wondered if he'd ever get a chance to open it and use its contents. The last plane to New York, the Redder Than Red Eye Special, left at midnight. Would he manage to track down the danger here in time to prevent it, and would he be able to do *that* in time to be in New York tomorrow at noon?

The hell with tomorrow, tonight came first.

The important thing was, Would this cab ever get him to that parking lot on the beach?

Would he ever see the yellow Porsche that was waiting there for its rightful owner?

He was Teddy Stern now. Howard Bluestern would have to wait. He was Teddy Stern and he was going to find Diane and the big son of a bitch she was working with and he was going to get to them before they wrecked everything for him and Jo Anne, out somewhere with her parents now, laughing somewhere, happy somewhere, oblivious to the evil that lurked all around her. Even if he'd had the time, he wouldn't have known how to reach her. And if he *had* reached her, what could he have told her? That they had allowed their love for each other to lull them to sleep?

He felt the careening cab swerve northward onto the coastal highway, and he uttered a silent prayer that he hadn't awakened too late.

SHE LISTENED to him talking to himself like it was *her* he was talking to, but it was all for his own benefit, to bolster his confidence, to make himself believe that he really knew what the hell he was doing, which he didn't, of course. She kept her eyes on the highway and drove very carefully, not trusting herself or the darkness completely, because she wasn't all that sober. Not that she was loaded or anything. She just wanted to make damned sure that she didn't run a red light, or wander over the double yellow, or do some other silly little thing that would bring one of those sneaky patrol cars out of the shadows and up behind her with the red lights flashing, and some macho blue-eyed blond-haired smartass in a badge and a uniform sauntering up to the car and frightening her totally to heart-stopping death by saying, What's that in the back of the car there, lady?

So she watched the road and the opposing traffic and with half an ear and half a mind she listened to him going on about how he was going to *toy* with Howard, play *games* with Howard, milk him slowly, make him twist and turn before tightening the screws and taking him for the whole mint and more, and how, after it was over, he was going to buy himself a business somewhere, in the Middle West somewhere, the hell with California, he hated it here, the phonies and the pretenders, he was going to set himself up and have a good life for himself with all the things he had never had, and she listened to him rambling on and on, with her half an ear and her half a mind, and not once did she hear him say anything about *her*, not once did he bother to include *her* in his plans, he wasn't even making believe any more, she was cast aside, worthless, good for nothing at all, before he was even through using her, and that pleased the hell out of her, it really did, that he was so dumb and careless and unfeeling and cruel that he would talk about himself and his future as though she didn't even exist any more. It would have been awful if he had said anything nice about her. That would have been the worst thing he could have done right now.

She turned left off the highway at the three-way light and made the long climb up the curving road to San Vicente Boulevard and drove east for a mile until she reached the tree-lined block where she lived, and not once did she interrupt him, she let him do all the talking, and certainly there was not a word out of Teddy, riding so cold and silent and lonely behind them.

She brought the car to a stop at the entrance to the garage beneath her apartment house, and she had to poke Bruce in the arm to get him to stop talking, and she pointed to the glove compartment to remind him about the remote-control box. He took it out and pressed it, and when the wrought-iron gate rolled to one side, she drove forward and down and brought the car to a careful stop in her assigned parking space near the elevator and turned off the motor. And in the sudden silence, with all the traffic far away now and Bruce quiet for the moment, she thought that she could hear the wild beating of her heart and the blood pounding through her veins, and she was afraid that Bruce would hear it too, but it was all in her imagination of course and the only thing that she heard was the iron gate rolling closed behind them.

They sat there for a moment, glancing about at the ghostly rows of empty cars in the dimly lit garage. There was no one around. Bruce looked over his shoulder at the blanket-covered body, and then at Diane.

"Well," he said. "Shall we?"

She felt the blood leaving her face. Her mouth was dry. She was afraid to speak, afraid to let him hear her voice. She nodded her head.

He opened his door and, grunting, squeezed himself out of the car into a standing position. "Go on upstairs, open the door and come right back down," he said to her.

Diane reached for her handbag, opened it, and started rummaging through it. She sat there behind the wheel, glancing about her as though searching for something.

"Well come on," Bruce said impatiently.

"Oh my God . . . " she moaned.

"What is it?"

"You're going to hate me, Bruce," she pleaded.

"What do you mean?"

"I did a terrible stupid thing," she said. "I left my house keys upstairs in the apartment. They're not here."

He leaned down and stared at her. "Look, this is no time—"

"I *mean* it, Bruce."

His face grew dark with rage. "Gimme that bag."

She held it out to him through the open door. He snatched it away from her and ransacked it savagely, then threw it back at her. "Son of a *bitch* . . ." His hands flew to his pockets. "Wait a minute, didn't you give me a key the other night?"

"Yes, but I took it back yesterday while you were asleep."

"I don't believe this," he whined. "I don't *believe* this. What about the super? Go get the super to let us in."

"He doesn't live here. He goes home at six."

"*Jesus . . . Christ . . .*"

"Bruce, you can get that door open, can't you? If anyone can do it . . ."

His sweating face twitched nervously. "Do you have something plastic? A credit card or something?"

"Yes, yes." She opened the glove compartment and took out several gas-station cards. "Mobil, Chevron, Texaco . . ."

"Gimme one, *any* one." He snapped his fingers frantically.

"Can you do it?" she said.

"I think so," he said, and grabbed the card from her hand.

"Go on up. I'll wait here," she said.

"No, I want you to come with me," he said.

"But, Bruce, somebody's got to stay here with—"

"Never mind that, you're coming with *me*. Now come *on*."

"But why?"

"Suppose someone sees me and thinks I'm trying to break into your place."

"That's ridiculous."

"Goddam it, are you gonna get out of that car?"

"I still think—"

"*Lock the fucking car and come on!*" he shouted fiercely.

They went up in the elevator to the third floor and walked down the hall to her apartment. She stood at his side, glancing about nervously as he knelt at the door and worked on the latch with the plastic credit card. No one was around. Everyone was behind their own closed doors watching their television sets. She could hear the racket reverberating through the hallway. The noise had a familiar, comfortable sound to it . . . loud sitcom voices raised in unintelligible dialogue, interrupted by sudden bursts of studio laughter. It helped to ease her tension a little. Without it, she might have fainted with fear.

She heard Bruce muttering to himself. She saw his neck and his back soaked with sweat. "It's not working," he was saying to the door. "It's not coming, I can't do it, what're we gonna do . . . ?"

Suddenly she pulled her hand out of her pocket. "Oh my God . . . look . . . Bruce . . . the key . . ."

"*What?*" He struggled to an upright position.

"In my pocket all the time." Quickly she inserted the key in the lock and turned it and pushed the door open and went inside past him and snapped on the lights and went to the sidetable and opened her handbag.

"Let's go," he said in the doorway.

"Come here a minute, *quick*," she said with urgency.

"There isn't time. Come on," he said, coming in.

Quickly she stepped to the freezer and twisted the handle of the powerful airlock and raised the lid to its upright, open position, and an icy white mist rose from the wetted-down, empty box.

"What the hell are you doing? Close that thing," he said angrily, moving at her.

"No, it has to be open," she said calmly.

He pushed her aside and leaned forward to grasp the lid.

"*Bruce . . . look!*" she shouted.

He turned his head, startled, and his eyes went wide. "*Wait a minute! . . .*"

"For *what?*" she cried with savage triumph, and pressed the nozzle of the slim and ugly brown spray can an instant before he began to shriek in dreadful agony.

THE PORSCHE HUMMED over the highway at seventy-five, eating up the distance hungrily. He was in sport shirt and jeans now and felt more like himself, with Howard folded away neatly in the luggage compartment, his attaché case resting beneath the shirt and tie. The changing of costumes in the dark and deserted parking area had reminded Teddy of the original switch that had started all this a week ago, and *that* was totally beyond belief.

A *week* ago?

Not a *year*?

He knifed into the darkness of Old Malibu Road and saw the lights up ahead and heard the music that was too loud from within the house even before he got there, which was the way he had left things, and that gave him heart, but not as much as he needed.

Inside the house now, with the radio turned off for sanity's sake, he glanced about with darting eyes, looking for telltale signs of intrusion, sniffing the air for strangeness, and found it quickly in the kitchen, and reacted to it with instant alarm, until he realized that it was Mrs. Mahoney's doing. His written message was gone, and so were the strippers from the refrigerator, and that was as it should have been, no cause yet for the quickening of pulse and the icy clutch of anxiety in the pit of his stomach. That was pure anticipation, and he knew it, and he could not put it off for one more moment. He had to face it. He had to step out onto the back porch.

The white monstrosity hummed and rattled and shook its sides as though it were laughing at him, mocking his fears and apprehensions with its dinginess, its ordinariness. But he did not fall for the ruse, he would not be put off guard, he knew that the big box was about to betray him and he was ready for it all the way, steeling himself for its fatal revelation as he kneeled down now and removed the padlock and pushed back the cover and looked inside for the damning disorder that would meet his eyes, and not for a moment did he relax his vigilance or ease his defenses or allow a muscle in his body to lose its tension as he saw with what care each frozen package had been placed exactly where he had left it, and he knew, nobody could fool him, he knew, as he lifted each package out, what would be waiting for him at the bottom of this freezer, he could see in his mind's eye the shininess, the whiteness, the emptiness of a bottom that no longer had anything to cover it and conceal it, and he quickened the motions of his hands because he wanted to get to the certainty, to the emptiness, as fast as he could, get it over with, know the worst, which was all he could expect, for he had been careless and overconfident and deserved what he was getting now, and he was ready for it and here it was now, he had arrived at the bottom and was ready for the emptiness, and he stared down at it now bewildered, for it had the shape of a plastic suit carrier and it was the same one that he had originally placed there and Howard's body was inside it, but he knew better than to trust what his eyes were telling him, it was an illusion filling up emptiness, that's what it was, obscuring for the moment the gleaming white bottom that he knew was there, and he reached down and felt with his own fingers the illusion of plastic and the illusion of the frozen hardness of the body inside to assure himself that he was only imagining this, merely wishing it to be true, but his hands told him otherwise, they refused to lie, the illusions were reality, they could be touched and felt and were cold to his fingertips, and he became filled with confusion because this was not what he had feared and expected, and he was not ready to handle it, and he was shocked at the sound of his own uncontrollable laughter as a wave of relief flooded over him, and then shame and embarrassment at laughing this way in his dead brother's presence, and so he quickly covered Howard over again with snow peas and lamb chops and broccoli and codfish and brought the lid down on the freezer and fixed the padlock in place and went inside to the living room to pour himself a drink.

He was puzzled, and didn't know how to think his way out of it yet. He was pleased and relieved and almost elated, but mostly he was puzzled. How could he have worked himself into such a state of panic over nothing at all? Was he cracking up? Was the strain of playing two roles finally getting to him? Or was it *more* than nothing at all?

Diane and the big guy had been looking for *something*.

What was it?

He sank down on the sofa and toyed with his drink and thought about it and thought about it and toyed with his drink some more, and finally, slowly, it began to come to him, and he only smiled at first, and then he laughed a little, not a lot, because it was sort of ridiculous rather than funny, so silly really that it couldn't *be*, could it?

Was Diane still looking for nothing more than that damned *tape* he'd invented and threatened her with? Was it only *that*? Nothing *important*? No intent to destroy Jo Anne and himself? All that trouble, all that skulking around, over something that never even *existed*? All *his* panic over nothing more than child's play, foolishness?

Oh God, if only he knew where to reach Jo Anne now. He would have loved to share it with her. The joke wasn't only on Diane and that hulk of a man, it was on him too. *He* was the one who had missed his plane and gone a little berserk and was going to have to face the board of directors tomorrow with no sleep at all after a night of homework on the Bloodshot Special. His luggage was on its way to New York, but *he* was *here*, playing cops-and-robbers with no one but himself.

He didn't know where Jo Anne was, but he did know where the bathroom was, because it was his own house, and not the first time he had had to take a leak either. All that excitement over nothing at all can do it to a guy, plus a little tequila on the rocks, of course. He went into the john and unzipped his fly, and when he was all through, he pulled the zipper up again, and had a little trouble with it, had to tug on it a bit because it was a new zipper, very new and shiny, they were the kind that gave you trouble, but let's not think about zippers now . . .

Why the hell was he thinking about zippers? What were zippers doing on his mind?

Not zippers. *Zipper*.

One zipper.

But which zipper? Which was the zipper he was trying to think of?

The zipper on the suit carrier.

The zipper on the suit carrier in the freezer.

The zipper that gave Howard his only privacy.

But what *about* the zipper? What was there about that zipper that was worth all this attention?

Well, hadn't it seemed a little *shiny* just now?

So what?

Well, hadn't it usually seemed *dull* every time you'd looked down into that freezer before? Dull from being glazed over with a thin coating of ice?

So?

When you looked down at it just now, the zipper was *shiny*. There was *no coating of ice*. The ice was *missing*. The zipper looked like it had just been *opened . . . recently . . .*

Recently?

Yes.

But Howard was there. I saw him.

No you didn't. You didn't look. You're always afraid to look.

He's *there*, Teddy said, shaking his head in protest. He's *there*, he said aloud, hurrying into the kitchen. How long was this nonsense going to go on, for Christsake? He's *there*, he said, as his fingers fumbled with the lock and he got it open and threw back the lid and tore at the frozen packages and hurled them out of the way and seized the metal tab of the zipper that was too shiny and unfrozen. *You're here, Howard*, he cried to the yielding plastic as he ripped it open and cried *Howard* to the red and raw and revolting beef and the gleaming calf flesh that gaped at him bloodily, and he turned away from it and rose to his feet slowly, numb with shock.

Gone. The body was *gone*.

Diane had taken it. She and that man had taken it.

Diane had discovered, somehow, that she *had* committed a murder, and was trying desperately now to cover it up. Of *course*.

Dazed, Teddy went into the living room, trying to sort it all out in his head.

Did she know who her victim really was?

How *could* she know?

Only he and Jo Anne knew.

Diane *didn't* know.

She had to be assuming now that it was *Howard* who was still alive, *Howard* who had been hiding the body, *Howard*, who was probably planning to wreak some sort of vengeance on *her* for his brother's death. Anything she would do now would be based on her belief that she had killed *him*, Teddy Stern, whom she had loved in her own crazy way. She had spirited the evidence of her crime away, she and that man who was helping her. She was fighting for her *life*, trying to prevent accusation and exposure that would *never come*, but *she* did not know that. How *could* she know it?

He went to the telephone and dialed her number, my God, he never thought he'd be calling that number again. He had no idea what he'd say to her, he could never reveal his plans, his and Jo Anne's, but he knew he'd have to find *some* handle on that wounded, hurting, frightened mind to bring it under control, for there was no telling what she'd do now, what *they* would do, there were two of them.

He needed Howard back.

He needed to assure her that she was in no danger of exposure and never would be.

He needed Howard back.

He had to get to her before—before what? What was she going to do now?

He looked down at the phone in dismay. Her line was busy, he could hear the signal.

He thought of his Porsche poised on the road outside. He could be in Brentwood in no time at all if he really let it out all the way. He'd take her by surprise, startle her, catch her off balance. He'd confront her and use her guilt as his trump card and get Howard back and have everything under control again, back on the track again, on schedule, according to plan, *his* plan, not Diane's.

His and Jo Anne's.

He knew Diane. He'd know how to handle *her*. She was easy.

He heard her busy signal and hung up the phone and hurried to the door . . .

And a hundred and twenty-five miles away, Millie McWorter, who had initiated *her* call a full two minutes earlier, stood in her bedroom and let Diane's phone ring a few more times before she too gave up, but only temporarily, knowing that she'd be trying her daughter again and again.

OH HOW HE LOVED sitting there in the steaming sweat-filled disco at the little table all by himself with the music pounding in his ears and the Scotch warming his blood, feeling their eyes on him, knowing they wanted him, every one of them did, he could see the love and the longing and the lust in their eyes as they gazed at him over the shoulder of whomever it was they were dancing with, and only he and they knew what they were doing, ignoring their partners, ignoring their pickups, ignoring their lovers, for they wanted *him* instead, every last one of them hungered after *him*, because he was alone and alluring and unspoken for, and looked back at them with eyes that promised unutterable delights, and the loving that was going on between him at the table and them out on the floor was far more exciting than any of the quick little shootoffs they would have afterward in the curtained booths or out on the floor as they writhed up against their partners in perfectly timed, well-disguised, slow-moving rhythmic copulation, and he was glad that the big tall blond named Bruce hadn't shown up yet, because this was heaven and he didn't want to let go of it, he just wanted to sit there in solitary erotic splendor and feel them all to their very depths and be a part of all the loving that was going on before him, knowing that each one of them who closed his eyes against sweet rising inevitability, mouth opening, cry of painful joy unheard beneath the pounding music, had been looking at *him* and thinking of *him* and was *still* thinking of him, even as the contorted features relaxed and the eyes opened finally and looked toward the little table and saw that the one who was alone, the alluring one, the unattached one, was still gazing at him and smiling faintly at him and moving his lips imperceptibly in what was almost a kiss, blown across the smoke-filled, sweat-filled room to let him know, to let them all know, that he had received their love and thanked them for it and returned it in every possible way. He would wait there like this for Bruce all night, if he had to, for he was loving every minute of it . . .

HE SWERVED into the well-remembered block and jammed the Porsche to a stop at the curb not too far from the entrance to her building. He hadn't been here since their earliest days together, right after he had first met her, when he'd drop her off after dinner at Joey's, or after a movie and a midnight bowl of chili at Joe Allen's place. Soon had come the invitations upstairs for a nightcap (who was she kidding?) and after that, their first wild couplings in her roomy bed, the best sex they would ever have together, some of the best he'd had in his whole life up to then, up to the time they began to hate and fear each other, after she'd moved into the beach house with him, when he had begun to sense that the invasion had the intent of permanency to it, and she had begun to taste and smell the fear in his kisses and had developed a rightful fear of her own that he was obsessed with the idea of getting rid of her. After that, they had become hopeless together.

He took the elevator to her familiar floor and walked down the hall to her familiar apartment and stood outside her well-remembered door, listening for sounds of her on the other side, and he heard voices, and they were not known to him, and he thought for a moment that he might have come to the wrong apartment, but he could not have forgotten so soon, and then he realized that the voices were coming from a television set, and he looked at the button that would ring the doorbell, and then he looked down at the doorknob and noticed for the first time the key that was still in the lock, forgotten there by someone who had been very distracted or very much in a hurry at the time.

Quietly, cautiously, he turned the key, pushed the door open, and from the hallway peered into the apartment. The lights were on, the television set was playing, but no one, apparently, was there to watch it. He stepped into the foyer, called out Diane's name, and getting no response, went quickly to the other rooms, looked in and found no one there.

He walked over to the TV set, turned it off and glanced around the living room. The piece at the far end of the room struck him immediately as something new, something he did not remember from the old days, and at first he thought it was a chest of some kind, just another exotic piece of furniture, because this was the living room. And it wasn't until he moved closer to the chest that he saw what it really was, and seconds later knew for *whom* it was, and while he couldn't fathom immediately to what diabolical uses they would be putting the frozen body, his angry bewilderment suddenly gave way to a rush of hope at the realization that he was all alone here now, that he had lucked out and could thwart their plans, whatever they were, by literally snatching their intended victory from the jaws of his almost defeat.

He stepped to the white enameled box, studied its new and special design for a moment before attacking it, and then he seized the handle of the airlock and twisted it hard to the left, breaking the airtight seal and enabling him to lift the huge lid and look inside and see Howard's body, which he knew would be there beneath the steely cloud of ice-cold vapor that rose up now to chill his face and sting his nostrils, and when the freezing mist cleared, he saw the enormous body staring up at him with its horrified ice-covered eyes and the puffy face contorted in a final hideous grimace of ugly jagged teeth, the mouth frozen open as though still gasping and sucking for the air that was not there, and the massive head enveloped in a long blond crown of crystalline hair turned to snow, and he knew instinctively who had done this, he didn't have to know how or why, and it was clear in his mind now, despite the shuddering revulsion that had seized him, that if he didn't find her at once, find her and Howard, for they would surely be together, all would be lost, if indeed it hadn't been lost already.

He had to find her. But *where?*

Certainly not here. He must never be linked to *this* horror, which was hers.

Where would he find her?

With urgent haste he took out his handkerchief and wiped his fingerprints from the enameled white box and from the television set. He was working on the front door when the telephone began to ring.

He turned sharply and stared at the phone. Could it be her?

Never.

He looked at the phone and waited for it to stop ringing because it couldn't be Diane, but it didn't stop ringing, it kept on ringing as though whoever was calling had a desperate need to reach Diane and would never give up, almost as desperate a need as his need to find her, and as the phone kept ringing he found himself drawn to it, and he walked over to it slowly, and with the handkerchief covering his hand, he very quietly and carefully picked up the receiver and stopped the ringing and brought the receiver to his ear and listened, saying nothing.

At first there was startled silence at the other end, the shock of desperation being suddenly rewarded, and then a woman's voice, and for an instant he thought it *was* Diane, except that this voice was older, though similar to hers.

"Hello, Diane? . . . Hello? . . . Diane, answer me please. . . . Darling? . . . Please . . . Diane . . . *I know you're there.* . . . Won't you please *say* something? . . . Listen to me, darling, I want you to *promise* me you won't take that plane up tonight. . . . Did you *hear* me, Diane? I don't know what kind of dangerous flight you were talking about but I'm terrified, Diane, I'm scared to death. In your state of mind, in your condition, I *forbid* you to—"

He took the stairs down two at a time.

chapter

25

"THIS IS HEAVY," Lou Poliano said, smiling at her.

"I told you it was," she said, her heart in her throat.

He had worked the horrible death-bundle out of the back of the Datsun for her, and together they were carrying it across the tarmac of the dimly lit field toward the blue-and-white Cessna tied down on the upper ramp. The bulging plastic carrier was freezing to the touch, and added to the chill within her as she watched the security guard's lined and leathery face for signs of suspicion. But all she saw were his aging eyes upon her, and the steadiness of his fond and hopeless gaze.

"My missus buys two steaks at a time," he said.

"My mother won't go to a market more than once every other *month*," she said.

"This should last her a year," Lou said. "I hope she appreciates it."

"She better," Diane said.

They were at the plane now.

"All right, honey, let go and give it to *me*. Just step aside."

"Are you sure you can manage?"

"We'll soon find out," he said.

She glanced about nervously. Nobody was coming. At this hour of the night, takeoffs and landings were blessedly sporadic. The rows of parked and empty planes were eyeless, unobserving. Across the field, on the far side of Runway 21, the huge windows of the control tower were deceptively dark beneath the tiara of red lights, as though no one were behind those windows, peering out, watching. At the southern edge of the field, atop its tall steel mast, the beacon light silently swept the black sky with alternating beams of yellow and green, beckoning the nightbirds to come home and rest.

It felt too safe here. She didn't trust it at all. She had a sudden vision of a shrieking, overweight, whining corpse rising up out of a white-enameled coffin and coming at her out of the darkness, and it frightened her badly. She needed a drink. She needed one right away. But the fresh, unopened fifth of Wild Turkey was still in the car, and she couldn't go near it while Lou was around.

"How does this look, honey?" he was saying.

She turned. He had pushed the cold and bulging garment bag up through the open door on the passenger side of the plane, onto the seat that she had already shoved back into a reclining position.

"That's perfect," she said.

"Think you can take it from here?"

She nodded and said to him, "How can I ever thank you, Lou?"

"Don't be silly, honey. It's always a pleasure."

Impulsively, she stepped close to him and kissed his weatherbeaten cheek.

"Oh, honey, honey," he said, with an ache in his voice. She was such a sweet, beautiful creature, unlike anything in his whole life.

He turned and walked away from her, because there was nothing else he could do. He was supposed to be in his booth down at the gate. He'd get fired if people came through unchecked.

INTERMINABLE goddam red light.

For *what*? There was nothing coming.

He jammed the Porsche into second, rocketed across Montana with a shriek of burning rubber, and was halfway to Wilshire before the sound of his frantic passage died down behind him.

SHE TOOK ANOTHER SWIG of the fiery courage, capped the bottle, and tossed it back onto the car seat. Then she picked up the lead-weighted, nylon-webbed belt and started for the plane again, wishing she could move a little faster. So far so good, but you never knew who would come by in that damned red Ford Pinto from the Security Office near the refueling area and start asking questions.

Excuse me, miss, but you can't keep your car there. If a plane wants to taxi through—

I know, I know, but these scuba-diving belts weigh forty-eight pounds each, and I didn't want to have to lug them all the way up from the parking area.

You're not going scuba diving tonight?

Of course not. I need those belts to strap around Teddy so that when I dump him out of the plane, he'll sink out of sight forever.

Oh, I see. A friend of yours?

He was once.

Look, I don't mean to be nosy, miss, but how are you going to get him out of the plane?

Through the open door, silly.

You'll never get that door open more than an inch against the wind pressure up there.

You think I'm crazy, don't you? Everyone does. Well, how about I unlatch his door, and I reduce airspeed to just above stall, and I bank sharply to the right, and I give him a shove, and about two hundred and fifty pounds and gravity do the rest? How does that grab you, huh?

That shut him up. That shut him up *good*. He didn't say a *word*. He wasn't even *there*.

She dumped the heavy belt onto the rear seat of the plane where the other belt was and said to her passenger, "I'll be right back, don't go away." Then she went over to the Datsun, got in, drove it down to the parking area on the middle tie-down ramp, grabbed the Wild Turkey, locked the car, and hurried back up to her wild Cessna.

She had to pass up the preflight inspection of fuselage and engine. There simply wasn't time, and she couldn't keep Teddy waiting or he'd lose his cool. She removed the three tie-down chains attached to the wings and the tail, pulled the two wooden chocks away from the main wheels, and tossed them to her left a safe distance away from any possible sucking sweep of the propeller. Then she climbed up into the pilot's seat saying, "Hello again," leaned across him in his zippered plastic privacy, closed and latched his door, raised the back of his seat to an upright position, and securely fastened the safety belt around his midsection. She didn't want him sliding down onto the right-hand set of rudder pedals or falling forward against the yoke on the passenger side. She didn't want him flying the plane with his set of dual controls, not in *his* condition.

Not that hers was all that terrific either, she decided, glancing down at the bottle at her side. She strapped herself in, closed and latched her door, and took a deep breath.

Okay. Let's see now . . .

BUNDY DRIVE was mean and treacherous, inviting you to race along next to the curb and pass at high speed on the right, then suddenly throwing a parked car in your path and daring you to stay alive. Teddy saw death waiting for him, swore aloud, swerved to the left, cut off the car he had just passed, ignored the horn-blasting rage behind him and surged forward, snaking in and out of the maddeningly unhurried drivers up ahead.

At Olympic Boulevard the light had gone amber. There was no way he could beat the red. He jammed his foot down on the accelerator, shot through the converging traffic, heard their howls of protest, zoomed toward Pico, hit the intersection as it was about to come up green, almost took off the rear of a car that just managed to escape him, ate up Pearl and Ocean Park and a changing light at National, and then he was racing along the curving edge of the airfield, just outside its cyclone-fenced boundaries above and to his right.

Suddenly a roaring bird swooped down at him from out of the night and he ducked involuntarily as the plane brushed over him and thumped to a landing out of sight. Up ahead he saw the sign: SANTA MONICA AIRPORT. He screeched to the right onto Airport Avenue, sped toward the gate, then suddenly slammed on the brakes and brought the Porsche to a shuddering stop and peered through the windshield.

Parked broadside in the entrance to the field with a barrier: in front of it was a red Dodge pickup truck with AIRPORT POLICE painted on its side. And inside the brightly lit booth beside it, a gray-haired security guard was moving around.

Think fast, think fast.

Do you know exactly what you might be getting into?

No.

Do you want your own name, your *real* name, or *Howard's* name, linked in any way with that frozen death mask you left behind in Brentwood?

No.

And because of that, with *Diane?*

No.

Danger, right?

Yes. Yes.

Fast, for Christsake.

He glanced to his left. The low-slung office building was lit up outside but dark inside, and its vast parking lots at the far end behind him were open and empty.

Quickly he made a U-turn, entered the driveway and took the yellow Porsche and its license plates to a safe hiding place behind the building. Then he slammed the car door behind him and started running toward the airport gate.

THE COCKPIT was a blur, the instrument panel fuzzy. She took another deep breath and brought them into focus. Come on, Diane. Stop looking around. *Do* it. Push the red mixture control in to full rich. That's it. Now crack the throttle. Good. Reach down, no, not there, *there*. Pull the lever opening the cowl flaps. Okay, left side of the instrument panel. The red master switch. Flip it on. *Flip it on.* That's right. Now did you remove the lock from the shaft of the control column? Of course you didn't. Well do it. *Jesus*, Diane. Where's the key? It's in your hand. Stick it into the ignition switch and— Wait a minute, are your feet on the top section of the rudder pedals? What're you going to do, start the engine without the *brakes* on? All right. Clockwise. Turn the key. That's it.

The propeller started to crank around . . . once, twice, three times.

Suddenly the engine sprang to life.

LOU POLIANO stepped out of the booth into the floodlighted entrance to the field and glanced around, slightly bewildered. Where the hell had the guy come from? Usually a car pulls up and somebody lowers a window . . .

"Can I do something for you?" Lou said, looking the man over carefully.

"Yes," Teddy said quickly. "I'd like to go through if I may."

"You an owner? You have a plane here?"

"No, no. Actually I—uh— Maybe you can tell me, would you know if a *Miss McWorter* has come through here tonight? She's got a—"

"Ya mean Diane?" Lou Poliano's face lit up. "Just a couple of minutes ago I helped her load some meat onto the plane."

"Meat . . ."

"Hey, I *thought* I recognized you. You're Teddy Stern, aren't you . . ."

"No, I'm—"

"Sure, I seen you on TV a lot, Mr. Stern. Diane used to tell me when to watch for ya all the time. I'm Lou Poliano. Lemme shake your hand."

"I have to get to her right away, Mr. Poliano."

"Lou. Please."

"Can I go through?"

"Where's your car?"

"Back there, across the street . . ."

"You coulda brought it in here. I woulda let you park over there."

"Look, I have to say good-bye to her before she—"

"Wait a minute, I'll see if she's still on the ground. You may've missed her, y'know." He took a small walkie-talkie from his belt and flipped it on. "Santa Monica ground, this is Unit Twelve."

The male voice came back: "Go Unit Twelve."

"Charlie, I got a friend here," Lou Poliano looked squarely at Teddy. "A friend of one of our regulars. Diane McWorter. The blue-and-white Cessna? Four two seven four eight, I believe. She take off yet?"

"Hold on."

Lou studied the actor. He seemed pale and tense in the bright lights. Lou wondered what was troubling him.

"Unit Twelve, Santa Monica ground."

"Go ahead," Lou said.

"No request for clearance yet."

"Roger." He looked at Teddy. "Still here, you're in luck, but you better hurry." He pointed off. "Up there on the upper ramp and to your right."

"I know," Teddy said, and started past him.

"Wait a minute. Ya gotta sign in, Mr. Stern."

"Goddam it, *must* I?"

"Take ya a second," Lou said easily. He reached through the open window of the booth, took out a clipboard and handed it to Teddy. "Name and address and who you're visiting."

"Shit," Teddy said.

THE COUGH and the catch that exploded into the steady thrum of the engine had always been her moment of truth, galvanizing her into instant alertness and the carrying out of the necessary procedures.

She heard the sound of the engine now, and responded.

First she turned on the instrument panel lights, then the three navigation lights on the wing tips and tail, then the red flashing beacon on top of the vertical stabilizer. She fast-checked the ammeter, the oil-pressure gauge and the fuel gauge too, and noted that her tanks were three quarters full, far more than she'd need for the hundred-mile dash out to sea and the hundred-mile dash back home.

Reaching up, she threw the switch that turned on her transponder and her radio, and then she dialed up the ground control frequency and pushed the press-to-talk button of her hand microphone.

"Santa Monica ground, this is Cessna four two seven four eight at the upper tie-down area, taxiing for takeoff."

She recognized the answering voice as Charlie's. "Cessna four two seven four eight, Santa Monica ground. Taxi runway two one. Altimeter two niner niner five, wind one seven zero degrees at ten knots." And she could have sworn she heard him add, *sotto voce*: "There's somebody here *looking* for you, Diane."

But she knew damn well that it was only her fevered imagination because Charlie would never fracture a regulation like that, and anyway, why would anyone be looking for *her* when all she had done really was kill the man on the seat next to her, you couldn't say she had killed *Bruce*, she had merely closed and locked the lid of the freezer after he had groped and stumbled and tumbled into the thing, no reason to believe her ears *or* Charlie's words for that matter, but it certainly wouldn't hurt to have just a *little* one now to chase the willies away, g'bye willies, g'bye Teddys and Bruces.

She put the cap back on the bottle and set it down again and reached past the control yoke and flipped the taxi light on, because she wanted to get the hell out of here. But first there was something she had to do. She slowly eased in the throttle while keeping her feet on the brakes and listened to the growing roar of the speeding-up engine. *That's* what she wanted, that great and marvelous noise that chased everything out of your head. God, what a sound, she could come with it, she could come. And she looked straight ahead through her windshield to the tower far off across the runway, and she could imagine them up there peering at her through their binocs and saying what the hell is that girl doing racing her engine that way, and she had half a mind to press the mike button and tell them I need it, I need it.

And as desperately as she needed it, suddenly it wasn't working for her any more, because she was not just *hearing* phantoms, like Charlie's remark, she was *seeing* them too, running toward her out of the darkness, calling out to her with silent lips and throat, unheard in the roar of the engine. She saw him out of the corner of her eye and knew at once that he was a phantom because he was really right there beside her, on the seat beside her, he couldn't be out there on the ramp running toward her, and she knew that right behind him would come another phantom, a towering one with long blond hair.

She had to get away from this one, he was coming too close. He was ducking under the wing. He was pounding on the cabin door. He was looking in at her with his staring eyes. He was looking right past her at himself, at *himself*, and he was shouting at her with his phantom voice and she couldn't know what he was saying because *her* noise was louder than his could ever be, and she didn't *want* to hear him, she didn't want to *see* him ever again, because he was all crumpled and horrible and dead and *she* had killed him and that's why she was going to ditch him now. Get out of my way, she cried . . .

THE PLANE was beginning to roll.

She hadn't heard a goddam word he had said, and the plane was beginning to roll.

She had just sat there and looked at him with those large, startled eyes of hers, and Howard beside her and the bottle of Wild Turkey between them and those weighted belts on the back seat behind her advertising her whole plan, and she hadn't heard a word he had said, and the plane was beginning to move now and he had to stop it, he had to prevent her from taking Howard away.

He grabbed a wing strut and tried to hold on, but the backlash of the propeller was too much to withstand, blowing him apart and blinding him with its windstorm of rocks and sand. He fell to his knees, saw the left wing passing over him, and knew that she was going to veer to the right. She was going to get out on the taxiway and head for the runway and get Howard away from him forever.

He had to stop her.

He rose up and charged at her rear assembly as it came toward him. He got there before she could make her turn. With one hand he seized the leading edge of the horizontal stabilizer, and with the other he clamped onto the trailing edge of the elevator, braced his feet against the tarmac and struggled for purchase, battling the Cessna with all his strength, fighting the thrust of its powerful engine and the rocks its propeller hurled at him, gritting his teeth and cursing his feebleness but not letting go, and then she gave him more of her noise and more of her power but he just shouted into the blast of air that she gave him and refused to give up, he hung on and finally he forced the plane to give in to his will for a moment, to capitulate and veer to the left for a moment, just far enough and long enough for the powerful wash of its churning propeller to suck up one of the discarded wooden wheel chocks, flip it into the air, smash it about and cut it to pieces in one blinding blur of its whirling aluminum blades, and Teddy caught the full sting of it, the sting of wooden slivers and, worse yet, small fragments of metal, like shrapnel, and he cried out in pain and stumbled back and the plane broke free of him and he fell to the ground and saw everything slipping away from him, the blue-and-white Cessna bearing Diane and Howard rolling swiftly away from him on the forward thrust of aluminum blades whose nicks and gouges were too young yet to be noticed, or to matter.

As he lay there on the asphalt, Teddy's eyes went to the bits of soft metal scattered about him, and the pit of his stomach went cold with foreboding. He looked off at the plane that was too far away from him now and he struggled to his feet and began to run after it, tired as he was and half-hearted as he was, he ran after the plane, knowing that he would never be able to catch up with it, or change Diane's mind even if he did.

SHE SAW HIM.

She took her eyes off the dark taxiway ahead of her for one dangerous instant and saw him in her rear-view mirror.

She knew who he was now, and no longer a phantom either. The power of his struggle, the force of his resistance had convinced her of that. It had to be *Howard*, it *was* Howard, she should have known it right away, and the only thing she hadn't figured out was how he could be *here* now when he was supposed to be in New York. He was here, and he had come after her, and he was not going to let her get away, even now he was pursuing her, but it would do him no good, he was too far behind and she was rolling too fast for him as she bypassed the preflight safety check area and taxied right up to the head of Runway 21, braked the plane to a stop, dimmed her red instrument lights, switched her radio to the tower frequency, and hurriedly picked up her mike.

"Santa Monica tower, Cessna seven four eight ready for takeoff."

And Charlie came right back with "Cessna seven four eight cleared for takeoff. Say direction of flight."

"Straight out departure for seven four eight."

"Is that a right turn at the shoreline?"

Diane hesitated. "Naturally," she said.

"Straight out departure approved, and have a nice flight," said Charlie.

Stop dawdling, said the rear-view mirror.

Howard was closing in fast, she had to get away.

She flipped on the landing light, set her directional gyro to two-one-zero, rolled the Cessna forward, made a left turn onto the runway, looked straight ahead at the road to infinity that stretched out before her, and then she began to push in the throttle and gently ease the control yoke back as the engine responded and the plane surged forward and she heard the deep throaty roar of her power plant, and heard something else that she had never heard before but paid it no mind, for there was too much to concentrate on right now and it was only a slight and passing tremor, and the Cessna was racing down the runway, gathering speed, gaining momentum, faster and faster went the blue-and-white bird until finally it decided to soar away, to leave the ground and climb into the night sky over Santa Monica and head west toward the Pacific Ocean, and when it reached the water's edge far below, it did not make a right turn at the shoreline. It made no turn at all.

HE SLOWED DOWN only long enough to watch her climb into the blackness beyond the runway's end. And when she became nothing more than a winking red light in the sky, he started running again, toward the control tower, a lonely outpost on the dark and deserted field, his last and only hope.

CHARLIE BLAKELEE loved working the night shift. He found the dimmed-down interior of the tower soothing to his keyed-up senses. He could look out into the darkness and really appreciate the breathtaking panorama of Santa Monica and suburban Los Angeles, sparkling with thousands of lights in the distance beyond the enormous windows. He even enjoyed the view *inside* this room, especially when Maxine Worth was the other controller. He liked the fit of her jeans and her long auburn hair and the sweetness of her voice and face.

She was peering through her binoculars at the Cessna that had just taken off and was climbing out over the dark Pacific. "Naughty naughty," she was saying, and not to Charlie either.

"I give TRACON thirty seconds," he said darkly, and ran a nervous hand through his sandy hair as he watched the progress of the plane on the Brite Radar screen that was linked by microwave to LAX.

"Two thousand and she's still climbing," Maxine said.

A loudspeaker squawked. "Santa Monica, Los Angeles Approach."

"There it is," Charlie said. He turned to his communications console, picked up the phone, punched a button, and said, "Santa Monica. We know."

"Who is it?" Los Angeles Approach Control demanded.

"Cessna four two seven four eight," Charlie replied.

"What does he think he's doing?"

"It's a *she*, and I don't know," Charlie said. "She promised us a right turn at the shoreline."

"Can you get her out of there?"

"I can try," Charlie said, and hung up. He picked up his Electro Voice hand-held mike and said, "Seven four eight, Santa Monica Tower."

No answer. He tried again. And waited.

"Come on, McWorter," he muttered under his breath.

Nothing.

"Seven four eight, Santa Monica tower. Will you respond please?"

There was a long moment of silence, and then Diane's voice came through the speaker, distant and indifferent. "Seven four eight."

"How do you read the tower?"

"I read you."

"Do you realize you've entered Los Angeles air space?"

"Tough," she said.

"Say again?"

"It occurred to me," Diane said.

"Request you vacate immediately," Charlie said.

There was no reply.

"We are asking you to vacate immediately," he said.

Silence.

Maxine Worth lowered her binoculars and turned to watch.

"Seven four eight, Santa Monica tower, did you *get* that?"

Again nothing.

Charlie Blakelee frowned.

A buzzer sounded in the room. The downstairs intercom. Maxine Worth glanced at it, startled. "Who's that?"

"Find out," Charlie said.

She stepped to the Teletalk, pressed a button. "Tower."

"Look, you don't know me." The voice was urgent. "I'm a friend of the pilot of that Cessna that just left here. There may be an emergency on board. Can I come up, please?"

"I'm sorry, sir, but we can't admit—"

"No, *let* him," Charlie Blakelee said quickly.

"Wait for the buzzer," Maxine Worth said to the intercom.

"Maybe he can help," Charlie said. "Don't ask me how."

Teddy heard the buzzer, pulled the door open, and hurried into the building. He tried to dash up the spiral staircase but it went on forever,

longer than his strength could last. He was out of breath when he made
the last narrow turn at the end of the climb and emerged into the great
pentagonal room.

A sandy-haired guy with a lean intense face was having an agitated
conversation on the telephone, and a good-looking red-headed girl was
peering out toward the ocean repeating something over and over into
a hand-held microphone.

"Seven four eight, do you *read?* Do you *read?*"

Diane's number.

"Hello?" Teddy said.

They ignored the hell out of him.

"Seven four eight, Santa Monica tower . . ."

"We're not just *close*, we're practically in *bed* with you," the guy
shouted into the phone before hanging up.

The redhead turned. "Charlie? . . ."

"LA changed its traffic flow fifteen minutes ago," he snapped.
"Too hectic to let us know. Did you *get* her?"

"Not a peep."

The man's lips tightened. He turned to Teddy. "I'm Charlie, that's
Maxine. You said emergency. What is it?"

"That plane. Seven four eight," Teddy said.

"Diane McWorter . . ."

"I think her propeller may be damaged and she doesn't know it."

"Oh dear," Maxine Worth said.

"That's nice. That's just beautiful," Charlie Blakelee said. "LAX
has just had a wind shift. They're bringing everything in on an easterly
approach. That means a skyful of 747s and DC 10s stacked up over
the ocean thirty to forty miles out, and your girlfriend is flying right
into their space with a lousy prop, you say?"

"Jesus," Teddy said.

The redhead was calling Diane again and getting nowhere.

"Foolish question," Teddy said. "Is Diane's receiver on?"

"We don't know," Maxine Worth said. "It was."

"You've *got* to get her to come back here," Teddy said.

"Thank you very much," Charlie Blakelee said, with bite.

The loudspeaker called out, "Santa Monica, Los Angeles."

Charlie grabbed the phone. "Santa Monica."

"Your plane is fifteen miles out at five thousand feet. We've given
her as traffic to everyone. What have *you* done?"

"Talked to ourselves," Charlie Blakelee said.

"We got a dozen inbounds out there. Two thousand lives."

"What do you want me to *do*, Los Angeles?"

"Close down your goddam airport, for *good*."

Charlie Blakelee slammed the receiver back in its cradle and stared at it. Over at the western window, Maxine was still calling Diane. Blakelee looked at Teddy.

"Is she smashed again?" he said in a low voice.

"What?"

"Come on. No bullshit now. Has she been drinking?"

"It's a possibility," Teddy said.

"Possibility," the other man said, shaking his head.

He walked over to the redhead and took the microphone from her and called Diane a few more times and said in a gloomy voice, "She's probably out of range by now."

"Can *I* try?" Teddy said.

"No, we can't do that," the controller said quickly.

"Why not?"

"Because we can't." He felt Maxine's eyes on him. "*What? What?*"

"Nothing," she said, turning away.

"Maybe she'll *respond* to *me*," Teddy said.

"Maybe she won't," the controller said.

Maxine turned. "Charlie? . . . ."

"All right, all right." He handed the mike to Teddy. "Go ahead."

Teddy took the mike and pressed the button while they watched him. "Diane, this is Teddy. This is Teddy, Diane, are you listening?"

"She's seven four eight," Charlie said.

They waited, and heard nothing but silence.

"Tell her anyway. Tell her about the inbounds, the traffic," Charlie said.

"Diane . . . seven four eight . . . if you're hearing me," Teddy said. "There's a lot of airline traffic coming in from over the ocean and you're flying right into their approach patterns. Will you please turn around and come back, Diane?"

Suddenly her voice came through the speaker, blurry and indistinct. "Don't you ever give up?" she said slowly.

"Hey," Charlie said.

"Don't you ever stop trying?" said the voice, with bitterness.

"Diane, Diane," Teddy cried. "Your propeller is damaged. Do you know that?"

"What else, anything else?" she said in a mocking voice.

"Get her *out* of there," Charlie Blakelee cried.

"Diane, listen to me carefully now and try to understand what I'm going to tell you. On that terrible night last week . . . . Do you know which night I'm talking about? . . ."

"Yes, yes, yes . . ." *So sadly.*

"Get her out of there!"

"Diane, this is *Teddy* speaking. It wasn't *me* on that night, it was *him*, Diane. He was *me* that night, I swear it, Diane. Do you understand what I'm saying . . ."

"For Christsake, what *is* this?" Charlie Blakelee moved at the microphone.

Teddy pulled away from him, "Diane, I'm *here* now, I'm *not* beside you. That's *him*, not *me*. *I'm here*, and I *forgive* you, forever and ever. And if you turn around and come right back, I promise you I'll help you. I'll do everything I can to help you and protect you. Will you come *back*, Diane, will you?"

And he meant it, goddam it, he meant it.

Tensely, he waited.

He and the tight-lipped controller and the girl with the auburn hair stared at the loudspeaker and waited and waited, and finally they heard Diane's voice again, and she was weeping, and she said, "You'll say *anything*, you bastard, won't you. . . . You'll say anything to get him back . . ."

And they heard her choking back her tears, and then abruptly there was nothing, as though she had dropped her microphone, or turned off her radio.

"Diane? . . . Diane? . . . Please . . . Diane? . . ."

But it was useless.

He knew it was useless.

Even though, somehow, for reasons he would never quite understand, he had meant every word he had said, she would never believe him, never.

It was useless.

The loudspeaker was silent.

He gave the microphone back to the other man.

"At least you got the traffic information to her," Charlie Blakelee said in a quiet voice, shaken.

Teddy nodded, sick at heart.

"That other stuff, I didn't understand a word you were saying to her."

"Neither did I," Maxine Worth said.

"Just as well," Teddy said.

"There's nobody out there with her, is there?" Charlie Blakelee said.

"No, she's all alone," Teddy said. "God, is she alone."

chapter 26

SHE SAT in the dim glow of the shuddering cabin with her cold and shrouded victim beside her, far out over the lonely sea, waiting for the confusion in her head to subside, for she could not think, waiting for the tears to dissolve, for they blurred her eyes and made the stars seem to move and come closer, and she could not understand that yet. There was so much that she could not understand. If only she could stop crying . . .

Why had she left her radio on?

Hadn't the throbbing hum and chatter of the vibrating propeller shaft been enough for her to listen to?

Why hadn't she turned the radio off sooner?

She never should have responded to the sound of his voice. She never should have let him say the things that he had said to her.

He had left her torn with tears of hope and fear, for he had said everything that she had been longing to hear, and she wanted to believe him now, how she wanted to believe him, but she was so afraid of trusting him ever again.

He had said that he was *Teddy*, that she had never really *killed* him, that it had all been a tragic mixup on that awful night, and she wanted *so much* for it to be true.

Teddy *alive*.

Oh, how she wanted that to be true.

He had said that he forgave her, forevermore, for the broken body on the seat beside her, and she wanted that to be true too.

Diane forgiven.

If she would turn around now and fly back home to the uncertain world of her own making, he would do everything he could to help her and protect her. He had promised her that, she had heard him say it, and oh God how she wanted to believe him, how she had longed for that, for as far back as she could remember.

Someone to help her.

Someone to protect her.

Someone to rescue her from all the problems that she had never been able to solve.

Who else had ever promised her anything like that, and with such feeling in his voice? She had heard it. He had meant it. And she had denied him his sincerity. Why had she done that?

Believe him, Diane.

Turn around before it's too late. There *is* no answer out here, only danger. *Believe* him.

She flew through the pitch-black sky over the dark Pacific, less alone now than she knew, less alone than she had ever been before, coming closer to decision, flying swiftly toward resolution, unmindful of the wrenching quiver of her engine and of the distant sound approaching, like thunder.

Give up, Diane.

Don't fight it any longer.

Trust him.

Don't be afraid.

Trust him, and give yourself over to him.

Go back, Diane, go back.

And suddenly she said *yes*, and a feeling of great gladness swept over her, for she had made up her mind, and she knew that the decision was a good one. There would be penalties and punishment for what she had done, she had no illusions about that, but she'd be able to bear them. She would not be alone any more. He would help her.

Quickly she switched off the automatic pilot and took the yoke in her hands and planted her feet firmly on the pedals that controlled her rudder and made ready to roll out and turn for the flight back to land. And all at once, before she knew what was happening, the moving stars suddenly came down out of the west with a tremendous roar, and they were upon her, they were heading right at her with incredible closing speed, and the collision was inevitable, there was nothing she could do . . .

But her reaction was instantaneous and she banked steeply to the right and dove toward the water and heard the giant airliner pull sharply up and away, and she had no time to feel the fear that was in her, for she was too busy trying to take the Cessna out of its terrible fall.

She pulled back on the yoke.

She pushed on the throttle and gave her engine all that she dared.

She heard the rising pitch of its whine and she shouted at her propeller, demanding that it take her back up out of this perilous dive, and it was an exorbitant demand, and the propeller answered back with everything that was left in its wounded imbalanced blades, and they did not fail her, her injured propeller, nor her straining engine either, they brought her up and out and back into level flight, facing out to sea, and then she saw more moving stars coming down in the distance to the right of her, and she knew that they would be upon her very soon, so she did what had to be done, and did it well. She made her rollout and turn, and headed for home.

And that was when it happened.

It was then that the slow and secret disintegration of the propeller hub finally revealed itself. It was then that the failing metal finally gave out from the cumulative fatigue of imbalance and vibration and the sudden stress of a dangerously exorbitant demand. The mounting bolts that had been slowly working themselves loose had finally succeeded in tearing free, and suddenly the whirling propeller simply clattered and clanked and went flying off into the night and disappeared from Diane's startled view.

A cry escaped her lips.

Her heart faltered, then beat firmly again.

Calmly she held her blue-and-white bird under control. Cleanly and smoothly it glided through the darkness, unencumbered by the drag of the aluminum blades.

She shut off the engine, for it could do her no good now, and she liked the sudden quiet that she found herself in. She had done that many times in the past, shut off the engine, just for the sudden hush, the peacefulness, though always at much higher altitudes, not at two thousand feet, which she was just passing through now, and not at night, not over the pitch-black ocean.

She tried calling the tower to let Teddy know that she had believed him and was coming back, she didn't want to talk to anyone else. But she knew she'd never raise the tower, because she was much too far out.

It was so quiet here, so peaceful. There was only the soft rustle of wind passing around the fuselage.

She was glad that she had decided to go home and face her life. She would not have wanted this to happen while she was running away from herself.

Now she heard the distant thunder of another airliner making its descent above and behind her, and then the thunder grew louder and passed over her and was before her, and she saw the big plane heading for its haven on the landfall that was far beyond her reach.

She hoped someone in the plane had seen her.

It would have been nice to know that she had been seen.

She glanced at her traveling companion on the seat beside her and felt sorrow for what she had done to him. He had no choice in coming on this trip. At least she had made her own decision to be here.

She snapped off the overhead lights, and the lights on the instrument panel too, and sat there in the dark in the silent, down-drifting plane.

She thought about her mother, and was glad that she had called her.

She was glad that she had had the talk with Teddy too, and glad that he had said what he had, for it made it easier now for her to believe that he would help her out of this problem too. He had promised her he'd help her and protect her, and she had decided to believe him, and that made it easier now, much easier now.

I believe you, Teddy, I know you'll help me, she said, as her Cessna, her friend, her blue-and-white bird, neared the end of its final descent.

She knew that she should be filled with fear now, but somehow she was not.

Something good would happen and she would be saved.

You cannot go through your whole life without something good happening even once.

This would be it for her.

Something good would happen now.

This is what she told herself, and it suffused her with a wonderful feeling of peace and trust and faith and lovingness toward everyone and everything in the whole beautiful world, especially toward herself.

And she held on to that feeling even as the landing gear finally hit the water, and even as the blue-and-white Cessna smashed over onto its nose, and even as the windshield cracked and the sea rushed in on her with merciful haste, and then she could no longer hold on to any feeling at all, and the plane sank swiftly beneath the waves and began its long journey to the ocean floor.

She was not damaged in the crash. There was not a scratch on her lovely body, nor on her pretty face either, with its wide, dark eyes and its vulnerable expression. The safety belt had held her in a tight embrace, and would hold her that way forever.

And Howard Bluestern would always be there too, on the seat beside her.

She would never be alone.

HE DIDN'T WANT to hear any more. He didn't have to.

He had known how it was going to end even before she went off the radar screens at LAX, and the co-pilot of the Honolulu inbound reported hearing her Emergency Locator Transmitter go on on impact and then vanish from the air in less than a minute. He knew that it was all over, even though it would be another fifteen minutes before the Coast Guard helicopters would sweep the area with their powerful searchlights and find nothing, not even a trace.

Charlie was terribly sympathetic and kind to him, and so was the girl, who cried softly and tried to hide her tears. Charlie confessed to him that he had talked to Diane many times over the air but had never met her, and had secretly admired her crisp, biting sense of humor, and her way of bending regulations a bit. He wanted to know what she looked like, and Teddy told him, he told him how petite she was and how attractive she was, and that was when the girl named Maxine started to weep.

They didn't ask him about Howard.

No one ever would.

No one would ever know that Howard was gone.

Only he and Jo Anne would know that, ever.

And they would never tell.

He didn't know when he had made that decision.

He didn't even know if *he* had *made* it.

Perhaps the decision had made itself, and he had accepted it.

That's the way it seemed, anyway.

Howard Bluestern would never die.

Teddy would not let him.

Howard Bluestern would go on living as long as Teddy was around. And Teddy Stern would go on living too.

They'd be in this thing together.

For Teddy there was no way out now, and he really did not want one.

He knew how Howard would have wanted to live out his life and he'd see that he did, as a good man, a successful man, an achiever.

There was no question about it.

He knew exactly how to play this role. He'd been doing tryouts for a week. And like all good roles, it would challenge his every skill, and that was something he had recently learned to welcome, too.

Teddy said good-bye to them now in the control room, and thanked them.

He put an arm around Maxine Worth's shoulders and he shook
Charlie Blakelee's hand and they said they'd be talking to each other,
and then he went down the long spiral staircase and out into the cool
night air under a starry and moonless sky and started across the dark
field toward the distant parking area where he had left his car.

The space on the upper ramp where Diane's blue-and-white Cessna
had been tied down was empty now. It had been such a short time
ago that she had been right there, peering at him out of the cabin
window. He could still see her face, large-eyed and frightened, a
bruised young woman without defenses, for all the harshness of her
words and deeds.

How strange it was, he thought, that she, she of all people, should
be with his brother now, for they had never liked one another, not
since the night they had first met, about a year ago, at some large
affair at the Beverly Hilton that he could no longer remember, with a
few thousand people milling about spilling drinks on each other.

Take care of her, Howard.

Take care of him, Diane.

He was glad that the security guard was no longer at the gate when
he went through. He saw him driving slowly across the field in the
red pickup truck, in search of trouble no doubt. Teddy would not have
wanted to talk to him now, nor have the man see the tears that he
knew were in his eyes.

He got in the yellow Porsche and drove to Los Angeles International
Airport, and changed his clothes in the men's room there.

Then he went to the phone booth and called Jo Anne.

She had just walked in, and he hated to do it to her.

He tried to soften the blow, as much as he could, soften the shock
of the events of an evening that, for her, had not even existed until
now.

He couldn't tell her everything. There wasn't time.

He had a midnight plane to catch.

But he told her enough, enough to make her understand, and weep
with anguish, for everyone, including himself and her.

"Oh my darling," she cried softly.

But she understood what had to be, and why.

"I love you so much," he said, fighting the tears in his eyes.

They said good-bye to each other finally.

Then he strode quickly toward the boarding gate with his attaché
case in his hand.

Howard Bluestern was on his way to New York now. He had business there. And in a few days he would be coming back and continuing the good work that he had started in the early weeks of his regime. He was up to it. He felt fully up to it.

And when he returned, he would see to it that his brother Teddy would begin to have every opportunity too, in *his* career. He had denied him too long. He would help him now at every turn. For he loved him really. Just as Teddy, he was certain now, loved him too.

Settled in his seat in the forward cabin of the jetliner as it leveled off and flew eastward through the night, he began to think about the future.

The first thing he would do when he got back to town would be to cancel his personal life insurance policy. Marvin Gerber would scream like the stuck pig that he was, because he'd be losing at least four, maybe five years of handsome commissions. But he couldn't think of any guy nicer than Marvin Gerber to whom it could have happened.

Next he would have David Stanner installed in a flattering but harmless position at the studio, and after a decent interval transferred to the company's London offices. He'd never get back into the United States. Scotty Seligman had friends in the State Department. They'd see to that.

Mrs. Mahoney would fit in very nicely in the Bel Air house as a steady housekeeper. She'd like the roominess and luxury of the place, and it was closer to where her family lived too. He could get someone else to come in one or two times a week at the beach house, because he'd hardly ever be there except on weekends. Which meant that he'd probably be getting rid of that old freezer on the back porch. He wouldn't be needing it. Never had.

And even before he returned, he was going to insist that the board of directors move Jeff Barnett and Larry Hough up to vice-presidencies, for they deserved it. He would threaten to resign if the board refused, just as he was going to threaten to resign unless they agreed to turn down every single one of the projects he had previously proposed, which had aged in a matter of weeks, and instead, approved the fresh new film packages in his attaché case. Time moved more swiftly than ever in the new Hollywood, and unless Winthrop Van Slyke and his board members understood that, maybe *they* had better offer to resign. Either way, he was going to lay it into them, and make them beg for *his* acceptance of *them*. And when he returned to California, he and

Hough and Barnett would run the studio as a troika. It would give him all the time in the world, whenever he needed it, to be away from the place.

He planned to let the tennis court fall into disuse; he'd go in for boating instead. He'd get something nice, not fancy but nice, and keep it at the marina, and disappear at sea for days at a time, like Jim Kelly used to do when he was running Paramount. It would spare him the awkwardness of being around while Teddy was appearing in something important that Sam Kramer had landed for him at the studio. And Kramer would be doing a lot of that in the future, getting Teddy solid roles, with stature, all over town.

Most of all, he thought about Jo Anne.

Of course he'd keep her as his secretary as long as she'd let him, because she was a loyal and loving secretary, and God knows he would need her all day long, and even more than that. But he'd never stand in the way of her life with Teddy, if that were the life she chose.

Maybe it would be premature to force her into making any choice at all. She hadn't seemed to feel the urgent need for marriage yet. And most important of all, she had seemed to like Howard as much as she liked Teddy. Why rush her? Why not wait until she decided that she wanted children? Then she could make up her mind. There was plenty of time.

Either way would be fine with him.

Meanwhile, the three of them would have one of the town's nicer relationships. Both brothers would obviously like her so very much, and each would fold her into his individual social life, and she in turn would obviously like each one of them equally well. Most people in the community would rightfully assume that she simply couldn't make up her mind. They'd never be surprised to see her at a party with Teddy one week and at a screening with Howard another. One of them would always discreetly remove himself from the picture when the other was out on the town with her. Which was why no one would ever see the three of them together. But Hollywood being Hollywood, there would always be someone who would swear that he or she had seen all three of them together.

And that person would be right.

Because they always *would* be together . . .

His revery was interrupted by a stewardess. "What would you like to drink, Mr. Bluestern?"

"Nothing, thank you," he said, smiling at her.

He didn't drink, really.

Oh, maybe a very weak vodka martini now and then, just to be sociable. But that was about all.